Road to Nowhere and
Other New Stories from the Southwest

Road to Nowhere and Other New Stories from the Southwest

EDITED BY

D. SETH HORTON AND
BRETT GARCIA MYHREN

UNIVERSITY OF NEW MEXICO
ALBUQUERQUE

18 17 16 15 14 13   1 2 3 4 5 6

LIBRARY OF CONGRESS CATALOGING-IN-PUBLICATION DATA

Road to nowhere and other new stories from the Southwest / edited by D. Seth
Horton and Brett Garcia Myhren.
pages cm
Includes bibliographical references.
ISBN 978-0-8263-5314-6 (pbk. : alk. paper) — ISBN 978-0-8263-5315-3 (electronic)
1. Southwestern States—Social life and customs—Fiction.
2. Short stories, American—Southwestern States.
3. American fiction—21st century.
I. Horton, D. Seth, 1976– II. Myhren, Brett Garcia.
PS566.R63 2013
813ʼ.0108979—dc23
2013004242

Contents

Introduction

D. SETH HORTON AND BRETT GARCIA MYHREN

ONE OF THE PROBLEMS WITH TRYING TO LOCATE THE SOUTHWEST IS that it is both too familiar and not familiar enough. On one hand, what we think we know about the Southwest often gets in the way of knowing it. On the other hand, without points of reference or prior experience in the region, we are even less likely to understand it. Consider, for example, how the narrator in "Trust," Paula McLain's story in this volume, describes a remote bar in the desert, a place so difficult to find that "you could go there only if you'd been there before." The way this description circles back on itself, drifting toward paradox, elegantly and concisely illustrates the puzzle and the pleasure of trying to understand southwestern space.

The point of this essay is not to resolve these difficulties, even if such an endeavor were possible. Complications make the Southwest more compelling precisely because they remind us that no one knows exactly where the place ends or begins. If forced to offer general guidelines, we would suggest that the Southwest includes Arizona and New Mexico; parts of California, Nevada, Utah, Colorado, Oklahoma, and Texas; and the northern regions of Mexico. These are, however, flexible guidelines, and our tendency is to be more inclusive rather than exclusive. We like the example of Texas folklorist J. Frank Dobie, who suggests, after offering his own definition of the Southwest, that it can be expanded to include "anything else north, south, east, or west that anybody wants to bring in."

Resolving the complications of the Southwest is certainly not the point of the stories in this anthology, either. Fiction does, however, offer one possible lens through which to see and understand places. If it is difficult to locate the Southwest, it is somewhat easier to describe a few of the themes that recur in these particular stories, which are saturated with the kind of understanding that comes only from intimate familiarity with a place. This is not to say that these writers "love" the Southwest in the same way that chambers of commerce tend to love it. The relationship to place in these stories is more prickly and complex, like the smell of sagebrush after a rain, a scent that the narrator of "Arboretum" describes as "at once fragrant and repellent, something like the smell of your hand after you licked it."

The threat of violence, sometimes imagined and sometimes actual, often lurks in the background of these narratives. Whether the characters cut new roads through the desert, kill cattle on a drought-stricken ranch, or haul a mysterious animal bone from a canal, the shadow of the sinister is never distant, a theme that resonates with the historical context in the Southwest. The war between the United States and Mexico in the middle of the nineteenth century is only one example. In fact, much of the history of the Southwest, from at least the sixteenth century onward, can be read as a series of invasions. In addition, images of the Southwest often glorified or sensationalized violence. While the writers of the stories collected here have a very different relationship to violence, the cultural legacy has deep roots.

There is also a sense of unease that permeates many of these stories, a sense of dislocation or isolation, of people out of place. For example, in Brad Watson's "Visitation," the protagonist realizes, while gazing around a restaurant in San Diego, that "there wasn't a single person in the entire place with whom he felt a thing in common." Some of these people have come to the Southwest to find themselves. Others have come to escape themselves. Some of these characters are transplants and immigrants; others are longtime residents. This combination of quest and flight, of local and foreign, produces a series of collisions that leave characters frayed and uncertain at the core. Like violence, these themes also have long historical trajectories. For example, much of the early literature on the Southwest involved travel and observation. From Cabeza de Vaca's sixteenth-century epic of survival to twentieth-century tourists in the "Great American Desert," the story of the Southwest often describes strangers in a strange land.

Many characters are uncertain in the present because of their unease with the past, and they rely on anonymity or disguise to shelter themselves. Because of a frequent association with desolation or isolation, people go to the Southwest to hide things or to do things they could not do under the watchful eye of "civilization," an idea echoed in atomic testing as well as the annual Burning Man festival. In this landscape, young girls try to abort the products of incest, and macho boys act out repressed homosexual desires. The Southwest, however, does not always provide the kind of escape or cover that these characters seek, and the consequences of past actions rupture their lives with the same implacable force ascribed to southwestern heat and light. In such a psychologically charged geography, dreams and visions might be expected, and they do at times appear. Yet if the visionary suggests a sacred element in these stories, the profane and mundane are never far behind. In one story, a young immigrant, struggling through an attempt to create a chile farm, imagines a visitation, not from the Virgin but from his ex-girlfriend in Mexico, a vision of an entirely different sort.

Perhaps because the Southwest often carries the burden of stereotype, many of the stories resist the standard tropes. The wonderfully titled "Lubbock Is Not a Place of the Spirit" shows this resistance to stereotype in the narration of a young man who embarks on a hilarious and disturbing tour of love and local politics. Who would have thought a story could deftly incorporate Jodie Foster, constipation, assassination, and bumper stickers? Another story with a mixture of the comic and sinister, "23 Months," leads the reader from a conventional house party to a space-age sleeping pod and finally to a terrible revelation beneath the "funny green-skinned trees" of the desert. And Kirstin Valdez Quade's story, "Portrait," is a poignant reminder that seemingly iconic images of the Southwest don't necessarily reveal the truth about the region.

Many of these writers remind us in other ways that the contemporary Southwest is not the "Old Southwest" of previous generations, especially if that prior image draws from conventional narratives, like gunfights in the sagebrush. Today's Southwest contains multitudes: Russian mail-order brides who dream of babies crying in the desert and painters who deliver the ashes of the dead to places like "Choking, Nevada." This Southwest is indeed a place of ranchers, Native Americans, and Mexicans; but it is also a place of rock collectors, palm readers, and drug dealers. In short, it is a place so difficult to imagine that you would likely find it only if you had been there before. Fortunately, the group of writers assembled here is willing and able to take you.

Because this is the second volume in the *New Stories from the Southwest* series, stories considered for inclusion had to be initially published between January 2007 and December 2011, thus beginning where the prior volume ended. In keeping with our flexible view of the Southwest, our other conditions for inclusion were more elastic. Instead of trying to represent all groups and regions of the Southwest or trying to determine how long an author has lived here, we felt it was more important to find stories that best revealed fresh insights into the contemporary cultures of the region. As the prior discussion suggests, each of these stories has something to offer in that regard. That kind of insight, while difficult to define, seems far more important than, for example, where an author currently eats breakfast.

Throughout the five years of our research, we read almost four hundred North American journals and magazines, nearly two thousand individual issues, in search of those stories that best illuminate some aspect of life in the Southwest. We are particularly indebted to the editors who provided us with complimentary subscriptions to their literary journals. We would also like to thank the many writers, including those we were unable to anthologize, for making us rethink, ponder, and debate the contours and limits of this most interesting of regions.

Advanced Latin

SALLIE BINGHAM

WHILE SHE TALKED, LUKE WATCHED THE SUN GLINT ON THE CARS IN the parking lot and, further off, the snow on the Sangres turning red. It was rush hour and the highway that passed the shopping center was thick with cars.

She'd come in an hour earlier, to take her first lesson—he offered two trial lessons for fifteen dollars, losing money on the deal but catching a few permanent clients—and now she was telling him she wanted to learn how to dance because of how she used to live.

Horses, he heard, and children, and knew that meant a big house somewhere and a husband who would never be mentioned, or if so, just to laugh.

Across the parking lot, he noticed a woman in a short skirt and tall black boots walking away from her car. She had the thighs of a dancer and he wondered if she was coming to his studio. But she turned left at the last minute and went in the sporting goods store. It didn't matter; these days, he had plenty of customers, and some of them had even better legs.

Meanwhile Mrs. Lewis went on talking about dancing as a girl at parties given by her parents and their friends. She didn't call them debutante parties but he knew that was what she meant. He had several customers practicing waltzes for just such occasions.

Finally he made her sit down next to him on the bench that ran all the way down the long wall of his studio, under mirrors that had cost almost as much as the floor. The bench was padded with blue acrylic and it opened, in sections, for storage. There were old dance shoes in there, bits of rainbow-colored costumes. Once a year he opened the benches and threw everything out.

"This is the way we do it," he said, and he showed her several lesson plans. Johnny, his floor manager, thought it was better not to show them the options in writing, but Luke knew they never read the contracts anyway. They rode along on his voice, waiting for a chance to sign.

The dance lessons were sold in blocks of ten, twenty, or more, and they were expensive, especially if the woman wanted to work with Luke. For the others teachers, the charge was less, but it all added up to a substantial amount, paid for on the spot, in advance, by check.

Mrs. Lewis took a check out of her purse and wrote out the larger sum and he saw she wasn't going to make a notation on her stub. In fact she didn't have a stub. The check had been loose at the bottom of her alligator-skin purse.

"When do I start?" she asked, her face lifted up to him, as though he was going to shine on her, or rain.

"Tomorrow, two o'clock," he said, checking his schedule.

"I only know a few steps from parties. Jitterbug, mainly."

He'd noticed, dancing with her, that she held herself badly, back arched, shoulders up, head too far forward. The tall ones usually did.

"That doesn't matter," he told her. "I'll start you over, from scratch."

She smiled. "Daddy danced with me every evening for a week, trying to teach me the waltz so I could get married. But he decided it was impossible. Or I was."

He imagined her father's arms, the cut of his suit. So many women were taught to dance by their fathers, then came to the studio to be fixed.

"Did you waltz at your wedding?"

"Yes—no way out. We stepped all over each other, and I ended up crying."

He liked her face, its brightness, the worn skin covered with a skillful layer of makeup. He liked it when the older ladies made an effort, wore the right kind of shoes, and short skirts, if they had the legs.

"Tuesday at two o'clock," he said, writing her name on his appointment sheet.

During her second lesson, it began to rain and he wondered if he'd remembered to close his car windows. It was a secondhand Chrysler with fifty-two thousand miles on it, but the previous owner had kept it in good shape. He sent Johnny to check. Johnny came back running because it was raining harder now. He said the windows were closed tight.

Luke nodded and went on teaching Mrs. Lewis the rumba, which was the way he usually started them to see if they could move their hips, or learn to. She laughed when he called it Cuban Motion, but then she tried to mirror the motion he was making, drawing in at the waist and releasing one hip smoothly, then shifting to the other side. She had some flexibility in her long torso, which he could see because she had worn a leotard. He thought she might have gone out earlier in the day when the sun was still shining to buy the leotard and the short flared skirt that was like the ones his women teachers wore.

He put his hands on her waist, then slid them down to her hips. It was the first time he'd touched her and she stood for it patiently. No woman ever objected in words to being touched, but some of them reared back. He remembered his mother warning him against touching girls and wished she could have lived to see his studio, bought with a big bank loan he was now paying off, five instructors instead of the two he'd started with, and Johnny to take care of the business end.

As he counted out the beats, he felt her moving her hips more smoothly. He went to put a CD in the stereo, and when he took her in his arms again, he felt the difference that music nearly always made. The tune was an old one from the fifties and he knew she'd heard it at slumber parties and later at her first teenage parties.

She sighed. She wasn't doing the rumba anymore, but she was on time and enjoying herself and he didn't correct her.

"You move well," he told her. It gave him satisfaction to find that movement, that flexibility. He thought she might decide to really work at it, take more lessons, turn out to be serious. Those were the ones who paid the bills.

That evening when he was watching TV at home Pauline asked how the new one was doing and he said there were possibilities. Pauline had been his partner when he was performing, and she kept an eye on the women who came in.

A few months later he planned to take five of his most advanced students, or at least the ones who could afford it, to a competition sponsored by his old studio in Denver, and Mrs. Lewis—Cindy—decided to go along. She bought herself a couple of gowns from the one good dress store at the mall, and a week before the competition, she brought them to the studio and tried them on for Luke, running in and out of the bathroom, bra straps showing, wearing sneakers. He liked the turquoise-blue stretch but told her to take back the gray silk because it didn't move. He knew she was not the kind of woman who took clothes back and he thought the gray one would probably end up in the back of her closet.

At the competition, he was too busy dancing with the students to pay much attention to any one of them, so it wasn't until the last day, when it was all over, that he had a minute to sit down and chat with Mrs. Lewis.

She looked tired and her azure eye shadow was smeared up into her eyebrows. She was wearing the blue dress, which she'd done quite well in—he reminded her of that—but she'd taken off her dancing shoes; her bare feet, in nylons, looked twisted, several toes turned under.

"I didn't do as well as I expected," she said. She was looking down at her coffee, turning the mug in her hands. "I let you down."

"You did exactly what you were supposed to do."

"Oh, why do you say that?" she wailed. "At least be disappointed."

Surprised, he took a sip of water. "But I'm not," he said.

"That's because you don't care," she said.

He wished Pauline was there, to put an arm around her shoulders.

"I do care," he said. "You have a lot of potential."

"You say that to everybody," she said. "I've heard you."

He sighed. It was late; the hotel coffee shop was empty except for a waitress swabbing the counter. The chandeliers overhead were lit with hundreds of little bulbs and the light shone mercilessly on her face.

"I want you to care," she said.

He told her it was time to go to their rooms—they were leaving early the next morning, in the rented van, to drive back to Santa Fe—and then he left to find the other instructors, who were having a party on the twenty-fifth floor. All of Denver lay spread out beneath the windows and he wondered if things would be different in a big city like this one, then remembered his days at the franchise and knew it was always the same.

Their own men don't do anything for them, he thought, standing at the window with a beer in his hand, but then, why should they? These women always leave.

On the way home in the van, Cindy barely said a word.

July Fourth was party time at the studio and the staff worked late the night before, putting up red, white, and blue paper streamers and little American flags, in bunches. The big summer stars were all over the sky when Luke locked up, and their size and grandeur made him think of his father, who'd never gotten around to applying for citizenship; the jobs he worked didn't require papers. When he turned sixty, he started drinking, and one night, late, he told Luke, "Your life will be nothing, like mine, and you won't even have a good woman like your mother." Luke had told him that he was already making a better life, as a dance instructor at a big-city franchise, but his father had only laughed. Dance instructors, he said, were just toys for rich women.

Luke went home and slept and was back at the studio early.

Students sometimes contributed flowers or other decorations to the parties, and Luke was always quick to check the accompanying cards, in case there was one he needed to slip in his pocket. So when the balloon cluster arrived, butting in the doorway—six big heliums, red, white, and blue, with a basket of flowers attached by ribbons underneath—Luke went right over. He had trouble finding the card lodged in the basket of flowers until Johnny pointed out the little envelope. Luke slipped the card out and read it, and then put it in his pocket.

Cindy Lewis wore a tomato-red dress to the party, with two thigh-high slits, and Luke noticed how much more muscular and shapely her thighs were, after six months of dancing, and also that she was wearing matching tomato-red silk underpants. He thought she had probably never worn red pants before, even for her husband.

"Thank you for the balloons and the flowers," he said when she asked him to dance a cha-cha. The balloons were lounging up near the ceiling, and the basket of red and white carnations bobbed by the dancers' heads.

"Did you read the card?"

"Of course. Thank you." His mother had died ten years ago, and his father, weeping, had said, "Now I have nothing." Luke had stood silent, his hands hanging by his sides, watching his father cry.

"I meant it," Cindy Lewis said.

"I know you did." Pauline had stopped sleeping with him at Easter, moving onto the sofa so she could have her space. Luke didn't know if she was going to change her mind; she'd done that two or three times. And the only independent studio in Albuquerque had just come on the market. Leasing it would mean running back and forth a lot in the car, but soon he would make enough money to replace the Chrysler with a Land Rover.

"Aren't you going to say anything more?" Cindy looked up at him with her damp, blue eyes, the lines like decorations, and he thought how pretty she was before he thought how pretty she must have been.

"No," he said.

"Oh, I know all the women are in love with you," she said, and then the cha-cha was over and he left her to put on a quickstep.

At the end of the party—he always ended them at nine thirty, so people could go on to the bars and dance places around town, where they could eat and drink and smoke cigarettes—she came over to give him a hug and tell him good night. She'd already taken off her dance shoes, and in her boots, they were exactly the same height.

"I meant every word," she said.

"There were only three words." He remembered the billboard on the way to Albuquerque that advertised some local restaurant; the sign showed a man in big, clumsy-looking hip boots, standing in a stream in a swarm of mosquitoes. There was a puzzled look on his face.

"You can't send me notes like that," he went on.

"Is it against studio rules?"

She was smiling and twinkling, and the dampness was gone. Now her eyes were expertly outlined with pencil and shadow.

"Yes," he said, turning away. Pauline, on the other side of the room, was calling him to help close up.

"I won't accept that," Cindy Lewis said, behind him. He'd known that was what she would say, that she would never accept a rule she didn't want.

That night, in bed with Pauline, he thought about his father saying that Luke would never have a life, or a woman as good as his mother. He had a life but he was still in hock to the bank and would be for years. His father had never believed a man could make a decent living teaching people how to dance.

He hated to have to sit down with Cindy and talk to her, but he knew it had to be done. And at her next lesson, too.

It was a Wednesday, late afternoon, very hot; the studio door was propped open, and the sweet, soft smell of gasoline and dust drifted in. The air-conditioning was on the blink again, and people were complaining.

Cindy Lewis was wearing a short black skirt and a sleeveless leotard. She'd stopped wearing black tights since he'd recommended flesh-colored hose. When they sat down, the blue acrylic bench subsided a little, and Luke knew he needed to prop up that section. Something underneath was broken.

"I don't want to hurt you," he said.

"You're not hurting me."

"I mean, what I'm going to say."

"I know what you're going to say. Just don't say it."

"I don't need to?"

"No," she said, looking at him, and he saw she'd started to use maroon eye shadow with a pencil to match. "But I won't give up."

"You have to," he said. He felt as though he was trudging through mud.

"No, I don't." She spoke crisply, and he thought that was the way she must have spoken to her children, her horses, her employees. "It's a free country."

He trudged another step. "If you're going to keep on taking lessons . . ."

"Is it Pauline?"

"No," he said, heavily. "It's me."

"You think you have to earn everything, don't you," she said, and as she moved her arm onto the back of the bench, he smelled her deodorant, sweet and strong. "You think there's no free lunch."

"There is no free lunch," he said, and he thought of the franchise in Albuquerque, and the new Land Rover, with leather interior and automatic windows and a radio that could pick up stations as far away as Chicago.

Later he would think, She broke me, but it was not as simple as that. In fact she went on taking lessons, five or six a week, and although Pauline was concerned about her—Pauline saw through people fast—Luke persuaded himself that everything was all right. Cindy didn't send him any more balloons, or flowers, or notes, and neither of them referred to the talk on the blue bench. Perhaps she'd decided it was hopeless, and was ready to concentrate on her dancing. That was all they talked about: her footwork, her frame.

In fact Luke was closer to several other students that summer, especially the married women who seemed securely moored. One of them, a handsome blond named Lucille who'd been coming to the studio for years, one of their bread-and-butter students who would never win competitions but would work hard and re-up every time their block of lessons was finished, came and told him—this was early fall—that a rumor was going around.

Luke was used to rumors—the business of dancing ran on gossip—and so he laughed and hoped she would not tell him. But she did. She was his friend, she said, and as his friend she thought he should know what was being said.

"I know already," he said, leaning down to tie his dance shoes; they were sitting on the blue bench, the one that caved in, and he reminded himself, again, to prop it up. "Either I'm sleeping with my students or I'm gay."

"It's not that," Lucille said. "I wouldn't pay any attention to that kind of thing. No, they're saying you've got a problem with cocaine."

The word was one that had swung in and out of his life, like a moth attracted to a light and then disappearing. In fact it was a word he almost never said, as though saying it would prove something. But he knew it.

"That's ridiculous," he said, "with the hours I teach." He was at the studio ten or twelve hours a day, first to arrive, last to leave, and sometimes he had to clean up, too.

Lucille just looked at him. She was a therapist, and he imagined she knew something about drugs.

"It'll blow over," he said.

"I don't think so."

"Why?"

"I'm hearing it everywhere."

He thought of Daisy Middleton bringing in her twelve-year-old daughter, a little fox in a skimpy dress, then sitting on the bench to watch during the girl's lesson; that was one of their rules. Parents had to accompany minors. Daisy Middleton, who'd told him she was pleased to find he ran a decent place. And all those physicists from Los Alamos who looked as though they'd never gotten dirt under their fingernails.

He asked, "Who started it?"—then suddenly knew.

She told him. "She swore me to secrecy—"

"She's mad at me," he said, as though that would solve it, end it.

"You've got to do something," Lucille said, and later, when he told Pauline, she said the same thing: "You've got to do something, Luke, you've got to stop it. It could ruin the business."

He remembered his father, then, with a spit of rage, as though his father, twenty years dead, had caused this to happen.

"I'll speak to her," he said.

"That won't do any good. She's already told a lot of people."

He knew then what he would have to do, and he armed himself for it, trying to imagine how his face would look to Cindy Lewis, who suddenly seemed a stranger, although he had touched her everywhere and taught her everything he knew. He tried to remember how his voice sounded, in his own ears—his voice which his mother had always liked. But it was impossible to imagine it all because he could no longer see Cindy's face, which had been turned up to him, at the beginning, as though he was going to rain on her, or shine.

"I wonder how she came up with that," he said, in the dark, to Pauline, but Pauline, being wise, didn't answer.

The next evening when his ten or twelve best students—not the best dancers, but the ones who came a lot—were gathered for their Advanced Latin Class, he made them all sit down on the blue benches and settled himself on a little stool in front of them. He'd never seen the stool before, and he didn't know where it came from; he'd put his hand on it, in the back room, and known it was exactly right.

Sitting on the stool, he was a little lower than his students, and when he began talking, he found himself looking at their knees.

"There's a rumor going around. I want you, my core people, to stop it whenever you hear it. It could ruin me," he said, and suddenly, without knowing he was going to do it, he put his head down on his knees.

They sat studying him, silent as cattle.

He said a few things after that, and several seemed shocked or said they were sorry, but really it was all done when he laid his head down on his knees. In twenty years of teaching dancing—and there had been trouble before, of various kinds—he'd never done anything like that in front of his students, or his staff. In fact he'd never done anything like that in front of Pauline.

And still he hadn't been able to see Cindy Lewis's face, although she'd been sitting right in front of him.

They filed out, after his speech; no one said a word, as though they were the ones who were shocked, or frightened, or shamed. In the doorway, Cindy glanced back at him, with a little smile, and he thought she was pleased. She'd done it now—brought down the house, or nearly, and he wondered if the same impulse had made her break her marriage, leave her husband, lose her children, shattering her own life as easily as she'd tried to shatter his, as though it was all paid for in advance, with no stub for the notation.

In the weeks that followed, no one cancelled their lessons, and he never heard the rumor mentioned again—Lucille told him she hadn't, either—although now and then when he saw two of his women talking quietly in a corner, or crossing the parking lot together, deep in conversation, he suspected they were discussing what he'd said or what they'd heard, which began to seem like the same thing.

The danger passed, and everything went on in the same way, or would have if he'd let it go at that; but he found he couldn't face dancing with Cindy Lewis, looking at her averted face, knowing what she'd done.

And so he told her to leave. It was done quickly one evening in October. He had his checkbook out, and he wrote her a check for the lessons remaining in her contract, which she wouldn't be taking.

"I wish you the best," he said, holding out his hand.

"You can't accept anything, can you?" she asked. "I could have done a lot for you."

"I don't need you to do a lot for me."

"Oh yes, you do," she said, and then she was gone, flashing across the parking lot, her short skirt swinging.

He stood watching her walk to her car, and then Pauline called him, and he turned around to get the students in Advanced Latin on their feet. But he could still feel Cindy Lewis striding away from him across the parking lot with her short skirt swinging as though she had indeed offered him something infinitely valuable—but what was it?

Pauline would say the moon.

On the San Juan

RON CARLSON

HE WAS AS HAPPY AS HE HAD BEEN ALL DAY, SWIMMING IN THE RIVER with his students, when he missed the eddy opposite their campground on the river, and he felt the muscle of the cold current grab his stomach and pull him past the five rafts where they were beached in the sandy willows. He was wearing his California swim trunks and his life preserver. He was barefoot for the first time in four days, having peeled his wet tennis shoes off when they'd landed after the day's rafting. He felt the river over his shoulders now and he put his head down and swam seven hard strokes, but when he looked up, he was even farther from shore. The rafts seemed small and far away, and he saw the trip leader, Sarah, stand up, wave, and call his name.

It was a writers' trip down the San Juan River, and he'd been talking to the bright young women for three days. He wanted, as always, to say something new about writing, something that might make it possible for them to write with more force, and the sunny afternoons under the cottonwoods had gone well. They were terribly bright and funny girls, and they were old and young three times every hour. They reminded the man powerfully of the girls he'd taught years ago, women who now had grown kids. He was godfather of two of his old students' children.

The San Juan River was running at four times its usual flow from the heavy snowmelt runoff, and the brown river had made for efficient rafting and some tricky landings. "Coming in hot," was the cry when the raft refused to slow near the bank, and all rafters knew to prepare for the bump and watch for the thrown lines.

The man had been in the city too long. He was successful, of course, but there was little sweetness in that for him. He was a good writer and appreciated for that, and he was friendly and easy to like, and he flew around the country a little too much now and he was weary. He'd signed up for this odd river venture to get into the wild and to sleep on the ground and to get bug-bit and sunburned and go two days then three in a row without washing. And to think.

All morning in the raft, he'd been thinking about the woman he loved. He had taught himself not to think about her because it was painful, and he had lived in that pain for a thousand days. He had trained his mind not to think of the woman or her new life.

But the river and the old rock mountains had disassembled the man's training. The rocks didn't care what happened to the man and they hadn't cared a thousand days ago and they wouldn't care in a thousand years. Everywhere he looked in the magnificent canyons, he saw rocks that didn't care and wouldn't care long after the man had had his little life.

When they would pull in daytimes, he hiked with the class to the pictographs and the petroglyphs etched in the rosy sandstone on the cliff walls and he wondered at the figures there, the powerful chests, the hands, the spirals and the figures hovering around the creatures. When he looked at the careful spiral, the man could not help himself: he thought of his tangled heart.

Last night he could see the woman he loved, her face, a face he knew better than any other face in the world. He tried not to think of her, but now she was there. So he sat in the rocks by the canyon camp, and he wrote her a letter and each sentence was hard to write. It seemed like it would have been easier to carve a pictograph—some picture of a man trapped in a spiral unable to find his way.

The girls on the trip were good writers; they were careful with words and with each other and they respected stories and they wanted to learn. They bent over their notebooks when they sat in the sand in a circle under the desert cottonwoods. Sometimes a raven would land above them on a branch and thrum for a while like the opprobrious headmaster. They also inked designs on their knees and elbows: stars and letters and figures. One girl connected her bug bites into a funny bicycle; another put an elaborate starburst around a wart on her knee. They all wove hemp string bracelets for each other, some with beads. One girl painted a fish onto the shaved head of the other teacher on the trip.

The man thought he was funny and he would urge his students to find some paper to write on instead of each other. This wasn't funny, but still he cajoled and pushed them, even when they wanted to stop or sleep with their heads on each other's stomachs. Write the story, he'd say. Push. Write it. It will unfold.

In the letter the man opened his heart carefully. He didn't want to spill it. He loved the woman, but he didn't say that. He said she was in his dreams and that was true, and he told her how she appeared in the dreams glad to see him and how they talked sweetly, ordinarily, and made plans. He loved how ordinary their talk was, how free from blame, and he loved making plans. In the letter he said something strange. He said, *We should be together. I would move heaven and earth if we could be together while we are alive together on this planet*. When he reread it, he realized that he meant it. But he also knew that like all the other letters he had written, he would not send it.

All that morning as they had drifted the San Juan River, the man scanned the red tiered cliffs for bighorn sheep, and he thought of the woman. Now he had started thinking of her, and she wasn't going away.

Late that morning, one of the other boatmen, Will, had rowed his raft up to where the man rode in the raft with his boatman, Lisa, and they plotted a quick water attack on Lyn's raft. Will and Lisa were boyfriend and girlfriend. The man smiled. A water fight. It was a bright day in the desert world, and a water fight seemed right. There weren't enough water fights in the man's life.

Even better, when they pulled onto the hard sand beach at Ledge Rapids, they unpacked the rafts, set up the kitchen, and then everyone jumped in the river. It was safe against the bank in the eddy and everyone was standing on the submerged sandbar and then floating in big strange circles in the eddy. The man was happy to remove his cowboy hat and his shoes and step into the water with all of his students. He was pleased with the trip, how much good writing had been begun, and he knew tomorrow he would be back in the world.

The eddy turned and caught him and sent him upstream three times, and then he missed it as the real river current held him fast, and Sarah called his name, and the man felt himself begin to disappear.

He took a deep breath and put his head down and swam again ten furious strokes, but when he looked up he was still trapped and being taken. Sarah ran along the narrow shore, and now the man saw Will running with the throw rope. Two hundred yards below, the river turned, and the man had one chance to strike near the shore. He breathed deeply in the cold water and swam hard again and his arms burned, and now he was closer to the shore, but Will had vanished and the man could not get a breath. The man hit a willow and grabbed at it and missed and then found an underwater branch and slowed himself. The river was a power he'd never known. It pushed him past the willow and his bare foot struck a rock on the bottom; he was going fast and it hurt, then another, but he wanted to strike something or the river was going to take him downstream to a future he could not see. He felt trapped in a spiral of forces, deep in the spiral, tangled and powerless, without air, and unable to move himself or earth or heaven.

Then he saw Will running the strip of sand along the river, dodging the willows and the rocks, and he saw Will throw something and the red and yellow rope bag was then in the air, a red and yellow thing in the blue sky. It looped up and out for a while. The man's heart beat in his shoulders and forehead and his mouth was in the river, and then the rope bag sat down without a splash in front of the man's face and the man saw something he would never forget: his hand closed upon the rope.

Will pulled and the man bumped the bottom and then stood and he pushed forward with the rope in his hand and then he stood again on dry ground.

The man was dizzy and confused and things seemed now to be happening out of order. He kept checking to make sure he was not in the river, and when Will tugged the second time, the man let go of the rope. Walking back along the sand to camp helped. Walking always helped.

A minute later he sat breathing in Sarah's raft while she looked at his punctured foot. She chatted with him about her life on the river and she told a story of having been bitten by a snake and the story helped. The man was breathing normally now. He loved how ordinary she made it all sound, even his incident, the rope throw, the bandaged foot. The man's stomach was churning, but his heart had subsided so that he felt weak. He could feel his students watching quietly, and one finally came up to Sarah's raft and said, "Are you traumatized by going down the river?"

"Probably," the man told her. Actually he felt drained and euphoric. He was certain now that he would send the letter. He was alive.

"You should write a story about it," the girl said. Later, while he was writing this story under an umbrella on the sandy beach, the girl would give him a string bracelet with three green beads. "That's my assignment for you. Write the story for this evening. Write it. Go ahead. It will unfold."

Dear Shorty

Eddie Chuculate

ON THE FIRST REGULAR BUSINESS DAY AFTER THE LABOR DAY HOLiday, hotel/motel rents at Old Orchard, Maine, drop nearly in half. Canadians in hideous skintight Speedos, Boston bluebloods, and leather-skinned Florida expatriates go home to gear up for fall, leaving the beach and waterfront businesses deserted. Roller coasters and fish-and-chips huts shut down, Vacancy signs in English replace No Vacancy signs in French, and locals get their beach back after the good weather's gone. I had driven all the way across the country, from San Francisco, to get there, to a room for $150 a week, so close to the water I could hear the waves break as I lay in bed. What a lonely feeling that is, at the edge of the earth, the edge of your hopes, to look out over a balcony as a spooky nighttime fog creeps in, and to not be able to see the water but only hear it, hear it boil to a hushed roar, then release. A landlubber from Oklahoma, I equated the emotion to hearing the late-night swish of trucks vanishing down the highway when as a kid I tried to sleep in a house we lived in along U.S. 69. I was in Maine almost a month before I broke down and called home, and my cousin told me they had found Shorty, my father, slumped over on a toilet at a city park, unconscious, with bottles of Listerine scattered about his feet. She said he was in the hospital, near death.

"Finally," I said.

My cousin gasped at the other end of the line. I wonder what she must have thought. I hadn't meant it like that.

I went down to the beach to ponder the situation. A full moon was pulling itself from the ocean, cut off at exactly half at the horizon waterline. The tide had slipped out and people here and there with rolled-up pants cuffs were quietly digging at clam holes with long-spaded shovels. The moon laid down a copper-colored stairway across the Atlantic, and the clam diggers made long shadows. I sat on a log smoking a cigarette and laughed out loud at the thought of Dad and his bottles of mouthwash. He had always said he had the nicest-smelling breath of any drunk in town.

My dad is the only person I know who could get drunk three, four times a day. Watching him get drunk was like watching one of those time-lapse films where snow melts, grass sprouts, flowers bloom and then wither away all in a few seconds with clouds rushing overhead and shadows underneath. Dad would start out with the shakes, red faced, then be happy and talkative after a few drinks, hitting his stride, then be completely wiped out with a face that looked melted, then pass out all in a matter of a few hours. He'd wake up after about an hour or so, so-so sober, shaking, wanting to know where his bottle was. I'd pick it up from behind the couch, half-full. Dad was half-white, which makes me a quarter white, I guess, but I don't claim it.

Shorty's second language was English; he grew up speaking Cherokee. He'd sit by quietly while fellow drunks rattled on in Cherokee (*I wonder if this white man here has a drink?*) then startle them with his own fluency. *Some people don't know their ass from a hole in the ground*, he'd say, jokingly, drawing bewildered stares and hilarious laughter. He'd start talking in Cherokee when he was drinking and I'd have to remind him I didn't understand. First of all I was raised on my Creek side and knew more Creek language than Cherokee; second, he was slurring and I certainly can't comprehend slurred Cherokee.

When I was a kid, I'd ride the Tulsa city bus with him and he'd pass out in back. The driver would have to come back and wake him up when we reached our stop because I didn't know where we were. Once I drove down to Tahlequah and went on his rounds with him. The first stop was Mac's Hamburgers, where he sold a brick of commodity cheese each month, still sealed in a brown box. The second stop was the liquor store for a fifth of Kentucky Deluxe. The third stop was the drugstore for the bottle of generic mouthwash—for when the whiskey ran out, which was sooner than later. The last stop was the abandoned house where he and his running mates drank and passed out. It was a sagging wooden house with boarded-up windows, set off from the street in a grove of locusts. There was no furniture or lights, but three or four guys had little pallets in different sections of the house made from blankets and clothes from Goodwill, and each drunk was afforded the privacy of his own room and space as if this were all legitimate. The water didn't run and there was no gas or electric, but who ate? The owner was driving by and saw the red swirl of cigarette cherries through the darkness and called the police. Again. After a night in jail the cops made all the winos go back to the house and clean up the bottles, cans, and trash. A photographer from the paper came along and in the picture that ran on the front page the next day my dad was laughing, stabbing a piece of trash with one of those long orange spears they gave him.

That was my dad. A kind-hearted old Joe who gave all the drunks haircuts if someone could come up with scissors. Shorty had a nice Cherokee Housing Authority home about three miles out but preferred to stay in town in the park, culverts, or vacant houses because it meant a shorter walk to the liquor store. It sounds absurd, but it's true. The brick house was brand new and my uncle—Shorty's fraternal twin brother—turned the garage into another bedroom with a bay window and King woodstove, and installed a cedar deck with a swing on the front porch. It was the nicest Indian home anyone never had. Shorty would make the long, hungover walk back to it two or three times a month to shower up and try to eat something, or scavenge for my aunt's Scope, then it was back to rumbling in the jungle.

But I never tried to make judgments about my dad. If he wanted a drink, I'd buy it. There's times he'd passed out on me and before driving home I'd stuff ten or twenty bucks in his pockets, which I now realize was dangerous: That ten bucks is something even your bestest drinking buddy will roll you for in Tulsa or Tahlequah. Don't tell me God protects the young, the innocent, and the young innocent drunk.

There's times we'd pull the chairs out under the shade of the oak trees during the evening and he'd give me and my buddies haircuts. The price was only a half-pint of whiskey to calm his nerves. I always stepped up first because I knew that toward the halfway mark of the bottle he tended to get a little sloppy; though early on it was a pleasure to watch him operate: the way he held the scissors with pinky extended for balance, the sharp snip of blade against comb, the easygoing joking and laughter. "My God, son, who's been cuttin' your hair?" he'd say once you sat in his chair. "It'll be tough, but I'll try and straighten it out. Now on, you come to me." They were the same lines he delivered to customers when he and my grandfather Ed ran "Chief's" barbershop on Eighth and East Broadway in Muskogee in the 1960s. The shakes were what eventually cut his barbering career short. He'd shake before he got well, then too much medicine would have him shaky again. It was that middle ground he strove for.

However, there were times he was so deep in his bottle he'd totally forget who I was or where I came from or what the hell I was doing with him. We were sitting under a tree in the park on Downing Street and he looked up from a far-off reverie and told me to get the fuck away from him and to leave him alone. Point blank. This after I'd taken the trouble to find out where he was living, made up an excuse to miss work, drove down, then patrolled all over town asking various drunks if they knew of or had seen him. I admit it stung at first but I got used to it. He'd forget what he'd said, and start joking and laughing, and this was infectious. After he said it, he fell back on the grass and passed out for a while. I sipped on a beer and smoked a few cigarettes, watching kids splash around in the creek. As long as I was with him, I figured, people or cops would just think it was someone catching a nap on a lazy summer afternoon. About an hour later he woke up and wanted to know where his bottle was. I showed him.

"Goddamn, son, I'm sure glad to see you," he said. "How's Flo and Zeke doin'?" My grandmother and grandfather had both passed away two years hence—something I told Shorty each time I saw him.

"They're doing about the same," I told him now. "Drinking beer, cooking out, driving around in the country."

Shorty grinned and drank. "I sure do miss 'em," he said.

I guess you could say my dad was a classic case of wasted talent. In 1966 he was lead guitarist in a rock-and-roll band at night and cut hair during the day. He'd drag my mom along to gigs in bars and they'd let her in even though she was only eighteen because they were married. He also played piano growing up and could play both instruments by ear. It was said he could hear a tune once on the radio and play it right back for you on his guitar. My mom told me she'd seen people cry when Shorty played and would get into a particularly long blues riff.

In later years—after hearing tales of his virtuosity, which he never talked about—I brought a guitar down to him and he started out well enough, sipping on whiskey, laughing and strumming. It was a simple wooden acoustic I'd picked up on a steal at a pawnshop in Muskogee. It had a brown leather case and a set of pearl-colored picks that stated "Damn I'm Good" on them. He cocked his head, concentrating, and quickly tuned what I assumed was an already-tuned guitar. It sounded like springs warbling. He played with a dreamy expression and when he hit a difficult spot he'd close his eyes tight

and grimace and stick out his tongue just a little. He played the guitar well—
there were no sour notes, uneven tempos, hurried rhythms. He raised his
eyes, beckoning me to join in. I never did. "Lay down Sally, let me rest you
in my arms. I been tryin' all night long just to talk to you." He played the
entire song, humming along at the vocals he had forgotten. I strum a little
myself and realize that particular song is a difficult tune for even an accomplished player but before I knew it Shorty had ventured off into some other
composition, something half-bluesy and half-classical. His happy expression
vanished and, shutting his eyes, his brows came together. I watched his hand
flash up and down the neck, his fingers knitting along the strings, which
made anguished birdlike squeaks when he switched chords. Trancelike, he
continued, pivoting his left foot this way and that, digging in for traction. He
was making the old guitar sound brand new. His pick popped off but he kept
racing forward at an unbelievable speed, stopped instantly, and somehow
massaged the strings so that absolute silence struck. He waited a couple beats
then launched back into the familiar opening of "Sally," only slower, comi-
cally slower, an arpeggio, a dying out, and his grin returned. He hit the last
note, bent the strings, and made them cry, and when the sound finally faded
he handed the guitar back to me and picked up his bottle—his new favorite
instrument, his real labor of love. I sat there spellbound as he took a long
drink. He told me it'd been at least twenty years since he'd played.

Problem was, he couldn't—or wouldn't—stay off the hard liquor—plain and
simple. Don't even think about coming at him with a beer, that "Oklahoma
three-two horse piss." He was one of those people who couldn't handle their
alcohol yet drank more than anyone around them like it was some sort of
contest. He'd vomit in bars or restaurants, then order a double. When he
started throwing up on the walls at home and telling my mom to clean it up
and after all the drama swearing no remembrance, she left him. It would be
easy to say the divorce spun him into a depression he never came out of but
the fact is he was drinking himself into oblivion before, during, and after
their marriage.

    It all started with Edward, a well-liked and talented full-blood Cherokee
Baptist minister who was kicked out of the church for drinking on the pulpit.
Yes, my grandfather was among that generation of full-blood Indians suck-
ered into the Christianity hoax and taught that Indians and their practices

were heathen and evil. They told Ed that they were officially here now to save his soul, praise God. The Christians stood on their mountaintops, generously handing down favors. Ed reached up and received one of them and was blessed. Can I get an amen? Never mind that in this worldview 1.3 billion Chinese are going straight to hell.

It's said the drinking didn't begin until the Coolwaters came to Indian Territory, present-day Oklahoma. You can trace the progression of alcoholism in my family like a flying arrow and I'm the bull's-eye. Anyone other than an idiot could have seen trouble coming when me and dad began hooking up when I got my license.

I had a midnight-blue 1977 Lincoln Mark V—a smooth-enough car on the highway but a pain in the ass on crowded city streets like those of downtown Tulsa, where every other street is one-way. It was my first time driving in Tulsa and there I was sharing nips of whatever rotgut Shorty happened to be drinking at the moment, lost, drunk, and happy as a fool can be. Shorty was supposed to be issuing directions but that's kind of hard when you can't keep your head up. He sat engulfed by the couch-like backseat, his feet barely reaching the floorboard. The party came crashing down when I bumped into a little Honda Civic at a four-way stop. Details are still sketchy, but I remember sitting handcuffed in the back of a police car watching a wrecker slowly pull my Lincoln up onto its flatbed. "Hey!" I shouted at the cop, "My dad's still in there! He's in the backseat!" The officer jumped out and waved down the driver, peered into the tinted windows of the car, and the next thing you know Shorty is stumbling out, wincing and groggy, looking all around him like—as he would say—"What in the hell?"

Shorty didn't have custody of me or my sister after the divorce, but we made periodic visits to Tulsa, in part to satisfy my paternal grandmother, who was always howling about "visitation rights, visitation rights" and blindly took Shorty's side in whatever argument. We lived in southern Oklahoma then, in Tishomingo, so the trips to Tulsa were time-consuming, costly affairs for a family living in the Chickasaw Nation housing projects. Shorty still held a job then, working on a Tulsa street crew. Once, he took me to OTASCO on Southwest Boulevard across from all the fuming oil and gas rail yards in west Tulsa. It was my tenth birthday. He had credit there and told me to pick out whatever bike I wanted. He was surprised that I picked out a knobby-tired

BMX model over a more costly ten-speed but it didn't really matter because we were notified at the counter that his credit was maxed, so I settled for a rod and reel and a Pepsi. Then it was across the street to the liquor store for a pint, which had him mumbling and walleyed before the bus arrived to take us back to the projects on Commodity Hill.

Shorty was a puzzle, a curiosity to me at that age, like a crow fascinated by a shiny object. He always seemed so troubled, so genuinely sad—seemingly on the brink of tears or breakdown each time we visited. Sitting, he'd pull me to him and I'd relent to the rough whiskers, the sour breath, the incomprehensible language: "I love you, son, don't you ever forget that, you hear? Tell your mother I'll always love her." His guitar-calloused fingers would caress my face, then pinch my cheek.

For all his weaknesses and faults, Shorty possessed qualities which won him if not friendship, then respect, among his peers. There are no real friends among the brotherhood of the town drunk and homeless because anyone will do anything for a drink: borrow money with no intention of paying it back, hide liquor in camp, hock your watch, pull that five-dollar bill out of the shirt pocket of your passed-out self. If you've got a few dollars everyone's complimentary, kiss ass, and a barrel of laughs. Broke on the street, though, this same guy is a pain in the ass, a leech, an extra bottomless throat. However downtrodden, though, Shorty was easygoing, quick with a joke, and nonjudgmental. He wasn't cocky—though he could adopt a little pimp bounce when feeling good, which made the uninitiated think he was arthritic or crippled—and was self-effacing to a fault. At a bar once I asked what happened to the woman he had been living with. "Took off with some other jackass I guess. Hell, I don't know." A lot of guys would act like they didn't care, but with Shorty, he truly didn't. He only cared about his next drink. You couldn't draw him into gossip-mongering about friends or family and he was proud of all the wild onions, crawdads, and cheap beer he'd consumed as a kid.

When I was in my twenties we landed in jail together again, this time in Tahlequah. I had hunted all over town for him before finding him at Hobo Hill earlier that afternoon. Hobo Hill was a homeless squat near the creek littered with rotten mattresses, flattened boxes, empty wine and whiskey bottles, and empty blue pouches of Bugler tobacco. I found him there, leaning against a tree trunk, passed out with a pink splatch of vomit on his shirt. I shook him by the shoulder and he woke up mumbling. He didn't even look up to see who it was. After he finally came around he wanted me to take him to the vacant house—he had another shirt there, he said. His eyes looked like they were about to bleed but as he gathered his wits he adopted a sly grin. "How's Flo and Zeke?" he asked.

After a stop at the liquor store we let ourselves in the rear of the house. Big Cheater was there, along with Tony Sixkiller and Bob Dragging Canoe. Another of Shorty's friends—Earl Davis—was passed out in the corner covered up with old coats. We started in on grape MD 20/20, which was OK since Shorty stayed coherent longer when drinking wine. It had been years since I'd actually had a decent conversation with him. All the boys were in good form too—no loudmouths, sloppy drunks, or pains-in-the-ass troublemakers who don't get a backbone until they get a good buzz on. Shorty was telling us about a certain minnow—a Jack Simon—that they would trap with pop bottles in the Illinois River when he was a kid and take to Lake Tenkiller, where the bass "just attacked those little minners," as Shorty put it.

I took the bottle from Sixkiller, gulped, and passed it on to Shorty. He drank, then went over to wake up Earl in the corner to get him an eye-opener. He nudged his shoulder repeatedly with his foot before bending down and discovering that Earl was dead, curled up in the fetal position. Everyone else hit the road, but Dad walked to the convenience store on the corner and asked the guy behind the counter to call the cops. We walked back to the house and shared the half pint while we waited on them. Before you knew it there were cop cars, fire trucks, and an ambulance in the front yard. Dad knew the officer but he said we were both drunk—which I readily admitted—and trespassing and that we'd both have to go to jail. They knew where Shorty lived and knew we would have to traipse through the middle of town to get home. They put us in the same cell and I was going to offer the only bunk to him but Shorty went immediately to the floor and was snoring before I could even pull my shoes off. I couldn't get Earl Davis's image out of my mind. His eyes were open. Other than that he looked normal, with a ball cap and new Wranglers and boots on.

I drove down to Tahlequah once and convinced Shorty to come back with me for a visit with Flo and Zeke. He hemmed and hawed, deliberated like he had other important plans. Like look for a job. Take a shower. Sleep. Apply for food stamps. Eat. Forget it. Open the bottle and the lid. He was dressed for the streets, layered in shirts and jackets and all wrapped up in comfy-looking powder blue coveralls. Such zany coordinated Salvation Army outfits I'd find him in. Somehow, though, at times he managed to pull it off. A V-necked beige sweater over a secondhand blue oxford, cuffs rolled up midway to elbow, of course. Red scarf thrown in for good measure. A baggy pair of brown polyester golf slacks and oxblood loafers without socks or strings. Street *GQ*. When he had the pimp walk working he was dangerous. I had asked him when he was fairly sober and on a Sunday because I knew he couldn't get a drink easily, and was flat broke. He had half a pint held over from the previous night, and I had two more of his "halfers" hidden in the car trunk in case he got terribly sick. He looked clean enough but it wasn't until he was in the car for a few minutes with the windows rolled up that I realized just how ripe he was. His coveralls covered everything except his stench. At Flo and Zeke's we tried to convince him, subtly, of his condition.

"Shorty, there's a washer and dryer there in the garage in case you might want to wash your clothes while you're here," Flo told him as we sat around the kitchen table drinking tallboy Schlitzes.

He ignored the comment, lost in conversation with Zeke about some long-ago fishing trip at Haskell Lake. Shorty laughed, shoulders jiggling like shock absorbers.

When he left the table, Flo and I whispered to each other about how best to get him into the shower. Zeke apparently never noticed the smell, protected by a bubble of his ever-present Prince Albert smoke.

"Hey," I tried, "why don't you strip off those coveralls and let me throw them in the washer. They look filthy."

He joked and laughed it off, until I finally gave up subtlety.

"Dammit. You stink," I had to tell him. Even then, he thought I was joking.

Shorty finally showered a couple of days later. It was a testament to his good-natured personality, and his relationship to us, that he was allowed to hang around that long, considering his condition. I sometimes find myself getting angry with my dad, thinking about lost chances, what could have been, et cetera. I'm angry, then I keep remembering the good things about him—his unassuming nature, the constant kidding and jokes. Even in the throes of depression and addiction, he managed to find humor in his condition. By chance, he ran into my sister at the clinic in town just after she had her first baby.

"He's got your eyes," she said.

"Red?" he inquired.

❧

In Maine I sold the '87 Toronado for scrap and bought a ticket to Tulsa, thinking there was a good chance I'd arrive before the postcard I had sent him last week, wherein I kidded him about drinking mouthwash. *Dear Shorty: If you're going to drink that shit at least step up to top shelf. Drink orange-flavored Listerine. It never fails where kidney failure is involved. Ha ha.* I signed it, *Your son, the only Cherokee ever mistaken for Chinese in downtown Portland, Maine.*

The Amtrak stopped in Boston, New York, and Chicago, where I called the hospital. They would only tell me he was still hospitalized. I already knew that, I said. From there I had to switch to a bus; I got off in Tulsa hunched over like an arthritic thirty-six hours later. I took a cab to the hospital, wondering if Shorty was going to make it or not, and when I arrived at his room he was sitting up in bed reading a newspaper and joking with the nurse.

"How are you doing?" I asked apprehensively, scanning his supine figure for tubes, hoses, machines making hissing noises. There were none. His face looked flushed, reddish, but his eyebrows were bushy and eyes bright. He looked fresh as a daisy.

"Without," he said, then laughed. "I'd feel a whole lot better if that nurse was sitting on my face. Goddamn, son, it's sure good to see you. How's Flo and Zeke?"

❧

He told me that Supertramp, a World War II veteran who collected a hefty monthly pension and picked out one drunk a month to present a crisp, clean hundred-dollar bill, had selected him a few days ago. He said he had bought a gallon of Old Crow for the occasion and remembered going to the park, then the next thing he knew he woke up in the hospital. He knew nothing of mouthwash scattered about his feet.

I couldn't believe he was still drinking the stuff; it says right on the bottle not for human consumption and if ingested induce vomiting immediately.

"How can you drink that shit anyway?" I asked.

"Practice, practice, practice," he said.

He said doctors told him he was in an alcohol-induced coma when the ambulance brought him in, and he said that that was the object. They had hooked up an IV for rehydration and before they released him prescribed an experimental drug that would help him quit drinking.

"Quitters never win," he said.

We tried living together after that. I really didn't have anywhere else to go, had a few bucks saved up and it would be nice to really get to know Dad, I thought, and get some solid carving time in. He mainly stayed in the garage-turned-bedroom off the kitchen, where he had a mattress laid across milk crates, a woodstove, a lamp, and his own private entrance. He passed the hours strumming on the guitar, practicing chords, getting halfway through a composition and starting all over again, sometimes playing the same riffs repeatedly in the middle of a song. I could tell when he became frustrated because he would play all the strings at once then slap the guitar, making a hollow thunk. The door would slam and I'd see him outside smoking a cigarette, wearing that silly Kappa Kappa Gamma sorority sweatshirt he'd found on the side of the road near the college.

He'd stand in the backyard burning trash in shorts and house shoes. His spindly legs made his potbelly seem huge in proportion to his body, which shook when he laughed at one of his own jokes.

"Have you seen Roy Orbison's new guitar?" he said.

"No."

"He hasn't either."

⁓

One afternoon I was lying on the couch listening to a storm move through. Cool wind fluttered the curtains, backed by a far-off rumble like bass drums. As evening fell, I dozed while reading a magazine article about trapping arctic foxes. A pink strobe of lightning awoke me; the rattling that followed shook the house. Dad was strumming along in the garage, deep galloping notes that echoed the thunder. I got up to shut the windows and he switched to a light, airy rhythm that matched the steady rain. When the storm passed and it was only sprinkling and dripping off the sides of the house, blinking in the sunlight, he played the high strings, made them tinkle like a banjo.

⁓

I started out for town the next day, cutting through a pasture, careful to avoid Deliverance, the retired bucking bull that had chased Shorty once and almost caught him. My aim was only to have a few beers at a bar in town and see if I could meet a woman and either go to her place or bring her back home. But there were only about a dozen ball-capped farmers sitting along the bar, not at all talkative, so I drowned my sorrows in pitchers of beer. There was a liquor store down the block so I went for a pint of schnapps before it closed. A little while later I went back to the bar but the door was locked. I kept walking down the street past a department store, a jewelry store, a hamburger joint. I walked across the street to an Indian art gallery and stood there looking at the paintings. They were typical Trail of Tears–themed prints, blanketed warriors staring off into space, riding slouched over on horseback. There was another typical subject: A warrior has died and is lying on his burial stand, but up in the atmosphere, damn, there he is again, atop his painted pony and shoving a spear in the air. Flowing hair, fierce scowl, *Warrior Spirit* title, et cetera, et cetera. As I was taking a drink a light inside blinked on and there was a guy drinking out of his own bottle. He had shoulder-length gray hair and a gray beard and wore paint-splattered white pants and a flannel shirt. He toasted me through the glass and we laughed. He opened the door and invited me in. After he heard my name, he said he knew my dad, introduced himself as Jefferson Dreadfulwater Jr. He wore thick glasses.

"I've drank many a bottle with ol' Shorty," he said.

He had several unfinished paintings on the wall; one had forest animals linking hands in a circle. In the middle was a rabbit reading to the assembled from a Cherokee-language Bible. Another painting had a background of Florida swamps painted in rich dark green with vines hanging in the foreground; there was a canoe outlined in pencil in the middle of the Everglades. You could smell all the fresh acrylic paints.

After I told him I was walking home, he said to forget about it; he would drive me in his 1957 Chevy. He wanted to see "ol' Shorty" and have a drink with him. We stopped for gas and beer at the last store on the way out of town. I was at the pump when he came running out lugging a giant box of beer, yelling for me to hop in. The way he said it, he meant now, so I dove into the backseat and he spun out on the gravel, the car whipping itself onto the asphalt. He roared down back roads with the lights off, whooping and hollering. He tossed a can of beer over to me in the backseat. I had never bothered to climb in front. At Shorty's we saw that the nozzle from the gas pump was still dangling out of his tank, shredded from its hose.

At home Shorty pulled out his guitar and Jefferson just so happened to have his harmonica. They played tunes all night and drank and told stories on each other. We finally passed out after the roosters started crowing next door, and when I woke up both Jefferson and Shorty were gone. There was a note stuck on the fridge, saying breakfast was inside, signed by Shorty. Hungry, I opened the door but it contained nothing but six cans of beer with another note tacked on: *LIQUID DIET. HA HA—SHORTY, YOUR DAD.*

Living in such a backwoods environment was about to drive me crazy. There was absolutely no traffic and I knew it was time to leave when impulsively I jumped from the couch to the window after hearing the first vehicle come up the road in three days. It was the denim-clad vegetable farmer in the red truck who lived about a mile away and went to town once a week like clockwork. I never knew if Dad was in the house or not: mostly he kept to himself in the garage, tinkering on the guitar or snoozing. He came and went through his own entrance, popping in to see if I would drum up dinner or not. If not, he just went to sleep. I never saw him lift a spatula; a fork, yes. If I didn't make a meal, we had sandwiches or commodity meat: cow, pig, or chicken.

I had thought that this period would give me time to paint or work on a sculpture but instead it just gave me time to wish I were somewhere else. Instead of working, I found myself daydreaming about the party I'd throw after winning Best of Show at the Heard Museum in Phoenix. Back to nature, getting to know your roots, living the simple life: to hell with that. Yes, he had been sick as a dog, but Shorty seemed OK now; he didn't need me and I hardly saw him anyway. I had imagined heart-to-heart talks or lengthy discussions about family history, but all I got was the same old baby stories: how I'd fallen into the lake while they were fishing, and how he was carrying me through the backyard drunk on his shoulders and nearly decapitated me on the clothesline.

I heard the Cherokee Smokejumpers were recruiting firefighters and more important heard it was easy to pass their fitness test. All you had to be was 1/128th Cherokee and jog a mile in fifteen minutes. Even someone like me, who had traded running for beer and cigarettes, could manage that. I got my

pick of Montana or south of Albuquerque, where some Indians had delib-
erately set a fire on their reservation covering about half the state so they
could get work. I had heard of guys that fought fires all summer only to come
home and get burned for all their money after getting drunk because they
had no bank account and everyone knew they were carrying thousands of
dollars wadded up in their shoes. Either that or they'd buy a car and total it
within a week or let someone borrow it who never came back. What a miserable feeling that must be, waking up with a hangover and an empty sock, or
your car in Arizona with a different paint job. But I just saw it as a free trip
to Albuquerque and then to Santa Fe, where there was a girl I wanted to see.

Later that summer the fire was always with us. I sat at an outdoor table at
the Ore House in Santa Fe smelling the char of faraway smoke and watched
as ash settled in the drinks of diners under rainbow canopies. Tourists and
natives alike were unwittingly drinking down the little flecks, chatting and
nodding toward the sky. Smoke had blotted out the sun, squeezing it into
a tight blood-red circle and turning midday into a carnival of underwater
shadows. "Flores, flores para los muertos," chanted an old Hispanic woman
selling flowers, pointing a bony finger at the noon eclipse. She turned and
looked right through me. "The world is coming to an end," she said in a
shaky voice. I saw rot in her teeth and fear in her eyes.

What lightning and arsonists had accomplished north and south, two
German backpackers matched with an unextinguished campfire in the
Jemez Mountains. I chose the Los Alamos fire but quit after a week upon
seeing two things: an eagle that had scorched its tongue black on a chunk
of glowing coal, squawking and jumping around with wings outstretched,
and a big juniper as tall as me that had turned completely into ash and
simply disappeared in a poof! when I tapped it with a stick. I had sucked in
enough smoke over the past few days that I could smell it even after shower-
ing. I collected my first and last check and caught a ride back down to Santa
Fe with a scientist from the national lab, just one in a caravan of thirty-
five miles of cars in a three-hour trip that normally took forty-five minutes. Now cashy again, I invited a girl I went to school with at the Indian
arts college who had remained in town but stayed in touch through e-mail
to lunch on the plaza. In this ebullient state (helped along with Seagram's
and 7UP) and with her looking at me over her glass with those smoky dark

eyes, I jotted a quick postcard to Dad, who had no cell phone, landline, or computer. *Dear Shorty,* I scribbled, *just wanted to let you know that your prodigy is relaxing at a fine restaurant in Santa Fe, New Mexico, with a fine woman, fine whisky and a fine wine. Wish you were here. Does your liver still quiver? Ha, ha.* I signed it, *Your son, also without a phone but in love with long distances. Jordan.*

~~~

A silversmith, Cynthia was a Seneca from Syracuse who had just finished six months of special studies at the Smithsonian. The art market was brutal for her that summer, so she found a job taking care of a handicapped pair who had, by a new law, been freed from state institutions and given their own housing in town, under the supervision of workers like Cynthia. They were her "clients" and they were "special." In college Cynthia spun some of the most astonishing jewelry the faculty had ever seen. An eight-piece set of her Spanish-silver spider-design rings was on permanent display at the contemporary art museum on the plaza.

Five years later she had slowed down on drinking, but understood and didn't mind if I brought my beer over to her clients' house as long as I kept it in a cup—lest someone from the state show up. Cynthia was in charge of Dianne, a twenty-two-year-old redhead with the mind of a three-year-old, and Nathan, a thirty-year-old Taos Pueblo Indian confined to a wheelchair after a car wreck when he was a teen, who was now "slow" because of it. He gave me high fives and watched pro basketball on TV. Dianne wore shorts, pink straw cowboy hats, nose-picker boots, and a squint-eyed expression, which was either a smile or grimace, I could never tell. All Cynthia had to do was cue up "Super Freak" on the CD player and Dianne would squat and sling her giant purse back and forth between her legs or whirl it around her head. This was any time day or night. Stripped across the top of the jambox on masking tape in big black Magic Marker were the words "DO NOT PLAY COUNTRY MUSIC!!" Dianne would not tolerate country-and-western music, throwing a fit any time she heard it.

Workers like Cynthia rotated in three eight-hour shifts and since she had afternoons, all she had to do was drive them around to the park, ski lodge, or DeVargas Mall and feed them supper, which without fail was either Whataburger, Homeboys Pizza, or Mucho Macho burritos from Allsup's. But Cynthia took her job seriously and I would sit out with her drinking a beer on the wheelchair ramp while she wove Nathan's hair into one long braid as the sun slipped behind Mount Taylor in a golden explosion. After her shift, as we would ride north back to her trailer on the pueblo, the fire glowed red like a crown on the mountain to our left.

On weekends I sat with her under the portico of the state history museum on the plaza as she peddled her wares. Tourists from New Zealand, Australia, or the U.K. would make the most brain-dead comments, wondering aloud where they "might find all the buffalo and teepees" or "Where does the Trail of Tears start?" After a few minutes of this I'd set off on my counterclockwise circuit, going for beer at Evangelo's ("We Proudly Do Not Serve Budweiser Products"), Catamount, El Farol, and the Ore House. I'd return to the plaza about $100 poorer and join in the long line of jewelry-fondling tourists, chatting with the Pueblo artists who sat in groups along the wall. They unfurled little velvet carpets and strategically situated their menagerie of silver and gold earrings, turquoise bracelets, coral necklaces, and stick pins fashioned in shapes of lizards, bear cubs, or bolts of lightning. Within their borders tiny diamonds were set, which blinked in the slants of light shooting through the wooden beams under the portico. If people were serious about buying they came through the line two or three times or knelt and inspected a piece instead of just wandering by avoiding eye contact. You learned to smile and look straight ahead and became familiar with an odd array of shorts, short-shorts, sun hats, sunburned legs, crutches, smear-faced kids, hairy arms, hook arms, drunks, and the annoying heavy thump of bass from teens cruising around the block.

After I returned I sat in for Cynthia at her spot while she went for lunch at The Burrito Factory. As soon as she left an Aussie wife inquired about a pair of clever pendulum earrings Cynthia had forged from silver and lapis lazuli. They were stylized storm clouds from which dripped three thin strings of turquoise symbolizing rain. In my slightly intoxicated state I doubled the price tag to $300 and talked her into a nice set of beaded baleen hair barrettes. I polished it all up and handed them over. Cynthia about fainted when I showed her the $500 cash, whereupon we rolled up the goods and headed for the casino. Sometimes we doubled or even tripled her jewelry money but usually just broke even or lost a little; I didn't care as long as there was money to roost at the bar and play video poker, and beer left in the ice chest when we got home to sit in back and watch for satellites and shooting stars.

I had painted my first landscapes and portraits at the art school and sold a few here and there in gift shops around Albuquerque. I even placed in a couple shows in California. But they paid next to nothing compared to the alabaster sculpture of a mountain lion that a Santa Fe gallery had sold on commission, but that check wouldn't come for a few weeks. It was as if I had carved it in another lifetime, it seemed so long ago. Cynthia kept all my news clippings in a scrapbook, and programs from shows and openings; stuff even I no longer had. She didn't care if I stayed at her place and worked during the day; the problem was I kept feeling antsy and liked tooling around town with Dianne and Nathan, nipping on a pint of peppermint schnapps and slipping Nate the occasional shot. Cynthia cracked that she should receive a raise considering she now had three clients to look after.

One afternoon Cynthia loaded up all three of us and we took off for her trailer to get her checkbook. She was driving the state-issued Plymouth Voyager, rigged with a lift so Nate could easily slide out of his chair and into the co-captain's seat. I sat behind Nate next to Dianne, who squirmed like a junior high kid as we took hilly 285 North past the veterans' cemetery and topped the hill next to the Santa Fe Opera. The fire still smoldered to the west, covering the mountain in a blurry shroud of smoke. The haze did to the normally fantastic blue sky what water does to whiskey. Thinking I might try to mix that color someday, I took a long drink of blackberry brandy I had found rummaging through Cynthia's cabinets and almost spewed it on the back of Nate's head it was so strong.

Cynthia liked to speed. Nathan's hair fluttered out the window while the green-gold of juniper and sandstone streaked by. Next to me, Dianne slapped her legs and made goofy faces, twisting her head this way and that. Cynthia held a cigarette and the wheel in her left hand and with her right fiddled with the radio, cutting through commercials and news static about the fire until landing on a familiar Eagles tune. "Well I'm standing on a corner in Winslow, Arizona, such a fine sight to see, it's a girl my Lord in a flatbed Ford, slowin down to take a look at me."

A little further in the song, at a part I eventually found out was a one-time departure for the band and unprecedented in rock music, there is a big banjo solo, as pickin' and grinnin' and hoedown as anything that ever emanated from the set of *Hee Haw*. Midway through this bluegrass-like riff, Dianne went apeshit and slapped me across the mouth right as I was taking a drink, busting my lip and splashing blood and brandy all over my face. Before I knew what hit me she had jammed her hands down her pants and was smearing crap over my hair, yelling and screaming like she was in agony. Blinded, I pawed the air in front of me. Cynthia turned to see what the hell and Dianne, eyes full of fury, yanked down on Cynthia's braid like it was a rope.

"Country music! Country music!" Dianne wailed, gnashing her teeth.

When Cynthia swerved to avoid rear-ending a Jeep, she overcorrected and in her panic stepped on the gas. We hit a pothole, bouncing in the air, which threw Dianne onto me again as the boxy vehicle hopped from left to right, Cynthia fighting the steering wheel. There was a curve and a dip ahead that rose up in front of us through the windshield like a slow-motion movie but at ninety miles an hour. The zippered yellow line stuttered then swirled away as if vacuumed. We shot off the highway and rocketed up a ditch that launched us hanging in midair until we crashed and sprang forward like a charging bull and teetered onto the side. Upside down and with Dianne sprawled in my lap, a wheel rotated wobbly above me. The impact knocked out every inch of glass but we were all strapped in and were OK. Sounds crawled back slowly: the grinding of the tire, slush of traffic, scuttling footsteps, a dreamy siren, and, lastly, from the Eagles, "Take it easy, take it easy, don't let the sound of your own wheels make you crazy." A grasshopper landed on a rock in front of my face, twiddled its front legs, and flew off. With its big bubble eyes and antennae it looked like a Martian.

"That goddamned country music," Cynthia moaned.

I didn't feel it appropriate at the time to argue that it was actually rock and roll. The music seemed both absurdly loud and just plain absurd out there in the desert.

Highway patrol, ambulances, and a fire truck arrived, jamming traffic one lane five miles all the way to Santa Fe. But since the wreck ended up on Indian land, Pueblo police handled the scene and what a scene it was: Cynthia dazed and stunned, wild haired and shaking as she smoked a cigarette; Nate unable to walk, sitting on a rock with one lens missing from his eyeglasses; Dianne curled up in the fetal position, hyperventilating and pounding her thighs; and me, half-drunk, reeking of brandy with a split lip, bloody shirt, and crap streaked down my face. A cop fanned his face theatrically, wondering aloud how much I had to drink. I told him nothing, that the stench was from a previously unopened bottle that broke in the crash. It was only after he had taken my name and info that I remembered I had an old warrant out of the pueblo from back in college. As I sat on the ground hoping they'd miss the warrant, Nate gave me a thumbs-up as they hauled him away on a stretcher. I made all kinds of promises to myself if they'd just please miss the warrant: quit drinking, start working out, get a job, paint more, go to church, give to the needy, volunteer. I heard the cop calling in my details but because of the wind and radio traffic caught only snatches of the response. So it was without much surprise that he returned from the vehicle carrying handcuffs.

Ten years earlier I had been arrested after I punched my girlfriend in the face in a drunken fight over money. I had wired her $250 (which actually costs $300) from San Francisco earlier that summer after she phoned begging because she was about to lose her new Probe. The court set up a preliminary hearing and let me out after I'd sobered up and we got back together and more or less dropped the subject. For a while she went around dramatically wearing a giant pair of Jackie O–type sunglasses and was left with a scar no wider than a fingernail sliver that she rubbed cream on three times a day. I truly was sorry, but in the back of my mind thought I wasn't entirely in the wrong considering she'd promised to reimburse me, then laughed in my face when I asked for it back. Plus we were both drunk, I reasoned. When the court date rolled around I was in San Diego, California, of all places, at my friend's reservation in the hills around Barona, where it snowed on Easter. I raised a beer at a party and pleaded not guilty.

The upshot was I had used my get-out-of-jail-free card back in '98. I got to see Cynthia once then didn't see her again for three years. I was shipped off to the city jail in Española, then to Los Alamos because Española was overcrowded with heroin tweakers and the pueblo didn't have its own lockup. At my initial arraignment it seemed the whole tribal judicial system turned out: there was a two-man/one-woman team of prosecutors, the judge, a bailiff, a judge's assistant, a court reporter, tribal cops, Los Alamos city cops who had transferred me to court in a van, and secretaries wandering about. The white judge wore a black leather vest and turquoise rings and had his silver hair pulled back in a ponytail—maybe this qualified him as indigenous, but he looked more Harley than honorable.

"I said ten years ago we would go to the ends of the earth to find you," he said and sentenced me to six months in jail for failure to appear, with four suspended, and set court on the domestic for two months off. I spent a furnace-like August and September in Los Alamos with a cell mate from Mexico City. We were in a small two-prisoner cell with one bleary Plexiglas window that had "Fuck Niggers" scratched on it diagonally across the middle. I kept wondering if it were a ringing endorsement, like "Eat at Joe's," or a racist condemnation. The toilet was so close to the beds you had to turn your head while the other guy took a dump. Other than that there was just enough room to do push-ups if you wiped down the floor around the commode.

With no books or magazines other than the Bible or the monthly *Watchtower*, there was plenty of time to think, write, or draw; the only problem was you had to yell "C.O." to get a guard to come and sharpen the little yellow scorecard pencils. It took a few weeks but I finally read the Bible front to back. I reckon I understood a great deal of it, but it wasn't what I'd expected in some places.

I jotted a note to Shorty, albeit in a less enthusiastic tone than I had written to him from Santa Fe. *Dear Shorty, Well they finally caught up with me in New Mexico like Migso said they would. I'm writing from the unfriendly confines of the jail in Los Alamos. I don't know if I ever told you but I had an old warrant here. Anyway I've got a court date in October and I'll find out then. Hopefully they'll give me time served and I'll be out. Don't be surprised if I am knocking on your door pretty soon. I hope you are laying off the Kentucky Deluxe but if not drink one for me.* I signed it, *Your son, high and dry in Los Alamos, New Mexico.*

Cynthia wrote that when she drove from Santa Fe to see me they wouldn't let her in because she was wearing shorts. *I might have incited a riot, ha ha.* She said the state had retaken custody of Dianne, but Nathan was doing fine. The only visit I got was from a tribal defender who said he had good news and bad news. The good news was that the ex wouldn't be testifying because she had moved out of state and they couldn't find her. The bad news was that tribal prosecutors had picked up the case. They had our old statements, my tape-recorded drunken confession, video, photographs, and officer affidavits to work with. If I was lucky and wrote a good enough letter of apology and pleaded no contest I might be released on time served. He said if I pleaded not guilty I would without question be returned to jail anywhere from six months to a year awaiting trial, depending on the judge's mood. There would be no bond because I had left the state and not shown up the first time. This judge especially did not like that.

"They're all over this like ants on a cupcake," he told me. "Yours is the only case they have right now they can really sink their teeth into. Of course it didn't help going to the West Coast ten years ago."

So I spent the remaining weeks artfully crafting an insincere letter of apology, trying to show off my vocabulary and insinuating that I wasn't just another common criminal off the street. Stuff like, *It is with much chagrin and embarrassment that I compose these words of sorrow to you today, Your Honor. I apologize to you, the court, the alleged victim and to the whole pueblo for my inebriated and regrettable actions that fateful night some ten years ago.* Atop my bunk I read the lines back to Fernando lying underneath me.

He resumed humming his Mexican ballad as they shut down the lights a level: not ever off, just lower. At my place in Exodus, the River Nile had turned to blood and goggle-eyed bullfrogs were bombarding Egypt in torrents.

～〇

Coming down in the van for court I was astounded how the fire had decimated the land. That time of year aspen and cottonwoods would be changing color, with brittle maroon, lavender, and peach-colored leaves fluttering against a turquoise sky. Instead it was gray and colorless, with monotonous stands of chalk-white trunks angling down steep slopes; ash upon ash, a mountainous holocaust.

Again, I was shocked by the number of people in the courtroom for what I believed to be a Mickey Mouse, kangaroo clusterfuck of proceedings. But I played the apologetic, reformed-offender role to an Academy Award–winning tee, bowing my head sorrowfully, shuffling my feet, frowning, saying in soft, subordinate tones, yes sir, no sir, pardon me? How did I plea? I glanced at my defender, who winked.

"No contest, Your Honor."

The same Harley-Davidson-looking judge sliced open my apology letter with a pocketknife and gave a speed read up and down, front and back, three brown sheets of Big Chief notebook paper. Never even blinked. I thought he would have read it admiringly weeks ago. He tossed it aside like junk mail.

"Mr. Coolwater, it's obvious to me that you are a bright young man, but one attempting to pull the wool over this court. A no-contest plea puts the onus on me, and while your plea is neither an admission nor denial of guilt, you, sir, are guilty. Yes, you may be sorry. Sorry for getting caught. I'm sentencing you to five years in the Indian Detention Center, suspending four on the condition of good behavior and another legitimate letter of apology, this time without your attempts at artistic hocus-pocus. Good luck."

I left New Mexico for Keams Canyon, Arizona, in the backseat of a Bureau of Indian Affairs cop car dressed in the smelly street clothes I was originally arrested in. They let me use the restroom at an Allsup's outside Bernalillo, recuffing me in the front so I could urinate. "I hope you got a piece of ass last night," the driver laughed, handing me a Coke and chips, "because there ain't none where you're going."

Going up Highway 666 north from Gallup, watching painted pinto ponies prance in cactus-scrub pasture dotted with water tank windmills, I thought that even though Dad was a big drunk, he never seemed to get in messes like this. I considered myself a good enough Joe, followed the do-unto-others rule, had a college education, didn't talk in movies, and was nice to cats, but here I was facing five years like any random crackhead.

The thing that struck me about the detention center—other than looking more like a library than a jail—was how easy it was to escape. Three inmates bolted the first two weeks I was there. The only problem was they were Hopi and the jail was on Hopi land, so they couldn't hang around the reservation because sooner or later they'd be caught and face more time. So those that went for it headed south straight for Flagstaff then to friends or relatives in Phoenix, sometimes settling in Scottsdale. But the rest of us gathered at the end of AA meetings and sang "Our God is an Awesome God" by God knows whom, led by a Korean woman with manly hands and hairy knuckles. For TV it was either the Winter Olympics, where figure skating was popular for the chance crotch shot on falls, or the local news, where the white weatherman couldn't pronounce the names of the Indian towns he was covering: Polacca, Hotevilla, Kayenta, Shonto, Ganado, Shongopovi.

It wasn't too bad—we weren't in little cells but in a wide-open dormitory-like setting with our beds lined up against the walls facing a commons area where we sat playing cards. There were about twenty-five of us in lockup, evenly divided among the young gangsters with garish multicolored tattoos, walking around with one pants leg rolled up; the middle aged with sensible haircuts and kids and a wife at home; and the old guys, veterans of overseas wars who had their Social Security numbers tattooed on their backs lest they be found dead in a gulley with no ID.

I sailed right along the first nine months, lost about fifteen pounds on a red beans and skim milk diet, read every book in the library, and drew pictures on every blank page I could find. I only wrote Cynthia and Dad; I didn't want the rest of my family to know where I was. But with Dad I didn't care. He had been locked up for drunk so many times he was the unofficial jail barber for inmates and cops alike. They actually let him out on a regular basis to go get the scissors sharpened at the drugstore down the street and maybe pick up some talcum powder or Mennen and he'd come right back in time for lunch, all chipper and smelling of mouthwash.

You got into your routines and there were stretches where time went by fast. Little things became major benchmarks and you actually counted the days until you could go outside and wash tribal cop cars or go up to the village and kill chickens for the old ladies or chop and stack wood for them. You were there so long you saw alcoholics come in with bloated, red faces and blood-shot eyes and leave slimmed down with their confidence and skin tone back.

It seemed every guy there was a master artist. Most of them were allowed to carve kachina dolls for a couple hours each night in a special workroom. The intricate but feather-light wooden figures were posed in some sort of dancing action, with a foot in mid-step, or an outstretched hand clutching a yellow-and-blue stick snake. I had a nightmare one night that they all came alive and were walking about the room with their scary masks and wild-eyed expressions. I didn't know anything about kachinas but I carved some styl-ized bears and horses and sent them to Cynthia. The dried cottonwood root was super easy to whittle.

The prisoners gave their figurines to family to sell, then you'd see those same inmates with new Nike basketball shoes, digital Walkmans and CD players, and colorful baskets of Doritos, M&Ms, Skittles, Gatorade powder, and ramen noodles. But the carving was cut off after someone got into a fight and was caught with an X-ACTO blade he had smuggled out of the workroom.

Mostly I talked to Psych Mike from Santa Clara Pueblo. Me and Psych Mike, and the occasional Navajo, were the only non-Hopis in the place. I was nearing in on three months left and had begun to think of the letter I was going to rewrite the judge when I got into a fight on the basketball court. It was always crowded out there on the cement slab; people would randomly play, take a shot, then walk around the perimeter, doing jumping jacks or push-ups. The old men sat under the shade of a tree in the corner and smoked roll-your-owns. It was a sunny spring day but had snowed briefly that morning, leaving puddles on the slick concrete. I was thinking how the sky and the high-desert terrain looked just like it did around Glorieta as you rode the train through the Sangre de Cristos heading toward Denver: clumps of juniper and sage underneath a magnified blue sky where everything was sharp and etched in clear lines. I was staring at three ravens swaying on a willow branch when the overinflated ball rocketed off my forehead with a ringing *whaaang!* and staggered me to one knee.

Everyone on the court started laughing and the one who threw it, a lanky long-haired teenager who was howling the loudest, shouted, "Shoot it homeboy, you were open! Ha ha ha ha ha!" I pretended to walk it off while the laughter subsided and play resumed, but something inside me began to roil, merged with the stinging on my face and the echoing in my ear, and formed something called fury banging against the back of my skull. Bolts shot out my eyes. The silver in my teeth vibrated. But I jogged calmly back onto the court, joined the flow of the game up and down, offense then defense, until I finally had the ball in the clear. I dribbled and pulled up for a jumper but faked and held the ball. While everyone looked skyward for the shot I pivoted and fired the Spalding as hard as I could, grunting, like a pitcher stepping into a fastball. It wavered on a straight line like a bullet or missile. The teen's head snapped back and he dropped to the ground like he'd been shot, me on top of him. I pounded his pretty face four or five times before someone kicked me off him and jumped on me and there was general melee until the officers came and broke it up.

Psych Mike brought it up first; until then I hadn't even thought of it.

"Well there goes your good behavior," he said.

Oddly the teen and I became pretty good friends after that. It was he who came up and apologized first after a few weeks when he was sure no one was looking. Around the other gangsters he mad-dogged me and acted like he wanted to beat my ass. I told him not to worry about it and we shook hands. He was actually a pretty likable guy, sort of like a little brother. We always teamed up in dominoes and were workout partners lifting weights. The scary thing was I think he enjoyed the whole brawl. He was in jail for committing the grievous sin of bootlegging whiskey and beer on the reservation, where it is outlawed. He said he and his cousin would drive to Winslow and bring back Bud Light, Jack Daniel's, and Coors by the case and sell it out of a shed in back of his mom's house. They would quadruple their money, selling cases of beer for seventy bucks. But their operation came crashing down when they sold to an undercover cop who had videoed the whole thing on his cell phone.

At nights—where I slept in fits and starts for weeks, convinced the teen would sneak over and stab me with a buck knife—I began to think of what Psych Mike had said. The possibility that I be let out after a year hinged on the condition of good behavior. Since my canteen had been cut off and I couldn't watch TV or play basketball for a month, somewhere something had been logged on my record. I went around asking anyone who'd listen—inmates and guards alike—what they thought would happen. Some said not to worry about it, that it was minor and in three months I'd be drinking a beer on a sandy beach.

Many, though, said I'd screwed up, that I might as well get settled in for four more years. The teen said I was fucked. Psych Mike said he'd write. The big-bellied Hopi guard who fell asleep at his desk all the time and sneaked us cigarettes (he'd walk by and pretend to drop them out of his pack without noticing) said to make out a will and laughed his ass off. I daydreamed through the next few weeks thinking about it. Psych Mike would be talking to me for fifteen minutes straight until I realized I hadn't heard a word he'd said. "Four more years, four more years," paraded through my thoughts like a presidential campaign chant. It was after about a month of this that I decided to escape.

Behind women, partying, and how you landed in jail in the first place, escaping was the next-most-talked-about subject. Without fail, if someone had his mouth open he was talking about one of the above. There were two ways to make a break for it. The most complicated involved playing sick and setting up a nurse's appointment for the next day. One of the guards would drive the sicklies in a white van to the clinic at the edge of town about ten minutes away, always after breakfast but before lunch. But before then you called one of your relatives or friends and told them when you would be there. And when the guard wasn't looking, which was always, you went out the back and jumped in a car and were long gone. But I didn't know a soul between Oakland and Albuquerque and no one within a million miles willing to drive all day and night to the middle of the Hopi Reservation and aid and abet a jailbreak.

So that meant the second option: simply crawling out of the ceiling. I never knew if it was a case of the guards not knowing how, or if they knew and didn't care, but about a half dozen had broke out in ten months. Every time someone escaped, guards usually just went around the perimeter of the fence, banging it here and there with nightsticks, or made their rounds inside our quad, checking underneath our bunks and going through our underwear when the answer was right above their heads.

～⌒

Before I broke out I wrote a letter to Dad, hinting that I might be coming back soon. *Dear Shorty, What kind of bird don't fly? Can you believe it? I've almost done a year, but my time in the Indoorsmen Society as you call it is running short. Right about now I fancy a drop. That's British for I need a drink. Learned that in a book. Yes, they have books here and I've read all three of them. I've lost about twenty-five pounds so when I make it back we'll throw a hog in the fire or something. Get those clippers ready because I need another haircut, or did you hock them again for a jug?* I signed it, *Your son, Jordan the Jailbird, in Arid Zona.*

～⌒

It was common knowledge among inmates that one single ceiling panel near the rear of our wing entered into a crawl space that traversed diagonally across the guards' control booth and past offices leading to the weight room. On the roof of that room was one of those cone-shaped silver exhaust fans that spun like a top in the wind but other than that served no visible purpose. It wasn't bolted down or hooked to anything and could be pushed off its base and returned snug. The teen knew all this because his brother had fled a few months earlier and was now living temporarily in Tempe. The plan was for us to make it to his house on Second Mesa about twenty miles away, where his uncle would drive us off the rez and into Flagstaff. We had each saved three or four baloney sandwiches and cookies for the journey, and I had that check for five hundred Cynthia forwarded me from the gallery.

After the guard made his bed check, walking by each bunk with a clipboard, sometimes stopping to chat with a prisoner who, chances were, was a relative, the lights were dimmed to a foggy dull yellow. We waited a few minutes then stacked the plastic chairs underneath the ceiling panel while someone looked out. The teen went first, pushing the panel up and over and lifting himself up like you'd do doing dip exercises in the gym. I knew it was game-on when he reached down to grab the sandwiches and the flashlight I had filched from someone's house in Polacca when I chopped firewood for the old ladies. I had a split second to change my mind but didn't. The only reason I was doing this was I thought that as a nonfelon offender the only way I'd be caught and returned to jail is if I went back to the pueblo, which as far as I was concerned no longer existed. I figured if the Hopis could do it and go no farther than Phoenix, they sure as hell wouldn't come after me in the Tenderloin.

Inching on my knees through the narrow tunnel, trying to be quiet and not cough from dust and mouse turds, with my heartbeat thumping in my ears, I envisioned them below hustling to get the chairs back in place and get into bed so they could act like they'd been asleep in case a guard came back. And when the officers came around asking each inmate what he knew about the escape—which they would as soon as count right after breakfast—I imagined them with newspapers flipped up, ignoring questions, or on their stomachs faking sleep, as I myself had done in six interrogations. By then I'd be on a bus halfway to San Francisco, somewhere near Twentynine Palms thanking God and Greyhound I was gone.

A silver spray of stars greeted us on the roof, where we replaced the fan and crawled on our bellies to the edge of the building. There were no vehicle lights for miles all around, no one in the parking lot or walking around in the yard. It sounds like out of a Western, but far off a coyote howled, then a bunch joined in a chorus. Following the teen, I jumped, dropped, and rolled from the one-story structure, and jogged after him hunchback-like down a trail between two junipers and into an arroyo. A whole spider web of these miniature canyons connected the reservation and the teen was on intimate terms with them. They were seven or eight feet deep so you were invisible to anyone on the highway and with the moon and cloudless night it wasn't hard seeing in front of you. The teen never said a word. I just followed him in a light jog like we were two suburbanites out for a moonlight run next to some big-city river walk. We ran until we came to the spot where his cousin had left a sack of clothes in a plastic white grocery sack. We stopped and changed, burying the blaze-orange jail suits under piles of rocks, and quickly ate the sandwiches. He had told his cousin over the phone in Hopi that I was about as big as he, the cousin, was, so the jeans and T-shirt fit well but he had left a pair of tan alligator-hide dress shoes that looked absurd but not as bizarre as my linoleum-brown jail slippers. We started off again due west, walking at a steady clip, with the teen sometimes scrambling up a slope out of the canyon to get his bearings. He motioned me over and pointed at his starlit mesa, which rose in black silhouette in the clear night—close but yet so far.

The more we walked the farther away the mesa seemed to appear, like a big chess piece on the retreat. Since we had to follow the snaky ancient river-bed, we probably walked three miles to every one in actual distance. I kept hearing things scurry away across rocks and crash into the brittle weeds.

"Lizards. Could be timber rattlers, though," the teen said, and laughed in the silence when he saw my expression.

Slowly, then with startling clarity, I began to see my breath in the pre-dawn chill and as it grew light the teen nodded toward an adobe house with a yellow porch light near the edge of the mesa. The light was on only at certain times, he said. We stayed under cover of the arroyo until we were right next to the house.

"There's my dog, Apache," the teen whispered, pointing at a brindle-colored pit bull who came charging at us when we crawled out onto the rim of the little gorge. I thought it was going to attack but when it saw the teen it whimpered in a low howl, barked once, and jumped up with paws on the teen's chest, tail thumping the ground. The teen scruffed his head and let him lick his face. The dog went to me for a brief instant but went right back to the teen, so happy he began to piss. The dog, not the teen. There was an orange van; apparently we were to creep in back and wait until his uncle came out at dawn. But there was a note stuck in the driver's door. Under flashlight it read: *Sorry nephew, but you are on your own. Can't risk it. Keys and money under the mat. Be careful and call. They'll come here looking. You know what to do with the van.*

I took a leak myself as the sun lit up a gold horizontal streak to the east and the first icicle of light jabbed my eye. I inhaled the delicious smell of burning pine and exhaled memories: a warm, squishy squirrel belly, Grandpa's .410, the World Series in daytime, scotch and water. A thin thread of smoke curled from the chimney atop the house. The structure had a quaint oddball mixture of brown adobe, modern oak doors, window screening, plaster, white cinder block, red brick, aluminum, and tinted windows, like it had been masoned together carefully over the decades by Picasso in a cubist fit. With cars and trucks parked at odd angles here and there and bikes and toys scattered across the yard, which overlooked the sweeping canyon floor we had just covered, it looked like a very comfy place to make a life if you weren't an escaped convict. The land slanted downward from the mesa and in its undulating sameness created the illusion of illusion. What seemed close was far, and vice versa. Leg muscles still twitching after the six-hour walk, I squinted to see the arroyo we had crossed but it was impossible, covered under a vast blanket of juniper, shadow, and mist.

The teen said it was about two hours to Flagstaff and there were two hours until bed check at the jail. He let Apache in and started the van and when he floored it I fell back ass over teakettle, chair and all. The teen laughed, saying his uncle usually took out the passenger's chair to let his dog stand up front when they went on their rides, so the seat was never bolted down. Sorry, he said, but he forgot. But the moment lightened the mood. I for one was jittery with the sensation of freedom, cool clean air, money, a ride, real clothes, cigarettes, and a bottle of Tvarscki vodka the teen found under his seat. We had actually made it! The teen was going to see his girlfriend in Phoenix and start a new life. They wanted to have babies, he said. Said he was sick of the reservation. I at that moment would have traded places with him; the sight of the house and smell of the smoke had struck a chord in me. It spoke of stability, roots, heritage, a sense of belonging and a middle finger at the modern world. The kid, he'd be back, like a moth to flame. Me? Who knew?

Carefully observing the speed limit and wearing sunglasses, caps, and seat belts, we made it to Flagstaff, taking a big drink when we crossed the reservation border into Navajo country then Coconino County. The teen took me to a trading post at the edge of town that always bought his "dolls," as he called his kachina carvings. His uncle had left him a doll wrapped in towels in a toolbox in the back, and the owner let me cash my check without ID after the teen vouched for me, but I had to buy something. The only ID I had said, "Indian Detention Center, Jordan Coolwater, D Pod." So after the teen sold the owner the kachina for $100, I bought it right back for $125 and everyone was happy. I tried to give the sculpture back to him at the depot where he dropped me off but he said to keep it as a memento, and wrote down his uncle's telephone number inside a book of matches in case I ever wanted to contact him. We were both a little drunk and talking like two old college pals who wouldn't mind if either ever dropped in on the other unexpectedly— fugitive escape warrants be damned.

"If you get caught you don't know me," the teen said.

"Know who?" I said, which caught him off guard a moment, then we both laughed.

"One more thing," he said.

"What's that?"

"Keep your head in the game when you're on the court."

He drove off, with Apache hanging out the window barking at buses and trains.

I tried to buy a ticket on the Southwest Chief for L.A. to connect with the Coast Starlight and up to San Francisco but Amtrak wouldn't sell without ID. The only other option was the Greyhound next door, where the agent said the next westbound bus was that night twelve hours later, but there was one eastbound in an hour. By now my buzz was wearing off and I broke out in a sweat every time I saw a cop car cruise by or station security staring at me. Calmly as possible I bought a one-way ticket for Tulsa, trying not to shake as I forked over the money. The agent never asked for ID, only inquiring if I had bags to check, but the only thing I had was that kachina doll. I bought the *Arizona Republic* and kept my head down until I got on the bus.

We dropped down out of the Coconino National Forest onto flat I-40 as we reeled in the Arizona towns: Winona, Winslow, Holbrook, Sun Valley, Chambers, Chetco, Allentown. I didn't relax until we crossed the state line into New Mexico, where I got off at smoke-break stops on the dark desert highway with the other down-and-out, who seemed clones of other fellow rejects I had ever ridden a Greyhound with: the old black man busing it to Chicago to visit his daughter because he's never flown in a plane and isn't about to start; the separated mother of two with eyes framed in blue mascara so that she looks like a ghoul on her way to "Grandmaw's" in Tuscaloosa; the soon-to-be-blown-up-in-Iraq army recruit on his way to South Carolina to report to his base; and the hard-looking parolee with his monster quads, neck tats, pillowcase full of clothes, and release papers en route to "any-fuckingwhere but here."

I got off in Albuquerque to buy a different set of clothes and take a shower at a cheap hotel on Central, insisting on a second-floor room so some crackhead wouldn't try to crawl in my window off the street. I checked in as "F. Scott Fitzgerald," hoping that the Nepali behind the counter hadn't studied early twentieth-century American literature. I thought about a haircut but decided to save my money and have Shorty do it. I also thought about calling Cynthia, but forced myself to block that out of my mind. That was hard because it had been a while and I kept thinking about her long brown legs that clamped around my back and her tight lithe body that squirmed so much it felt like you were being screwed by a boa constrictor. But she lived adjacent to the pueblo, where right about now even the judge himself was probably out prowling for me on his Harley.

After a nap I walked back down to the bus station in the gray premorning light and caught the Chicago-bound 4:45 that would stop in Tucumcari, Amarillo, Elk City, El Reno, and Oklahoma City. I swallowed three sleeping pills with a half pint of lemon-flavored rum in the station bathroom before I boarded and slept blessedly all the way to Oklahoma City, where a sunglasses-wearing undercover cop in street clothes boarded with a German shepherd and I thought about running for the door. After going up and down the aisle, sniffing in every row, including mine, the dog froze and whimpered on a duffel bag two seats up from me and when the rider got back on the bus after buying soda and chips, he was handcuffed and driven off in an OCPD squad car. "Well, looks like he's going to have a little layover in Oklahoma City," the driver said wryly as we backed out and headed up the Turner Turnpike to Tulsa.

⌒

I never thought I'd say I was glad to see Dad's house again. I stomped through the pasture in twilight and saw the porch swing on the cedar deck and my uncle's truck in front. The house seemed choked in greenery after spending two years out in the desert: There was thick grass that needed mowing, leafy enormous trees hanging umbrella-like over the house vibrating with locusts, and fields beyond ripe with jungles of Johnson grass and corn. Gnats hung in clouds over the gardens and farther out, in the pasture, I saw the big humped form of the bull swinging its tail.

I tried the door but it was locked so I knocked and saw my uncle pull back a curtain and peer out, owlish in his glasses. He opened the door with a big smile.

"Where in hell you been you nutty thing you," either one of us could have said but it was my uncle said it first.

"I was searching for Shangri-La but wound up in this hellhole," I said walking in. I pulled out the whiskey I had bought in town for Shorty. "Where's he at? It is drink-thirty I'm afraid."

I drank and sat down. Uncle had already fired up his little one-hitter. He held up a finger for me to wait as his cheeks ballooned and he spewed out smoke.

"Oh fuck, you haven't heard have you?" he said and sat down and kind of buried his head in his hands, then reached for my bottle.

I took it as a rhetorical question.

"Shorty's dead. We buried him six months ago yesterday."

My uncle was the biggest bullshitter ever to walk the earth, and all the dope had made him paranoid and a little dingy, but his voice had the ring of truth. Still, I sat in silence waiting for the punch line or for him to jab my arm and tell me to load up, let's go get him from the park like we'd done a hundred times before, but that never came. I took another drink and slid the bottle over, never taking my eyes off him, checking his expression and waiting for him to break into a grin. He didn't. "We tried to reach you but no one knew where the fuck you was," he said.

As we drank he told me that Shorty had repeated the procedure that nearly killed him last time: drink mouthwash and pass out in the park. This time no one found him and no ambulance was called. After the temperature dipped to fifteen degrees he simply froze to death during the night leaning up against a tree facing the Illinois River, which had skimmed with ice around the banks. My uncle knew this because he discovered him; he knew all his drinking spots and had driven around until he found him. He knew it was him from a distance by the orange wool cap he always wore. Uncle showed me the little program they printed for his funeral. *Donald Everett 'Shorty' Coolwater*, it read. *Born 1945. Called home by the Lord in 1999. Barber.*

They listed me as an honorary pallbearer and my hometown as Muskogee, Oklahoma, although I hadn't lived there in fifteen years. But none of this sank in until my uncle brought out the sack of letters and postcards I had been sending him from all over the country, the majority of which were unopened, some at least five years old and postmarked from places like Black River Falls, Wisconsin; Ethete, Wyoming; and Macy, Nebraska. He had scribbled musical notes and snatches of lyrics on most of them in pencil.

I shook my head and almost cried but instead began to laugh, my uncle looking at me crazy. But he started laughing too and the more we laughed the louder we got, laughing at each other laughing, looking at each other and thinking the same thing: Shorty was getting the last laugh. Those who have coexisted with a drunk may understand.

Whoever said things happen for a reason is a damned fool or an evolution theorist. Things happen for no apparent reason whatsoever. Or at least they did to me. In the box of mail that had been waiting on me at Dad's was a packet from Cynthia and something from California that I thought had to have been put in the wrong box but was correctly addressed to me. Cynthia had enclosed digitized color slides of my artwork that had been scattered all over New Mexico, Arizona, and Nevada, and a letter saying she hoped I didn't mind but she also sent them to an artists' colony in the Bay Area. The letter from the colony offered a scholarship to join a two-year workshop which afforded visual artists time to work on projects. Everything was paid for except housing but you received a monthly stipend. Two more weeks and I would have missed the deadline for accepting.

So I'm back in San Francisco again where daily walks take me to the end of Municipal Pier, which curves out over the bay like a backwards apostrophe. From there you can see Chinese immigrants catching Dungeness crabs in wire baskets baited with bacon, or watch sea lions barking and wrestling on the docks, putting on a show for tourists, who in turn are aped by mimes or scared stiff by pranksters jumping from behind fake bushes. Sad-faced clowns offer tricks along the wharf, as do prostitutes on the corner of Geary and Leavenworth. Sometimes I look at Alcatraz and think of Psych Mike or the teen, or look at Golden Gate and the fog and freighters flowing underneath and wish Cynthia were here. I still write postcards to Shorty, but don't mail them and keep them in a drawer under one of his old badger-bristle shaving brushes. It keeps me half-sane. It's not the craziest thing anyone has ever done in this town.

The Hooferman

Natalie Diaz

I STARTED BELIEVING IN THE HOOFERMAN THE NIGHT BOY PULLED THE rope from the old canal—it lifted from the dirt inches at a time—until a hoof and leg appeared at the end. Boy hollered as loud as my cousin Wendell and I. We all ran from the creosotes and smoke trees to the streetlight across the road. The rope and leg didn't move. The bushes were still. Boy walked over, cool-like, grabbed the rope, and drug it back. The hoof scraped the asphalt. We huddled, inspecting it—it was boney and dry looking. It smelled salty. I thought it was a horse leg, but didn't know why it'd been in the canal, or on a rope. Wendell bet it was a goat leg, but none of us had ever seen a goat with a leg that big. Boy said he knew what it was. *Hooferman!* he screamed. He swung the rope over his head, letting the leg fly.

We watched him, whirling in circles, flinging that awful leg. Blue-brown light slid across his mouth and teeth. Boy was crazy. Everyone knew it. He had no parents except for two even crazier uncles. We left him under the streetlight, swinging at nighthawks.

We went to Wendell's. There was a party in his backyard. Boy's uncles brought a white hobo with them. I'd seen the hobo before at the Colorado River, down by the bridge. He had a dog he said was part wolf. The dog wouldn't let anyone near him, not even Boy's uncles. The backyard filled with people and music. Wendell's auntie set up her drum set outside the washroom and played along with the stereo. She closed her eyes and pushed her face toward the sky, hair whipping in every direction. When I stood too close, I lost track of my heartbeat in all the drumming.

Wendell and I ate hot dogs and argued about Hooferman. *He's not real,* I said. *My dad saw him,* Wendell said. *My dad said only drunks see him,*

I replied, *and it's really the devil they see*. Wendell told me, *Your dad can't see him because he's white*. My dad is Spanish, but I was hungry so I didn't argue. Plus, I heard trouble in the front yard.

One uncle had led the wolf-dog away with hot dog buns and potato chips. The hobo should've left then. I wanted to tell him to go. *Where's my dog?* he asked Wendell's mom. She looked away. Wendell's auntie started drumming again.

He should've left before the uncles shoved him into the gravel. Before they kicked him. Before one found a rock the size of a cantaloupe and smashed it down on his head. Smash. Smash. My heart fell in time. I dropped my hot dog in the dirt and ran. Wendell yelled, *Don't call the cops*.

I ran home like something was behind me. I passed Boy, walking toward Wendell's, twirling the leg in the air. *Hooferman!* he cried out. And I knew he was right.

Lubbock Is Not a Place of the Spirit

Murray Farish

I HAVE THOUGHT ON NUMEROUS OCCASIONS THAT THE BEST THING TO do about Clive is to kill him and then bury him out in the desert somewhere. Clive is problematic because he knows the following things that I wish he did not know:

1. Allison is not really my girlfriend.
2. I've been telling my family that Allison is my girlfriend.
3. I have a series of pencil drawings of Allison in various poses.
4. I have written a series of love songs to Jodie Foster.

Clive knows the last of these four things because one night I shared a small number of these songs with Clive, and he pretended to listen intently and honestly, only later to claim he would turn my songs over to the police. He knows about the third thing because when I'm out at class and he's sitting in the apartment supposedly writing a treatise about human consumption of natural resources, he instead spends his time going through my possessions. He knows about the second thing because one time I was on the phone talking to the man who claims to be my father—whose corpse is lately on my mind—and Clive heard me tell him that Allison is my girlfriend. He knows about the first thing because one time I was on the phone, pretending to talk to Allison, and Clive sneaked up on me and snatched the phone away and heard the dial tone. And then he sent me to the liquor store, because he is a bully of the intellectual and spiritual type, and he inspireth not.

Clive says my brother called three times and where the hell have I been? He needs skim milk and a carton of Marlboros.

I have been to the following places:

1. English class; had the following experience after English class:
   Teacher: It's John, right?
   Me: It's John.
   Teacher: Where have you been?
2. The Golden Galleon, where I ate one-half of one-half of a Raiderburger with cheese. Left when I began imagining the hot globules of deep-fried fat pocking the pink skin of an infant.
3. The filling station.
4. The grounds outside Knapp Hall, where Allison lives.

Call your brother, says Clive.

This is the fourth day in a row that I have been unable to have a bowel movement.

Clive says—your brother called again today. Clive rarely leaves the apartment and never watches television, but today when I come home Clive is watching President Carter on television, talking about the economic crisis. Usually, when I want to watch television, Clive groans. Clive subscribes to at least fourteen different magazines, nine of which I pay for. I own a Gibson guitar.

Song for Jodie #143 (a ballad)

> *I wouldn't have you on the streets, my little one——*
> *I wouldn't have you out there on the streets*
> *The nights I'd have you in between the sheets, my little one——*
> *And rub the temples on your lovely head*

Today at the English class the teacher taught a poem called "The Passionate Shepherd to His Love," by Christopher Marlowe. He also said that Christopher Marlowe was a spy who was killed in a tavern brawl. He also returned a test I did not take. I think Allison did well—she seemed pleased, and smiled a half smile, the bottom corner of one top tooth showing. *Fetching* is a word I'd like to use to describe it.

Today I'm at home when my brother calls. Clive says—you get it, dammit. My brother says—How's school going have you talked to Mom and Dad lately how's Allison?

Look, I've got some work for you, my brother says.

I've got something I need you to do and you need something to do, he says.

A job would be good for you right now, I think, in a lot of ways, he says.

I'm running this guy's campaign for the House of Representatives, and I want you to come work for us, he says.

I just want to work long hours, I tell him.

No problem, he says.

Clive distinctly remembers giving me a check for his half of the rent. Today I spent twenty minutes in the bathroom. I had the need to move my bowels, I felt the pressure, but when I sat down nothing occurred. I strained. I stopped straining and rubbed my lower back, in the kidney regions, for quite some time, which is a technique. I tried straining while standing up to produce something, a beginning, some breach, some peeking of a head. After twenty minutes I managed to produce one small rock of feces, brown and cracked and cakey.

More than 200,000 Americans, mostly men, die on toilets every year.

I want a job where I have to work long hours. I can't sleep nights. Allison was out tonight, with that little slut roommate of hers. They were out until nearly 2:30.

≈⌒

Song for Jodie #156 (a ballad)

Come live with me and be my love
Come live with me and be my love
Babe—————————
Come live with me and be my love
Without you I can't seem to move
There's more in me than you can ever see from where you are . . .
So come and live with me and be my love.

≈⌒

My brother sends me out armed with literature. Fliers and bumper stickers in a milk crate at my feet. The candidate's face on a sign. He grins. He has Lubbock on his mind. From Lubbock, For Lubbock. I stand at the corner of Broadway and Tenth, near Sneed Hall, holding my sign, armed with my literature that I keep in a milk crate at my feet. If anyone comes up and asks questions about the candidate, I'm supposed to be polite and give them some literature. I'll work anytime, anywhere. The city's motto is: *Lubbock!*

≈⌒

Spoon-benders and other psychic phenomena. Christopher Marlowe was a spy. Clive asks why haven't I paid the phone bill. Clive says he distinctly remembers telling me to pick up some paprika and Marlboros. Clive is writing a treatise on human consumption of natural resources. Clive knows about Allison.

Today I saw her leaving her biochemistry class. I was standing on the corner of Broadway and Tenth with my sign for the candidate and my milk crate full of literature and bumper stickers. The following experience occurred:

A lady comes up to me at the corner. A lady who is probably fifty years old, and dry. She asks me why she should vote for the candidate. She's wearing pants. Black polyester pants tight on her dry hips and flared out around her legs. And a white shiny shirt with ruffles. What does he stand for? she says. In the case of this experience occurring, I have been instructed by my brother, director of campaign operations, to say the following eight things:

1. The candidate believes in America first.
2. The candidate believes in lower taxes.
3. The candidate believes in God.
4. The candidate won't raise your taxes, like the other guy.
5. The candidate understands Lubbock.
6. The candidate puts Lubbock first.
7. The candidate thinks it's high time we took this country back.
8. The candidate asks for your vote for the House of Representatives.

Then I'm supposed to give them some of the literature I have in my milk crate.

But when the Dry Lady asks me, I can't think of any of these things. It's all in the flier, I say. I hold out a flier, but not a bumper sticker. Bumper stickers are more expensive and should only be given to those who specifically request them, number one, and number two, my brother says, I'm supposed to get some kind of feel for the people who specifically request bumper stickers, to try to gauge how firmly they support the candidate and how likely they are to actually go out on Election Day and vote. He says there are lots of people who just want to take a bumper sticker and then not do anything about it. Not even put it on their car. Why, I don't know, he says, but it's true. People just like to get things of value, however small, as they're walking around town. Especially college students. Which is why we don't want to give out bumper stickers to just anyone and everyone.

Here's what I think, the Dry Lady says. I think you don't know *what* he stands for. I think he doesn't stand for anything. I think if he stood for something you'd be able to tell me straight out. I think you just lost my vote.

Just take the flier, ma'am, I say.

I don't want anything to do with your flier, and I don't want you people knocking on my door anymore, either, she says. I've had it with you. She either said that or How sad for you, I couldn't tell which. She walked away, her dry legs bone-clattering up Tenth, and got into a gold Valiant parked there on the street. I was sweating terribly.

So now I'm back on the corner with my sign, and Allison is walking with her slut tramp whore roommate toward Bledsoe. Her light blond hair shines even in the thin September twilight. Her friend is a toad of blood.

Song for Jodie #151 (a ballad)

When you feel the terror of existence
I will comfort you like a child
When you feel awed by my insistence
Then I'll know your blood is running wild
Chorus:
When you mewl just like my little kitten
I'll know I have you
When you cry————————
When I leave————————
Then I'll know I have you.

✑

Clive is drunk. He sends me out for more Evan Williams bourbon. He distinctly remembers writing me a check for his half of the rent. He remembers where he was sitting when he wrote the check. Among Clive's magazines:

1. *The New Yorker*
2. *The Nation*
3. *Screw*
4. *Southern Living*
5. *Guns and Ammo*
6. *Harper's*
7. *Foreign Affairs*

Clive tells me that in twenty years the world will run out of carbon dioxide. I got the wrong size bottle of Evan Williams bourbon and now I have to go get more. My feet hurt from standing on the corner all day with my sign. And because I either erred or perhaps willfully disobeyed his instructions and didn't get the right size bottle, I have to pay for the whole thing.

Or else he'll call my parents and tell them the truth about Allison.

✑

Today in the English class the teacher talked about John Donne. A poem called "The Flea." It's about how this girl should stop holding out on him, since he's been bitten by a flea and she's been bitten by the exact same flea, and inside that flea their blood is all mixed up, so why should she be so prissy about letting him have sex with her. Allison didn't seem impressed by the argument. Allison does not exist in a world of blood and fleas. The teacher returned another paper at the end of class. Again, I didn't hand one in so I don't get one back. I knew this one was due, but I was working, standing on the corner with my milk crate holding the sign for the candidate. Last week, when I should have been working on my paper, I was holding my sign. Anytime, anywhere.

∼)

All my life needed was a sense of somewhere to go. The teacher has stopped asking why I haven't been coming to class.

∼)

Clive.

Clive distinctly remembers giving me a check for his half of the rent. Clive has no friends, no one ever visits Clive, no one ever calls Clive, Clive never goes anywhere or sees anyone. Clive refuses to let me look at any of his magazines, even though I pay the subscriptions on more than half of them. Although—sometimes when I'm in the bathroom, struggling with a movement, he slides a dirty picture from *Screw* or *Leg Man* or *Oui* under the door. Have fun, Clive says.

∼)

There was a rally for the candidate and my brother told me to come, first to hold my sign and act like I was just some person who came to the rally. Then he said, no, I have a better idea—you should come and pass out literature. Then the day of the rally he calls back and says, Listen, I've got a better idea.

He says, At the rally, the candidate is going to take questions from the audience. Except they're not really questions from the audience. Actually, my brother says, the candidate is only going to call on people from the campaign, but who are pretending to be people who just showed up to the rally. Do you get it? he says. Do you think you can handle it?

I tell him, All my life needed was a sense of somewhere to go.

Yeah, he says.

That night at the rally at the VFW hall, there are about thirty people there, and at least half of them work for the campaign. I recognize them from the headquarters, where I go every morning to get more fliers and bumper stickers for my milk crate.

The candidate is short. Shorter than he appears on the sign, which is just a picture of his head. But he looks taller on the sign.

The candidate says—I love Lubbock. I'm practically *from* Lubbock. I think Lubbock is God's country. Are you tired, he says, of the government getting your tax dollars? Are you tired of the liberals in Washington, D.C. telling you how to live your life, and giving your money to deadbeats and dropouts? Some people clap, mostly the people from the campaign.

The candidate says—Do you want a congressman who believes in God? Isn't it time we started listening to what God is saying to our hearts, instead of what those liberals are saying to our heads?

Now I'll take some questions, the candidate says. I raise my hand, but just as I do, I notice the Dry Lady in the crowd. The candidate points his finger at me and says, Yes sir, you there. Good to see the young people out tonight. You might could use a haircut, but still, good to see you. He chuckles. Go ahead, sir, you may ask your question.

The Dry Lady is looking at me. The candidate is looking at me. My brother, who has been following the candidate around the stage with the microphone cord in his hands, is looking at me. I suddenly can't remember the question I was told to ask. I suddenly panic.

I suddenly need to have a movement. I have gone to the clinic at the university and have gotten literature that says that people who have trouble with their bowels should never ignore the need to have a movement, and should never resist the urge to go. It was a pamphlet, which also listed a number of techniques.

The candidate and everyone else is still looking at me. The candidate is still smiling, but I can see the smile changing. His eyes are hardening, and his lower lip is coming up, flattening the smile into something else. It feels like the candidate is standing right on top of me, and now he doesn't seem short anymore. I have to go.

I turn and run, the crowd parts, I'm waving my arms and shouting. I don't know what to shout, so I shout, *Lubbock! Lubbock!* At the door of the VFW hall are three people who work for the campaign. I turn back toward the candidate and my brother. I want to say something, *I'm sorry*, something.

But one of the people standing by the door grabs me and pushes me out into the night.

I'm off balance now, but still running. Energy policy. Oil drilling. That was what I was supposed to ask about. Clive says the police would be very interested in looking at over 175 songs about a fourteen-year-old girl, even if she is a world-famous actress and my chances of actually meeting her are—and you have to understand this, he said—absolutely zero. I'm running to my car, trying desperately to clench my rectum, the movement is coming on its own now, and there's nothing to be done.

I stop between two cars, a Malibu and the gold Valliant that I know at once is the Dry Lady's car. I hurry my pants down and squat there in the parking lot.

I wait.

Nothing happens.

Allison. A long time goes by.

I strain. I push so hard I start to fall, and then when I try to stop myself from falling, my feet catch in my pants legs and I *do* fall, and when I fall the movement comes, hot and wet and smelling of metal, and it's on my legs and I'm trying to kick myself free from it. I can hear other people in the parking lot now, coming from the rally. I can see the Dry Lady in the lead. I crawl underneath her car, then crawl again underneath several other cars, until I get to mine.

I have a gun at home.

Clive does not know about the gun.

Clive does not know about the gun because I have concealed it very cleverly.

At the door of my car, I finally pull my soiled pants up, and then I drive to the filling station, where I buy two gallons of gas.

～⌒

When I get home, Clive says—Your brother called three times why haven't you paid the rent what's that smell?

～⌒

We all want different lives. Clive, my father, my brother. The candidate wants a different life. Even Allison. Why can't we have them? Why can't I give them to us?

I am more than I appear to be. I am waiting for the sun to shine. A long continuous chain, then suddenly, there is a change.

~~~

Today on the corner the Dry Lady comes back again. She is wearing tan polyester pants of the same cut as before, and again the white shimmery ruffley shirt, and this time there is a red scarf around her hair.

I've opened my mind some to your candidate, she says. He's beginning to appeal to me. I saw him talk at the VFW hall the other night. He's young and dynamic. He says what he means and he means what he says. I believe in him. He's the kind of guy you'd like to have a beer with. I liked his answer about oil drilling, she says.

I say nothing.

I think your candidate has a bright future. I'd like one of those bumper stickers, please, she says.

I begin sweating again. It's late October and still 85 degrees in Lubbock. *Lubricious* is a word I'd like to use to describe it. Pistons churn. In Colorado, it's snowing.

I'll have one of those bumper stickers, please, the Dry Lady says now.

I've been standing here on this corner every day for eight, nine, ten, twelve hours a day for weeks. My studies are suffering. When people come by and ask me questions about the candidate, I give them a flier. Some people ask for bumper stickers and I give them to them. But the Dry Lady? No. I will not do it.

Here is a man who stood up.

~~~

On the day after the rally at the VFW hall, when I went to pick up more fliers and bumper stickers for my milk crate, my brother called me into his office.

The candidate was in my brother's office with another man I didn't know.

What was *that* all about? the candidate says to me. Your brother said you were reliable. He said, we can put him to work. I said, why not, help the guy out, get him a little spending money, college student and all. I trust your

brother. Your brother says, John's smart, he works hard. He just needs direction. I say to myself, that is one thing I've never had a problem with. Direction.
I've always known where I'm going. But I know how to take advice, too. I know
how to listen to the opinions of others, how to use those opinions to shape a
consistence. Your brother says, Stick to taxes. Taxes, taxes, taxes. I trust him,
but I like to give 'em a little Jesus, too. What do you think?

He's asking me.

I'm sorry, I say. I messed up. I really am interested in your energy policy,
too, I say. My roommate and I have been having an interesting debate on
this exact topic. It was the perfect question for me to ask you. In twenty years
we're going to run out of carbon dioxide.

Exactly, the candidate says. Your brother said you were smart. I think
you're weird. What do you think, Karl? he says to the other man, who stares
at me without answering. Weird John, the candidate says. From now on that's
your name. Weird John. Or how 'bout, Johnny Weird?

He stops for a moment, thinking. I can see him thinking. He's thinking
about what to do to me. All I want is to get my literature and stand on the
corner with my sign. The other man is still staring at me also.

Nope, the candidate says, finally, decisively. Weird John it is.

He stands up and he and the other man move past me toward the door.
Don't fuck up again, the other man says, his back to me. Then they are gone.
My brother, who still hasn't said a word, sits in his chair, staring into his
desk lamp.

Give me one of those bumper stickers, right now, young man, the Dry Lady
says. Her scarf is a swirly red-and-purple paisley. She points at the bumper
stickers in the milk crate on the ground near my left shoe. I move between
the Dry Lady and the crate, nudge the crate backwards with my heel. I still
have not said a word.

What are you, some kind of idiot, the Dry Lady says. Are you nuts? Are
you retarded? I'll have you know I am an extraordinarily influential Lubbock
voter. And I'd say you just lost my vote. And I'm calling the campaign. I'll talk
to the candidate himself about you. I can't believe that the nice young man I
saw speaking the other night would have anything to do with you. I believe if
he saw this he'd throw you in jail. That's where you belong. You fat jerk.

I still have not said a word. I have a gun at home, and from now on I'm bringing it to work. From now on, I'm bringing it everywhere. Lubbock is lubricious. Clive does not know about the gun.

Here is a man who stood up.

A small crowd begins to gather at the corner of Broadway and University. Five or six people. Some of them I've seen before, walking around. We don't want to give bumper stickers to just anyone off the street. But today I give each member of the gathering crowd a bumper sticker—the couple of students who have wandered by, wondering what all the yelling is about, the guy who runs the sandwich shop across the street, the taxi driver, the old professor who shuffles by every weekday at this time, his briefcase scuffed and worn. I have to actually move out of the crowd to hand him a bumper sticker, and he looks confused at first, and backs away, putting up his briefcase in front of his chest, and when I move toward him, the Dry Lady goes for my milk crate.

Here is a man who stood up.

I dive back into the small crowd and lunge for the milk crate. The Dry Lady's hand is nearly inside the crate, she nearly has her hand on a bumper sticker when I land on the crate, and her, and we're rolling out into Broadway. The Dry Lady is slapping at my head and my hands, and I'm trying to cover the crate and push her away and stand up all at once, and instead we both roll over again, farther into the street, and horns are honking, and the milk crate upends, spilling fliers and bumper stickers into the street, where all the people who have gathered, many more, most of them students, have now run into the street to grab the literature.

The Dry Lady is screaming and scratching at me. She scratches my face terribly, from just below my right eye all the way across my mouth and down onto my neck. Other people are grabbing at us now, hands on me, pulling, grabbing, kicking, several people.

When they finally pull us to our feet the sleeve of the Dry Lady's shimmery shirt has been torn from her shoulder, her scarf is gone, and she's bleeding heavily from her mouth. My milk crate is still in my hand, but it's empty, and people are running everywhere with fliers and bumper stickers. There are two men yelling at me and a man and woman are leaning in to talk to the Dry Lady, who is touching her hair with her hands and breathing quickly. My face hurts very badly and there's something wet in my shoes. But the Dry Lady does not have a bumper sticker, because here is a man who stood up.

You stay here with him, one of the men holding me says to the other one.

I'm going to go get a cop. The other man holding me is very small, and when I turn to look at him it appears he has no interest in holding me. I pull my arm away from him, and he says, wait a minute, buddy. But I don't wait. I walk back to the corner of Broadway and Tenth. We've rolled around for nearly half the block.

Across the street, on the campus green, a group has formed around a hipster guy in a striped pink shirt, who is holding my sign with the candidate's face and jumping up and down. The students all seem to have bumper stickers, and they're peeling them and sticking them on their shirtfronts.

Allison is at the edge of the crowd, with her little slut roommate who is letting another hipster boy stick the bumper sticker to her rear end. Soon the hipster with the sign has formed his group into a parade, and he's off, leading the students in a happy march up the hill toward Bledsoe Hall. Allison looks back over her shoulder, once, for a brief second, and she recognizes me. She looks at me, and in that moment, for the first time in what has to be months, I smile. I know I'm smiling because it hurts my mouth where the Dry Lady scratched me. Allison is about to smile back, but just then that little bitch monster of a roommate comes to her and pulls her away, and off they run, chasing the hipster with my sign and laughing. I watch them finally disappear over the hill.

Up the street the man from before is coming back with a cop. I turn toward the campus, where some people are still milling around, and looking away, I move quickly toward the English and Philosophy Building. I plan to ask my English teacher for asylum if I have to. I perform several acts of tactical evasion, including blending in with a crowd that has gathered to hear someone recite Shakespeare, and I cross from there into the cafeteria, and back through Lowndes Hall to Eighth Street where I've parked my car. I've escaped.

It is one week until Election Day. I don't believe that one should devote his life to morbid self-attention.

~⌁⌁

Song for Jodie #186 (an urgent ballad)

When you smile at me
I know you're just a child
I know you're just a child
When you smile—

ᐤᐤ

Clive says—The police called, your brother called, the landlord called, when
are you going to pay the rent, have you seen my latest copy of *Field and
Stream*, what happened to your face?

ᐤᐤ

It's 2:15 a.m. outside Knapp Hall. Allison is inside, her light is out. This is the
third time I've walked around the dorm tonight. I can't sleep nights. I haven't
had a solid bowel movement in over a week. I feel something is building here.
This afternoon, fighting with the Dry Lady, I felt that if someone killed me,
if a cop or something walked up and shot me dead on the streets of Lubbock,
Texas, it wouldn't mean anything, that they wouldn't even file a report or give
me a funeral.

I am not a person like other people.

After the fight with the Dry Lady, my brother said I couldn't stand on
the corner anymore. He said the police had come to campaign headquarters
looking for me. He said, why can't you just do one thing right, John? He said
he was being demoted.

This is the third time now the security guard has seen me pass the front
doors of Knapp Hall. He comes outside and stands on the steps, looks at
me. I keep moving toward the corner of the building. I keep looking up at
Allison's window. I keep looking at the security guard, because I want him
to. I really do. I want him to, just this once.

I have the gun tucked in my windbreaker. From now on I carry it everywhere I go. It finally made sense to me after I killed Clive earlier tonight. The
whole thing, for the past several weeks at least, has been planned by someone
who means me harm.

I think a person ought to be like other people. I don't have that exactly
right.

Anyway, I left Clive dead on the couch with four holes in his chest.
Later, I will take him out into the desert and bury him.

Hey, buddy, the security guard says. The security guard is slim and wiry.
I have always had great respect for the wiry.

Hey, he calls again, coming farther down the steps. What do you want
around here, pal?

This is what I've wanted, what I want. So why do I keep walking? I suddenly think that maybe this wiry security guard has kids. That, even if it is a plan, and my brother and my father and Clive and the candidate and the hipster and Allison and her roommate and the Dry Lady are all involved, this guy's just a security guard who would be working here whether they ever launched their plan or not. At the very least, my studies have suffered irreparably, and you don't have the right to do that to other people. For any reason.

I keep walking, putting my head down. I only want to check one more time, to make one more circle round, then I'll go to my car, drive home, put Clive's body in the trunk, and take him out to the desert to bury him.

Now the security guard is coming toward me. I can hear him behind me, feel him reaching for me.

What's the problem, buddy?

I turn.

Jesus, he says, what happened to your face?

I point to Allison's dark window.

You see that bitch up there in that window?

He turns to look. I move my hand inside the pocket of my windbreaker and take it out. He looks back at me. He does not have a gun, but he sees that I have one, and he puts up his hands and begins to back away.

Take it easy, buddy, he says now, his palms facing me, shaking. I fire one shot just past his ear. Lights go on in Knapp Hall. The security guard falls to the ground and curls into a ball with his hands over his head. I fire one more shot at the front door. The bullet makes a tiny hole the size and shape of a nipple in the glass before continuing its trajectory through the building, unseen. More lights come on. The light in Allison's room comes on. I see her face in the window. I hear voices around me.

It took three days to find a good spot to bury Clive. Texas is large. I was surprised at how I felt when I put Clive in the ground. I was touched by the look on his face and the sadness I experienced, which I think must be like the sadness other people might experience in a similar situation. After I buried him, I said a few words over his grave.

The night I buried him I stayed in a motel in Plainview, where I had an exquisite and perfectly natural bowel movement. Almost a foot long, well turned, smooth, colored in an appropriately normal way. It left no seepage afterwards, and I felt so light I could fly. I thought at that moment—this is how people always feel.

~~~

When I get back to the house the next day, Clive is there, reading a magazine, acting like I hadn't shot him and buried him in the desert at all.

The police have been here every day, Clive says. They say you are a fugitive from justice, he says. I showed them your songs about Jodie Foster. I'm actually pretty impressed by your emergence, Clive says, but they told me if I see you I'm supposed to call them right away. Also your brother has called over and over again. The landlord came by and said she was going to evict us if we didn't pay this month's and last month's rent by the end of the week, so I called your father.

Whose corpse is lately on my mind.

He sent me the money for the rent, Clive says. He wired it Western Union yesterday afternoon. He wanted to know what was going on with you. He wanted to know why you were acting so strange. He said the police had called him, too. I told him about the night you pooped your pants. I told him you got in a fight with an old lady. I told him I thought this was a very bad sign. I need you to drive me to the Piggly Wiggly to pick up the money.

Clive says this, who is dead and buried in the desert outside Plainview, Texas. For all the mysteries surrounding this case, I am almost positive of that one fact.

He wanted to know about Allison, Clive says.

What did you tell him, I say, reaching inside my windbreaker for the gun. I've already killed Clive once, I think, so what's the big deal?

I didn't tell him, John, Clive says. I think you have to tell him, Clive says. I think you're a pretty all right guy, you know, you're just having some problems with things. I don't think you like Lubbock very much, for one, and I don't blame you for that. And I don't think you like yourself, or your family. I think you need some help. But you've been a good roommate to me—you help me with my errands, and you don't watch too much television, and after you get out of jail and get your other problems sorted out, I'd be happy to have you for a roommate again, so long as you can talk your father into paying your half of the rent while you're away.

I take my hand away from the gun inside my windbreaker.

Thanks, Clive, I say.

He's coming here, Clive says.

My father?

Yes, he said he was going to drive out this morning. He'll be here to-morrow.

He's coming here?

Yeah, Clive says. You ought to get this place cleaned up. But first, take me to Piggly Wiggly. I'll wait a couple of hours before I call the police.

～

This time I drove Clive well into New Mexico, dug another hole near Vaughn, and buried him again. We drove all night, me and Allison, with Clive dead in the trunk. Allison liked the mountains and the desert landscape. She said it reminded her of the hills in Ernest Hemingway's story "Hills Like White Elephants," which I know we were supposed to read for the English class.

I didn't read it, I say.

No, she says. You wouldn't have.

When Allison and I get back to Lubbock we make love in the front seat of my car in the dorm parking lot at Knapp Hall. She'd invite me in, she says, but after I took a shot at the security guard, it isn't safe for me around here. She kisses me deeply, holding my penis in her hand, then she scampers from the car and up the steps to her dorm.

I'm still watching her when she stops and comes back to the car.

Come and get me tomorrow, she says, and take me to vote. And after that we'll kill my roommate and you can move into the dorm with me.

～

There's a rally that night for the candidate at the ballroom of the Lubbock Ramada Inn. I have the gun in my windbreaker. The crowd at the Ramada is a good bit bigger than the one at the VFW a few weeks ago, and I see some people I know, but more that I don't. I have on a green baseball cap I bought at a filling station in Roswell, New Mexico, where Allison and I stopped on our way back from burying Clive.

The candidate is standing on the stage in front of the ballroom. One more day, he says. I thank you for your support, he says, and I ask you for your vote. I see my brother in the crowd holding a sign just like mine. There is a man standing next to him who claims to be my father. On the other side of him is Clive, whom I am frankly surprised to see, since I have killed him and buried him twice in two different states.

I can still smell Allison. Of all the things that have happened, I was gladdest to determine that she was not involved in the plot. Christopher Marlowe was a spy. I have my hand on the gun and I'm moving toward them. I will shoot my brother once, my father, three times, and the candidate, twice. But in what order? I should probably shoot the candidate first. I will also have to shoot Clive again even though this apparently doesn't do any good.

It's hard to believe how calm and happy I feel. But then, maybe it shouldn't surprise me. This is it. This is what my life has been moving toward. Pure force. And then, the end.

Song for Jodie, #200

(a ballad—poss. title: "The Last Song?")
You don't know me but
You'll never know me now
You'll never know how
Much I need you
How much I need you—

I am within ten yards of my brother and Clive and the man who claims to be my father. They have not seen me. The crowd seems to part from the force of my will. My hand is on the gun. I am going to kill them. And after that, my life will be different. I will never be a person like other people.

But when the candidate says, I'd be happy to answer some of your questions, I stop. I look to the stage. I am wearing a green baseball cap. I raise my hand. The candidate is looking directly at me.

You there, he says. The young fellow in the baseball cap. Nice to see the young people out here tonight, although my momma always told me to take my hat off indoors. He chuckles. I take off my hat.

The candidate is looking at me and smiling the smile from the sign. He is waiting. People are turning to look at me. My brother and Clive and the man who claims to be my father. They are all looking at me, one hand raised for the question, one hand still on the gun.

What do they see? Do they see a man who stood up? Do they see a person like other people? They're moving toward me now, not just my brother and Clive and the man who claims to be my father. The whole crowd, the candidate, Lubbock itself. The whole entire world, all those dead babies and those old men who died and all the women anyone ever loved and all the women who went unloved and the animals and the stars and the distant planets—it's all moving toward me and I can feel myself in the center of it. I am no longer God's lonely man. I just need some help, some direction. I can be redeemed. I *can* have a different life.

I look back to the candidate, he is still smiling, still waiting patiently. He is looking at me as if he admires me, as if he knows that I *am* a person like other people. At that moment, whatever else the candidate may ever do in *his* life, he's heroic. He has saved not only his own life, but my brother's and Clive's and the man who claims to be my father's, and probably mine, and at this moment I would do anything in the world for him. I realize that holding my sign in the heat and the dust and the rain and the sweat for six weeks, every day for eight, ten, twelve hours a day, that is nothing. That's the least any man should do for his candidate. You get a job, you become the job. If he could look into my soul and see the gun in my hand, and he asked me to pull it out and kill, I would do it, without hesitation. If he sent me to war, I would go. I am his, and he is mine, and I will never forget the goodness he has done for me, and the goodness in his beautiful heart.

Go ahead and ask your question now, son, he says. I love him. My brother and Clive and the man who claims to be my father are here now. I am ready to ask my question.

We need to drill for more oil in this country, I say. I spent thirty minutes at the filling station tonight for two gallons of gas. It seems like your opponent doesn't care about people like me. He wants us to keep depending on Arabs for our oil, when we've got good American oil right here in Texas. My brother reaches me and puts his hand on my arm. The man who claims to be my father is on the other side now, and they're leading me, gently, away from the stage and toward the door. I look back up, one more time, to the candidate, who smiles and says, Thank you, I'm glad you asked that.

It's three months after the election, and I'm in Colorado now, staying, for the time being, with the people who claim to be my parents. I have decided that there's very little virtue in not accepting them as such—what good would it do? These two people have actually been very nice to me, for most all of my life.

I've gotten letters from Lubbock. The prosecutor there has decided not to bring charges against me for assaulting the Dry Lady. When the police went to interview her, they found that the Dry Lady had turned her entire house into a shrine for the candidate. There were bumper stickers and posters and signs and hundreds of little candles lit all through the house. The D.A. told all of this to my father—she said she was trying to light a candle for every person who had voted for the candidate on Election Day. You could feel the heat from the front yard, and she was, the D.A. said, about a half dozen votes away from burning the whole neighborhood down. He said she was actually employed by the campaign in some obscure way, that they were investigating her for vote fraud, and that bringing charges against me would only muddy the waters. He told my father that the Dry Lady was obviously unstable. I didn't bother to disagree, but I knew exactly how she felt.

My father wrote a large check for a scholarship to help campus security guards take evening classes at Texas Tech, and a smaller one to replace the front-door glass and some plaster at Knapp Hall.

Clive has also written, and his letter was very nice. Although he said he sold most of my things, he is keeping my Gibson guitar and my songs for Jodie, which were returned by the police. I'll just hang onto them for you, he said in his letter, and you can get them when you come back to school. Then, in a PS, he said—maybe I'll just hold onto them for when you're famous someday. Ha Ha, Clive wrote.

Which is fine, because I won't ever be going back to Lubbock again. Dr. Croon at Clear Branch has agreed with my assessment that Lubbock is not a place of the spirit, and he's also pretty much convinced old nutso me that there's no sense in writing any more songs to Jodie, or to anyone else, for that matter. I don't really know how to play the guitar, for one thing.

I haven't heard from Allison, but Dr. Croon says I'm better off without her. Dr. Croon says hard work is its own reward, and he provided me with a job with the grounds department at Clear Branch and a prescription for stool softener, and more than anything, this has had a healthful effect on my day-to-day outlook. *Salutary* is a word I would like to use to describe it.

The other day I got a letter from the candidate!

I'd written him a while back, before I checked out of Clear Branch, and I told him how very sorry I was that he'd lost. If my terrible behavior cost you even one vote, I will not be able to forgive myself, I wrote him. I thank you from the bottom of my heart, I wrote him, for the kindness and the chance to serve on your campaign. It was, I told him, the proudest work I'd ever done in my life. I hope, I wrote, that I didn't let you down. The fear that I had failed him, I said, has been the one regret I had been unable to shake since coming to this place.

The other day I got his reply. Dr. Croon delivered it to me, his breath huffing in white puffs to the north parking lot, where I was shoveling snow. I opened the letter there and read two sentences, two sentences I've read again and again, for every nuance and intonation in them.

Cheer up, Weird John, the candidate wrote. There's always another campaign.

Here It Was, November

Laura Furman

THE MARIAN FOSTER TODD ARCHIVE WAS AMONG THE HOLDINGS OF THE New York Public Library, but when she was diagnosed with her terminal illness, Marian sold her few remaining papers to the famous archival center in Austin. As ever she was desperate for money. Marian made many appearances in that capacious Texas library. There were references to her in letters and diaries in Austin's Sexton, Lowell, Auden, Bishop, and Creeley collections, for she was more comfortable with poets than with fiction writers like herself. A letter from Salinger to a family friend quoted a line from one of Marian's first published stories, and a postcard from Olivia Manning to Ivy Compton-Burnett mentioned meeting Marian in London and finding her more intelligent than expected. Marian lived to be an old woman and she put her oar in literary waters at an early age. One of the photos I planned to use in my biography was of young beautiful Marian smiling arm in arm with old broad Willa Cather in front of the Plaza Hotel. Marian prized that photograph above all others, even the glamorous ones taken by Irving Penn for *Harper's Bazaar* two decades later.

My biography of Marian Foster Todd, the capstone of my career, was all but written. Five years before, early on in my research, I'd gone to Austin, not yet convinced that I could undertake such a life. Two biographies of Marian had been published in her lifetime, neither one successful nor, understandably, thorough. Now I knew the type of chocolate she preferred and that she claimed to sleep well only on ironed, white sheets. All the separate bits of Marian Foster Todd were collected and assembled for those who would not read her letters and diaries, would not hear the voices of those who knew her, might not even read her beautiful stories. Through my biography, the woman who had lived and died would live and die again.

The present trip to Austin was my final sojourn in the familiar country of archival research. One document evaded me and I hoped to find a trace of it in Austin, a certain letter to Marian Todd Foster from her dearest friend, Sandra da Rocha, the renowned poet who lived her final decades in Pomfret, Vermont. The correspondence between them was frank and intimate. Marian and Sandra, incomparable women, practically bled into each other's veins; even Marian's affair with Sandra's husband hadn't strained their bond to breaking. What snapped the spine of their friendship was Marian's habit of arranging to visit and canceling at the last moment. Meticulous and elaborate planning would drag on for months about when Marian might arrive, bringing what and staying for how long, but this didn't stop Marian from sending a telegram or, later in life, picking up the phone to cancel the visit, often on the very day she was expected to arrive. She did this to all her friends. Her favorite excuse was that she'd finally become involved with her work after an unbearable drought and couldn't possibly interrupt it. According to Marian's ethos, the excuse of work was sacred, but she never understood that there was at hand a causal relationship: Marian arranged elaborate and burdensome visits then cancelled them in order to force herself into work anew.

When Marian cancelled a visit a short month after the husband's unexpected death, Sandra wrote a blistering message of farewell and they never spoke again. I longed to find the entire letter and quote it directly rather than rely on Marian's account, but the original letter was missing. It was Marian's custom to preserve her correspondence, even the most painful documentation of lost friendship and love, but not this particular letter. The carbon copy it was Sandra's habit to keep of every letter she wrote, major and minor, was nowhere to be found, but her farewell to Marian was partially drafted in Sandra's daily journal, so it was possible to approximate the contents. Sandra's papers were in Boston and I'd trolled them thoroughly.

My previous books had taught me that the first loyalty of the biographer was to truth, not to feelings or reputation. Marian Foster Todd quarreled eventually with everyone who meant anything to her, supplying me with decades-cherished grudges to narrate and tangled emotions to sort. One puzzlement was the failure of her sophisticated friends to understand that what Marian did to one she would in time do to all; each considered himself or herself the single exception to Marian's cancellations, disappearances, and inconvenient reappearances. Why had each not been prepared for the moment when Marian would act exactly like Marian? The answer lay partially in Marian's personal charm, partially in her talent for finding friends whose need for love and inclusion was almost as great as her own. Marian's childhood had been spent among people who fought constantly and bitterly; she felt safest when she was stirring things up for people she liked. The reenactment of abandonment revived her spirit.

Marian justified her manipulation of others, her ruthless need for fulfillment on her own terms, as living in the service of her art. But others have lived lives just as lonely, made love just as difficult for those brave enough to try, without self-aggrandizing justification.

In the libraries and archives where I'd spent my adult existence, one's personal life was meaningless; only books, documents, archives, and collections, only the catalogued counted. The reading room in Austin was a favorite, a granite bunker built into the hill below the main tower. In the anteroom hung the oil portrait of the pale young woman whose parents created the library in her memory; the visitor paused, then got on with her work. Time took on another quality altogether in the reading room; there I moved from obscurity to darkness.

The biographies that made my reputation were of other, relatively minor figures in twentieth-century American letters. Long ago I left academia, the little world I knew best. I worked alone, independent of an institution, with sparse financial backing. Through uncompromising research and skillful telling, my books made the lives of my subjects crucial context for understanding twentieth-century American literature, or so the reviewers asserted. Academic journals treated my work with respect. The books won prizes. In this, my final effort, the stakes were considerably higher. If I succeeded, Marian's place as an important, even canonical, novelist would be secured. Though the biographer was always an ancillary figure, my name and Marian's would be coupled after my death in a lasting sisterhood.

For the biographer, the final clue to character lies in the yet unread—the scribbled note, the diary page, a notation on the margin of a draft—until the day when even the most devoted portraitist of the dead says, *Enough!* Working in the service of the dead, biographers quit their labors only when the sole remaining task is the impossible—resurrection.

The guesthouse I rented in Austin lay at the back of a large, pleasant lot canopied by ancient live oaks; the guesthouse had a miniature kitchen and laundry, as well as a holly hedge to screen it from the main house. My landlord on my previous visits to Austin was a professor of astronomy. He'd since gone to join his stars, and a young academic couple now owned the place.

I unpacked my wardrobe—one skirt, one pair of dress pants, one pair for daily work—and started a list: soy milk, coffee, other necessities. Though I had acquaintances in Austin, I had no interest in alerting them to my presence. In the past my visits to archives were occasions for the eager continuation of a friendship—this one in London, that dear old soul in Massachusetts. At the present moment, silence and loneliness were preferable; human warmth might tempt me to confide.

How many times in my scholar's life had I forced strange rooms to welcome me and, however temporarily, to become my own? In the past five years, in search of Marian Foster Todd, I'd breached the solitude of rented rooms and borrowed apartments in England, Ireland, and France, in New Haven and in Troy. Day after day I'd waited for the doors to open, anxious to secure my customary seat, my little home, all in the name of research.

The end of my travels was New York, my rent-controlled and by no means small apartment on the Upper West Side. Once I left my native state, I didn't advertise my beginnings except to say, *Oh, the middle of the country*, on the rare occasions when anyone asked. As a biographer, I was expected to answer questions on the smallest detail of my subject's origins; in exchange I was granted immunity from curiosity.

Like Marian Foster Todd, I never married. Once I came close but I resisted. My fate lay elsewhere, I thought grandly. My family had dwindled over the years to a cousin I heard from at Christmas. My friends in New York were dear but I expected nothing from them.

In the guesthouse mirror, I looked through my present face for the past one, and waited for the two to merge. The essence of a person stays intact from birth; I was the same as I was at eight when I checked in the mirror, trying to see myself as others saw me. But the body changes. When I looked at my hands now, I didn't see them clutching the handlebars as I pedaled along the streets of my riverbank village in my unnamed state. They looked like my father's hands, steady on the steering wheel of his ancient Studebaker, resting across his chest in his coffin.

Marian left behind a string of male and female lovers, and Dorothea, her daughter. Dorothea's father was a handsome folk singer of no great talent who left before the birth of his child. In one of her last interviews, Marian said that she was brave until Dorothea was born, and then she knew, looking at the helpless baby, that she'd never write again if she stayed. She handed the infant over to a relative of the father's and promised never to communicate with the child. The crystalline moment of relinquishment reminded one of Marian's finest short stories.

When I phoned Dorothea from Austin, she spoke in her low warm voice of her plans for my visit—our Albuquerque mornings would begin with a walk through the nature center and a visit to the café I liked; we'd take a tram ride to the top of the mountain; her garden was prepared for my inspection, the sturdy desert plants eager to hear that I admired them. I hoped this visit to sleep where Marian had died. The bed was swaddled in white covers and pillows, placed so that Marian could view the passing day without having to raise her head. There, Marian suffered the end of her beauty and the final humiliations of her body. The room opened onto Dorothea's garden. The view was silver, lavender, and misty green against the blue adobe wall.

Dorothea said, "You'll be so happy here with me."

We had years of letters and phone calls between us as well as my two previous trips to New Mexico, the first to persuade her to reveal the story of herself and her mother, the second to show that I was sincere in my affection.

"Yes, yes, how wonderful, I can't wait," I said.

It didn't seem as though we'd have enough time—or I the stamina—to do all that she'd decided we must, but I hated to tell Dorothea how exhausted I was after a day doing nothing more strenuous than reading. Dorothea would have done anything for me. The careful work of not taking advantage of her was all mine.

In Dorothea, as in so much else, Marian Foster Todd was a lucky woman, and I shared some of her good fortune. Their separation and reunion bestowed shape on a life that might otherwise appear to be one capricious lurch followed by another, the only constant Marian's struggle to write.

With the fearsome diagnosis still fresh, Marian understood that she needed a place to die. She arranged to give a reading at the University of New Mexico, and contrived to meet Dorothea and to inspect her house behind its blue adobe wall. Dorothea lived in New Mexico, unmarried, in her late forties, working at a clerical job with the goal of early retirement in the state system. Her adoptive parents were dead. She'd spent years nursing them through their final illnesses, one and then the other. Meeting Marian's high standards in every way, Dorothea found herself in possession of her long-lost and dying mother.

"You'll be here soon," Dorothea said.

"Yes, I can't wait to be there."

"I wish you'd gone to Austin second."

"My stay might have to be extended. If I find anything new."

My warning, my hedge against Dorothea's greater energy, alarmed me, and I wondered if I'd gone too far. If everything went smoothly, Dorothea was fine, but *smoothly* meant no break to her routine. Life, even a life like Dorothea's, wasn't like that.

When she was a child, Dorothea fell off her bike and a piece of gravel lodged in her cheek. It looked like a cunningly placed birthmark, but she considered herself disfigured. More beautiful than her famous mother, she allowed no photographs to be taken of her. Whereas Marian strived, even at her poorest, to dress strikingly, Dorothea wore ironed shirts over jeans in winter, white T-shirts over shorts in summer. On the third anniversary of Marian's death, her *Collected Stories* was published to great acclaim, and the Albuquerque newspaper assigned a reporter to a profile of Dorothea, sending her first into terror that she'd have to talk about herself, next into burning guilt that she'd let her mother down. In the end, Dorothea referred the reporter to me. "Do what you have to do," she said, her cheer restored, her anxiety lifting suddenly. "You always do." Dorothea's tone was fond and a little amused at my thoroughness, my hard labor that would benefit her more than it ever would me.

"Oh," Dorothea said. "We'll go to Acoma Pueblo. And the little church in Chimayó where the pilgrims leave their shoes.

"You'll love Acoma," she said. "It was where Willa Cather set her enchanted mesa. Marian told me."

It wasn't true that Cather had based her famous New Mexico story there. Dorothea didn't read, and Marian often misremembered.

In my apartment far away in New York, the radio played softly to discourage burglars, dust settled on every surface, and the black phone waited at attention for the call from the specialist, telling me to call for his diagnosis. Once given a name, my disease would take over and there would be little left to my life but the treatment protocol. Was it any wonder that I refused to check the messages waiting for me?

When Marian was on her way to what she called her last real disaster, she didn't wait for bad news but pursued it as aggressively as she ever had a man or publicity for her books or a teaching job to spare her another minute of living from hand to mouth. Her doctors, all of whom I'd interviewed, started out by admiring Marian. Only Dorothea had been patient enough to sustain her mother's leaving of the world. All human actions are self-serving; there must have been something appealing to Dorothea about sustaining Marian through her illness. Dorothea would have been within her rights to send Marian packing. Dorothea wouldn't discuss her decision with me, saying it was only natural for her to care for her mother when she was old and sick: "Who else would take care of her?" Dorothea didn't know that someone else would have appeared, as someone always had for Marian.

Who would appear for me? When the phone call caught up with me, when I heard the expected words, who would care for me when I was unable to care for myself? There was no Dorothea in my life to soften the mortal blow.

When I died someone would empty my apartment, and that someone would dispose of my small art collection, cabinets of papers, thousands of books. My jewelry was worthless. My clothes were hopeless. No vintage treasures hid in my closet, only the most utilitarian packables and washables. My only hope was that close to the end there would be a kind of friend to take on my leftovers, though I'd lived long enough to know that there would come a time when this wouldn't worry me any longer. My possessions, which I went through every year, subtracting and adding, would no longer be my concern.

In Austin, I swam in Barton Springs, and here it was, November. Leaves from the water's surface clung to my head as I passed the lifeguard stations and the deserted diving board. At the deepest part, where the springs entered the pool, I pushed down into the water where the most beautiful colors waited and I imagined that death would be like this but without the effort. Then I struggled up to the surface, gasping for air. My body, it seemed, wanted to live. When I showered in the bathhouse, I found clumps of algae and leaves clinging to my body. I could have pressed down to feel the tumor. It would do no harm. My doctor had shown me the method and demonstrated the correct pressure to use. Still, I felt no desire to know its shape or to probe its private life.

Once you've done biographical research, once you've written a life, you understand the obvious, that you don't know anyone else, not really. You can't.

Now I knew the answer to the sophomoric question: *Is it possible to know one's self?* The disease was my biography. Soon enough it would expose my life's secrets to me, its only reader.

～○

The table I claimed as my little home was at the back of the reading room. While I squinted at a barely legible note from a once-famous professor approaching Marian to teach at his university (an event that never transpired), I became aware that someone stood at my side, a shaven-haired youth, barely a man. He wore the ill-fitting cotton jacket of a reading-room runner, and he spoke my name in a hushed tone.

It occurred to me that my doctor was more resourceful than I'd imagined and that the news had reached me even here. I shivered, suddenly aware of how cold the room was. The boy swiveled to reveal that he held a box with a call slip stuck in it.

Across the elegant room, past the other scholars bent over papers, books, and small computers, the reading-room supervisor, an amiable woman who bred corgis, was waving to me. On a previous visit, I visited a litter of new-born corgi puppies and considered taking one back to New York with me; a ridiculous idea. She was smiling; she'd sent the runner over and was watching for my reaction. I waved back, pantomiming delight.

To be present when new material was released to public examination was nothing short of a sign, and I paused to consider Marian's orchestration. The present moment—the release of the box to public scrutiny—was exactly seven years from the date of Marian's death in Albuquerque. According to the terms of her will, all of her other papers were made available immediately upon her death; only the box before me had been forbidden. Familiar as I was with the ins and outs of Marian's decisions, I wasn't aware of the existence of new material.

Three letters in white envelopes and a spiral-bound notebook. Marian carried such notebooks with her to compose stories, but she was just as likely to use the pages for grocery lists, inventories of her wardrobe, or as a diary for recording daily events. Her formal journals were hand-bound, an annual gift from an old friend in London even after they ceased to speak.

There, in the notebook, in Marian's beautiful hand, was something like a love story, set in New Mexico, time period undefined. A month after a kind of troubadour and a beautiful naïf meet, they marry against the wishes of her family. He takes her to his ancestral home, a once magnificent adobe on the edge of town. There they live alone.

They enjoy one month of happiness.

One night the husband tells his bride that he's leaving. She says that she'll go with him anywhere. He insists that she stay. She must trust him. He has his reasons. She awakens alone to the sounds of morning in the large house, then hears an unfamiliar noise, a repeated shrill cry. She decides that it's an animal trapped in one of the empty rooms. In her long nightgown, barefoot, she wanders, trying to locate the source of the sound. Eventually, she opens the door of a room on the opposite side of the courtyard. There she finds a baby, perhaps six months old, in a wooden cradle that's rocking from side to side as the infant kicks and waves its arms. The baby is frantic, and, as the bride discovers when she lifts the child, wet, soiled, and hungry.

At this point, the story changes, no longer a melodrama but a more familiar Marian Foster Todd tale.

In time the bride discovers that her husband has another wife who bore their daughter and abandoned her, disappearing to parts unknown. Now that the baby's father is gone also, the discarded bride is left to care for the helpless, fragile, needy infant. The bride stands over the infant, knowing that if she accepts being the baby's mother, her life will be over at seventeen.

The ending is ambiguous and the possibilities terrible, an obvious homage to Chekhov's well-known "Sleepy," in which the overburdened servant, herself a child, strangles the baby in her care in order to get some peace. Murder isn't beyond the implications of Marian's story, the metaphorical death of the child bride or the actual death of the baby.

Though there was more to read, I closed the notebook, returned it to the box, and left the reading room, signaling to the room supervisor that I'd be back. It was lunchtime, and I wandered down the hill to the new computer sciences building. The café was crowded with faculty and students. I found a small table far away from the suspended television set with its mute display of news. My heart pounded. Adrenaline narrowed my throat.

The strength of Marian's work derived from her clear vision of the lives of her characters; it was impossible to say which she favored, for she created them with a cold impartial hand. The story in the notebook read more like a message than a work of fiction, but it was a message in a language I didn't know.

The midday sun and my heart's painful rhythm made my trek up to the reading room as difficult as scaling a mountain.

There were a few blank pages in the notebook, standard operating procedure, for Marian often reserved space for later amendments before beginning another story. The second was in a more familiar style.

An affair set in New Mexico, between a professional singer who's down on his luck and a young girl disillusioned about love because of an earlier betrayal. She hopes that in him she's found a truthful lover. The girl leaves her family and moves into his rented adobe at the edge of town. They enjoy a month of careful happiness, and she begins to trust him. One night he announces that he has to get out of town. She'll go with him, the girl says. He declares that he must travel alone. They quarrel bitterly, and she accuses him of planning from the start to leave her. When she wakes up the next morning, he and his few possessions are gone. In a skilled passage, the girl realizes how little he had with him and how easy his exit was. Hearing a noise from the next room, she hopes that he's come back, but instead there's a baby in a wooden cradle, no more than six months old, crying and, the girl finds, wet and soiled.

At first reluctantly, the girl cares for the baby. She begins to find meaning in her daily tasks and to feel a kind of love. After a few weeks, the baby's aunt and uncle appear. The uncle, a lawyer, explains that the baby's mother, addled by drugs, left the infant here with the father. Since he's gone too, they intend to raise the baby as their own. At that moment, the girl realizes that in this affair, she is not the heroine and has no rights at all.

The end is the best part: the girl's sorrow at losing the baby; her simultaneous recognition that she's had a narrow escape.

The second tale was more naturalistic, also less touching than the more sentimental and heightened version.

My back was giving its familiar library twinges. Closing the notebook, keeping its contents from prying eyes, I strolled past the portrait of the donors' daughter. Crowded on top of the card catalogues were busts of writers and poets whose papers rested in the collection. None, not even the most egomaniacal, would welcome a biographer; they were too smart for that. I inspected their well-known faces, some ordinary, some beautiful. Their disapproval rained down on me. When I embarked on the biography, I was convinced that Marian's was a story worth telling. Her reputation in the years following her death took a dive, as always happens, but by the time the book was finished,

I calculated, it would be the moment for a reappraisal of the work. By the time I returned to the reading room, I was considering another question: What of Marian's privacy? What gave me the right to know her secrets?

The third story in the notebook was a first-person narration in the confessional tone Marian had perfected in her most anthologized tale.

The narrator is a young woman, no longer a girl but much younger than her lover, a journalist from Los Angeles who's in her small town in New Mexico for an extended rest. He's just dried out and needs to be in a simple, cheap place in order to stay away from drink. The young woman is a fairly straightforward version of Marian at that age, with only geography and physical features changed here and there. She's the brightest young woman in town, discontent with her opportunities, without the means or momentum to leave. The man, even though he's a drunk and a has-been, represents her chance for a new life. His reluctance to become involved with her, given his age and condition, is conveyed with subtlety and sympathy so that when he does fall in love, the reader is moved. It is guaranteed that something terrible will happen. In Marian's stories, love is always prelude to disaster.

In the story's second act, the narrator shows her lover, for lovers they become, the beauty of her birthplace, which, in her discontent and restlessness, she has stopped seeing. He tells her stories of a larger, city life, the one they intend to lead together.

And then. The fatal *and then*, the turning of the worm, the curve in the road with only darkness ahead.

And then one day, the narrator awakens to find her lover packing. There was a phone call in the middle of the night but he assured her that it was a drunken friend. Now he tells her that he has to leave. He'll send for her as soon as he's settled. *But where will you go?* she asks. *How will I reach you?* He doesn't know. *I'll go with you.* He won't let her. He'll write. He promises.

The appearance of the word *promise* in Marian's work is another sign of doom.

The man leaves, and the woman is left to face the town alone; all the old biddies pronounce her used and abandoned. The man has paid for the house for the rest of the month, so she stays there, taking long walks and trying to decide what to do next: Go to Los Angeles to find her lover? Wait patiently for his return? Travel east to a different destiny? One afternoon she returns from a walk and hears a strange noise. In the living room, a baby in a wooden cradle, kicking and crying. When she lifts the baby she finds that it's wet and soiled.

She contacts a favorite cousin, a nurse at a nearby hospital, and together they care for the baby until a letter arrives from the man. The baby was born six months before; he's the father, his wife, hitherto unmentioned, is the mother. The wife is an alcoholic who left their infant daughter at the address she had for him, the rented adobe in New Mexico. Now the wife is gone, and the lover plans to disappear. The baby is the girl's to keep. But she doesn't keep it. She persuades her cousin, who's older, married, and unhappily childless, to take the baby, and she gets on a bus headed east. The story ends with a lyrical description of the desert between New Mexico and Texas.

It is problematic to seek in literature—drafts or finished work—the facts of a writer's life. It takes nothing from Marian's skill to say that she used her life in all her work, to assert that there was nowhere in her fiction an example of an event wholly invented. In my nearly completed book, I resisted the temptation to use the life as a map to the work or the work as a map to the life, but now I read the stories in the notebook with the iciness one feels on hearing confirmed a dreadful truth one has unconsciously suspected.

Often I wished that Marian had acted more nobly in her personal relationships, but nothing she did sickened me until she sought out Dorothea and persuaded her daughter to see her through her last days. Marian's final act was the one I'd struggled with, trying to maintain moral neutrality so that I could report the facts, leaving judgment to others.

Once I met Dorothea, I became almost reconciled to Marian's late-life claiming of her daughter. However self-serving it was of Marian, however calculated to gain a safe nest and a devoted nurse while she was dying, for Dorothea the reunion with her birth mother and the chance to care for her was the fulfillment of a life's wish. Before Marian, Dorothea had been troubled and lonely, without a sense of her place in the world, and she attributed this, despite her love for her adoptive parents and theirs for her, to her missing mother. She was nearly a recluse, working by day at a state office job, returning to her small, much-loved house and garden in the evening. Her parents had been her closest friends and now they were gone. Her dogs, her garden, occasional forays to the Four Corners or nearby pueblos: these made up Dorothea's quiet life. She confessed to me that, before Marian, she fretted that she didn't do enough either in or for the world. But then Marian appeared, and Dorothea's life suddenly had meaning; she became Marian

Foster Todd's daughter, her loving nurse, and, finally, her grateful heir. Dorothea's debt to the world was paid and her place in it secured.

Work dominated Marian's life, her process of procrastination and avoidance followed by total relinquishment to the work, and her constant struggle to meet her own high standards and her idea of herself. In the end, though, Marian's art was not enough. Marian had outlived many of her friends and all of her friendships. She hated her few living relatives. Seeking out Dorothea, finding her worthy, causing dramatic havoc in her daughter's life, appealed to Marian and gave the degradation of her illness and death a pleasing narrative shape.

It didn't seem so terrible. Awaiting my own bad news, I envied Marian. At the end of Marian's life, when she needed a daughter, she inserted herself into Dorothea's life, pushing aside the couple, now dead, who had nurtured Dorothea, replacing them with her glorious if dying self. Still, my biographer's abhorrence of literal congruence between life and work didn't mean that I couldn't connect the dots. In the cool, concentrated air of the reading room, my sad confidence grew that Marian was not Dorothea's mother. The stories in the notebook would break Dorothea's heart.

It was closing time. I put away the notebook, and carried the box to the desk, leaving it on the cart where it would wait for me until morning.

That evening, my landlady, a specialist in French medieval market practices, rushed from the kitchen of the main house as I unlocked the guesthouse, saying, "I didn't want to leave a note." Her denim apron protected a festive shirt from the local Indian store.

If a message is meant to get through, it will. I believed that the doctor in New York had phoned this young woman.

She said, "You must come to our party tonight." A cocktail party: a candidate for a chair and the spouse whom the psychology department would have to take on before the deal was sealed.

"Oh, my dear," I said. "I've had a trying day and a party's the last thing . . ."

As so often in my life, the other shoe dropped. She was inviting me pro forma so that the inevitable noise would have to be excused.

"But I'll try," I said, and her face brightened. "I'll have a rest, and I'll try."

The truth was, I couldn't bear to speak to anyone.

After a shower and a bite to eat, I retreated to the tiny patio where I wouldn't be seen by the partygoers. It was a pleasant night, warm for No-vember. That morning I'd had a swim but the muscles in my arms ached and my back complained after the day in the reading room. Perhaps it was not simple muscle fatigue but a harbinger of what was to come. The sound of laughter and the murmur of lecturing that passed for academic conversation formed the background to my thoughts.

If Dorothea was not Marian's daughter but the abandoned child of a former lover and his wife, then Dorothea represented not Marian's late-life acceptance of the deepest connection of all, but another connivance on Marian's part.

The story Marian told so often about looking at her baby and realizing that she'd never write again if she gave in to her maternal instincts—that was true. The twist, the turn, was that the baby she relinquished was not her own.

My discovery destroyed the heartwarming shape of my book. So often in my researches it seemed that Marian was a force rather than a human being, and that her own survival was all that mattered to her. To show her as a mother at the end of her life, to be able to say that she loved someone else—loved Dorothea, her daughter—gave Marian a missing dimension of human-ity. Now, in the light of my new findings, if I bought Marian's version of her motherhood, I'd be a sentimental fool. If I didn't, if I revealed the new material and proved my case as best I could, all received ideas of Marian's character would be altered. No longer would she seem a relic of the past; her ruthless-ness would mark her as a truly contemporary figure, and the sensational rev-elation would be the making of my biography.

Beyond my literary calculations lay the horror of what the revelation would do to Dorothea: to gain a mother out of nowhere, to nurse her and learn to love her, then to lose her to death, then to learn that she had been duped—Dorothea would be destroyed, though, as Marian once remarked, "People are so rarely destroyed."

By this time, the party was ending: early classes, babysitters, the stran-glehold and welcome embrace of domestic and academic routine. The night was over for me too, and I gathered my wine glass and the plate from my small meal and went inside.

As I washed the dishes and arranged my papers for the next day's work, I realized that, though I'd searched the official records and all of Marian's papers, there might be other evidence and living witnesses I'd missed. Marian might have planted such bombs in archives all over the country. Her carefully timed revelation, the new box released seven years after her death, might only be the first of many that one by one would diminish the worth of all I averred.

Little by little, my achievement, my life's work, might be discounted until it sat unread on library shelves, remaindered in bookstores, unwanted at any price.

~~~

On the three letters in the box, Marian's name and address were written at the top in blue ballpoint in block letters. There was no return address. Two of the letters were nearly fifty years old, addressed to Marian at the boardinghouse in the Village where she'd lived on her first arrival in New York. The first was brief:

> *Tinky told me what you did with the baby. It wouldn't be any use to ask what you thought you were doing. But I'll be a fool and ask. Couldn't you stand to wait for me?*

I'd never seen the name *Tinky* before. The letter was signed with only a letter: *B.*

The second letter was longer. It began with a Whitmanesque celebration of names of all the places B had been since he left Marian and the baby, then turned into a catalogue of hard jobs he'd taken and his chances for good fortune that turned bad, and then:

> *You like to hear the end of stories. My baby's mother is dead. They won't even let me see my baby. The so-called mother swears she'll fight me to the death. She has the money to hire a lawyer and you know me. Your words of love meant nothing and your promises less. You were my last chance and you knew it.*

B had managed to enrage her or at least to touch a sore spot; she must have replied to the first letter. If I'd received any of Marian's scathing prose, I'd have crumbled on the spot, but B evidently enjoyed infuriating her. He reminded her of their plans to raise the child and then:

> *Anyone would think you cared about the baby. Or me. You called her your own. I never figured you for a natural but you looked like for*

*once you cared for someone other than yourself. That's why I trusted
you with my baby girl.*

The third letter was much more recent, addressed to Marian at her last
New York residence. Two years before her diagnosis and the onset of the disease's symptoms, Marian signed a lease on a floor-through in the Village. The
beautiful apartment was meant to be the place where she would be a famous
and successful author, at home at last. It had been decades since Marian had
had a place of her own. She'd traveled in Europe and Latin America, perched
in San Francisco and Chicago, and of course found temporary shelters during her many stints as a visiting professor. For years, she'd called herself a
cuckoo bird, I thought in reference to her habit of living in other people's
houses, though now an additional meaning came clear: some cuckoos lay
their eggs in other nests and leave their young to be raised by other birds.

Marian's last apartment had white walls and pale furniture, polished
floors and soft rugs. Vases of flowers everywhere. She must have stood many
times at the front window where her view was of the redbrick, two-story houses
across the street, window boxes filled with geraniums and lobelias. She'd
described doing just that in letters. The oblique angle of observation appears
in her penultimate story, "Enfilade," when the main character is shocked to
see her former lover walking past, he unaware that she stands watching him.
Once again, Marian was a step ahead of me; I'd assumed that the story's vivid
moment was inspired by nothing more than the view from her front room.

His last letter was brief:

*No thanks to you no thanks to me the baby's grown to be a fine woman
right where you left her. Not a day goes by that I don't curse you for
taking her from me.*

If B's letters were to be believed, he'd entrusted his baby to Marian,
who'd relinquished her and fled. Marian wasn't Dorothea's mother. B's third
letter came at the first moment that she needed a daughter. She arranged
the reading at the University of New Mexico at half her usual fee, inspected
Dorothea, and saved herself. Throughout my years of research, I'd wondered
off and on how Marian knew that Dorothea was still in Albuquerque, but I'd
figured she was just lucky.

The stories in Marian's notebook would make an intriguing appendix to
my book. The lover was not a stock Marian male; he was a drunk and she had

no use for alcoholic men in her art. Babies appear only twice in Marian's work, but in those instances are adorable and savvy in a comical way. In none of the three versions was the baby appealing—not appealing enough for Marian to fight for, not appealing enough to keep.

Add the three stories to Marian's statements to interviewers about her moment of temptation before she abandoned Dorothea—so congruent with the drafts in the notebook—add the fact that she had reserved the notebook and letters until she knew she would be dead, and I had the possibility of coming as close to the truth as Marian would permit.

Nothing could stop me from publishing my new finds: early on, Dorothea had signed a form giving me access to all of her mother's papers and permission for me to photocopy and make use of whatever I wished. No one could have been more generous than she. Her signature on the permission form, and on all the notes and cards she'd sent me over the years, was rounded, childish, loving.

In the chill of the reading room, I had a moment of the sort of rare understanding that illuminates Marian's stories. The content of the letter I'd hoped to find in Austin—the farewell from Marian's dearest friend—was now obvious.

Sandra, the poet, alone of Marian's large circle, must have known Marian's secret. The entry in the poet's journal at the end of the friendship declared that Marian was incapable of love. The missing letter must have specifically condemned Marian for abandoning the baby entrusted to her, the infant who became Dorothea. Marian destroyed the original. Sandra must have destroyed her carbon copy out of a loyalty to Marian that endured even after she couldn't bear to be with her, and Sandra's loyalty held fast even after Marian so outrageously claimed Dorothea for her own.

B was Brandon Miller. Best remembered as the model for a heroic figure in Beat literature and lore, Brandon Miller was an Action painter of unfulfilled promise, and he was an alcoholic. They had been lovers when both were young and poor, before each moved to New York. By coincidence, both were living in Greenwich Village, only blocks apart, at the time of Marian's diagnosis. They had no contact, so far as I could tell from my exhaustive examination of Marian's date books, journals, and letters. Brandon Miller outlived Marian. Only a year ago, he died in the town where he was born, near Mount Shasta in northern California. In Miller's obituary in the *Times*, his liaison with Marian was mentioned, hers one name on a list.

When I last lunched with my editor in New York, she mentioned that a young writer, someone I'd recommended for a Guggenheim, was shopping around a proposal for a biography of Brandon Miller. When my fellow biographer came to Austin, as he would without question, and read the contents of the box, Brandon Miller's fatherhood of Marian's abandoned baby would make a juicy chapter. Still, no matter how Brandon Miller's biographer hurried, my book would be finished before his. The opportunity was mine to reveal Marian's dearest secret.

My book might cause the kind of stir that mere dogged research wouldn't, for I could unveil Marian as a fraud, right up to her last day on earth. Never a fraud in her writing, often in her life. The new material offered something better than a happy ending. Marian, on the cusp of obscurity, would be newly famous as the selfish and brilliant charmer she was in life. All her fiction would be brought back into print, and the young—some of them—who knew her name vaguely, her work even less well, would read her as a lifelong rebel and a devoted artist.

If my book succeeded, I would hold briefly what the world had to offer—modest fame for what remained of my lifetime; my book in all the bookstores and libraries; and, most elusive and unquantifiable, readers. My book would be something to leave behind, aside from my apartment filled with worn possessions of no value to anyone, not even myself.

I repacked the letters and the notebook in their acid-free box and, saying grateful farewells to the reading-room staff, I left a request for a copy of the notebook and letters to be sent to me in New York.

～⁍

November was half over. Winter would come even here. That morning, I'd felt a chill in the air and decided to swim in the evening. Now I had the energy only to walk through the dusty autumn streets back to the guesthouse.

My flight to Albuquerque was early in the morning so I packed that night. As usual after a bout of research, I had more papers than ever. My clothing returned to its place in the suitcase obediently. In no time, I removed all trace of the small rearrangements that had made the guesthouse my home. When I'd changed into my nightdress and performed my nocturnal libations, I lay in bed, overcome by an exhaustion irreparable by sleep.

Dorothea lived in a modest neighborhood in the North Valley of Albuquerque. Her house was hidden from the street by a high adobe wall, a blue that was fading with age into the most delicate shade of white. In back of the house, Dorothea tended a vegetable patch and an orchard. Small crisp pears came in autumn, apricots ripened in July. Her dogs patrolled the garden paths, and used afternoons on the back porch to guard the world. Butterflies visited Dorothea's garden, and birds of all kinds. Though you heard cars pass, dogs bark, music from neighbors, it felt as though you were far from the rest of the world. Inside Dorothea's house, the tile floor was cool. The blades of the ceiling fans rotated sedately. Only there would it be possible for me to rest.

Here was food for thought, thoughts for the night ahead.

To Document

DAGOBERTO GILB

MY GIRLFRIEND JENNIFER RUSHED IN TO TELL ME—I WAS STUDYING— that she'd talked to them, meaning *him* of course, the one we looked away from all the time, the one staring at us from his driveway, always standing there, a driveway to him like a beach, only you stood there. Staring. The narc, I called him. She called him *coolio*, which was kind of fun, but it made me think *culo*, which was not so fun. My mean sarcasm was something she never got or heard or listened to because she was a well-mannered white girl. Worse, I knew she really did think he was cool in some twisted-up way. I figured that was because she grew up without any danger, or any crazy, or any just plain wrong, so anything that wasn't like a family TV upbringing was not only fascinating but exciting. This also explained why she was with me.

"He invited us over," she said, thrilled. "Is that wild?"

"No," I said.

"Yes it is!"

"It isn't, Jennifer."

"Well, I'm going. You don't want to, you don't have to."

I'd already put down the book. It was always hard to study where we lived. Music going all the time, people in and out. Lots of dogs. Cats to step on or around. Beer, vodka, tequila. Drugs. Noise noise noise. I was the only one who kept it down. Vanessa and her mousy girlfriend had one room and my friend Ef, the other. He sold drugs with his cousin Richard, who was always in the house, sleeping on the couch. They paid the rent, meaning I didn't, which obviously encouraged me to stay. I was on the good path. Because it didn't pay well, to most I had a shitty job as a clerk at a motel and didn't get enough sleep, but I liked it. Studying was my newborn Christianity, and I read a lot there.

I had to go. It was how it was. She decided, I went along. She helped me. I'd never known anyone like her and she made me feel . . . like life was better. Soon, she said, she'd be leaving El Paso—meaning me, too, or the way I took it, that we'd be leaving together.

It was a few days later, a weekend night. The sky was tuned bright, the starlight above mirrored in the streetlight below, the raw desert in front of us as romantically Western as she saw it. They had a nicer house than we did. Maintained better on the outside anyway, the landscaping free of weeds, the decorative rock making the ocotillos and agaves seem ceramic-pot pretty, the paloverde lacy. The front door we knocked on was freshly carved Mexican wood. The inside was nicer, too, all new paint and furniture, like objects inside a frame. She was Natalie, he was Phil.

"I'm Jennifer," Jennifer said, "but please call me Jen. And this is Nino."

"Nino," Natalie said. "How unique a name."

"Is that short for something?" asked Phil.

I would have said no, but Jennifer thought I was taking too long. "Just Nino. Nino the *niño!*" She laughed, and they laughed, too.

"Around here Phil goes by Felipe," Natalie told me.

"Felipe!" said Jennifer, thrilled as ever with what I found irritating. The man was also shaved bald and wearing a light blue coat with wide lapels and a "hip" shirt—maybe cool in New York. She had on a black party dress. Older, she was still cute, so much that it was hard to see how they could possibly have matched up. We were both wearing jeans, though I washed mine, and Jennifer made me iron both the pants and my white guayabera, which I was glad I had. As usual, she was right. It didn't matter what she wore, she made it classy.

"Are you guys from El Paso?" Phil asked me.

"Nino is," Jennifer answered. "I'm from California first, then I moved to Maryland."

"I'm from Philly," said Phil. "I know, Phil from Philly. I know, I know."

"That doesn't work with Felipe, does it?" Natalie cheerfully said to me.

She was speaking to me because I hadn't said a word yet. I might have, I might not have as quickly as I should have, anyway, but in their living room I'd already gotten distracted. It was a spacious room, long pastel blue sofas and chairs circling a wall of glass—the drapes were pulled to their corners so that the panoramic view of the desert and city lay before. No doubt beautiful. But my eyes wanted to lock on the wall opposite, at a painting as big as most picture windows. Hard for me not to see it when I walked in because it was of a woman—a very attractive one—seated and completely naked, her face aroused. The painting blurry, a strange green and pink, at first I thought only my mind made it seem to be Natalie.

"Wine? Or beer, maybe?" said Phil. "I have gin, bourbon . . . I have it all. Name your pleasure."

"I can't believe we forgot to bring a bottle of wine or something!" said Jennifer.

"Yeah," I said, "I should have remembered." I would never have thought of it. "My fault, I'm sorry." I didn't look at her, but I was talking to Jennifer.

"Please," said Phil, "you're our guests."

"Wine, white wine," Jennifer said.

"Me, too," I said.

"You do not seem like a white wine man," he said to me.

"It's fine," I said.

We would eat very soon, but for the moment we all sat.

"Oh!" said Jennifer. "It's you!"

Natalie smiled. "Self-portrait."

"You paint? So do I!"

"It's Modigliani, but more now, more contemporary avant-garde," said Jennifer.

"He is my favorite."

They were hitting it off, talking in little screeches and exclamations. Phil was pleased. I thought he was proud that his woman was so hot and proving it in their living room's portrait. So I was more uneasy still. I didn't really like the wine, either, but it wouldn't have mattered what I was drinking. When suddenly the women were going to the kitchen together, and Phil and I had to be alone, lousy was even worse.

He refilled our drinks. I assured him I really wanted another white wine.

"So what about you, man," he said, being cool. "What do you do?"

"For money?"

"Well, usually."

"Only a crummy job. Nothing. At a motel."

He was smiling. "You have other work? For not money . . ."

I didn't answer quickly.

"You know, like your lady is an artist."

"I'm studying. I read. I like to read."

He chuckled like I made that up.

"For school? A grad school?"

"Yeah, maybe. But no." I didn't like to discuss this part of my life. "What about you?" Turning the subject. "What do you do?"

"Retired military."

"Military," I said. "Retired."

He waited, expecting more. Probably most people would ask quite a bit more. In fact, one detail was that he didn't seem retirement old, even if he did seem older. But I didn't care. I didn't want to ask more.

"A lot of people over at your place," he said finally. "All the time."

"Yeah, it's a zoo."

"Partying a lot."

"Not always. Not Jennifer and me."

"Not everybody lives there, though."

"No."

By now he was getting a little peeved. Like he wished dinner was ready. Like he wished I'd tell him whatever. Or maybe exactly.

"So what is it? How many people live there?"

"Roommates?"

It was like he either wanted to stand up or sit better than he already was.

"It's a three-bedroom," I said. "I have one of the rooms. Me and Jennifer. Then our other two roommates."

He drank his drink. I had barely sipped my second glass of wine. I was sure he would say something else, but then we heard Natalie.

"Nino, Felipe, dinner is servido'd!"

Jennifer was right behind her. "You can't believe how good the food looks and smells," she told me. "I think I'm in love with your wife," she told Phil. This made him feel much better, and that made me feel a little relieved, too.

The dinner was probably great, as excellent and unbelievable as Jennifer and Phil gushed, but I was too uncomfortable to do much more than pretend as well as I could. I probably didn't really like this food as much as they did. No tiny eater, I thought good was some eggs with chorizo, or rice and beans made right, avocado with lime, salt, and pepper with warm tortillas. Though she tried to act like it was no biggie, I knew it ticked Jennifer off that I was this way, and it didn't make me feel good that it did.

"I had fun, and I really liked her."

"I know."

"And he's so out there."

"Out there like a narc."

"I don't think they'd care. I bet they smoke it."

"Who'd want to smoke it with them?"

"I definitely would with her. I bet she does. I'll find out."

"With him, then."

"It doesn't seem like he would, that's true. I bet he'd be very interesting if he did."

"You gotta be joking, right?"

She smiled. She wasn't. I didn't for one second believe she'd want to hang out with him—even her, for that matter. Jennifer was just . . . this was how she was.

Not that I would smoke it with either of those people. I wasn't doing any with anyone. I had put that past me. Even Ef didn't smoke like he used to, not like his cousin Richard and Richard's friends. Not that he wasn't into the white powder some, enough. He did the blow. He insisted he was careful about it, and I believed him. Mostly. Efren was my closest, longest *camarada*. We were brothers. I wanted to believe him. The truth was that he'd been getting loose about his business. Was it because of blow? It was like he was getting it too easy, and he was moving it around too fast. Sometimes the house noise seemed like more than noise. Sometimes it sounded like stupid.

These two young guys coming over were proof. One had long scraggly hair that had braids in it that hadn't been unbraided in a year. Tattoos that seemed like a long-sleeve blue shirt from a distance. He needed food. I'd take him for a meth head, but he smiled too much and too calmly. His partner was a pretty blond, proud of the muscled cuts in his pecs and abdomen. In other words, he went shirtless. Only hippie beads. I was there when they were telling Ef that they felt like they were being followed at first, so they drove around until they lost those detectives. Ef sold to them.

"Are you losing your mind?" I told him after.

"I been doing business with them for a while," Ef said. "They've always been good for it."

"I never seen them before."

"You're not always around, *mano*. I'm telling you, they're good for it, and a solid quantity when they . . ."

"Are you joking? They even said they were followed."

"They said they *thought* they were. *Pero*, okay, I see what you're getting at."

"Like, if you saw them, if you were a cop, what would you do? You'd see where these stoned *idiotas* go, who they know, like that."

"You got a point, *simón,* yeah. *Pero . . .*"

"But what?"

"Come on, Nino. Lighten up, dude."

"Ay, you are *so* losing it."

"Look, serious, I'm practically done with the shit now. I know what you're saying."

"You're done?"

"Ya no más, en serio."

"I do not want to see their car here again, ever, okay?"

"Yeah, that's cool."

"They're a bust. I'm telling you."

"*Andale,* brother. I got it, I got it."

Jennifer didn't recognize anything as dangerous. She thought it was all an adventure ride. Material, paint strokes, color. Nothing in her life suggested that she was wrong. I never asked her if she'd even gotten a traffic ticket.

"Detectives," I said. "You heard of them?"

"How would anyone know? Aren't they undercover?"

"No. They drive unmarked cars."

"That's what I mean. That they look like cars, so how would he know?"

"They're as unmarked as a seven-foot quarterback, wearing plaid shorts and a camera, in, like, a cruiser painted plain brown."

"You worry too much."

"Right. That's probably it. Let's forget about it."

"It'll pass," she assured me.

After that we got on our way for a picnic in Cloudcroft with our neighbors, who'd invited us. Phil had a silver flask of cognac and we all shivered after taking swallows. Jennifer was very excited because she'd never been, and with the Mescalero reservation nearby—more excited. She and Natalie were still exuberant over each other, and Phil had got creepier since—it was hot in El Paso—they were both displaying much in their low-cut tops. And they did not shy away from the topic that was on his mind.

"You wouldn't like a nude beach?" asked Phil.

"I'm normal. Of course I like to see naked women. It's not tha . . . though probably they don't all look so good, and maybe it's best I didn't see that, either."

The women moaned critically.

Phil loved it. "Not all boobs are equal," he explained.

The women moaned.

"Not all penises are equal, either, Felipe," said Natalie.

Jennifer said, "*Uuu.*"

"What's yours like, Nino?" Natalie asked.

I was not good at this. Didn't like it ever, less so with these people who did not make me comfortable.

"Come on," she insisted. "You've seen what we girls have, what about you?"

"When'd he see you?" asked Phil, giddy. "What are you guys doing when I'm not watching?"

"Our painting, my darling."

"You are well endowed," Jennifer told her.

"You're a couple of handfuls yourself, my lovely."

Both of them seemed to be shoving their breasts forward.

"So what about it, Nino?" Natalie kept on.

"You're asking him to take it out?" cried Phil.

"I didn't mean that, but if that's what it takes!"

I didn't offer a word. I didn't move.

"It's big," Jennifer said to break through. "I've seen it up yummy close."

Both Phil and Natalie howled.

I hadn't drunk that much, and I didn't think Jennifer had, but she was drunk already. Clearly the flask was no aperitif for them. "Settle down, boys and girls," I said finally. "We're still getting there."

"He's no fun but probably right," said Jennifer.

"If he promises to show me later." Her hands were so close to her breasts, it was as though they were someone else's moving in for a feel.

Phil was still laughing too hard as the highway curved to the right, and he didn't turn the wheel enough, so the car wandered into the oncoming lane. We all heard car horns as he straightened it out fast.

After a few moments passed, I offered to drive. Phil's eyes were already locked on the rearview mirror. It was the New Mexico State Police, who finally lit it up. When the patrolman got to the window, Phil was perfect, driver's license and insurance already out: He lost his grip on the steering wheel; he was very wrong to be driving one-handed. He stepped out of the car, and the two talked by the trunk. Then he came back, shaking his head.

"He was a good man," he said.

"You didn't even get a ticket?" I said. I was sure I'd have been given a DWI test, and I only had a couple sips.

"One of those things," he said. "He understood."

I looked at Jennifer to say, *See?* without words, but like Natalie, she hadn't sobered up as Phil had.

"Look, I don't mean to piss on the party, but I feel like we should turn back. Cash out while we're ahead."

"Poop on," Jennifer corrected me. "The expression is *poop on*."

She and Natalie giggled too much again. All was well. I offered to drive. He wouldn't hear of it. A flask—a second one or refilled?—came out again in Las Cruces. By the time we pulled into his driveway, I was the only one not fresh-start happy to be back. All seemed completely forgotten by Natalie and Phil by the time they were pouring a second bottle of red wine, our picnic laid out on the outdoor patio table. Natalie was bombed. Jennifer, either because she didn't know how not to be agreeable or because she was, kept up. Phil, his crude slobber virtually drooling down her cleavage, didn't seem to disturb her, and Natalie, bumping and pressing against me whenever possible, didn't provoke, either. Though it was true I didn't adore the Gucci food, I got up to leave because I was done for the day.

"I'm not ready yet," said Jennifer.

"Stick around, man! There'll be plenty of time to study later," Phil told me, but then looked at them—an inside joke.

Which did the job of irritating me. Pissed me off. Jennifer didn't move to slow me down even a little as I turned away to leave.

"Wait wait wait," Phil said. Then, slowly, "Wait, wait, wait."

I stopped. I was outside his front door.

"Look," he said. He tried to reach his arm around me, but I dodged it. "Look," he said. "Listen." He was drunk, trying to sound like he was just cool. "You shouldn't go. You shouldn't, man." Did he wink? "Look. Nat. You know? You know, man, you know! She likes you."

"Your wife likes me," I said.

"Come on, man. You go with her, you know. She wants that. You'll like her."

I was about to laugh. I had enough time to bounce around what to say. I mean, I might choose to have sex with this man's wife, though not right then, and not interested at all, really—but whatever, it wouldn't be as much for *his* pleasure as mine in fucking him over by doing her.

"I'll take care of Jen," he said.

My ears heard that faster than I did. So did my arms and my hands and my voice. "Fuck you, you asshole!" I straight-armed his chest with both hands, tumbling him into the front door loud and hard.

"What are you doing?" he yelled. "Are you out of your mind?"

As he steadied himself—"Wait a minute, hold on a minute"—it seemed like he was coming toward me aggressively, not backing away. It could have been to reach out kindly. Who knows? I didn't care. I hit him solid—first a left to stun him, and then a right that, I'd have to admit, punished and slammed him.

Both the women were at the open door screaming. I couldn't say if it was at me or about him. His nose and mouth were bleeding. I went home.

And yes, I was mad. No doubt that had something to do with my bad reaction when I walked in and saw those two dopers in the house again. They were standing in the living room when I asked, probably too loud, what they were doing here again.

"I don't have nothing to do with it," Ef said, backpedaling from all of it completely.

"It's me," said Richard. He stood up straight, which he didn't do so often. "I'm the one who told them. It's cool, Nino, honest."

"It is, *vato*," the blond said to me. He was wearing a torn T-shirt, his beads over that. "We got the message. Seriously, really. Like today, just now, we didn't park outside your house. We parked below the arroyo, and we hoofed it up. The little kids thought we were maybe desert aliens. It was cool."

These two walked a half mile through the peaceful family neighborhood, as inconspicuous as two ice cream trucks. Quickly I traveled beyond mad into controlled and steady. This was finished, it was time to move along. Even before Jennifer came home, I was packing. She was still dealing with what happened next door, which, it was true, seemed to me a less important past already. She was so furious at me, she said, truly embarrassed by me. Even as she was going on, though, I caught fascination growing in her voice, the thrill of a ride. Here was an adventure she had witnessed and lived through. The Old West! Her Chicano boyfriend when she lived on the *frontera*! I'd loosened two teeth, not broken his nose, even though it took a while for them to stop the bleeding there. We even started smiling.

"God, I would never be with him," she told me. "I can't believe he even thought it was possible."

"Glad to know it'd be okay if I was with her."

"She is a turn on," she said, giggling. "Pretty hard to not want to get naked with her."

It had never crossed my mind what she might be thinking. Talking about the colorful incident and about sex-starved Natalie made Jennifer, still a little drunk, affectionate. In bed, whatever I wanted to do was fine with her.

"We got no choice now," I said. "We have to leave. They're out of control."

"We'll go to my place," Jennifer said.

"You mean you still have the apartment?"

"Of course," she said. "Where did you think I did my work? When I slept? Here?"

"I guess I assumed you gave it up once you lived here."

"When you're at work, those crazy hours you get, I'm there. I'm there a lot."

"Here I thought you were at the college."

"I wouldn't get in this bed if you weren't in it."

"Never thought about it once."

"Such a strange man you are. You read too much."

"All the time you could have been with Phil."

"Or Natalie," she said.

We were on our way for the last few boxes two weeks later when, as I was about to turn into the street, I caught sight of the buzzing hive of police cars in front of the house. Phil stood out like a rodeo clown. I was driving slow enough that I could straighten out the turn.

"We'll know in a minute, but I don't think they saw us. I don't think he did, either."

"My camera's still there!"

We headed back to her apartment.

"I can't believe I left it there. I don't want anyone to take it."

"You can get it back if they did."

"I can't believe I left it. I don't know why I brought it last time."

"To document," I reminded her. It'd been the first time I ever heard that phrase used. "Us here, this time and place on the Texas border." I remembered it like a book title.

"I already took most of the pictures I wanted. It's why I forgot it."

At her friend's apartment, we waited on news. I didn't think it was such a good idea for her to call and ask Natalie. After a few hours, I finally reached Ef's sister. Everyone at the house was arrested, at least nine people. It was four ounces of cocaine and a good stash of marijuana. The coke deal was arranged by a friend of a friend of Richard, who was really a narc. What she understood, they had a warrant for me. At the least, it meant I'd be picked up and need to have a lawyer, with all the jail time and expense between. She didn't hear anything about Jennifer's name.

"What?" I asked. She was as upset as I'd ever seen her.

"One time he asked," she said. "And I told him."

"Names?"

"Everybody's. Everybody who lived there. Yours, and mine, too. Last names. It seemed like harmless conversation. That he was curious, the same way I would be."

"That's all you told him, though?"

"Yes," she said. But she wasn't done. She wasn't quick with it, she wasn't done. "I talked too much to Natalie."

"He's not the narc, but he could have called it in."

"Me, too?"

"He was pissed off at me." I was thinking, and she was crying. "But just as likely dealing with those *payasos* Richard let in."

"I'm sorry, I'm really sorry, Nino! I'm scared now."

"We're all right, especially here."

"You think they'll be looking for my car?"

"There won't be an all-points bulletin."

She was on full alert. "They won't know where my apartment is. I never told her about that."

"Jennifer," I said, "*cálmate*, take it easy."

But she couldn't, or she did in another way: She had her girlfriend and the boyfriend of get all her things from the apartment, even the camera from the house—it was still there—and she was gone in three days, driving to California, or Maryland, or somewhere, she couldn't tell me, even as she kissed me good-bye. I quit my job at the motel, which is to say I never showed up again, not even to get my last check. I had her apartment free for the next three months, until I got worried by the second angry letter—not from the landlord but from her grandfather, who was still paying the rent but said I would have to leave or else. Or else? He'd stop paying. Her? He didn't say he knew, but he knew I was there, he knew my name to mail the letters. I never heard from Jennifer again.

And so rested the twenty-five-year-old memory of the rich girlfriend way back when I'd never imagined using airports and rental cars. I'd been to Phoenix a few times, but it was already years ago. I didn't like it then and still didn't. Sedate as it was, the hotelish lobby layout seemed hard to follow. Maybe it was why retired types were hired to nice it up to people like me who looked lost. A half hour before takeoff, I was afraid of being late for the flight. The old man in the blue vest at the elevator who came over to me seemed more like a Walmart greeter.

"No," I said. "I'm fine, thanks."

"But what I'm saying . . ."

"It's all right," I said, rushing to an escalator. I thought I heard what sounded like my name, but I dismissed it. Since I had frequent-flyer-premium advantages, I got through what would have been a long screening line fast, just in time to hear the explanation that the flight would be delayed for about forty minutes.

Which was okay. I bought a turkey and Swiss sandwich from the *mexicanos* working there, asking if they were miserable in Arizona because of the new law. They both laughed when I said how it wasn't fair that pretty papers covered turkeys and big cheeses so fast and for so little coin. I found a vinyl seat across from the gate, near two East Indian Americans and a man from Dallas who knew one of them: This afternoon flight was always late. Nobody thought there should be weather issues, but there was rain here, wind there. Like almost all, only a few of them women, each had a computer open on their lap, the Dallas man with his Bluetooth earpiece blinking, him talking, typing, both.

Moments before the first-class boarding call, the old man greeter approached. Many people were already standing near the gate.

"Excuse me, sir, but do you have your documents?"

I was not prepared. Some seconds passed, and people sitting around within range both stared and looked away. I stood with my bag.

"You don't remember me?"

I had no choice but to walk toward him to get to the gate.

"Probably better that you don't recognize me," he said.

I'd passed by him, but it wasn't like I could go too far.

"It's Phil," he said from behind me, pausing. "Felipe. Of Felipe and Natalie."

I turned. It could not be the man I knew. He was so old. Overweight, he was fragile, beaten.

"We've been here for years," he said, maneuvering closer to me. "She's had cancer. It's been tough, on both of us."

His teeth were from a museum or an archeological dig. I moved to the other edge of the business attired—dress shirts and silk ties, pleated slacks and shined dress shoes that never scuffed, executive leather briefcases— waiting for my time in the line. I was so not interested.

"Nino, are you doing . . . better?" People stared at him, then me. It wasn't true, but it seemed the only conversation. "And Jen? We still think of her. You both."

My group was next. "I didn't mean to make you mad. It's Arizona."

He was pathetic, and I knew others felt bad for him, that I was heartless. I was relieved when I finally handed my boarding pass to the airline attendant, who ran it over the laser beam and thanked me. I was almost in the chute.

"I'm sorry," he said louder so I'd hear.

On an aisle seat, alone still, I was cramped anyway. Was he sorry about Arizona, or possibly about what happened back in El Paso? I wished I could have upgraded. I rubbed my closed eyes and planned to sleep. I knew I would never see him alive again.

23 Months

Caitlin Horrocks

I MET THIS GUY AT A PARTY, IS WHAT HAPPENED. BUT THAT SEEMS LIKE a lousy way to start a story. I don't want anyone operating under false pretenses. The juicy part's not all that juicy. I arrived at the party alone and he told me about the pod people and I told him something I had never told anyone else and then I was home alone before two thirty. That's pretty much the shape of the thing.

The party. I counted twenty-one people when I got there. It was a funny number because you could tell Miranda had expected a lot more, and I felt a little embarrassed for her. A little glad too, because it was a new thing to see Miranda embarrassed. But twenty-one was enough to spread through the house and out onto the back patio, at least a few people in every place, so it didn't look so bad. I'd meant to show up at ten thirty, two hours late, so people would have had some drinks and be easier to talk to. But I got lost when I got off the freeway and ended up pulling in at eleven.

Miranda gave me a tour of the house, low and stucco, with huge bathrooms. She had two roommates and I wished I knew people to move in with, to afford to rent a house like this. She introduced me to some of her friends. How brave, a few said, you came here on your own, how brave. And of course what they meant was, how sad. How sad that you don't know anyone and had to come alone, a woman alone at a party, all dressed up with Google Maps directions in her car, sipping a half glass of wine and is there anything sadder than that?

One of the bedrooms was almost bare, filled with brown cardboard boxes and a double bed with a green comforter. "One of my roommates," Miranda said. "He's moving out next week."

"Where's he going?"

"Prison. For awhile." She paused before saying it, but not too long, because it might be rude to tell tales on your roommates but it was also fun to have a great story, to be able to say: My roommate's headed to prison.

"What did he do?"

"He was in a car accident. He caused a car accident. But he hadn't been drinking."

"You go to prison for that?"

"His girlfriend died. They'd been driving to Tucson to visit her parents. He was speeding. A lot, I guess. Her parents asked for jail time."

I'd never been in the bedroom of someone who had killed someone else. "Is he here?" I asked.

"Out back, last I saw," Miranda said. "On the patio."

Isn't that something, I thought, to be at a party with a guy who killed his girlfriend. Everybody eating and getting drunk and making nice, and there he is, that guy with the glass of Chianti, he killed his own lover. I wanted to go find him. I wanted to talk to him. It seemed like a good way to spend the party, knowing a secret about somebody and him not knowing you know and maybe telling you about it anyway, just because he wants to, because you're a girl he wants to tell things to.

"Thanks for the tour," I said, and Miranda asked me if I'd be okay schmoozing around on my own. She wasn't so bad, really. I could see how she'd let me stick close by her the whole night if I wanted to and she wouldn't try too hard to ditch me. It made me wish more people had come to her party.

Miranda and I weren't friends. We both worked for the Arizona Hospital and Healthcare Association. I had my own cubicle where I researched funding opportunities for member hospitals. It was not interesting. I had a cousin who had put in a good word for me at AHHA and I'd been hired over the phone a month earlier. The job wasn't worth coming halfway across the country for. I wasn't all that good at it, and they probably wondered why they'd bothered to bring someone like me all the way from Minnesota when there were people like Miranda here in Phoenix who could do my job twice as well and who made sure everyone knew it. I don't care all that much about the public health, really. I kind of feel like people should just look after themselves.

My cousin had me over to his house in Scottsdale when I first arrived. He has a wife and two kids and a big house. After he'd gotten me a job and fed me dinner, I think he figured he'd pretty much done his duty by me, and I guess he had. He worked in a different part of the building and I never saw him. I checked the weather in Minneapolis online every day: 22 degrees, 17, 2, -5. It made me feel better about being where I was.

I walked back through the living room and kitchen. I passed the food by. If you're the girl alone at a party you don't want to be the girl alone at a party eating. The patio was just this long rectangle of cement. There was a wooden roof with Christmas lights tacked up all along the edge and a porch light on the wall beside the back door and other than that it was dark. Just beyond the edge of the patio the light gave out in an almost perfect line. Cement and a few inches of grass and then darkness. There was no moon and I squinted to see the bodies standing out on the lawn, smoking. You could catch the lit red ends of cigarettes moving up and down. It was February and the weather was soft and warm and it was still strange to me, the way winter felt sweet in the desert. It had rained that afternoon and the air had a spiky, grey smell someone would finally tell me was damp creosote the week I would leave Arizona for good.

On the far left side of the patio, this guy was standing by himself, and I knew that it was the roommate, the accidental murderer. Nobody else came near, like he was quarantined. He had a quiet face, black hair. He was wearing jeans and a green T-shirt. If he'd been lying on his bed he would have matched the comforter. The T-shirt was oversized, the shoulder seams falling partway down his arms, and while he was probably just wearing an oversized T-shirt, it made me wonder if he'd been heavier once, if there was less of him than there used to be and he filled up his clothes in a different way now. I was wearing a black dress and felt stupid. It was too formal for standing in a backyard with a plastic cup of wine.

I was a fat kid, and it makes me notice certain things now, like the way people wear their clothes and the way girls here are thin and hard and all one color, an orangey brown. It makes me notice people who are fat like I used to be and that makes me feel good but also embarrassed, because I think: That's the way I used to look, that's the way I used to move, taking up too much room in the world. I'm glad I'm not fat anymore. I like being able to walk up to some guy, a nice-looking one, and stand beside him and feel like I have a right to be there.

"I'm Leah," I walked over and said to him. "I work with Miranda."

"Sasha," he said, which I'd always thought was a girl's name. He was leaning against the house, looking out at the yard. I thought about saying, I hear you killed your girlfriend. Instead I said, "It's dark out there." I say a lot of dumb things.

"Yeah," Sasha said. "It's dark."

"How do you know Miranda? Or did someone else invite you?"

"I live here," he said, which of course I already knew.

"So you can tell me what the yard looks like," I said. "When it's not dark."

He thought about this for a while. "We have a trampoline."

"Yeah?"

"Yeah. You can't see it from here, but it's out there."

"Does it work?"

"Sure it works. It's a trampoline."

"The springs could be broken."

"They're not," he said, and I wondered if he was annoyed because I'd implied that his trampoline was all busted. He took a drink of his Newcastle. "There's a grapefruit tree, too," he added. "Behind where they're smoking."

"Really," I said.

"Do you want some grapefruit?"

"No thanks."

"Sure? Miranda and Sam don't like them. I've juiced some but the rest will just stay on the tree."

"Why not juice the rest? Shame to waste them."

"There's only so much grapefruit a guy can eat," he said, which wasn't what I was going for. I know why they'll go uneaten, I wanted to say. I already know about you.

"So holler if you decide you want some grapefruit. I'll grab you a plastic bag."

"Okay."

We stood there awhile. For a guy who had killed somebody, he wasn't very interesting. Someone had set up their iPod with some little speakers on the patio picnic table. People kept walking by and changing the song.

"There's a garden out there, too, a place I think used to be a garden. The dirt's all turned under but none of us planted anything."

"You could plant stuff now."

"I don't think you're supposed to plant now. It'll get hot soon."

"I forget. The seasons are all backwards here. Spring comes and everything starts to die."

"Where are you from?"

"Minneapolis."

"So I guess you got a lot of snow," he said.

"Yeah, I'm used to snow." I put my cup to my lips and tipped it back but it was empty. I swallowed anyway, to make it took like I got something, but I forgot that I was drinking out of a clear plastic cup. Sasha was watching me and he seemed glad that my drink was so visibly gone, that I had to leave now to get another if I wanted something to sip on like a normal person.

"I'll just go get some more wine," I said. "You need anything?"

"I'm okay."

~~~

The back door opened into the kitchen and the wine was lined up along the counter. The bottle I'd brought was half-emptied, the plastic cork stuck back inside. I poured a cup and read the magnetic poetry on the fridge. They seemed to have two sets, dog poetry and French poetry. *Dobermans sont grandes*, I read. *Vous mangez chew toys.* I wondered if there were poems they'd taken down, if they'd taken words like *car*, or *road*, or *girlfriend*, and hidden them in a drawer somewhere until the day Sasha left and they could stop watching the things they wrote. If I'd taken Spanish in high school instead of French I'd be in a whole different salary bracket with the AHHA now. Je suis stupide.

~~~

"I tried to mingle," I announced, even though I hadn't. Sasha was still standing where I'd left him. "It was a bust. I tried to take myself off your hands but I don't know anybody. Sorry."

"That's okay," he said, in a tone of voice like it wasn't, really. "But I thought you were Miranda's friend."

"We just work together. Do you have a dog? You have magnetic dog poetry on your fridge."

"Miranda has a Lab. It's probably around here somewhere but it doesn't like crowds. It usually hides in the bathtub." He said it like he was jealous, he was tempted, to go fight the dog for its bathtub and be alone, but then people would come in to pee and it would just get awkward.

The patio was getting crowded, people arguing over the music, a bunch of girls wanting to dance and Miranda trying to keep things mellow. I was hoping Sasha would suggest we go somewhere else.

"You want to see something?" he asked.

"Sure."

"Follow me," he said, and stepped off the patio into the grass. I followed him, keeping his back in front of me, the person-shaped darkness that showed up against the dark of the yard. He didn't go far, just to the high wooden fence at the back of the property. We passed the trampoline, the smoking people, and the grapefruit tree. I felt trusted, that the yard was as he'd said it was. It was quieter away from the house. "Wait here," he said, and went behind a small shed that stood in the corner. He came back with a stepladder, kicked its legs out so it stood flush against the fence. "Climb up, look over," he said, and I set my wine down in the grass beside the ladder. I thought he'd maybe take my hand, touch my arm or my back to steady me, but he didn't.

There was a narrow dirt alley behind the house, black trash cans and blue recycling bins lined up along either side. It smelled warm and dirty, food softening in plastic bags, animals staking out their territories. The only light came from a streetlamp at the end of the block, dim and orange, and a floodlight in the yard across the alley. Sitting behind the neighbor's fence was an enormous silver pod, like an old Airstream trailer, but slicker, no seams or antennas or visible doors or windows. Just smooth metal walls, a trailer-sized lima bean. It had a circular hole in its top left side. The branches of a tree poked through, lit from underneath. The tree was green, not the leaves but the bark, the funny green-skinned trees they had here.

"What is it?" I asked.

"The neighbors are architects, built their own pod. There was a thing about them in the paper, and a whole feature in some architecture magazine."

"They live in it?"

"They sleep there. They use the kitchen and bathroom in their regular house, but the rest of the house, they knocked out all the walls, anything that wasn't load bearing, made it into studio space."

"It doesn't seem very comfortable. Living in a pod."

"I think you'd either bake or freeze. And then when you wake up you have to go outside just to take a piss and start some coffee."

"What's the point?" I asked.

"Search me," he said, and smiled just a little.

"They make cool neighbors, at least. I should come to more parties here."

"Miranda and Sam are moving when the lease is up. They're looking for a place for just the two of them. No more pod people."

"You could find new roommates." I was still on the ladder, fingers hooked over the tops of the fence boards. They were rough and smelled damp and I knew I'd have the smell on my hands, of soaked wood and splintery fence.

"I won't be here, when the lease runs out."

"Where will you be?" I asked, because I could.

"Prison," he said, but he looked so sad to say it that it wasn't much of a victory.

"What did—it's none of my business."

"Reckless driving. Someone died. Twenty-three months."

"I'm sorry," I said.

"I'm sorrier. But then I guess that's the point."

"When do you leave?"

"Day after tomorrow. Yesterday was my last day at work. I drop my stuff by the storage place tomorrow and then report for—whatever, Monday morning."

"Are you scared?" I asked.

"Yeah."

"I'm sorry," I said. "For being so nosy. I don't know what's gotten into me. I'm not normally so nosy."

"I don't want to leave," he said. "Is that wrong? That I don't want to go?" He was staring straight ahead into the fence, the cracks between the boards seeping light from the pod planet onto his face.

"No," I said. "I don't think so."

"I think I'm supposed to welcome it. I'm supposed to do my penance and be graceful about it, but I—I've been punished. I feel like I already have been. And she's gone, regardless. She's just gone."

I was a little disappointed in him, that my murderer was so selfish, that what he really wanted was just his life back. It didn't seem like a very worthwhile confession. It didn't seem like much of a way to end the party. I wondered what I should say to him next, if it should be comforting, or something sharp, to remind him of his crimes.

"And Miranda's having a goddamn party. She said she'd had it planned for ages when my reporting date got pushed back. Then she said she wanted to throw me a going-away thing but it's not like I want everyone Miranda's ever met to know."

"So it's a secret going-away thing where no one knows you're going away."

"They probably know. They probably all know, everyone at this party," he said, and looked at me like he was so thankful, so grateful that I was a stranger. "They're out of town, the pod people," he said. "Asked us to pick up their mail for the weekend."

"You guys? All the way around the block?"

"There's a gate. We're the closest neighbors if you cross the alley."

I waited for him to offer, because why else had he told me the pod people were gone, but he stayed quiet. "I'd like to see it up close," I said finally. "The pod planet. If you don't think they'd mind."

"I think it would be okay. Wait a minute." He headed back towards the house and all of a sudden I felt silly standing on top of the ladder at the edge of the yard by myself. I could hear someone being sick near the grapefruit tree. Sasha came back with a bottle of wine, two cups. He held his right hand out flat and bounced his palm up and down so a set of keys jingled.

"For the gate?"

"The house and the pod. I can give you a tour."

We crossed into their yard, shutting the gates behind us. Sasha opened the pod, the doorframe marked with puckered ridges of welded steel, a little round, flat lock like a car door. Inside was a single room with curving silver walls, a futon mattress on the floor beside the tree. The bedding was all hospital white, blinding; Sasha and I sat on the end of the mattress and I took up fistfuls of the duvet while he poured the wine. "Down," I said. "The comforter and pillows. Real birds in the bedding."

"Architecture must pay okay," he said, and we got drunk for a while. We were pod people, in our thin-shelled home, the walls shivering a little with the noise from the party. We owned a green-skinned tree and bedding so full of feathers it could fly off on its own. At some point we put down our cups and lay down on our backs, side by side.

"Are you seeing anyone?" Sasha asked me, and thinking about it, it was kind of a weird question, because in two days it couldn't matter to him whether I was or wasn't. He wouldn't be in a position to see anybody.

"Not really."

"What does that mean?"

"Someone in Minneapolis. But only sort of."

"We don't have to do anything."

"I know. I'd like to," I said, and reached my hand out so it touched his and our arms made a V on the bed between us.

"Why?" He looked at me and meant it.

"I don't know. Give you a send-off?"

"You've got a guy in Minnesota."

"He hit me," I said, and Sasha, the sad-sack murderer with the grapefruit tree, became the only person I ever told. "My cousin got me a job out here. Just to get away for awhile."

"You're going back?"

"Maybe."

"You shouldn't."

"You're saying that because you're supposed to. You've watched a bunch of domestic violence PSAs."

"Still. You shouldn't go back."

"What if I deserved it?"

"I'm sure you didn't."

"You don't know that. I'm not a very nice person."

"I'm sure that's not true," he said, and pulled his hand out from under mine so he could pet me with it, just brushing over my knuckles, down my wrist, smoothing the little static-y hairs on my arms.

"It is," I said, and I rolled towards him, closed the V of our arms into a long straight line. Neither of us said anything else for a few minutes, just did the usual things, the kissing and the fumbling with each other's clothes and before Sasha pressed inside me he asked, "Is this okay?" and I nodded. I waited for a couple more minutes, his forearms under my shoulders and his face a little sweaty and his ear right above my lips and then I whispered to him that I'd known all along.

"Miranda told me," I said. "When I got here. She told me about your girlfriend."

Sasha raised his head, stared at me betrayed, and for an instant I wanted to brush his sad hair out of his sad eyes and take it all back. Then he closed his eyes and kept moving, hard, like he couldn't let go or didn't want to, and he went on so long I started to hurt. "You knew," he said, pushing, angry. "The whole time."

"The whole time."

"Maybe you did deserve it. When your boyfriend hit you."

Sasha finished and rolled away from me so that our heads were on separate pillows. I turned to look at him but he was staring at the ceiling, and his nose was longer, sharper in profile than I'd thought it was.

"I think I did," I said. "And if that's true, then it means he didn't do anything wrong."

"Maybe you should go back."

"Maybe I should," I said, but I was still lying beside Sasha when he said, "I meant you should leave."

"Oh. Okay."

I got up, started pulling my dress back on. He tugged the duvet up over his legs and watched me. I stacked the empty cups beside the bottle and found my left shoe beside the tree, the toe edging over the hole in the trailer floor above the spreading roots. I was standing at the door, my hand on what looked like the stainless-steel handle to a refrigerator, when Sasha asked me, "Do you still love him?"

"I think so. I want to."

"Then maybe you're right. Maybe you shouldn't fuck things up."

"Thanks," I said, and pushed my way out of the pod down the steps to the yard. The door fell shut behind me and as soon as my eyes adjusted to the light I was walking through the grassy yard of the pod planet to the driveway, down to the sidewalk, and around the block to my car. The party drifted in and out of earshot, snatches of music and laughter and conversation. I was scared to be driving, worried about cops and the way the world spun a little when I turned my head, the lights along the freeway haloed with a furry glow. I was glad to make it home. I woke up with a bruise in the middle of my forehead, plum-round and tender to the touch, and it took me until Sunday evening to realize it was from pressing my head too hard against the tap, from being sick in the bathroom sink.

Two months later I quit my job with AHHA, and two weeks after that I moved back to Minnesota. Miranda and I never became friends, and we didn't pretend we'd stay in touch. I never knew Sasha's last name, or the names of the pod people, and I wouldn't be able to find that house again if you flew me into Phoenix and gave me a rental car, Google Maps, and a month. When Sasha got out of prison I was shoveling snow, sharing a bed with a man I told myself I wasn't afraid of anymore. I told myself everything was fine again, and it became true and stayed true for four good years, and when things weren't good anymore it was for a whole other set of reasons. I never told him about Sasha. There were a lot of things I never told him, which was maybe a part of our problems, but someone told me once that I seem like a better person when I keep my mouth shut. It sounds mean, but it was pretty good advice.

I figure it works the other way, too, though—that if you *are* going to tell a story you should try to make it good, make yourself look nice. So the pod people thing, I've already decided if I ever tell it to anyone how it should go. How I arrived in Phoenix unattached and outgoing, brought bagels and coffee to the girls in the office my whole first week, and made friends with them all. How Miranda even asked me to come early to her party to help set up, and how I brought little hors d'oeuvres from Trader Joe's and warmed them in the oven and they were a big hit. How I'd already read about the pod people in *Architectural Digest*, because I read that kind of thing. How I didn't even get tipsy before Sasha and I went to the pod planet, and how the sex when we got there was incredible. And then we didn't say anything afterward, nothing at all, didn't try to be funny or mean or smart. Just slept all wound up together in our own private cell, my head on his shoulder and his arm not even tingly when he pulled it from under my waist in the morning. We woke up together on the pod planet, I'll say, and it was fine and happy and fearless, to be a pod woman with her lover, woken by the sun slanting through the branches of a paloverde tree.

And then I'll say, The End, and it'll be a story sweeter than the truth.

Trust

PAULA MCLAIN

THE HAPPY ENDING WAS A DIVE BAR OUT IN THE DESERT THAT HAD NO address and no signage. Basically, you could go there only if you'd been there before. The logic of this appealed to me for some reason, and so I agreed to go with my friend Kendall after work one night, though an hour into our driving around finding nothing but vast stretches of desert that looked perfect for burying a body or two, I asked Kendall if she was sure she could find her way back to the place.

"I have a perfect sense of direction," Kendall said, arrowing her Mazda into an empty cul-de-sac where, for a split second, her headlights illuminated the silver-yellow eyes of a coyote before it flinched away. "This looks familiar."

"It's a dead end."

She put the car in reverse and then paused a moment to stare me down in the dark car, her forehead wrinkling prettily. "You, my friend, have real trust issues."

"Maybe," I countered, "but I'm a good dancer."

"That will only get you so far," she said. "Look at Mishelle."

Mishelle was Kendall's roommate, and we all three cocktailed at the Situation Room, in Scottsdale, Arizona. Mishelle used to be ridiculously fun to go out with, but recently she'd come to a personal impasse over whether or not to marry her longtime boyfriend, Stewart, and she'd lost all sense of adventure.

"He's asked me three times," she told us over giant rum drinks recently, her face sullen, hair lank. She hadn't even wanted to go out, we had to drag her. "I always say the same thing, that I'm not ready."

"If you're not ready, you're not ready," I said.

"Sometimes I worry it's the only thing I can think of to say." She sighed. "Who's ever ready, anyway? Right? Am I right?" She stabbed listlessly at her drink with her straw while she talked.

"Not to be aggressive or anything," I said, "but have you ever thought you really and actually might not be ready?"

"Maybe. But I'd still like to come up with a reason that's completely profound, that no one's ever heard of before."

"Like Virginia Woolf," Kendall said. "Now, she was an original."

Mishelle and I both nodded, pacified, but the bartender had overheard the whole conversation. "I'm pretty sure Virginia Woolf was married," he said.

"I'm so fucked," Mishelle said, and we ordered her another white witch.

I didn't know Mishelle all that well. She was really Kendall's friend, and who was I to give her advice, anyway? My relationships were all dead on arrival. I'd never been able to stick with anyone for more than four months, and I blamed my father for this. He left my mother for another woman when I was a toddler and after that became the blow-through-town variety, bringing me crushed stuffed animals from cardboard bins in convenience stores. We'd have a spaghetti dinner at a place near the highway, and I'd tell him about spelling tests or the new math while he'd nod at me slowly over his untouched pyramid of meatballs, as if he was trying to remember how, exactly, we knew each other. By the time I was twelve he stopped coming altogether, which was a relief, really.

The point is, my dad was a leaver and I was a leaver—and I'd more or less come to terms with this as a liability. But thinking about how Mishelle couldn't find a way to stand up for what she wanted or, let's face it, didn't have the first clue about what she had the *right* to want, made me feel tired. As Kendall and I barreled through the desert, I rolled down the passenger window. Hot air funneled in and out as if the car were breathing, taking it all in, the whole empty desert, which was also breathing. From Kendall's tape deck The Sundays yelled, "Here's where the story ends."

"I'm tired," I said out loud to Kendall.

"Then get untired," she said. "We're here."

Even for people without trust issues, the Happy Ending wasn't doing much to ease suspicion. The parking lot mushroomed out of a dirt side road and was just more dirt—hard-packed dirt and sand pushing out into the Joshua trees as the trees pushed back. The bar was an outbuilding with shingled siding and a corrugated metal roof that looked like someone might have sheared sheep there in some century or other before the sheep shriveled under their heavy skins and died. I could easily imagine the whole place going that direction: fading, shrinking, and then vanishing into nothing but a jawbone or clavicle. That's what the desert did to everything, what it was built to do, but no one seemed to notice or care, certainly not Kendall as she stepped up to the front entrance, bending to pet the two big bloodhounds that lounged there without a worry in the world.

"Hi, puppies," Kendall said in baby talk.

"You're buying," I said crankily.

"Sure," she said, and tucked her hair behind her ears.

Inside, everything was old raw wood—the walls, the flooring, and the bar, which angled out into the room in a lazy horseshoe shape. There were half a dozen listing tables, and these were mostly empty. The bar, however, was full—and full of men, the same variety of after-hours golfers that made up our clientele at the Situation Room. As Kendall and I walked up, they all pivoted to face us, tan mannequins on a conveyor belt.

"Ladies," the bartender said, fingering his cocktail towel in a friendly way.

"Ladies," one of the golfers echoed from his barstool. He smiled and combed his thumb over one eyebrow. It took me a half a beat to place him: Warren James.

"Warren," I said. "I haven't seen you in a while. Do you know Kendall?"

"Of course," he said, but didn't shift his eyes away from my face.

"Have you thought about my offer, Torie?"

I didn't like the way he said my name—it was too soft and measured, too familiar. "I'm sorry. I've been busy with midterm exams. I haven't had a minute."

"Of course." He blinked twice, in slow motion, and when his eyes opened again he seemed changed somehow. "You two have a nice time," he said, and then he took a fifty out of his money clip and laid it on the bar. "Take good care of my friends," he said to the bartender, and then he was gone.

"Wow," said Kendall. "He's a little intense."

"He's not that bad," I said, and then climbed into the seat he'd just left. It was cool and dry, as if he had no heat left over, none to share. "I'll have a Dos Equis," I told the bartender.

"Lame ass," Kendall said, smiling. "We'll both have mai tais, extra tall," she corrected. "Your husband's paying."

"Right," I said, and then looked at the money on the bar top, perfectly smooth and new, as if Warren had printed it himself. "Trade me seats, all right?"

～⌒)

Kendall had an asshole for a father too. Hers was some high-powered hedge-fund manager who had his assistant, Clarice, call Kendall on her birthday this year—on the wrong day, no less. The world was chock-full of fathers, all of them, seemingly, in low-slung 450SLs wearing golfers' tans and salmon-colored polos. These were fathers of another order from mine, maybe, since mine had been a garage mechanic. Or maybe every father was more or less the same sinkhole, minefield, muddy minor continent. That would help explain why I couldn't even begin to deal with Warren James. I needed to tell the man no, already. I knew it, but I just couldn't seem to make myself follow through.

Warren had been completely innocuous at first. He came in with the same group of friends for happy hour on weeknights, each of them indistinguishable from the others—same sunburned nose and chunky Rolex. They drank too much and dropped their cash and their sexual innuendoes and never failed to leave a ridiculously fat tip. Nothing unusual. Then Warren disappeared from the group for a while, and when he came back he came back alone. He sat in my section and watched me walk back and forth to the bar. Without his cronies, he didn't have much to say to me but still left nice money on the table, so I didn't mind him. And then one night he left me a job offer, written out in tiny, perfect print on both sides of one of his business cards. Apparently he and some of his associates had just opened a new nightclub in Tempe called What's Your Beef. I hadn't been in yet but had heard the servers there were clearing three hundred a night, sometimes more. "I could make you a lot of money" is what he said on the business card. And it was the phrasing that unsettled me, that *he* could make me money. I left the card on the table for one of the busboys to clear and forgot about it. I was good at willed amnesia. In fact, I considered it one of my superpowers, one of my most reliable strategies—maybe my only strategy. That was weeks ago, and he hadn't been back, and essentially I really had forgotten about him until the Happy Ending. But after that night I wondered if I was going to have the luxury of forgetting him again.

Warren was hardly the first to insist on himself, but it hadn't ever been a big deal. Nothing had. My life worked for me. I was a wreck at dating, but as a cocktail waitress I was first order. All I had to do was smile—smile at everything, and stand there a beat or two too long, rocking side to side in my three-inch heels and wraparound Danskin skirt and smoky eye shadow. I was game, a good sport, and it came easy.

What I liked best, and always had, was serving one guy alone. With him, I felt unreasonably proud of being the perfect courtesan, asking about the round if he looked like he'd had a good day, avoiding it altogether if he didn't, drawing out his jokes, no matter how long or badly timed, his one or two good stories. One wanted to play dirty hangman on a cocktail napkin. One wrote a recipe for Steak Diane on my wrist with my blue ballpoint pen. One showed me a long, staggered scar up his arm and said it was from a moray eel attack he'd barely survived off the Florida Keys.

"Wasn't there a movie about that in the seventies?" I asked. "The eel instead of *Jaws*? An eel on a killing spree?"

"That's right," he said. "That movie was about me."

I brought him an appallingly strong drink on his next round, and when he left he tucked his phone number into my hand and a hundred-dollar bill tightly rolled into a Coke straw. I never called him, but I kept the money for the longest time, way at the back of my underwear drawer for some thin day when I would need it for groceries or a bottle of really nice tequila.

I worked five nights a week, sometimes six, and worked so I could play. The only struggle, besides not looking like hell when I was dead hung over from the night before, was getting out of a shift by twelve thirty or one to get to another club while there was still some bar time to spend. The drinking mattered, obviously, but not as much as the dancing. The dancing was why we bothered with all the rest of it. Why we stood on the street outside Club Rio in our silk tank tops and Girbaud jeans, even in January. An hour or more pretending we didn't care if we froze to death to catch the last handful of songs. Once in, we'd order three tall anythings and leave them on the table to dance off the leash to The Cure or Psychedelic Furs or Siouxsie and the Banshees. And then I was happy. Deliriously, avalanchingly happy. It was the best thing I knew for as long as it lasted, every time.

It was on a night just like this, less than a week after our adventure at the Happy Ending, that I came home late and sweaty and euphoric to find Warren James on my machine: *clickslide*, then "Hi, Torie. Now that your exams are over, I wanted to put my offer on the table again. Let's talk, all right? I won't hold you to anything."

I wondered briefly if Warren had paid one of the busboys to get my last name, my phone number, and who it was, and how much it had cost. But it didn't really matter now. He likely had my address too. I erased the message and then lay in bed for the longest time with my eyes open, listening to the cockroaches trying to climb the stainless-steel wall of the kitchen sink, that scuttling and sliding, scuttling and sliding, then silence as the bugs gave up, finally, and opted for flight.

All my friends were waitresses and bartenders and cocktail girls, but they were other things too—part-time secretaries or students or girlfriends. Kendall did something with crystals and rainwater at a spa in the lobby of the Desert Princess hotel. Mishelle was a nanny and house manager for Alice Cooper.

"What do you mean by house manager?" I asked when she first told me about her day job.

"I pay their bills, make sure they have stamps and light bulbs and peanut butter."

"Peanut butter? There's a story, right, about him smearing his body with peanut butter at a concert?"

"That was Iggy Pop," she said. "The weird thing about Alice is he's totally normal. They're all really nice to me. Last year I went to Maui with them for three weeks' vacation. They went mini-golfing every day."

As soon as she said it, I could easily picture Alice Cooper mini-golfing with his kids or walking around with a rubber inner tube around his waist at the water park. It was the ones who looked conservative that harbored dark and freaky secret lives, like the men I served lines of perfect martinis, who drank them without slurring or spilling a drop and then walked a straight flat line to their cars like alcoholic robots.

Mishelle loved Alice and his family, but she was thinking about quitting because Stewart wanted to be sure she had time for him and their beautiful, as-yet-imaginary house. She and Kendall and I were all waiting for orders at the bar one night, debating the sanity of this, when the main lounge went quiet suddenly, table after table growing hush, as if each were a bright birdcage being covered, lightly and completely, with a sheet. We turned together, and there, striding across the room with an armful of pink roses, was a guy in a pretty convincing gorilla costume. He was singing a ballad, though we couldn't really pinpoint the song because of the mask. The room was happy to collaborate anyway. Everyone egged him on, all the way to the bar, where we watched, speechless, as he got down on one knee with the roses. Mishelle had to put her cocktail tray down she was crying so hard. Tables clapped. Someone turned off the British Open in time for everyone to hear her say yes, and when Stewart took off his mask, his face was slick with sweat and tears, and I had the thought, watching both of them cry, that tears and sweat were the same thing and that humans were just bags of saltwater. I thought I might be sick, suddenly. I didn't really know Mishelle, but I knew this wasn't how her life was meant to go, this passive slide that only looked like love to strangers. As my head spun, our manager came over and told Mishelle she could have the night off. The rest of us had to scramble to cover, which is why I was too busy to worry much about Warren when he came in and sat at the bar.

I didn't look his way, just tried to stay professional, and when he left an hour or so later, I was at the hostess stand talking to Monya, a busty and utterly fabulous Jewess with a head of high-gloss ringlets who looked like a Russian doll. Warren ignored her and said, "I'm starting to think you don't like me, Victoria."

Monya shot me a wide-eyed look and walked away to collect menus.

"It's not that," I said. "I just don't need a job. I like it here."

"Really?" He reached for a toothpick, unwrapped it, and tucked it between his molars. They were flawless, his teeth. I guess I expected that.

"Don't I look happy?" I tried to keep my voice steady, my eyes on line with his.

"In my line of business I find that most of the time people only think they're happy. They think that because they need to. Because they can't bear to imagine otherwise."

"I'm not sure I know what you mean?"

"I think you're afraid of change, Victoria. Maybe afraid of everything."

I felt the blood leave my face. "I have to cash out now. Nice to see you, Warren." When I walked away my hands were shaking, my knees had gone liquid.

An hour later Kendall and I were sitting out back in her car, splitting a bottle of wine while she tried to talk me into going to Long Wongs to toast Mishelle.

"Why?" I said. "This is terrible news. There's no way she should be marrying Stewart."

"No, but that's not less of a reason to get drunk."

"Tomorrow," I said.

"You bet your ass," she said.

When we'd killed the wine, I headed straight for home on back roads—shooting down Bell to Pima, where it was all desert, reservation land, and planned housing developments with elaborate names but no construction. I liked it out there. There was nothing but space and more space, shadows of cactuses on shadows of stark, arcing hills. Phoenix sunk down in the middle distance, like light in a bowl. I put Echo and the Bunnymen on the tape player and turned the volume up to ten—which is why the first time my engine made a loud, low *whonk*, like a sledgehammer on an anvil, I felt it more than heard it. I had just hit the pause button when it clunked again, louder, harder, then the car lurched and shuddered. *Shit.* I gripped the wheel as the body began to heave and decelerate. I had my foot to the floor, and it was getting no gas. Finally I wrestled it off onto the shoulder, where it went into quick and noisy death throes until there was no fight left. No steam rising from the hood, no click when I turned the key.

Shit and double shit. I was still in my uniform, which wouldn't do for a hike to the nearest house or any kind of hike at all. I slid my seat back and had started to change my shoes when I saw lights coming up the road behind me, slow and slower. *You stupid girl*, I thought to myself. My car was full of old *Vogue* magazines and empty Styrofoam coffee cups. Nothing that would work as a weapon—and I knew instantly that I would need one. I knew all the way to my now bare feet that this was Warren James, that he'd been trailing me from the club, and that this wasn't the first time. He'd planned everything to the letter. He'd done something to my car. It was all so terrifyingly clear—the whole trajectory, how every move and conversation had been part of it. And it was already over, in a way. Like the whole thing had been written out here on the desert before I was born, even, in vanishing sand. It was here. This story. Being trapped in the middle of nowhere with a man who would whisper *Are you happy?* in my ear like a poisonous vapor just before he hurt me. And I wouldn't be okay again, maybe ever.

The lights were nearing, easing up, cat and mouse. Five hundred feet away, then two. I kicked my door open and bolted like an animal, skittering dumbly into the night. The soles of my feet were instantly cut to shreds. The sand wasn't soft, nothing was. Everything I felt had a spine on it. Cactus. Cactus. Rock. I scrambled up an incline into blackness, jamming my elbow against something flinty, then my knee. I went down hard, clambered up, and then fell again. I felt my wrist snap, then a jangling pain shot up to my ear.

"Hello!" He was out of his car.

I spun around and looked down the dark hill to where he stood just outside the pointed rinse of his headlights.

"Are you all right?" he shouted up at me vaguely. I didn't think he could see me now, but he'd certainly seen me run, and I worried he could hear me, the serrated breath crawling my lungs.

"I just want to help you."

It was Warren, it had to be, but it also sort of looked like any man. Every man. To be really sure, I'd have to walk down there and deliver myself into his headlights.

He put his hand up to his forehead and faced the hill, a man wearing a shadow, a gorilla costume, the night sky like a secret skin. Just then, from very nearby, I heard the hard, scuttling sound of something coming out from under a rock. It might have been a scorpion, they were everywhere, I knew, as were snakes and Gila monsters and mean-tempered wild desert pigs.

"Will you let me help you?"

Suddenly it didn't matter what was out here. I was part of it now. Because whatever else it would mean for the rest of my life, the answer—and I could feel it flexing through every nerve of me—was no.

Arboretum

DAVID PHILIP MULLINS

THE SAPLINGS STOOD IN NEAT ROWS ALONG THE WINDING AVENUE, each leafless maple growing from a dark hump of soil that resembled a pitcher's mound, or a small grave. They rose six, seven feet above the sidewalk. With flashlights and a trowel, we uprooted the shortest one we could find and carried it off to our plywood fort in the desert. I was fourteen that year, and so was Kilburg. It was late on a Sunday—warm and arid, though summer was still two months away—and I'd left my house in the middle of the night without permission. Surrounded by cat's claw and schist rocks, the rickety fort sat stark and uninviting in the middle of a dried-up arroyo. Kilburg had said that all the outside needed was a little greenery, a few trees.

Earlier that evening, I'd learned that my father was going to die, and I was glad to be out in the open, away from home. Kilburg had convinced me to sneak out my bedroom window, to meet him at the end of our block at a quarter past eleven. Now he had me on my hands and knees, scooping rocks and hard-packed dirt, baked solid after a rainless winter. The drought that had begun in December had yet to subside. People joked that their faucets might soon run dry. Out at the fort, a twenty-minute walk into the Mojave wilderness that bordered our neighborhood to the southeast, the air sometimes smelled of the chlorinated swimming pools and freshly mowed lawns that were partially at fault for the city's water shortage. Beside me, Kilburg massaged his aching stump. He could stand for only so long before he had to remove his prosthetic leg, a hollow, plastic thing, a mannequin's appendage. He had diabetes and had lost his leg at the age of six due to a blocked artery.

"I don't know about you," Kilburg said, "but I sure could use some action." The leg, which had once matched the color of his skin but had faded to an unnatural ivory, lay beneath him in the dirt. He sat crouched on it as though it were a log next to a campfire. In one hand he held a flashlight, and with the other he kneaded his stump in a slow figure eight, avoiding the spot in the center where the skin had been knotted together like the end of a sausage.

"Action?" I asked, tossing a clump of dirt over my shoulder. "What kind of action?"

The sapling was balanced against the overturned paint bucket we used as a bongo drum. Behind us, the fort stood at an angle, leaning westward, undeserving of its name: it wasn't fortified in any way and appeared on the verge of collapse. Deep in what seemed to us an uncharted region of the Mojave—there were no trails, no cigarette butts or empty beer bottles—and concealed by the arroyo's high, crumbling banks, it was at least unknown to the rest of the world. Building the fort had been Kilburg's idea. We'd spent an entire Saturday wrestling with the sheets of plywood we'd found in his father's tool shed, shaping a door frame with his ancient jigsaw and dragging the sheets one by one through the desert to hammer them together, but in the end our construction was nothing more than four unpainted walls and a low, flat roof, less complex than your average doghouse.

Kilburg shook his head at the ground, the way he did whenever I asked him a question. "*Action*," he said. "*Chicks*. Jesus, do I have to explain everything?"

"Oh," I said, and lowered my eyes back to my work.

Travis Kilburg was tall and muscular, with long earlobes and a wide, open face. He wore a military buzz cut, and it seems to me now that his complexion always had a greenish tint to it—like the patina of an old bronze statue—his eyes dark and serious. He liked to talk about sex, about the many girls whose virginity he'd taken, though I knew he was a virgin himself. We both were. Neither of us had ever even kissed anyone. Kilburg was perhaps incapable of honesty, no matter what the topic, and I played along whenever he fabricated his exploits, as he spun tales of seduction and conquest.

I stabbed the trowel into the dirt and leaned to grab a few pebbles from the hole. I didn't mind doing all the work. It was taking my thoughts off the news my parents had delivered over dinner. According to my father's doctor, a rare lung condition—a fibrosis—was responsible for his chronic cough, for his labored breathing, which in the last couple of months had grown louder and raspier. My father explained that his lungs were in bad shape, their tissue inflamed. Without at least one transplant, he told me, swallowing the words as he chewed, the fibrosis would prove fatal. The only person I'd ever known to die was my grandfather on my mother's side. He'd had a heart attack two summers earlier.

"You bring the booze?" Kilburg said now. He put a licked finger to the air. "It's about that time."

"Just some schnapps."

The liter of Bushmills I often borrowed from my father's liquor cabinet had been half-empty when I'd checked it earlier that night, and I'd chosen a bottle of Dekuyper Peachtree instead, paranoid that my father might have secretly taken to watching the volume of his whiskey. I had a hunch that Kilburg might declare the schnapps an unacceptable offering, but he only shrugged and said, "Whatever, man. Booze is booze."

I held the sapling up to the beam of the flashlight. Dark soil clung to a knot of roots. A shiny worm writhed from the soil, twisting around like a periscope. I positioned the roots in the hole and scooped the dirt back in, patting it flat around the trunk.

"There," I said. "What do you think?"

Like the fort, the sapling leaned heavily to one side, in a way that made it look pathetic.

"Just as I pictured it," he said. "This place looks better already. When that thing grows leaves, we'll have ourselves a little color out here." He kneaded his stump harder now, as though working a pulled muscle. "Well, what are you waiting for? Let's celebrate."

I reached into my back pocket and brought around the bottle of schnapps, a pint. I handed it to Kilburg, and he uncapped it and sniffed the contents. He made a face, crinkling his nose, then caught himself and smiled. "Just what the doctor ordered," he said. "All we need are some women and we'd have a party on our hands."

"Tell me about it," I said, laughing through my nose the way Kilburg sometimes did.

He took a long pull, wincing as he lowered the bottle. Kilburg rarely discussed his health, and at the time I wasn't sure if having diabetes meant that he shouldn't be drinking. I'd never seen him test his blood sugar or inject insulin, nor had I ever thought of his illness as life threatening. He seemed, at any rate, to have a high tolerance for alcohol, or pretended to. He would do almost anything for attention. Just above the knee joint, his prosthetic leg opened into a kind of cup, and it was from here that he would occasionally drink my father's whiskey. Into the cup fit a concave socket, attached to which was a leather sleeve that laced up like a shoe. If Kilburg took a clumsy step as we crossed the uneven terrain of the desert, the socket would come out, popping like a cork, and he would pitch forward into the dirt. What's more, the knee and ankle joints creaked when he walked, and his stump itched and perspired and developed weekly blisters. He moved with the lop-sided gait of an arthritic old man. At school, kids tormented him, calling him Peg Leg and Gimp—especially two thuggish, athletic-looking boys in our class named Todd Sheehan and Chad Klein, neither of whom I'd ever seen without a wad of chew plugged into his cheek. They were both as big as Kilburg and tried to trip him whenever they had the chance. I assumed Kilburg, for his part, took out his frustration on other, smaller kids.

"College chicks," he said now, taking another pull. "That's what we *really* need."

We were still in junior high and I wondered if Kilburg had ever even met a college-age woman.

"I'd go to UNLV for the babes alone," he offered, "but my dad says college is for people who think they're too good to work."

Kilburg was the son of a chemical plant operator, and he often found a way to incorporate his father's opinions into a conversation. He was deter-mined to follow in the man's footsteps, to land himself a job someday at Kerr-McGee, where his father had worked for the past twenty years. Perhaps because my own father was an engineer, Kilburg needled me about being what he called a "richie," even though my parents shared a Mercury Capri that was nearly a decade old, even though we lived in a small ranch house just up the block. Both our fathers worked in the desert, but the Kerr-McGee plant was only twenty minutes outside the city. The nuclear test site where my father worked was more than an hour away.

Three years earlier, Kilburg's mother had run off with a gambler from Arizona, a man she'd met at a poker table. His father was tall and potbel-lied, and he glared at you with stony eyes, and when he spoke his black beard parted to reveal a mouth full of crooked teeth, many of which overlapped or were angled to such a degree that you could see their rotting undersides. Evenings, he nursed an Old Milwaukee in his Barcalounger until he fell asleep. More than once, Kilburg had shown up for school with a fat lip, or a bruised cheekbone, or a cut above his eye. When I'd asked him, the Monday after we'd built the fort, why his wrist was black-and-blue, he told me that a stereo speaker had fallen on him—knocked over by Tarkanian, his German shepherd—but I suspected the injury had been punishment for the wood that had gone missing from his father's shed. Still, Kilburg worshipped him, perhaps because the man was all he had left.

Presently, he switched off the flashlight, slipping it into a pocket of his shorts. "C'mon," he said. He handed me the bottle, scooting himself off the prosthetic leg and onto the ground, his real leg stretched out in front of him. Pushing with his hands, the way we eased ourselves down the sloping banks of the arroyo, he inched across the dirt and into the fort.

I crawled behind him through the low doorframe. A green shag rug, taken from a supermarket Dumpster, covered the hard dirt floor. Flashlights hung like inverted torches in each of the four corners, dangling from shoe-strings nailed to the plywood. One or another of the bulbs was always faintly flickering. Each month Kilburg stole the latest issue of *Playboy* from the 7-Eleven near our school, and our only interior adornment was a glossy cen-terfold of Bernadette Peters, thumbtacked to the wall opposite the door frame.

I took a sip of the schnapps, coughing as it burned down my throat.

"There you go," he said. He took off his shoe, a white sneaker whose mate was outside, on the foot of the prosthetic leg. "We'll make a man outta you yet."

Before long I had a terrific buzz going. My head had grown numb, and I was loose jointed, slurring my speech. The two of us lay flat on the rug. In the still air I could smell primrose and sagebrush and Kilburg's cheap drugstore cologne. He kept saying, "You drunk yet? You feeling anything?" I pinched my eyes closed and a kaleidoscope of color spun behind the lids. When I opened them, Kilburg was leaning over me, his breath warm on my face.

"Get off," I said, squirming, but he held my arms. I couldn't get free, pinned by the stiff weight of his torso. I looked away. Through the door-frame was the moon: white light in a black sky. When he put his lips to mine, I let out a grumble, doubtful at first of the tingling sensation that rained from the crown of my head to the tips of my fingers. Kilburg slipped his tongue into my mouth, and I gave in to the kiss. Soon he eased off me, touching my ears, my cheeks, the side of my neck. Then he forced his stump into my hip and gave a shudder when my erection brushed against his own. I brought my arm up around his neck, but he batted it away.

"Easy, lover boy," he said. He rolled off me, laughing.

"I thought—"

"*I thought, I thought,*" he mocked. "Relax. We're not fags, man. It's only practice for the real thing, for when we get girlfriends." Kilburg narrowed his eyes as if the answer to a troublesome question had finally dawned on him. "We're drunk, Nick. We're not thinking right. Don't ever tell anybody about this." He fumbled with his shoe, trying to get it back on. "You do and you're a dead man."

My father began taking a daily dose of prednisone, a steroid meant to decrease the inflammation in his lungs. Over the past several weeks he'd undergone a CAT scan and a bronchoscopy—procedures I'd never heard of—and already there seemed to be a lack of hope in his eyes, as if he'd predicted the ultimate uselessness of treatment. After dinner he read from newspaper articles about the drought, now the longest in the city's history, his voice thin and scratchy as he shook his head in disbelief. His hands had fattened from the prednisone and taken on a yellowish color, as though he'd soaked them in formaldehyde. How long did he have to live? The question troubled me, and yet my worry was often replaced by daydreams of being at the fort with Kilburg.

We continued to sneak out after dark, the course of each night the same. We hid behind the corner of an office building, or in the shadows of an empty strip mall, peering from the darkness until the coast was clear, waiting as motorists made their way up and down Eastern Avenue. To the trill of katydids—everywhere that spring—we dug a twiglike sapling from the earth, wrapped its roots in a plastic produce bag, and made our way by flashlight into the desert. By the end of May—as the days grew longer and the air even dryer, the sun scorching the valley with what seemed to be malice—our saplings numbered twelve around the fort. After planting one, we'd saturate the ground with water we'd brought in a plastic thermos. Later, we'd drink ourselves to recklessness and find new ways to express our attraction: unzipping, fondling, going farther every time, Kilburg always in control.

I concocted elaborate fantasies in which we spent entire weekends together, waking on the shag rug, unclothed in each other's arms. Not a day went by when I didn't think about him. I felt lucky to be more than just his friend, though I was convinced I wasn't gay, deciding on a precise distinction between bona fide homosexuality and my curious interest in Kilburg. Surely a person could be drawn, temporarily at least, to a member of the same sex without being a homosexual—surely there were explanations. Like Kilburg, I didn't want anyone to know about what we did at the fort.

Mornings, we walked together to school, through our neighborhood and up Eastern Avenue, past each of the humps of soil we'd emptied, caved in like little volcanoes. But when I ran into Kilburg between classes, he usually ignored me.

My mother started speaking of my father as though he were already dead. "Before long, it'll just be the two of us," she might say with tear-filled eyes. When I failed to cry, she'd insist I was in a state of denial. But if my father was around, my mother was all smiles, preparing his favorite meals, surprising him with tickets to a movie or a new set of golf clubs. She bought him watches, ties, books by his favorite authors, and—in June, for his forty-fourth birthday—a new Buick LeSabre, an expense my parents couldn't afford.

One night when I returned home late from the fort, around one o'clock, a light was on in the family room. I'd never been caught sneaking out, and I feared that my parents had finally discovered my absence. I crept between the shrubs to the window, squinting into a space of light where the curtains didn't quite meet. I saw only my mother. Her knees were drawn to her chest in my father's leather armchair. When she glanced up, I ducked below the edge of the window, holding my breath. But as I looked back in—cautiously, my heart hammering in my chest—I saw her staring down at the carpet. I kept holding my breath, and then I thought of my father, of what it would be like to struggle for air. I thought about what my mother had told me earlier that week, that soon he would need an oxygen tank to breathe, one he would wear all the time, like eyeglasses or a hearing aid. I imagined tending to him, what my mother would have to go through, fretting at his bedside. My chest heaved, and I let go my breath. We'd parted only minutes ago, but I realized I missed Kilburg, as though I might never see him again.

My mother got up from the chair, stretched her arms, and switched off the light. I walked down the block, but Kilburg's bedroom window was dark. He lived in a big split-level with wood trim and aluminum siding, out of place in our neighborhood of low stuccoed houses. A trailered boat took up most of the driveway and an orange '67 Mustang was parked against two bricks in the middle of the yard. A single agave grew beside the rusted automobile, the grass a sunburned brown. The development dipped along a hillside, and the distant valley was a bowl of glimmering light, the Strip a reddish flare that blazed across the land.

I walked around the side of the house, through the open wrought-iron gate. The backyard had never been landscaped, and patches of creosote grew from the wind-blown dirt. Along the cinder-block wall stood an abandoned lawn mower, two of its wheels missing. I sat down in an old blue wheelbarrow overgrown with dandelions and quack grass, as if, like the lawn mower, it hadn't moved in a hundred years. It was a school night, but I remained in the wheelbarrow for a long while, deciphering constellations that shone in the night sky, a skill my father had taught me. Kilburg was asleep in his bedroom. I wondered if he even liked me, or anyone else, for that matter. I'd never seen him completely naked, but I pictured what he might look like—a solid torso, two arms and a leg—and I unzipped my shorts.

The following morning I was running late for school. When Kilburg knocked on the front door, my mother told him to go ahead without me. Fifteen minutes later, I was making my way through the neighborhood when I spotted him at a corner. He should have been in class by now, but there he was, thirty yards away, surrounded by Sheehan and Klein and a third boy named Walsh, who'd been in my gym class the previous semester. Suddenly Sheehan swung at Kilburg, clipping him on the cheek. When Kilburg raised an elbow to shield himself, Klein took a step forward and kneed him in the groin. Walsh stood back and watched it all, howling and stomping his heel on the concrete. Doubled over, Kilburg stumbled to the left, then to the right. I waited for his leg to come off. Like a felled tree, he tipped slowly to one side. His textbooks spilled from his arms as he hit the sidewalk. I knelt behind a beat-up Impala. We were half a mile from school, and I considered running for help, cutting unseen through the desert and summoning the principal, then decided against it. I wondered what, if anything, Kilburg had done to provoke the boys. Billy Walsh was short and skinny, a loudmouth and a tagalong. I figured I could take him in a fistfight if I had to. But I'd recently chipped both my front teeth during a game of touch football, and I imagined Sheehan and Klein kicking them in entirely while Walsh held me from behind.

It was a hot, clear morning and sunlight glinted off the Impala's chrome bumper. As I leaned against it, I understood that Kilburg was really no bully at all. He was just someone to feel sorry for. Perhaps this, beyond his physical appeal, was what I liked most about him—the difficult home life, the unfair disadvantage of his disease. I suppose I loved him, or thought I did, and I waited to feel compelled to rush to his defense, to act as any good friend would. But the feeling never came.

I peeked around the bumper of the Impala, holding my breath the way I had in front of my house the night before. Some cars had slowed during the commotion, but none of the drivers had got out to help. Kilburg groped around on the sidewalk, trying to stand, but before he could get to his feet Walsh bent down and pulled off his prosthetic leg, tossing it as far down the sidewalk as he could.

Kilburg struggled to sit up, then dragged himself over to the leg as the three boys walked off with his textbooks. Almost as though he'd sensed my presence, he looked up the street a few times, squinting at the Impala, it seemed, as he held his groin. Every part of me wanted to help him, but if I revealed myself now he would know I'd been watching all along. And so I remained behind the Impala as Kilburg reattached the leg and limped off toward home.

He never did show up at school, and when I called his house in the afternoon there was no answer. That night I found him at the fort. He was sitting outside on the overturned paint bucket, rubbing his stump in his usual way. The prosthetic leg rested beside him in the dirt. Inside, the flashlights were on, and a dreary glow spread from the doorframe. The air smelled strongly of marijuana.

"What are you doing here?" I asked him.

His neck and arms were spattered with dime-size welts, as though he'd been pelted with stones. He had a black eye, and the side of his face, badly bruised, looked like the palm of a catcher's mitt.

"What are *you* doing here?" he said.

I sat down in the dirt. It seemed that not all of his injuries could have resulted from what had happened that morning, that some of them must have been his father's doing. I didn't know how to ask him if it was true that the man beat him.

"What happened to you?" I said.

He relit a joint, shaking his head as he looked down at the leg. The laces had come untied, he claimed, and he'd tumbled down a flight of stairs at the school library. He'd gone there to check out a few books on gardening, since all of the saplings we'd planted appeared to have died. There were fifteen in all. Many had begun to sprout leaves, but now the leaves hung from their branches like rolled parchment. There had been no end to the drought, and the water we'd brought to the fort hadn't been enough to keep the maples alive.

"Jeez," I said. I felt a revulsion for myself, a churning in my gut. "You look pretty bad."

"Thanks," Kilburg said. "I'll heal."

"Did it hurt? The fall, I mean. You in any pain?"

He took a hit off the joint. "I bet you don't even jerk off," he said.

"I jerk off," I told him. "Who doesn't?"

"Girls don't. Girls don't have peckers, stupid."

"Whatever," I said. "No shit, Sherlock."

He raised an eyebrow and glared at me. Then he handed me the joint, burned down to nothing. I'd smoked marijuana only once before, with a cousin at a family reunion in Illinois. I inhaled, pinching the joint between my thumb and index finger the way I'd been shown.

"Good stuff," I ventured, managing not to cough.

Kilburg strummed an air guitar. In a rock 'n' roll falsetto, he began to sing: *What I want, you've got, and it might be hard to handle. But like the flame that burns the candle, the candle feeds the flame.* It was a Hall and Oates song we both liked. *You make my dreams come true*, he squealed.

My eyelids grew heavy and a dense warmth surrounded me. I had a sense of time passing slowly. I was suddenly very hungry. "Awesome," I said, and laughed.

Kilburg took a breath. "Holy shit," he said. "I'm so goddamn stoned."

For a few seconds, neither of us spoke. The sun had set hours ago, but it had to be close to ninety degrees outside. Heat rose through the desert floor. A cloud of smoke hovered above the fort. It seemed to drift into the night as I extinguished the joint against the side of a rock. Kilburg mumbled to himself, gesturing with his hands. I couldn't make out the words. Already my forehead was throbbing, and I was glad I hadn't taken a second hit.

After a time, I heard him say, "I'm going to fuck you." Just like that, my high was gone, or I thought it was. "Yeah," he said, as though he'd reflected on it and made up his mind. He spoke slowly, his voice soft but emphatic: "I'm gonna fuck you."

In the distance a coyote wailed. The desert beyond the fort opened out in the milky light of a full moon.

"Stand up," Kilburg said, louder now. "Pull down your shorts."

I did as I was told, standing in front of him with my shorts and underwear bunched at my ankles. I felt the twinge of an erection, and soon it bobbed beneath the hem of my T-shirt. In a corner of my mind I could see into the future, into tomorrow or next week, when I would look back and yearn for this moment. I knew it would seem distant, fictional. Somehow I wanted to savor it, even though I was scared.

"Kneel down," Kilburg told me, and I knelt before him. He sat up straight, his real leg outstretched. He took my hands in his, and his thumbs trembled in my palms. He was just as scared as I was. The muscles flexed in his arms, while a vein bulged from the side of his neck. He tightened his grip, squeezing until it hurt. Then he grabbed hold of my head and pushed it into his crotch. He leaned over and put his lips to my ear. "First you're gonna blow me," he whispered.

I unzipped his cutoffs, resting my cheek against his knee, where I could smell the sharp scent of his groin. He took a deep, eager breath, but when I kissed the inside of his stump, tasting the salt of his skin, he flinched and pushed hard at my shoulder. I looked up at him. In the light from the door frame, he was working his jaw like an animal.

"Get away from me," he said, his face twisted in anger.

"What is it?" I said. Still kneeling, I smiled in a way I thought might comfort him.

"I'm not like you!" he hollered. "You make me want to puke. You make me hate myself."

"You don't mean that."

"Just shut up," he said, pressing his fingers into his eyes. "Jesus Christ."

I pulled up my underwear and my shorts and sat back down in the dirt. I looked through the darkness, and it struck me that all across Las Vegas, at that very moment, there were people having sex. When I'd turned twelve, my father had tried to broach the subject of intercourse, uncomfortably explaining that, beyond the fulfillment of desire, it was an act of love. But right now people were doing it, I was sure, in motel rooms and bathrooms and parked cars and storage closets, and they either loved each other or they didn't. I didn't know if it made any difference. It seemed possible that simply being with someone—anyone—was enough, and I had the idea that desire was nothing more than a form of desperation.

"I promise not to tell anyone," I said, sounding helpless. "I wouldn't ever do that." I considered taking off my shirt. To make my chest look more feminine, I'd plucked what few hairs I had from around my nipples, and I wanted to show him. "Trav," I pleaded.

"I told you to shut up," he said, and zipped his cutoffs. He pinched the knotted center of his stump, tugging at the skin.

I'm not sure what made me do it, but when Kilburg closed his eyes, as if he were trying to recall some vital piece of information, I told him my father was sick. "He's going to die," I said, crying now. I thought of how Kilburg's mother had left him without notice, and I wondered if he ever cried over her when no one was around.

He stared silently at his hands, his arms loose across his lap. Between low clouds the stars seemed to float through the sky like distant aircraft, flashing in and out of sight, faint in the light of the moon. I thought of them falling in slow motion, all at once—a blizzard of stars—down through the universe and into the valley, filling it up before melting away. For a couple of minutes, there was only the noise of katydids, a steady chirr that filled the air. A breeze picked up, stirring dirt around the fort. The clouds came swiftly together, padding the sky. I thought of the smell of sagebrush when it rained—at once fragrant and repellent, something like the smell of your hand after you licked it. Kilburg nodded his head. He seemed to have calmed down. He bent forward and picked up a rock, chucking it into the night.

"Why didn't you help me this morning?" he said.

I wiped tears from my face, looking him up and down.

"I know you were there." He lifted his chin. "I saw you behind that car."

I tried to think of an excuse for why I hadn't defended him. Kilburg pulled a flashlight from his pocket, switching it on and shining it at a Joshua tree. Heads of sagebrush rose up among the cat's claw. He pointed the flashlight at a small cluster of jimsonweed, swathed by long white flowers shaped like trumpets. He circled the weed with the beam and clicked his tongue.

"If you wanted to hallucinate," he said, "you could eat those flowers. Problem is, they might kill you."

"I'm sorry," I told him. But I was still thinking about my father. In my mind, as in my mother's, he was already dead. I pictured his last, gasping moments, then his wake: he lay in an open casket, done up with cosmetics to resemble the living, the way my grandfather had lain at his own wake two summers earlier. I saw Kilburg beside me at the burial and imagined that afterward the two of us would sneak into the cemetery at night and plant a sapling behind my father's headstone. I imagined Kilburg as an important part of my life, even though I could feel that this would be our last time together at the fort—that we were more or less done.

The breeze that had picked up grew stronger, sending a tumbleweed bounding past the fort and lifting a plastic produce bag we'd left in the dirt. A dust devil spun elegantly and died. I hadn't stopped crying, but I tried not to show it, blinking away the tears. I told him again that I was sorry. One of the tears landed on my forearm, and even though I'd felt it fall from my chin, I thought for an instant that after five long months it had begun to rain. But the clouds had already started to separate, exposing the moon and the stars, floating east toward Frenchman Mountain.

Kilburg knuckled his shoulder. He set the flashlight in the dirt and reached for the prosthetic leg, scowling as he pulled the sleeve over his stump and tightened the laces. For the first time it occurred to me that he had a potentially critical illness: if it had cost him his leg, I reasoned, it could just as easily cost him his life. I was suddenly convinced that, like my father, Kilburg wouldn't live long.

"I guess I thought we were friends," he said.

It was late, and I could feel that I was still pretty high. I was tired and I wanted to go home. Finally I stood, brushing dirt from my shorts, and offered Kilburg my hand.

"We are," I lied, because that seemed less hurtful than the truth.

Alba

KENT NELSON

ÚLTIMO VARGAS HAD BEEN IN HATCH, NEW MEXICO, ONLY SIX MONTHS, since March, and already he owned his own business to compete with Netflix, delivering compact disc movies and video games to ranchers and people who lived within twenty miles of town. He had worked out a deal with Señora Gaspar, who owned the video store, to pay him 90 percent of the delivery fee, and if he took out more than fifty videos in a week, a premium on the extras.

Último had a moped, which made it feasible. Gas prices were high, and the delivery fee saved customers money. Also, it was convenient—they didn't have to wait till they had an errand in town. Most of the customers were Mexican families who worked the land for Anglos, or Anglos who owned cattle or pecan groves. Último organized his schedule by time and direction to avoid random trips. It was a lot of riding on the moped, but he liked the terrain—the low hills, the bare mountains, pale blue in the day and silhouetted in the evenings, the vast sky. He liked seeing the fields of onions and chiles, the pecan trees, the alfalfa growing, the cattle grazing. He saw hawks, antelope, badgers, deer, and learned their habits.

In a few weeks he knew most of his customers—the Gallegos family out Castaneda Road, who grew green chiles, the Brubakers farther on, the widow woman, Señora Obregón, who still ran the Bar SW. The Michaels family was a mile east, the Garcias were on the other side of Interstate 25—they owned the bakery—and Tom Martinez lived in the turquoise trailer a mile past. Many of the families grew chiles—that's what Hatch was famous for—and marketed them to the co-op in Albuquerque or along the town highway, pickled or fresh, or in jellies, or as *ristras*. Everyone knew Último, too, the *chico loco* on his moped.

The more people knew him, of course, the more people knew about his business. He was strong, had a good smile, and was a natural salesman. He talked to the Mexican families in Spanish, asked where their relatives came from, who was left in Hermosillo or Juárez or Oaxaca. He talked to the Anglos to improve his English and to show he was a serious businessman. He expected great things of himself one day.

Último's English was passable because he'd worked almost a year in Deming before he came to Hatch. He'd washed dishes at Sí Señorita from six to two, and at four he mopped floors at the elementary school. In between he spent his off hours at the Broken Spoke, where he met people, even some women, like Brenda, who was a hairdresser, then unemployed. One night Último was walking home to his trailer at eleven p.m., and Brenda stopped in her Trans Am with the muffler dragging. She gave him a ride, and one thing led to another. He fixed Brenda's muffler and relined the brakes, and she fucked him like there was no tomorrow. After a month Brenda wanted to get married—she was pregnant, she said—and Último said why not. Two weeks after the wedding, when he found out there was no baby, Brenda ran off to California with a wine salesman.

To pay off Brenda's debts, Último used his meager savings and took a third job unloading freight at the train yard, though he still wasn't making enough money, or sleeping enough, either. One evening, after he had been threatened with eviction from Brenda's apartment, his boss at the school found him dozing at a teacher's desk. He was finished in Deming and he walked north with his thumb out, but no one picked him up. In two days, forty-six miles later, with nothing but the clothes he wore and a blanket he'd brought from home, he staggered past Las Uvas Valley Dairy and a few broken-down adobe houses and into Hatch, where he saw a HELP WANTED sign in the window of the Frontera Mercado. He went in and got a job stocking groceries.

Hatch was in the fertile cottonwood corridor along the banks of the Rio Grande, the interstate to the east, and open country in every other direction—ranches, pasture, rangeland. The days were getting warmer by then, and he slept in the brush along the river, shaved and washed himself there, ate for breakfast whatever he had scavenged from the *mercado* the day before. If he wasn't working, he spent sunny mornings in the park and rainy ones in the library. Then Señora Gaspar hired him to work the morning shift at the video store, checking in rentals, cleaning, replenishing the stock of candy bars and popcorn. He established a more efficient check-in, organized a better window display, and built a new sign from construction waste: GASPAR'S MOVIES, and in smaller letters, *Pregunte sobre nuestro servicio de mensajeria.*

"What delivery?" Señora Gaspar asked.

"Our delivery," Último said. "I have bought a moped from Tom Martinez."

Some of his customers ordered movies for the company Último gave them. Señora Obregón, fifty-five years old, had lost her husband and wanted someone to talk to. She reminded Último of his *abuelita* in Mexico, and he often made the ranch his last stop of the evening so he had time to sit on her porch and listen to her stories. Her husband had been killed two winters before when, as he was feeding the cattle in a blizzard, a fifteen-hundred-pound bull slipped on a patch of ice and crushed him. They'd lost a hundred head in that storm. Her children were in Wichita, Denver, and Salt Lake City, two sons and a daughter, and none of them wanted anything to do with the ranch. Señora Obregón dressed well, as if Último's presence meant something, and she offered him steak and potatoes, and always leftovers to take with him afterward.

Another person who ordered movies but didn't watch them was the Garcia's daughter, Isabel. She was seventeen, had bronzed skin, short black hair, and a good body. One day in June, she called the store and ordered *Babel*, "Pronto," she said. Último was alone, so he put a CERRADO sign in the window and took off on his moped. Isabel came to the door in a tank top. "Let me find the money," she said. She didn't invite him in, but she paraded around the room pretending to look so Último could see the sunlight on her body. She found the money and came back to the door. "Come again," she said and handed him a five-dollar bill.

Elena Rivera also called for ordered movies. She had lived all her life in Hatch—her family owned a small dairy that competed with Las Uvas—and she was married to a village trustee, Manuel, who grew chiles. Manuel was often there when Último came by, as was their son, Aparicio, twelve years old, who was sick. Elena Rivera thought it was good for the boy to see other people, and Último obliged her by playing games with Aparicio and telling him jokes. The more time Último spent with Aparicio, the more movies the Riveras ordered.

Último was born in the village of Ricardo Flores Magón and raised there with two older sisters without being aware much of the wider world. Growing up, he thought of his father, Fidel, as already old. He slouched, his face was wrinkled, and he wore a straw hat with the brim coming apart. The hat had a blue-gray heron's feather tucked into the sweaty red band. "This hat keeps me alive," his father told Último. "You don't know." His mother kept goats and chickens and a small garden, watered by hand, and made baskets from yucca fiber and marketed them in Chihuahua. Then his father disappeared, no one knew where, and money arrived from different places Último had never heard of. His mother said in the States money grew in the gardens like squash and beans.

Último was an altar boy—every boy was—but he had doubts about God. Último had been to Chihuahua with his mother once and felt the energy of the city, had seen the lights and the cars, the radios and TVs, the clothes, soaps, and a thousand other things, and why would God make such things that belonged to so few?

Último did well in school without much effort, and girls were kind to him, especially his sisters' friends, who came over to their house all the time. When Último was fourteen, the padre warned him of sins Último had never thought of, and when he inquired of his sisters' friends, they laughed and kissed him and showed him what pleasure a boy might receive from their hands and mouths. Último was troubled that God should not want him to do what felt so joyful.

So he passed his days reading and learning from the girls and playing soccer. When he was seventeen, his father came home for several months. He had a car and nice clothes and wore a hat that was useless against the sun. He told stories of Fresno and cotton picking, of Castroville, where artichokes grew, and Yakima, Washington, where apples were heavy on the trees. If a man was willing to work, he said, there was money everywhere.

His father wanted to take Último back with him to California, but Marta, the older sister, was pregnant in Buenaventura and needed help, and the younger sister, Lorena, couldn't be left alone. Most of the day she sat with their *abuelita* under the thatched awning, but sometimes without warning she screamed at a lizard or a bird, and once she'd torn off her shirt and run through the village crying out, "God is chasing me." Another time she took the knife she was slicing papayas with and stabbed herself in her arm.

The *abuelita* was too old to do what was necessary for Lorena, so when his father went back to the States, Último had to stay longer in Ricardo Flores.

~⌒

Elena Rivera appreciated how good Último was with Aparicio and saw no reason not to help a tall, good-looking boy who had gotten himself to the U.S. That's what she told Último one afternoon in September when he brought over a video of *Abu and the Giraffe* for her son. "What will you do when it gets cold?" she asked. "You can't sleep at the river all winter."

"Maybe I will rent from Hector Lopez when his pickers are gone."

"My parents have a vacant house at the edge of town," Elena Rivera said. "There is a spell on it, because a child was killed by a rattlesnake."

"The place by the dry arroyo?" Último asked. "It has tires holding down the tin roof."

"That's it," Elena said. "The windows are broken, and who knows what else is wrong with it. You'd have to do some repairs. Are you afraid of snakes?"

"Yes and no," Último said.

"Which?"

"No," Último said.

"Then, if you're interested, I will ask my parents about it."

~⌒

At the end of his days in Ricardo Flores, Último had a girlfriend, Alba, three years older, a friend of Marta's, whom his mother had gone to help. Alba was devout and shy, and she went to Mass every day with her mother. She wasn't one of his sisters' friends who'd shown him what pleasure was, and he knew better than to coax her or to try to kiss her. Instead, he asked to see her naked body.

"Once," he said. "I want to remember you when I'm gone."

"You can remember me with my clothes on," she said.

"I promise I won't touch you."

"You will look at me with lust. That's a sin."

"I might look at you with lust," Último said. "That will be my problem, not yours."

"Why would you ask this," she said, "when you know I cannot do such a thing?"

"There is no cost for a question."

The next day, as they walked outside the village, Último asked again.

"I have already answered you," Alba said.

"You might have changed your mind," Último said. "You might have decided there could be no harm in it because I will go to the States."

"When are you going?"

"Soon," Último said. "When my mother comes back from Buenaventura."

"In any case, where do you think we could do such a thing? Lorena and *abuelita* are at your house, and my mother is at mine."

"In the church," Último said. "There's a room behind the altar where we used to wait before Mass. No one is there in the afternoon."

She laughed. "You're as crazy as your sister."

"Only once," Último said. "I want to walk all the way around you so, when I am in the States, I will remember clearly your whole body."

"Without touching?" Alba said.

"Yes."

"It won't happen."

A week passed. Último tended Lorena, who was seeing the Virgin Mary in the clouds. He humored her, sang to her, told her she would live to be 103 years old. They threw stones into the ravine. Último read her stories from a magazine.

Their mother returned, grieving for a lost granddaughter. "It was God's will," she said. "The child was never well, but did it have to die?"

"God's will," Último said, "what is that?"

A few days later, Último filled two plastic bottles with water and loaded his backpack with food that wouldn't spoil—peanut butter, bread, cans of stew—and said good-bye to Alba at the *tienda* where she worked. "I am leaving tomorrow before daylight," he said. "I am going alone so I won't get caught. I promise I'll write."

"How will you find your way?"

"I am destined for great things," Último said.

"I have changed my mind," Alba said. "I will do what you asked."

Último said nothing.

"At two o'clock I have a break," Alba said. "I will meet you at the church."

"Promise?" he asked.

At two o'clock the next afternoon, Alba appeared at the church as she said she would. The room Último remembered was behind the altar, though he had forgotten how barren and simple it was. There was only one square window high up in the wall, and light fanned down onto the plaster of the wall opposite.

"You have to turn around," Alba said.

Último turned around and stared up at the light. He heard the swishing of clothes, a dress fall to the floor, then quiet.

"Now," Alba said.

He turned back slowly and saw her body, her small, dark-tipped breasts, her long black hair over one shoulder. She did not hide herself with her hands, but she lowered her eyes. He was aware of her face, the expression of chasteness, but of joy, too, as if she were both ashamed and glad of the moment. Último walked all the way around her so that, for a few seconds, his shadow fell across her body and then her body returned to light.

Elena Rivera's parents agreed to let him have the house in return for his labor fixing it up. An abandoned shack was what it was, with waist-high weeds in the yard. The door was padlocked, but Último looked through the jagged glass of the broken windows. Swallows had nested on the rafters, and the stuccoed walls were covered with graffiti—VENCEREMOS! VIVA ZAPATA! ANGLOS SUCK EGGS. There were three rooms, one with a sink, but no running water. The outhouse in back was functional, but it leaned two feet toward the dry arroyo where cottonwoods grew. A barrel stove had heated the place, but the barrel was in the yard, and the stovepipe was gone. Último tried the outdoor pump and gave thirty pulls on the long, curved handle. Dirty water came out, but in another thirty pulls the water came clear.

Early mornings in October, before he went to the video store, Último cleared the weeds and burned them. He borrowed tools from the Riveras— hammer, saw, chisel, level, tape measure—and bought plaster, nails, window glass, glazing compound, and a stovepipe. At night he scavenged for plywood, bent two-by-fours, one-by-fours with nails still in them. He fixed the hole in the floor, repaired the damage to the clapboard outside, filled rocks into the holes raccoons had made under the house. He scraped away the swallows' mud nests, covered over the graffiti with fresh plaster, moved the barrel inside, and cut the stovepipe to fit. He propped two fallen cottonwood branches against the outhouse to make it stand straight. The electricity was turned on. From his customers he cadged two lamps, two chairs, a mattress, and a card table. He saw no rattlesnakes—it was getting cold.

October 25 he moved in and not long after, an unusual thing: one evening he stayed for steak and green chiles at the widow Obregón's and drove home late on his moped. It was windy and dark, and when he pulled up to his shack he was chilled. The moon illuminated the tin roof with the tires on it, and the stones in the yard were silver. When he opened the door to his house, the moonlight came in with him, and there was Alba in the kitchen. She had on shorts and a pale blouse—he couldn't see what color in the dark—and her face was calm but conflicted with desire. "Let me make a fire," he said. "You must be cold." He turned on the light, but no one was there.

Último knew people claimed they'd seen Mary Magdalene and the Virgin Mary and even Jesus Christ, but this was Alba, an ordinary girl from Ricardo Flores. Despite the promise he'd made, he hadn't thought much about Alba. In Deming he'd written her several letters scrawled on torn paper, and he'd received three from her, written on a lined school tablet, the last of which offered him more of her if he came home. But he was with Brenda, and he hadn't written back.

The night after Último saw Alba, he came home from his last delivery with a keen anticipation of seeing her again. Perhaps she'd be at the table or lying in bed, or she'd be at the window looking west into the moonlight, but when he opened the door, the house was empty. He thought it might have been a difference in the clouds or the moon's waning by a single day. Several weeks went by, each night getting longer and colder, and he got over his disappointment and wondered whether he'd ever seen Alba at all.

It rained. At the Goodwill he bought a coat and hat and gloves. With the winnowing light, people had longer evenings to fill up, and he hustled videos even harder because Señora Gaspar was always getting in new movies and his premiums were good money. But with the cold and the early dark, deliveries were more of a burden. Yes, he was familiar with the signs, the location of the poorly banked curve on the Canal Road, the washboard gravel by Jaime Delgado's adobe house where seven people lived, but Último couldn't see the blue hills in the distance or the hawks circling or the silhouettes of the mountains, except as a jagged black line against the stars.

His solace was his house. Each day he became more used to it, more comfortable. The barrel stove was smoky, but it heated the rooms. He had built a platform for his mattress, and he slept well. For a couple of months, he sent money home to his mother and Lorena.

In December, Elena Rivera's parents asked for rent, starting the New Year. "You've lived there for free," Elena Rivera said. "What you spent for labor and materials has been accounted for."

"How much?" Último wanted to know.

"Two hundred a month. I've argued your case, but the dairy business is not going well, and they want what's fair."

"There's no heat," Último said. "No running water. I'm already paying the electric."

"That's why it's not four hundred," Elena said.

"I understand," Último said. "I will pay the rent."

At Christmas, Señora Gaspar went to Albuquerque to visit her son, and Último was left in charge. He opened the store, answered the phone, logged in the returned videos. He called the people whose DVDs were overdue and offered pickup service. Of course, Señora Gaspar needed someone in the store when Último was making deliveries, so at three her niece Rosa came in with a four-pack of wine coolers. When Último returned half-frozen from his pickups and deliveries, Rosa was sitting on the stool with a space heater under her reading comic books.

The next morning the till was short twenty-two dollars. To avoid suspicion, Último made up the difference from his own pocket. The next morning, another fifteen dollars were missing. He didn't know what to do. Señora Gaspar would be gone another eleven days.

Último was saved from one despair by another, because the next night when Rosa closed the store, she left the space heater on, and too close to the wastebasket. It melted the plastic and set fire to the computer tear-offs and then to the desk. It was three in the morning, and by the time the volunteer fire department arrived, the building was ablaze, the inventory destroyed, and Último's livelihood gone up in flames.

For several weeks after the fire, Último sat by the barrel stove and looked out the window at the gray sky. He bought a cheap bottle of red wine and drank it, but felt no better. He slept. Only a week before the fire, he had sent money home, so when he paid rent, he had no money left. His only possession to sell was his moped, but it was a mile to town.

He might have looked for his father in California, but where? Or, of course, he could have gone home, but in Ricardo Flores he could not do the great things he expected of himself. Then, on a dark morning, he was lying in bed, dozing, waking, pondering, when Alba came again. She was in the doorway to his bedroom, embracing the wooden jamb, hiding her breasts from view. He sat up and pulled his blanket up to cover his chest and shoulders. Alba's expression was no longer conflicted, but wanton and eager. Último called to her softly. She wouldn't come closer, so he stood up to go to her, and she disappeared.

He interpreted this vision of Alba as a sign to stop moping, and that afternoon he asked Señor Garcia for a job in the bakery. Último had to go in at four a.m., and each day he understood his mother's desperation. What had she thought? How had she endured the long journey to Chihuahua to sell baskets? What had she thought, leaving her children behind?

One of the Garcias was there, Mercedes or Alfonso, and Último helped prepare the dough, knead it, and put it into pans. Último learned to make *dulces* and *churros* and cinnamon rolls, and at six, they opened the store. Último brewed the coffee. There were three tables for sitting inside.

At eleven, Mercedes or Alfonso, whoever was there, took a break for lunch and left Último alone for an hour. He was not allowed to sit at the tables, but he might drink coffee in the back room, from which he could watch the store. One day, as he was behind the counter gazing at the street, Isabel touched his shoulder, and he jumped. She had come in through the back door from the alley.

"Are you alone?" she asked.

"I'm here where I'm supposed to be," he said.

"They say you're a good worker and do what you're asked. Would you obey me, too?"

"That depends," Último said.

Isabel slid past him, and he smelled her scent. "You don't come to see me anymore."

"I never came to see you. I delivered the movies you ordered."

"Hatch is the end of the world," she said. "I can't wait to leave."

"For me it is the beginning of the world."

She took a bite of a *churro*. "I'll think of something," she said. "Be ready."

On the day Último left Ricardo Flores he had said good-bye to his *abuelita* who was old, but not to his mother, and hitchhiked to Buenaventura, where he got a ride north to Las Palomas. In the evening he hiked west into the desert, and a three-quarter moon led him into the mountains. In the morning he hid in a cave, and the next night he walked again. He followed animal trails, and in the morning he was in the United States, at the edge of an encampment of RVs. All that day he watched what the people did there, who was leaving, and at mid-morning of the second day, he saw a couple on their way out stop their motor home at the restroom. Último ran from his hiding place, climbed the ladder to the roof, and lay down.

The ride was easy. He held on to a vent to keep from rolling off on the turns. Most of the time he lay on his back and looked at the sky, the same one that arched over Ricardo Flores, and he daydreamed of Alba—her bronze skin, her black hair, the shame and joy on her face as she revealed herself to him. Several times he raised his head to see where he was, but everywhere around him was desert and mountains.

Once they stopped for no reason Último could see, and he heard voices—questions and answers. Someone opened the back of the camper. Último didn't move. If he couldn't see anyone on the ground, no one on the ground could see him. Then the RV gathered speed again and kept going. A half hour farther on was a town with stoplights, where the couple pulled into a gas station. Último climbed down from the roof and ran.

One afternoon after work in the bakery, Último was in bed but hadn't gone to sleep yet. He'd gotten a raise of fifty cents an hour and was calculating how much he could send home when he heard the door open in the living room. For a minute he didn't hear anything more. Maybe it had been the wind, maybe Alba. Then the floor creaked. He opened his eyes, and Isabel Garcia came into the room.

"I thought of something to ask," she said. "Do you want to make love?" She walked to the bed and pulled her shirt up over her head. "Move over."

He moved over—he had no choice—and she slid in beside him.

Isabel visited every few days, and it wasn't punishment to feel her hands on him, her mouth, the weight of her body. He liked her sighs, the notes of pleasure she sang to him, the urgency she felt, but he didn't feel love. He felt an uneasy peace, and he slept after, but he worried about who had seen her car there, who might talk, and he knew his days at the bakery were numbered.

He went to talk to Elena Rivera. "I want to grow chiles," he said.

"Everyone in Hatch grows chiles," she said.

"That's the idea," Último said. "I want to be everyone. But I will grow the best ones."

"Do you know anything about growing chiles?"

"I will learn."

"And where will you grow them?"

"On the land around the house that has tires on the roof, on my land."

"You want to buy it?" Elena Rivera asked. "I laugh at you. My parents will laugh at you. But in case they don't, how much are you intending to pay?"

"Ten thousand dollars," Último said. "The house is barely a house, and there are rattlesnakes. Two thousand now, and a little at a time over five years."

"Will you be here in five years?"

"If I get the land."

"The land is full of stones," Elena Rivera said, "and the creek is dry."

"More reasons for your parents to sell."

"But how will you grow chiles there?"

"Magic," Último said. "I am destined for great things."

A week after he talked to Elena Rivera about the land, she came into the bakery. She bought two cinnamon rolls. "Aparicio likes to eat these," she said. "I'll tell him you made them."

"I did," Último said, "only for him."

"I talked my parents into selling," she said. "Who else, I said, would buy a house like that in a field of stones with tires holding down the roof?"

"Others like me," Último said.

"There are no others like you. They want fifteen thousand—three thousand now, and the rest in four years. They will charge no interest."

"Give me two weeks," Último said. "I will find three thousand dollars."

But he had no idea how he would get the money. He tried the bank, but, as he thought, he had no assets and no credit, and even Elena Rivera's recommendation got him nowhere. He thought of asking the widow Obregón for a loan, but that would change their friendship. He had only one other idea, and on a Thursday after work at the bakery, he drove his moped to Deming.

He went first to the Broken Spoke, where the bartender remembered him. "Your hair is longer," the bartender said.

"You've gained weight and look prosperous," said Larry Munzer, sitting on the same barstool he had been on a year ago.

"I am almost a chile grower," Último said. "Do you understand what that means?"

"You're almost a man," the bartender said.

"I'm looking for Brenda," Último said. "We're still married."

"She's back in town," Larry Munzer said. "She's started up the Hair You Are Salon. She married a nice guy from California."

"All the better," Último said.

Brenda was surprised and not at all happy to see him. The upshot was, in return for three thousand dollars, he offered her a divorce, silence, and for-giveness of the money he'd paid on her debts. She siphoned the money from her loan. It took a few days—Último had to ride back to Deming another time—but he signed the contract to buy his house and the land around it.

Before offering to buy the property, Último examined what he was doing. The cottonwoods along the arroyo were healthy, and, though the arroyo was dry, the hand pump in the yard was good. Último disassembled the pump and measured the well casing—fifteen feet, not very deep. He bor-rowed an electric pump from Tom Martinez and ran an extension cord to the house. Whether there was a stream underground or a reservoir Último didn't know, but the pump produced five cubic feet per second, which was plenty to irrigate five acres of chiles.

Now Último eyeballed the highest point on his property, figured out how he would get water to it, and then traded away his moped to Alex Tomar for the use of his tractor. On Sunday, when the bakery was closed, he plowed up the stones. The plow blade broke, and Último welded it. It broke again, and he welded it again, and he finished plowing in the dark. On Monday, surveying the field of loose stones, Último had more work than ever.

For the next two weeks, every spare minute, he carried stones. Aparicio helped. They gathered the stones into a pile, loaded them into a wheelbarrow, and wheeled them across a plywood trail laid out over the broken ground.

The wheelbarrow was too heavy to dump, so Último turned it on its side, and they heaved stones into the arroyo.

After work, Último had no time for siestas and no time for Isabel. He loaded and unloaded the wheelbarrow hundreds of times, each day creating more arable ground. Then one day when he came home Isabel was there and asked her same question.

"I can't now," Último said. "Come back when it is too dark to work."

"You'll be too tired."

"I'm too tired now."

"Would you want me to tell my father about us?"

"What have I done but what you wanted?" Último asked. "What kind of love is it if you make me?"

"Better than nothing," Isabel said. "Come inside, Último. I need you now."

When the stones had been carried away, Último broke apart the big clumps of earth with a hoe. That took another week. Then he borrowed back his moped and visited the widow Obregón and asked to buy manure.

"You can't buy it," she said. "I will give it to you."

"Can I rent one of your trucks to haul it?"

"I will lend you the truck."

"Thank you," he said, and he listened to her complain about her son in Wichita who worked for Cessna but never came to visit her.

Último spread the manure with a shovel, fifteen loads over ten days. He hoed furrows three feet apart and arranged a flexible plastic pipe to the highest point in the field north of the house and irrigated the dry ground so it could get used to moisture it had never experienced except as rain. He did the same thing from the highest point to the south.

He spoke to other chile growers he'd met when he delivered movies—the Gallegoses, who marketed their chiles to Safeway; to Arnie Yellen, who grew chiles on an acre behind his house and sold them on the highway; to Alfred Saenz, who was the biggest grower in the Hatch Valley. He talked to Ned Cruz, the owner of The Chile Store, who sold chiles year-round as paste and in powder form, dried, fresh, and frozen. In the library he read in Spanish and English about green chiles and red chiles, their growing seasons, the ways to keep insects off the plants, how to make sure the chiles flowered. He called the agricultural extension agent of Doña Ana County for recommendations and learned that the less water chiles had, the hotter they were.

As the weather warmed, the bakery became busier. Locals shed their winter isolation and moved around outside. Motels were full of spring travelers, and these people wanted *dulces* and coffee for the road. Último came in at three a.m. to make more bread, more cinnamon rolls, more *churros*. Even Isabel helped. She was at the cash register before school and came back for an hour at noon and complained the whole time.

Still, Último labored every afternoon on his land. He had carried the stones away but continued to find new ones; he broke clumps of earth smaller and smaller; he irrigated the ground. Then, finally, in April, he was ready to buy seeds.

There were too many choices—sweet or mild, hot, super-hot. A habanero was fifty times hotter than a jalapeño. There were bird chiles, Bolivian chiles, Peruvian chiles, all undomesticated, plus bell chiles, Cherrytime, Hungarian Hot Wax, Hot Cherry, red, cayenne, and serrano. And there were specialized versions of these, too, like Cherry Bombs, Marbles, and Bulgarian Carrot, as well as hybrids like Ancho 211, Thai Dragon, Conchos Jalapeño, and Serrano del Sol.

He was pondering what to buy when Isabel came over and asked him to go with her to Las Cruces to find an apartment. "I'm moving as soon as school's finished," she said.

"Is it all right with your parents?"

"I'm not asking."

"When do you want to go?"

"Now," she said, "right after you fuck me."

Isabel had read a newspaper ahead of time and had marked the ads, and by three o'clock she'd found a one-bedroom not far from the university. The manager of the building wanted a month's rent in advance, which Isabel supplied. "You can visit me anytime," she said to Último, "and you'd better."

"Since we're here," he said, "do you mind if I run an errand? I want to buy a hat."

They found a hat store in the Yellow Pages, and Isabel drove him there and waited in the car. He bought a straw hat with a brim to keep the sun from his face.

"You look silly," Isabel said.

"It's a hat like my father's," Último said. "Now I have to go to the university."

"I have a friend there," Isabel said. "I'll see if he's home."

Isabel let him off on the corner of Espina and Frenger, and Último found the Chile Pepper Institute of New Mexico State. He asked to see the director, and after a short wait was ushered into a small office and sat down across the desk from a young woman. "I am going to grow chiles in Hatch," he said. "I need magic."

He set seeds in the ground in rows three feet apart, each seed eighteen inches from the one he'd planted before. He marked every seed, fertilized it, and watered it by hand from a bucket he carried along. He moved on his knees from one planting to the next like a pilgrim crawling for miles to atone for his sins. It took him three days to plant the seeds—the experimental ones the institute was paying him to grow.

Then he waited.

So the water wouldn't evaporate in the heat of the day, he irrigated after sundown, again at midnight, and a third time when he got up to go to the bakery. On his break at nine a.m., he ran home and turned off the pump.

One afternoon he came home and saw two trucks parked along the arroyo, an old one and a new Dodge. He recognized Señora Obregón sitting in the shade with her hired man, Paco. Último came up, and they all shook hands.

"It was my turn to visit you," Señora Obregón said. "I see how hard you've worked."

"I have planted chiles," Último said. "I can offer you a drink of water. It is a humble house."

"I would like you to bring me chiles from the harvest," Señora Obregón said.

"I will be glad to," Último said, "but the harvest is far away."

"Closer than you think," Señora Obregón said. "That's why I'm here. How would you bring me chiles without a truck?" She nodded toward the old truck. "The tires are worn, and it has a hundred thousand miles of use. But it's a Toyota and has lived well."

"I am honored," Último said.

"The title is on the seat," Señora Obregón said. "Here's the key. Now you can visit me again."

May 21, a long day. Último had hardly slept because at two in the morning, something had made an eerie, quavering sound in the cottonwoods. He stepped outside with a flashlight and heard the unmistakable buzzing of a rattlesnake. He found the snake in the beam of the flashlight, coiled, with its head raised, its tongue flashing. Último got to his knees and shone the light into the snake's eyes. "I will leave you alone," he said, "if you will leave me alone."

The snake didn't answer, but Último believed they had made a deal.

He heard the quavering again—like a saw blade being played—and he skirted the snake and walked to the arroyo. The sound came from upstream in dark billowy trees, but each time he reached the place he thought it was it moved farther away.

The night was cool, but the stars were out, and as Último waited to hear the sound again, he urinated into the arroyo. Like every man in history who had done the same thing, Último felt the enormity of the sky, the deepness of space, and his own tiny greatness in the effort he had made in his field. Then the quavering came again from the trees nearby.

Último shone his light back and forth into the leaves until he found the shining eyes of a small owl. It was thirty feet away and a little above where Último stood, and Último made a deal with the owl, too, never to die.

Último lowered the light, and the bird flew deeper into the trees.

He set water and went back to bed, but still couldn't sleep because he felt the air move though the house, sweet air, humid with the earth's smell. He got up when it was still dark and went to bake bread.

At nine o'clock he drove his new old truck home and cut off the pump and sat for a minute on the smooth stone he had put down as a step to his door. He was wearing his straw hat against the sun. The snake's path was carved in the dust in the direction of the arroyo, and cottonwoods tattered in the breeze. Because he hadn't slept, Último felt part of everything that lived nearby. He remembered his mother and Lorena in Ricardo Flores, Marta in Buenaventura, his father in California, wherever he was, and wished they all could see him at that moment, tired and exultant.

He closed his eyes for a moment and leaned back against the door, and when he opened this eyes again, he saw tiny sprigs of green coming up through the soil. He stood up and ran into the field. The chiles were coming up, three feet apart in the rows and eighteen inches one plant from another. He knelt down in a wet furrow between two rows and kissed the ground, and when he looked up again, Alba was a few feet away, gazing at him. She wore jeans and a white blouse, and her expression was dreamlike, as if she had believed in him all along and was answering his call.

Fantasy Is That

Michael Onofrey

THE SINGLE-WIDE WAS IN A TRAILER PARK ON THE EAST SIDE OF LAS
Vegas, but Dwayne wasn't sure it was still Las Vegas. It was desert, it was
windswept, it was off Highway 147. He'd been there before, a year and a half
previous, but there had been no address, only directions via the cell phone.
It was the same this time, but this time it was Connie on the cell phone.
She was waiting for him.

He parked and got out of his pickup truck. He was rangy and wore a
short-sleeve plaid shirt and a pair of khakis. This was the end of the trailer
court, tenancy dissipating, spaces abundant. There was a chain-link fence,
and beyond that fence grey and black-limbed creosote grew at the base of a
craggy hill.

At the screen door he knocked. He felt grit beneath his shoes. He adjusted his bifocals. Overhead the sun beat down. He waited and then he
stuck his hand through a hole in the screen and knocked on the trailer door
proper next to the doorknob, a tinny feeling at his knuckles.

The door opened and Connie stood, looking at him. Then she said,
"Come in."

At a Formica-top table he sat opposite her, she with a cigarette and a
tumbler half-full of amber liquid, no ice. Her face was deeply lined. She was
a thin woman and everything about her was dry—hair, hands, fingernails.

"Bourbon, beer?"

"No thanks."

"Coffee?"

"No thanks. I'm fine."

She drew on her cigarette and looked out the window and pointed. Dwayne turned and looked.

"Right there. Right over there on the road. He was taking a load of laundry to the coin laundry, you know, in the trailer park here. The laundry was on the road. The basket was on the road. The laundry was dumped out. The basket was sideways. He was just there on the road, kind of crumbled. No one was around."

Connie was still pointing. Dwayne was still looking.

"Right in front of that empty space where the Wilsons used to live before they picked up and moved to Bullhead City. I've been looking at it for three days and three nights now, and you know what I'm thinking?"

Dwayne turned and looked at her. Her shriveled hand came down.

"I'm thinking that maybe I should put a bottle out there or something, you know, like people do, with flowers in it or something, like they did for Princess Diana."

A blue T-shirt advertising Steve's Tires hung from Connie's shoulders, collar of the shirt stretched.

"What do you think?"

"About the flowers?"

"Yeah."

"Sure. Go ahead."

Connie inhaled on her cigarette and then exhaled.

"Did you call?"

"Yes, I did," Dwayne said. "I'm having the body cremated. It'll be about five days before I can pick up the ashes. There's an office on Paradise Road. I stopped there before coming here."

Connie started coughing, scratchy yet infected with phlegm. Dwayne waited. The ashtray on the table was half-full, origins, according to an emblazoned rim, Elko, Nevada.

"Just taking a load of wash to the coin laundry," Connie resumed, voice raw, hand waving, cigarette a smoking wand, "and he drops dead—what—forty, fifty feet from the trailer. It was hot, but not that hot, not yet. The laundry's not heavy. We tote it down there all the time. I went out to check on some fish I was drying for the cat, and there he was."

Dwayne had heard it on the telephone three times and now he was hearing it again. Connie brought her cigarette up and inhaled. From down the length of the trailer a door opened.

She walked to the table and stood. Dwayne's eyes had followed her the entire way and now he was looking up at her, complexion brown, cheekbones high, eyes black. She was in jeans and a grey sweatshirt with the sleeves cut off. Her hair was short and black, and it lay against her skull like a yarmulke. At each ear a silver stud with a pinch of turquoise winked. It wasn't that she was beautiful. It was something else that had Dwayne stalled, something familiar, yet he couldn't put a name to it.

"This is my daughter, Lana. Lana, this is Jack's son, Dwayne."

"I'm sorry about your father," Lana said, but didn't look at Dwayne when she spoke. She looked to the side of him as if she were talking to someone next to him.

Dwayne only looked at her. Then he realized he should respond. He gave a weak, "Yes." Lana shifted her weight. She was gangly, but she was too old for gangly. She was late twenties, early thirties. Her face had contour, but her expression was flat. It was hard to believe she was Connie's daughter.

"Lana came out from New Mexico on the bus to give me a hand with the situation."

Dwayne nodded.

"I think I'll go outside," Lana said, and turned and went to the door and opened it and then opened the screen door and went out and closed the door.

Connie brought her glass up. Amber liquid flowed beneath a sere lip. On her face there were glasses, lenses smudged. She set her glass down on the table.

"I guess we got to talk, don't we?" Connie said.

Dwayne nodded.

"The trailer's in Jack's name, and so is the truck."

"Of course they're yours," Dwayne said. "It's just a matter of paperwork and time."

"I just can't get over it," Connie said.

"It's too bad you two didn't get married."

"I know, and I don't know why we didn't, but we just didn't. Do you want to look through his stuff?"

"Not particularly."

"I tried putting the important things in a bag. Let me get it."

Connie eased out of the nook and went to a closet and opened it and took out a plastic bag that had the name of a supermarket on it. She brought the bag to the table and set it down in front of Dwayne.

"Photographs and things," she said.

Dwayne moved the bag aside. Connie slid into the nook.

"I should be able to pick up a copy of the death certificate," Dwayne said, "when I pick up the ashes. That's what the lady there told me. After that, I guess I'll go to the DMV and try to get the truck put in your name, or maybe my name, and then your name. After it's in my name, I can sell it to you for a dollar or something. I don't want the truck, or the trailer. They're yours. They should be."

Connie ground the nub of her cigarette out in the ashtray. Dwayne looked beyond Connie and saw Lana standing at the chain-link fence.

"There's something else," Connie said.

"Oh?"

Lana was looking through the fence. Her hair was shiny in the sun.

"There's a checkbook."

Dwayne looked at Connie. Connie reached for a pack of cigarettes.

"It's in Jack's name."

"Not a joint account?"

"That's right."

"How much is in the account?"

"A little over eight thousand dollars."

"Eight thousand dollars?"

"Yeah."

"What about an ATM card?"

"I've looked everywhere. I never saw Jack use one. I don't know if he had one."

"No ATM card?"

"That's what I said, isn't it?"

Dwayne's hands were on the table. He brought them together and inter-twined his fingers. Lana was still at the fence. Connie lit a cigarette.

"I never saw Jack use any plastic, credit cards or anything. He said they were trouble."

"I'll go to the bank with the death certificate and work on that too," Dwayne said.

Connie set her cigarette on the lip of the ashtray and slid out of the booth and went to a cupboard below the kitchen counter and got a half-gallon bottle of bourbon and brought it to the table and set it down. She slid back into the booth and uncapped the bourbon and poured some into her glass. Her glass wasn't empty. She was adding strength.

"You sure you don't want a drink?"

"No thanks."

Connie twisted the cap back on the bottle and then pushed the bottle along the tabletop to where it settled next to the window. Lana remained at the fence. Connie picked up her tumbler and swirled it a couple of times and then brought it to her lips and drank.

"Well," Connie said.

Dwayne was looking out the window but now his view shifted to Connie. She looked back at him.

"Oh, yeah," Dwayne said. "You can have the checking account too. That's yours too."

"After it's in your name," Connie said, "you know, the account and all, if you could slip me the cash on the QT, I'd appreciate it. That way it won't mess with the welfare I'm going to have to apply for."

"Sure."

Connie picked up her cigarette and brought it to her lips and inhaled. Dwayne looked out the window. Lana was gone from the chain-link fence.

"Jack really liked you, you know. He always said, 'Dwayne's a stand-up guy.'"

At the first motel he stopped at he was told, "The No Vacancy sign's on. It's just hard to see in the daylight." At the second motel it was eighty dollars a night. Down the road, in front of a mammoth casino, a sign flashed: Rooms $49!

The casino was nowhere near the Strip and Dwayne could almost see its clientele as he pulled into the parking lot—the elderly, along with those plying a trade in this growing municipality, service-sector employees mixed in like confetti. At night there'd be a country-and-western band perched above a bar and an open lounge area, a drummer and a couple of guitars, maybe a female singer. The music would be loud and no one would be listening. Sweat-stained cowboy hats and baseball caps would bob throughout the casino amongst those seeking quick fortune and cheap drinks. In a twenty-four-hour coffee shop there'd be a middle-aged waitress with a twang chasing her words, stick-to-your-gut food, and highway humor plentiful. Sushi would be absent, but Mexican fare was a possibility. Dwayne thought he might find a decent piece of berry pie in there.

He selected a smoke-free room. In the elevator on the way up, a man who must've weighed three hundred pounds asked how his luck was holding.

At the window of his room he looked out. The view was similar to the one in the trailer court, but now he was six stories above ground. The chewed hills to the east glowed with an orange tint. It was late afternoon.

The room was cold. He found the thermostat on the wall near one of the two beds. He turned the air-conditioning system off. Down the hall next to an ice machine he purchased a can of Diet Pepsi.

It was a clean room, efficiency its hallmark. He picked up the plastic bag containing his father's possessions and dumped the bag out on the bed closest to the window.

A dozen or so photographs of varying shades of age, a wristwatch, a pair of glasses, a wallet, a couple of documents, a rosary, a deck of cards, an Indian head penny, and a Zippo lighter lay in a queer pile on a pastel bedspread. Regarding the checkbook, Connie had handed him that separately to mark it as important. Dwayne popped the tab on his can of Pepsi.

On a night table between the two beds there was a telephone. He circled around. Below a drawer on the night table there was a shelf that held a telephone book, white and yellow pages. In the white pages, under the A's, he found what he was looking for. He pushed some buttons on his cell phone and brought the device to his ear.

～⌒

At sunset he took a walk and found that he could enter the desert without too much trouble. He was forty-one years old as of yesterday. A dry breeze tweaked his hair.

～⌒

The men were about halfway down the hallway and they were standing in front of an open door, three men in short-sleeve shirts, each man with a Styrofoam cup. It was the basement of a church, fluorescent tubing on the ceiling. The men were middle-aged and they were chatting, but they broke it off to look at Dwayne as he approached. One man said, "Hi." Dwayne said the same thing in return and went into the room.

At a table he put a dollar in an empty coffee can that held other dollar bills. He pulled a Styrofoam cup from a stack and filled the cup with coffee from one of the two coffee urns on the table. He added milk and sugar. While stirring his coffee he looked at the room's arrangement, which was a bit different than usual, but he had seen it before. Instead of all the chairs facing the front of the room, where there was a desk, the chairs in this room were divided into two groups, each group facing the other with a wide aisle between the two rowed groups, the front of the room to the right or left, depending. The chairs were folding chairs. Altogether there were about sixty of them, thirty in each group. About half were occupied.

Dwayne dropped his coffee stirrer in a trash basket and walked over and sat down in the first row, the front of the room to his right, the wide aisle at his feet. On the chair next to him he placed a thick book.

He sat and sipped his coffee and he found himself eavesdropping on a conversation that was in back of him. As he listened he tried to imagine the faces of the people. He could tell that there was a man and three women, the women bold and playful, the man humorous. The man was telling jokes, stories that were funny. But then something changed. There was a pause, and then Dwayne heard: "How are you?" This was from the man who had been joking, but now he wasn't joking. Another man, a new voice, said, "Fine." "Fine?" said the joking man who wasn't joking. "Yes." A pause, and then, "How long's it been since you've had a drink?" Another pause, and then, "Five days." "Well, that's how you are—five-days fine."

Silence followed. Dwayne could feel tension crawling up his back like a snake. He wanted to turn and look but didn't because he didn't want to draw more attention to the scene than had already been drawn. He sat and he sipped his coffee.

One of the women spoke. She spoke to the assertive man, the jokester. But now the woman's voice wasn't bold or playful. It was conciliatory. She asked the jokester about his work and he replied in an accommodating tone. With this exchange Dwayne understood that the man worked construction, a framer. Another woman joined in, and in this way the tension eased, yet there was the man who had been humiliated, and of him there was silence.

The men who had been standing in the hallway came into the room. One of them walked to the desk at the front of the room and set his Styrofoam cup down on the desk. The only other thing on the desk was a thick book. The man sat down. His hair was sandy and thin, and it was combed straight back. On each forearm there was a faded tattoo. His movements were deliberate. He said, "Let's begin."

Someone sat down on the chair to Dwayne's left. Dwayne was looking at the man at the desk, who was to Dwayne's right. Dwayne tried looking down and to his left without turning his head much. He saw a brown hand resting on denim. He sat a moment and then he turned and looked. It was Lana.

"My name is Dave and I'm going to read a passage from the Big Book."

She was in the first row in the section opposite Dwayne and Lana. She wasn't fat. She was big boned and tall, mid-thirties, and what marked her appearance was a dress that said she had come from an office. Her hair was shoulder length and brown, her eyes large. She wore glasses. Black pumps were on her feet.

Dave had finished with the passage from the Big Book, and it was that time when people commented about the passage, or about anything that came to mind. It was that time after the newcomers had stood up and had told the group that they were alcoholics or substance abusers. It was that time when comments and confessions and stories were thinning. It was that time when things were winding down.

"I always had sex when I was drunk. I've been dry for two and a half years and I haven't had sex during that time. I think I'm afraid of it. It scares me. But it's not just the sex. It's relationship that scares me. I want to have a relationship without drinking, a meaningful relationship. That's what I want, but it scares me."

She was standing and now she shifted her weight. Her look, speech, and demeanor suggested education, her clothing, a sophisticated office, perhaps law or finance.

"I haven't met anyone, but I've thought a lot about it. I know it's going to be frightening, if it ever happens. It's strange, because I want to meet someone, yet I'm afraid of it.

"I imagine the day when I meet someone, someone I want to go to bed with. That first time—that very first time having sex without alcohol—that's what's frightening.

"I can only imagine it. I go over it in my mind again and again and again, and I imagine so many different things. I look forward to it. I look forward to that day when I meet someone. I want to meet someone, but it scares me."

She stopped talking but she didn't sit down. She stood. And there were no comments because there was nothing anyone could say.

Someone clapped, then everyone clapped, then people got to their feet and then there were women with their arms around her.

"Your mother wants to have a ceremony."

Lana glanced around. The coffee shop wasn't busy. There was only one waitress.

"When I pick up the ashes, she wants to have a ceremony, maybe outside. That's what she told me."

It was a well-lit coffee shop, casino just beyond its open doors. Lana looked down at her coffee cup.

"I'm curious," Dwayne said.

Lana brought the cup to her lips. Her lips were big and flat, and they curled away from her mouth and smoothed out without any rise or plumpness. She wore no lipstick.

"Why don't you look at people when you speak to them?" Dwayne said.

The cup came away from her lips. She swallowed and set the cup down on the table.

"Navajo don't look at people when they talk to them. It's not polite."

"Navajo?"

"My father was Navajo. I grew up in my aunts' house. Two aunts, one house, four cousins. Mostly, that's where I grew up."

"On the reservation?"

"Yes."

Dwayne's pie was finished, boysenberry. He had judged it mediocre. Lana still had chocolate cake on her plate.

"You left the reservation and came here?"

"No. I was in a place near Santa Fe, up in the mountains. A church group. I was there for nearly four years."

Lana picked up her fork and used it on the cake. Dwayne watched her as she put cake in her mouth. She didn't look at him, but she didn't dissuade him from looking at her. After she set her fork down, she said, "Is my bicycle going to be okay in the back of your truck?"

"Sure. With the camper shell on no one's going to bother it."

"I bought the bike yesterday. Someone in the trailer park was having a yard sale. I think they always have a yard sale. They were asking twenty dollars. They took fifteen. It only takes about twenty minutes to bicycle to that church. I can go to the basement during the week and upstairs on Sunday."

"Good idea."

Lana began to scrape chocolate icing from the surface of her plate with the fork.

"Do you want another piece of cake?"

Lana set the fork down.

"The church group helped you?"

"Yes. I was lucky. They let me work in the kitchen. I could stay on. Room and board and work. I could earn a little money."

Dwayne picked up his cup of coffee.

"I was torqued out on crank, methamphetamine. I had to leave that environment. They offered me a chance."

"AA was there?"

"Yes. And there were meetings in town."

The waitress came to their table and refilled their cups. Dwayne said, "Thank you." The waitress winked, her eyes laden with cosmetics.

"What do you do?" Lana asked.

"I paint houses and do handyman work in Los Angeles."

"That's the same thing your father did, at least that's what my mom said."

"Coincidence. I certainly didn't pick it up from him. He left when I was seven."

"Coincidence?"

"The only thing I picked up from him was alcoholism."

Lana put sugar and milk in her coffee and stirred it.

"So you're going to live with your mother in that trailer with the bourbon and the cigarettes?"

"I'll get a job and I'll get a small trailer and I'll put it on a space near hers."

Lana sipped her coffee. Dwayne watched her. After Lana set her cup down she looked around. The waitress was across the way at a table, her one hand on her hip while her other held a coffee pot. Her uniform was pink and she had wide hips. She was jawing with an elderly man who wore a string tie.

"Maybe I'll get a job here," Lana said.

The suggestion of a grin rose on Dwayne's long face. He said, "You get a job here, you're goin' be fighting off the make-believe cowboys who come in for the breaded pork chops and mashed potatoes."

Lana's hand was on the table near her coffee cup. She raised her index finger but kept the rest of her hand on the table.

"They bother me, I'll tell 'em my big brother will scalp 'em."

Dwayne's grin lingered. "Do you have a big brother?"

"No. No brothers, no sisters. Least none I know of." Lana was looking to the side of Dwayne. "Do you have any brothers or sisters?"

"No. The last of my family I'm having burned up now."

Lana looked down at her coffee cup. She picked the cup up and brought it to her lips. Dwayne watched as the cup came away from her lips and as she set it back on the table.

"Do you want to do something?" Lana said.

"Do something?"

"In your room."

Dwayne tilted his head.

"I'll go to your room if you have condoms. If you don't, then I won't go up there." Lana was looking at a place to Dwayne's right.

"Do you have a fantasy?" Lana said.

"A fantasy?"

"A sexual fantasy."

Dwayne brought a hand up and adjusted his glasses.

"Lots of them."

"Tell me one."

Dwayne's eyes went left to right. His eyes were grey.

"There's a full-length mirror. I sit on a chair. You stand to the side of me and a little in front of me. You're facing the mirror, so I can see your front and back."

Lana was still looking to the side of him.

"And, ah . . ." said Dwayne, and trailed off.

"No 'and ahs,'" Lana said. "Just say it like the lady did."

Dwayne sat a moment and then said, "Your hand goes down to stimulate yourself. I watch. You look at the mirror. There's a lamp on, a small lamp. It's on the night table between the two beds. The full-length mirror is on the wall to the side of the room's windows. The curtains are open, so there's a view of lights twinkling in the desert."

"I don't have any clothes on, right?"

"That's right. And I don't have any clothes on either."

"Anything else?"

"That's the fantasy. We take it from there."

Lana brought her cup up and sipped her coffee.

"That's fine. Do you have any rubbers?"

"I think the sundries shop in the hotel here sells them."

"I'll wait here."

Dwayne looked at her, but she only looked to the side of him. Dwayne started to scoot out of the booth, but then stopped.

"This is great and everything, don't get me wrong. But I mean . . . I'm just curious. Where's this coming from?"

Lana was looking to the side of him and she spoke without inflection.

"So much damage. It's time for fun."

⌒

They drove northeast on I-15 and then took 169 east and entered Valley of Fire State Park and looked at reddish sandstone cut into odd shapes by the whims of tectonic movement and erosion. After they were done with that they drove on a lesser road and entered Lake Mead National Recreation Area. At Echo Bay they stopped and looked at a campground, and then they continued south and lost sight of the lake midst arid hills.

At an unmarked dirt track they turned off the pavement for no reason, except maybe boredom. As they crept along they remarked about a morning of bureaucracy—social assistance, banking, the DMV. Lana said, "My mother wanted to stop at a flower shop, but we didn't, because we didn't see one."

Dwayne said, "Who's driving the truck?"

"My mother."

"You should be driving."

"I know."

The dirt road led to Lake Mead but they stopped well short of that body of water. They got out of the pickup and looked at the lake from a vantage point of height and isolation. The lake, put there without trees or greenery, seemed an aberration. The eye couldn't explain it.

"Hoover Dam did this," Dwayne said.

Lana brought a hand up and shaded her eyes. "Why are you bothering with this?" Lana said.

Dwayne cocked his head. "Bothering with what?"

"My mother."

Dry air was on their arms and faces like a hot cloth.

"It's the right thing to do."

"It's a hassle," Lana said.

"With my mother, a year and a half ago, it was all set up—joint accounts and a living trust for the house—a smooth operation. But my being here isn't the question. The question is: Why'd you leave New Mexico?"

Lana shifted her weight. The hand shading her eyes came down.

"I was afraid to leave, but I knew that someday I'd have to. This seemed right, this seemed responsible." She paused, and then said, "Responsible— wanting to do the right thing, a sense of grown-up."

Dwayne went to the rear of the truck and opened the camper shell and got a beach towel out and returned to the front of the truck and set the towel on the bumper. They sat down.

"After you clean up there's this sense of responsibility," Dwayne said. "It's like you want to correct things, like you want to do it right." He paused, and then said, "But it doesn't mean anything unless you're giving something up. Somehow, responsibility isn't a comfortable deal."

Lana stood up and went to the cab of the truck and got a plastic bottle of water and came back and sat down on the towel and unscrewed the cap from the bottle of water and raised the bottle and drank. She handed the bottle to Dwayne and he drank, and then he took the cap from her and recapped the bottle.

"I feel something," Lana said. She was looking at the lake. "I brought that box of rubbers. You can lower your pants. I want to sit on your lap, and I want to see this view like that."

～♪

The table was a couple of sawhorses with a piece of plywood laid on top. Dwayne had hauled the makings out of a shipping container that his father had used as a shed.

"That's just the way he did it," Connie remarked. "That used to be his worktable. How'd you know?"

Across the wide expanse of Las Vegas the sun had dropped in back of a range of mountains, twilight lingering, but it was still hot. Assembled were Dwayne, Lana, Connie, Hank and Lorraine, and Roy. Hank and Lorraine were like Connie, elderly and with tobacco-stained fingers. Roy, mid-fifties, managed the trailer court. A potbelly bulged Roy's floral-print shirt, while a wristwatch with a quantity of turquoise flashed at his wrist.

On the table there was a metal box about the size of a cantaloupe, its color bronze. Dwayne had expected an urn but was handed the tin box by a Ms. Witt in her office on Paradise Road. A bouquet of flowers lay on the table near the box. Two votive candles on either side of the box flickered. Fortunately, there was no wind.

"Well, I guess we can begin," Connie said. She wore a cream-colored blouse with ruffles down the front and at the wrists. Clean jeans were on her legs. She waited, as if someone was supposed to reply.

Lorraine said, "Oh, yes. Let's begin."

"Well, I just want to say good-bye to Jack," Connie said. "He was a good man. He took good care of me. We met about ten years ago, maybe eight years ago, in Mesquite. We came down here and started a life. We went fishing at Lake Mead and ate the fish. We had a good time."

She paused.

"Maybe he wasn't president of the United States, but he was a good man, and I know God has a place for him in heaven, because that's where good men go. If someone else wants to say something, I think that would be nice."

Everyone shifted their weight. Lorraine nudged her husband. Hank cleared his throat and began to speak in a shrill voice.

"Yes, Jack Crown was a good man. He could fix most anything. Lorraine and me had Thanksgiving dinner with Jack and Connie last year. It was real nice."

Hank stopped talking. Everyone stood. Connie looked at Dwayne. Dwayne said, "Maybe we could have a moment of silence."

Connie said, "That's a good idea."

The moment of silence ended when Lana said, "Amen."

"Well," said Connie. "I think we ought to have a little drink for Jack. I think that'd be the right thing to do. Here, let me get you all a glass and the bourbon. Lana, could you give me a hand."

Connie and Lana went into the trailer. Dwayne went to his pickup and came back with two cans of Diet Dr. Pepper. The bourbon was poured. Dwayne handed Lana a can of Dr. Pepper.

~~~

"That was nice of you to give your father's ashes to my mother. It means a lot to her."

They were in Dwayne's pickup and they were headed for the Strip. Dwayne had asked Lana if she wanted to see some paintings by impressionists. There was a gallery with a collection in the Bellagio, and there was an Italian coffee shop just across from the gallery that served espresso coffees and pastry. Lana said okay, but she also said that she didn't know anything about art. Dwayne told her that there was nothing to know. "You just walk in and look at it."

While stopped at a traffic light that was going through a sequence of events in the management of traffic, four lanes in either direction, two streets crossing, sixteen lanes squared off like armies at a crossroads, Lana said, "Do you believe in coincidence?"

"Sure."

"What do you think it is?"

"If I knew what it was, it wouldn't be coincidence."

Lana laughed. Dwayne turned and looked. He wanted to see her laughing, he wanted to see her smiling. She didn't hide it. Dwayne saw short teeth along pink gums.

The light changed in their favor. They started moving. It was three in the afternoon.

"That man who runs the trailer court, Roy, he told me that he's got a double-wide for sale, or for rent, whichever. He said he picked it up cheap. He said he was willing to let it go cheap."

"I can't afford a double-wide," Lana said.

"He told me this while we were standing around after the ceremony. It was after I told him that I was a painter and a handyman. He said my father did the painting and handyman work for the trailer court. He said his brother runs a trailer court over in Henderson. My father did that work too."

"Did he offer you a job?"

"He said he's looking for a painter/handyman."

"What'd you say?"

"I took his card. I told him I'd tell him something in a week."

They turned onto the Strip and then they sat in traffic and looked at people on the sidewalk, shorts, sunglasses, and T-shirts, bottled water epidemic. Lana brought a hand up and fingered the lobe of her ear.

"What happened to your father?" Dwayne asked.

"He was killed in a car wreck on his way back to the reservation from Farmington."

After looking at impressionistic art they went across the way and sat in the Italian coffee shop and had cappuccino and pastry. Floral designs decorated the crockery.

"What did you think of the paintings?" Dwayne asked.

"I liked the colors."

"That's one of the things they're noted for."

Lana brought her cup up and took a sip.

"Do you like these fancy coffees, these espresso coffees?"

"Yes, I do," Lana said. "Do you?"

"Yes."

Lana's eyes roamed. The coffee shop was busy. While looking at people, who were engaged in conversation and coffee and pastry, she said, "I like the fantasy we do. Do you like it?"

"Yes, I do."

"I always want the truth," Lana said. "Fantasy is that."

Dwayne had a piece of a sweet roll in his fingers and was bringing it to his mouth, but now he stopped to listen.

Lana raised her cup and brought it to her mouth. Foam nudged her upper lip. She drew the cup away and swallowed. She lowered the cup carefully and set it on its festive saucer, her fingers leaving the cup, her tongue collecting the foam from her upper lip.

Portrait

Kirstin Valdez Quade

DELUVINA IS WRAPPING THE CHRISTMAS TAMALES AT THE KITCHEN table with Francisca and Maria Esperanza when there's a knock at the door. A tall Anglo about thirty-five years old stands on the step, smiling with straight teeth. His sandy blond hair, mussed by the cold December wind, is in need of a trim, and he hasn't shaved in a few days. If it weren't for the teeth—and the dusty Ford parked under the cottonwood, its engine still clicking as it cools—Deluvina might have thought he was on foot, begging food, passing through.

"Buenos días, Señora," he begins. "Por favor, tengo una pregunta para usted."

"I speak English," Deluvina says with some sharpness.

The man's face relaxes as his smile broadens.

"What is your question?" Her voice is hard and she stands firmly behind the screen door, sure he is selling something, encyclopedia subscriptions or vitamin supplements.

"I'm a photographer in the Farm Security Administration, a department of the Works Progress Administration."

So he's official. Deluvina straightens. She likes transacting business: waiting upright in the leather chair in the lobby at the Bank of Commerce, writing her monthly check carefully when she settles her account at Marcone's Grocery, tapping her pen as she fills out the rare telegraph form at the post office. She pushes the screen open enough to shake his hand, surprised by how large and bony it is. "I'm Mrs. Arellano. Pleased to meet you."

"I've been traveling around the country, documenting how people live. I was hoping you'd permit me to take some pictures of you and your home here. It wouldn't cost you anything, of course." He looks around the yard at the sheds and barn, at the horses in their pasture and the goats in the corral. "Is Mr. Arellano here?"

"Not now." Deluvina touches her hair, which she twisted into a hasty bun this morning. There is chile smeared on the bosom of her apron, on the hem of her skirt. Of all days. Still, excitement flares in her. She hasn't been photographed since her sister's wedding in Raton two years ago. "He's over there in the sierra checking the cattle." She gestures with her chin at the mountains, unties her apron, then pushes the door open farther and smiles up at him. "Will you have some coffee?"

Deluvina leads the photographer to the parlor, noticing he must stoop to pass through the doorway. It's chilly—the stove hasn't been lit since Sunday—and Deluvina opens the curtains, which she keeps drawn against the sun. Pale winter light stretches across the faded green velvet of the couch and the starched doilies she crocheted as a young bride.

"Please," she says, and gestures for him to sit. "Do you take milk?"

"Thank you, ma'am."

As she turns to leave, she sees that he is looking at the altar on the shelf above the cold stove. The statues of the Santo Niño, Sacred Heart, Blessed Mother, San Judeo. The framed picture of Christ. Deluvina is glad the candles aren't lit. She doesn't want him to think her superstitious, old-fashioned, extreme.

In the kitchen, Deluvina repins her hair, tugs at the ragged sleeves of her cardigan—her oldest.

"Who is it?" asks Maria Esperanza. She presses a spoonful of marinated meat into the masa, wraps the cornhusk expertly, all the while breathing heavily through her mouth.

"A photographer. He wants my picture." Deluvina takes down cups, saucers, tea plates—two of each—from the cupboard of her wedding china, arranges biscochitos on her mother's silver-plated dish.

"Why?" asks Francisca. She squints and cranes her neck as though she might see him through the wall.

"He's come a long way, so don't you go bother him."

She hears a low cough behind her and is dismayed to see the photographer in the doorway of her kitchen, stooped, hands braced against the thick plastered walls. "Hello," he says, smiling his charming blond smile at Francisca and Maria Esperanza.

"Please! The kitchen is a mess! I'll bring your coffee." Deluvina waves at the table and the hired women dismissively. "We were just preparing food for Christmas Eve. The maids were."

The photographer instead comes into the kitchen, straightens, and introduces himself. "I'm a photographer for the WPA."

When he says this, Francisca giggles, covering her big horsy teeth with a hand. The WPA is a joke here. Pronounced in Spanish *El Doble-V-P-A. El diablo a pie.* The devil on foot. Deluvina shoots Francisca a look that shuts her up, then explains the pun apologetically to the photographer.

"The devil!" He laughs a joyful, unrestrained laugh, as though it were a joke Deluvina made up herself, and Deluvina cannot help smiling.

"The devil in a Ford," she says almost shyly. The spots of color in his cheeks remind her of a child's on a cold day.

Without being invited—Deluvina still stands with the tray in her hand, ready to usher him back to the parlor—the photographer pulls out a chair and folds his long legs under the kitchen table.

He was born in Washington, D.C., he tells them. He has lived for six years in New York, making his living taking portraits. This is his first time out west. He accepts the coffee Deluvina places before him, drains the delicate china cup, eats one biscochito and then another. "Delicious," he says and smiles up at Deluvina. "I love New Mexico." He gestures around the kitchen with his large hand. "Nothing like this sky anywhere I've been."

Maria Esperanza nods solemnly as he speaks, and Francisca smiles behind her hand. Neither of them understands him, but he looks at each of the three women in turn. Deluvina remains standing by the hot stove, sweating at her temples and under her arms, impatient, thinking Maria Esperanza and Francisca should have the sense to go outside and feed the pigs.

He loves taking portraits, the photographer says, but he also loves landscapes. "Some pictures are just pictures, and some are art."

Deluvina has never heard a man talk about art before. As a girl, she was praised for her sketches: horses and botanicals and landscapes she'd never seen, copied from the books at school. Portraits, too. When she was ten she won an illustrated volume of *North American Birds* for a likeness she'd drawn of the pope. The book is in the parlor, her name in calligraphy on the bookplate, beside the Bible, an atlas, a dictionary of home remedies, and her grammar and algebra texts from school. She'd loved drawing: the steady, sure motion of her hand, images taking shape on the page.

When he has finished his third cup of coffee and eaten most of the biscochitos, the photographer pushes the plate away and turns to Deluvina. "So I have your permission to take some snaps?"

Deluvina is relieved. "Of course. We can move to the parlor."

While he gets his equipment from the car, Deluvina hisses at the girls to clean up the kitchen. She sets water boiling for the dishes, covers the bowls of meat and masa with cloths. She is carrying a bowl to the pantry when he returns to the kitchen with bags slung around his body.

"Stop," he says, and places his hand on Deluvina's arm. He squeezes just a little, looks at her with green eyes. They are gentle eyes, she thinks, and something loosens in her chest. He takes the bowl and sets it on the table as if it were an infant. He removes the cloth, folds it, and presses it into her hands. "Don't mind me. Just go about your business."

"The parlor—" she says, but her voice trails, because the photographer is unpacking a shining black enameled camera and setting it on legs.

"Go ahead," he says, gesturing to the tray of tamales. "Go on with your work. Don't let me interrupt you."

The photographer takes some photos of the kitchen, of the dried herbs hanging from the vigas, of Maria Esperanza and Francisca with their heads bent over the tamales. He's getting the lighting right, practicing. Deluvina excuses herself.

In the cold bedroom she changes her dress to her clinging navy velvet; it's not right for the day, but it's her best, dark and sensual. She brushes her hair until it shines, coils it and fixes it in place with combs. Powders her nose and chin. Licks her finger and smooths her eyebrows, dabs eau de cologne on the exposed skin above her breasts. In the dim afternoon light, her eyes look soft. She tilts her head, looks out from under her lashes, gazes at her reflection theatrically, then breaks into a grin, embarrassed.

For so long she feared she had wasted her beauty out here, so far from town, surrounded by pigs and goats, the hired women and her inscrutable children. And Eduardo, too serious and hardworking, his affections never enough to transport her from her life.

She thinks of them—the children at school, Eduardo on his horse, gazing at cattle—all her intimate knowledge of these people she lives with. The dingy stain Eduardo's head leaves on the lace pillowcase. The particular smell of her son's breath in the morning, no longer sweet, not yet foul. Ofelia, sturdy and bright, but so easily frustrated, so ready to cry over minor injustices. Gloria, whose breasts are developing unevenly, the left one swollen under her dress.

But now, before it's too late, before her beauty has faded full away, the photographer waits in the kitchen—a handsome man, a good man. Her eyes are bright in the mirror. Carefully Deluvina applies lipstick, blots it, gives her reflection a final brave smile.

Her good heels are loud on the plank floor, but she is floating.

She stands in the kitchen doorway. Deluvina and Maria Esperanza are still wrapping tamales, eyes trained self-consciously on their hands. The photographer is behind the camera, peering, adjusting shining knobs. His long body is stooped, his rump in khaki pants so close Deluvina could touch it. There is something boyish and young in the long line of his spine, something vulnerable that makes Deluvina want to wrap him to her.

Touching the doorway to steady herself, Deluvina half-smiles. Beauty swirls around her as she waits. He will retain his composure. He will lift his camera, capture her.

The flash of the bulb, like something breaking, startles her. The photographer straightens, turns—Deluvina smiles uncertainly—and he takes her in.

He shakes his head, gazes a moment longer. "You misunderstood. I don't want you to get dressed up," he says. "I want to photograph you as you are."

"This is me," she tells him.

The photographer is still a moment, then nods.

She feels her voice rise. "*This is me.*"

He bites his lip. "Okay," he says. "I'm just about finished here. Where would you like to be?"

Deluvina sits on the parlor couch, watching the photographer adjust the tripod, peer through the camera. Behind him Francisca and Maria Esperanza stand in the doorway, gazing at Deluvina in her heels and evening dress, hands trembling on her lap.

"Ready?" asks the photographer.

Deluvina nods. Her throat is tight, and it is an effort to stretch her lips into a smile.

Years later, when she is an old woman in Albuquerque, Deluvina is on her way to the bus from the public library. She is holding three books in her hands—fat romances that will keep her occupied when she isn't watching her stories or working crosswords. Deluvina has kept her figure, but no longer puts the same care into her clothes, no longer even plucks the three stiff

gray hairs under her chin. On days like today, though, when she goes downtown, she puts on lipstick, fixes her hair, and wears low heels.

She is thinking she will plant tomatoes next spring when she is caught by
the photograph in a gallery window: a taut-mouthed woman looks up from
stirring an enamel pot on a woodstove. Behind her, a dirty window, casing
unpainted, limp tatter of curtain over a twisted wire rod. Below the ragged
hair and lined brow, haunted grey eyes gaze out at Deluvina standing on
the street.

It is an exhibition of photographs taken by the WPA's Farm Security
Administration in New Mexico between 1935 and 1941. Deluvina feels cold
and nauseated. She pushes through the glass door and finds herself in a high-
ceilinged gallery space. The floor is blond wood; the lines are clean and white
and modern. Photographs, framed and matted, are arranged on the walls.

She pauses before each picture, transported to a stark black-and-white
world of poverty that she does not remember, though some of the accessories
are familiar. A man walks a dusty road alongside his horse. A child sits on a
sidewalk beside a dirty cloth piled with beans to sell. A woman whitewashes
her house. Deluvina feels the crack of drying lime on her knuckles.

The captions are descriptive, anthropological. Spanish-American woman stringing chile. Spanish-American woman peeling peppers. Spanish-
American woman stirring a kettle of soap by the *horno*. Not a single name.

None of the photos displayed are of Deluvina's home—she is relieved
and crushed—none are even of San Juan. Likely none of these was even taken
by her photographer, though she cannot be sure. Deluvina knows from the
pamphlet she holds that over ten thousand negatives were shot in those few
years by scores of photographers "documenting with a compassionate eye the
plights of those disinherited by America."

The faces refuse to release Deluvina as she makes her slow way around
the gallery. They seem dirtier, older, more worn than any she remembers
from those days. Nothing near as sharp and glinting as her memory of the
photographer who stood in her kitchen.

Deluvina spends an hour in the gallery, sickened and mortified, but
unable to leave. Her ankles feel heavy, her body thick and slow. When she
finally pushes through the glass door onto the sidewalk, she is startled by the
sun and the bright-colored city moving around her.

Even in the most difficult days of the Depression, even during the hard-
est period of her marriage when she left her bed to stand in the dark kitchen,
weeping into a dish towel, Deluvina had never felt the way those people looked.

Never had her suffering felt universal and emblematic, a hollow-eyed symbol of the times, reduced to black and white. It had always been simply hers.

They hadn't captured the truth at all, these photographs. They glossed over everything that comprised a life—the longing and pettiness, generosity and resignation—turned their subjects from people into myths. Spanish-American women wrapping tamales. They used to talk as they cooked, she, Francisca, and Maria Esperanza. Once in an afternoon lull, they sat around the kitchen table and sipped sherry from jelly jars, and Francisca made them gasp with laughter with a story about her blunt Aunt Felia berating the priest. For all her scorn for them, they'd been Deluvina's friends.

Only when she is on the bus with her purse in her lap—books stacked on the seat beside her, the bus churning through the hot metallic tide of rush hour, bearing her toward the little stucco house where she lives alone with the framed school portraits of grandchildren she sees once a year—only then does she allows herself to think of the photographer.

In the years after his visit, Deluvina often returned to the memory of that day. In the beginning, Deluvina felt misunderstood, humiliated because she knew he had humored her by taking her picture. But that passed, and gradually she almost forgot that the hired women had been present, almost forgot that he hadn't asked her to come away with him. She had thought so many times of his hand on her thigh, his finger under the band of her stocking, the press of him against her, that sometimes she could nearly believe it had happened.

It was dishonest, she knew, this revision of memory—and self-serving. But she allowed herself the indulgence, the way other women allowed themselves a jigger of whiskey at night, because it was secret, because, she told herself, it couldn't hurt.

Gradually it became a story she recited to herself about how she had chosen to stay—how from love and nobility, from self-sacrifice, she had given up her chance for art and escape and excitement to remain on the ranch, in San Juan, across the table from Eduardo.

Now, passing strip malls and car dealerships, Deluvina wishes she felt used, betrayed, outraged. But she doesn't. Instead, she is overcome by the knowledge that she has lost something—not the photographer, who she knew even at the time (or soon after, at least) was nothing. Her picture did not have to be among those on the gallery wall for Deluvina to know what it would have shown: a woman dressed in her shabby best in the middle of the day, sitting on a faded couch in a dim and roughly plastered room. A woman giving herself sad and pointless airs, a woman imagining she had a choice.

Baby Mine

Ron Savage

A BABY IS CRYING OUTSIDE KAYTA'S BEDROOM WINDOW. THE CRYING began fifteen or twenty minutes ago, something far off and insistent. I want to see you, it says. I am in the desert, it says. I am waiting, and I miss you. Kayta leans closer to the screened window. Stars and a half moon are in a clear dark sky. The desert becomes cool at night and has the clean smell of a beach. A breeze rushes over Kayta's face. She can feel the sand prick her skin. Sand scatters across the highway in front of Mr. Killian's ranch.

Kayta is Russian and a skyscraper of a girl, six feet eleven inches in her bare feet. She has thick stubborn brown hair that hides the tips of her ears. Before marrying Mr. Killian and coming to America, Kayta was a giant among the men and women of her village. Everything about her is big. Big broad cheekbones and forehead, big shapeless legs, big shoulders and hips, strangers stop and look at her. You must learn to ignore them, Blind Margo had said. That's what the villagers call her mother. Then Blind Margo said, There is nothing normal about this world. There is nothing everyday.

The crying won't quit. It's distant, breathy. Kayta is stretched out on her bed now and looking straight up at the shadows. The clean smell of the desert has an added lavender scent from the wooden bowl of potpourri on her nightstand. She is thinking, Who would leave their baby in a desert? What sort of mother? The crying rises through the night and the moonlight. It's carried by the desert breeze.

Her new husband, Mr. Killian, has given Kayta her own bedroom. There is a king-sized four-poster bed with a pink canopy. The length of the bed has been extended to accommodate Kayta's height. A burgundy Persian rug covers the pine floor. Pictures of America are on the walls, a bright Houston skyline, the Statue of Liberty in oxidized green, the Colorado River bending through the Grand Canyon, the presidents cut into Mount Rushmore, Old Faithful shooting water and steam into a cloudless sky at Yellowstone National Park, and the Golden Gate Bridge seen through fog and spanning the San Francisco Bay. Beside the window is a large copper telescope on a tripod. Mr. Killian has even bought her a teak wood desk and a computer.

Kayta cannot sleep. The crying outside her window is keeping her tense. Is the baby alone in the desert? Is it sick? Is it hurt? Her English is not good but it is good enough to read newspaper stories and put together the pictures and the words on the TV news. She knows that people can do many different things to babies. Kayta's Viktor was eight months old when he left her. Left her, as if he packed a suitcase. Left her, as if Kayta was a child instead of his mother and Viktor didn't want to play anymore. She imagines he might come back should she promise him a better deal. Chocolate pudding twice a week. A more cheerful room. A CD player for stories and lullabies. Blind Margo had to buy the small wooden casket. Kayta wouldn't go to the funeral, either. She didn't want to see the dark hole in the ground or Viktor's wooden casket lowered into the shadows. Kayta had dreamed about the cemetery men with their unshaven faces and their rolled-up sleeves and their shovels. In her dream she had watched them smoke cigarettes and joke, tossing the dirt, hiding everything that mattered.

I've always been blind, Blind Margo will say this to anyone who wants her service. She will say, I tell futures not fortunes. Many people in the village go to her for guidance and don't care if she is blind. They don't care what she chooses to call what she does. Future or fortune, they say, do your business. Blind Margo is a short woman with thick ankles and small feet. Her husband died five years ago from stomach cancer and her grandson died last year from influenza. She is religious and still wears black and recites her prayer for the dead twice a day. Her graying brown hair is fixed in a long braid. A few strands stick out and catch the sunlight. Blind Margo will also say, Whether you see your future as fortunate is up to you. She likes giving an example from her own life. Blind Margo knew she would have a big ugly child months before Kayta was born but big ugly Kayta has a sweet disposition and that is a blessing. Do you see what I mean? Blind Margo says. A big ugly child can bring good fortune. Mother and daughter live in the village of Zov'kiv which is 115 kilometers northwest of Odessa. Seventy-six other people live in Zov'kiv and they all know Blind Margo. Most of these people have gone to her more than once. They swear by what she tells them, and they recommend her to people from other villages. What people say is this, Blind Margo can predict a future by feeling the bones in your hands.

The crying is a tiny sound. It's an on-again off-again sound. Kayta thinks, Maybe there are animals in the desert who come out at night and cry like babies. Kayta can't relax herself enough to sleep. She is lying in her extended king-sized bed and watching the shadows under the canopy. Kayta isn't sure if Viktor died of influenza or has followed her to America. The people of Zov'kiv believe babies are spiritual and have their own agendas. Maybe Kayta's Viktor has decided to join her and her new husband, Mr. Killian, in Lubbock, Texas, America. The land of the free. Anything is possible, Blind Margo likes to say.

I know I am much older than you, Mr. Killian said to Kayta in his first letter. He was responding to an ad Blind Margo had dictated to her friend Antosha. Antosha has a cousin who lives in Odessa and owns a computer. The ad was for Kayta, and Antosha's cousin put the letter on the Internet. The ad did not include a photograph. After three months of letter writing, Mr. Killian rented a jet and flew to Russia. Kayta was twenty-six then. Mr. Killian told her he had a young soul and loved tall wide-hipped women and that his cattle ranch in Lubbock was bigger than Zov'kiv.

Last Tuesday evening Kayta and her new husband celebrated his eighty-sixth birthday with a chocolate cake and presents. Later Mr. Killian took a pill and Kayta and her new husband had careful sex. You are a very experienced man, Kayta whispered. She and her new husband have been married for almost a year. Mr. Killian said how much he loved her wide hips. He is small and bony with white skin and no hair or at least no hair that Kayta has noticed. He smells of oranges and mothballs. Mr. Killian's bedroom is next door to Kayta's. He goes from bedroom to bedroom in a chrome and gray leather, electrical wheelchair. That Tuesday night Mr. Killian pressed the fleshy side of her waist between his thumb and forefinger and said she had no fat on her body. Kayta thanked him and said, Your body is like a smooth pebble at the bottom of a stream. Mr. Killian can say hello in Russian, *Privet*, and you are very beautiful, *Vy ochen' krasivy*. That same Tuesday night Mr. Killian told Kayta that her sweat smelled of licorice and that he loved licorice. Kayta thanked him again and smiled and nodded. She waited until Mr. Killian had climbed into his chrome and gray leather wheelchair and left the room before she looked up the word *licorice* in her English-Russian dictionary.

The first man didn't love her, Blind Margo says to her old friend Antosha. They sit in front of an empty fireplace on wood chairs that have burlap cushions. Her home is one room with gray stone walls and a blue-and-white throw rug over an oak floor. The room smells of last winter's ashes that haven't been swept from the fireplace. Blind Margo says, It's Kayta's size that frightens them, these men. Kayta's size makes the men feel like children. The first man climbed on my Kayta and gave her a baby and ran away. This was no man. This was a boy, a child.

That's the way boys are, Antosha says. What can you do? When I was a boy I couldn't leave the girls alone.

Antosha lights a cigarette and shakes his head. He shuts his left eye to avoid the rising smoke. Antosha has thick eyebrows and thick gray hair that goes its own way. He is a farmer with a farmer's face. Weather and cigarettes have creased his skin at the forehead and the cheeks and the corners of his eyes. Dark, tough skin. His hands are the surprise. Blind Margo has felt the hard calluses on his palms from the farming but she has also felt his long delicate fingers. The first time she touched his hands she said, What do you play? What instrument? Antosha told her the fiddle. In those days he farmed during the morning and played the fiddle at home in the evening. Sometimes people would ask him to play the fiddle at a wedding or a dance.

A small round wood table separates Blind Margo and Antosha. Centered on the table is an oil lantern and the flames are a deep yellow. Light and shadows wobble across the stone walls and the wood beams of the ceiling.

I don't know Kayta's future, Blind Margo says. Why is that? I tell futures, and my daughter's life is a mystery.

Futures are better told to strangers, Antosha says.

I knew my Kayta needed an older man, Blind Margo says. That much I knew. Young men are too crazy.

Antosha's cigarette is in the corner of his mouth. He inhales and releases the smoke then picks a tiny flake of tobacco from his tongue with his thumb and forefinger. He says, Don't kid yourself. Older men are crazy, too.

I had to buy the baby's casket, Blind Margo says. She reaches out and Antosha lets her grasp his hand, the hard calluses, the long delicate fingers. She can smell his scent. He smells of tobacco and pine from the forest. Blind Margo says, My Kayta won't let go of the baby. She didn't go to Viktor's funeral. She didn't cry, not a tear. You would think a mother would go to her baby's funeral.

Viktor is gone and buried, Antosha says.

In the ground, yes, Blind Margo tells him. In my Kayta's heart, no.

~~⌒

The baby's crying comes and goes. There are huffy gasps between the sobs. Kayta can barely hear the baby. This crying comes in through the open screened window on a breeze. Kayta thinks, The baby must be sick. Or afraid. If I were alone in the desert I would be afraid. What sort of parent would do such an awful thing?

An electrical whirring noise moves down the hall outside her room. It's too loud, too disruptive. Not now, Kayta thinks. She is lying in the four-poster bed and looking up at the shadows under the pink canopy. Even with the king-sized bed's extended length Kayta's bare feet hang over its edge. Her heavy long arms and legs, her wide hips and big shoulders, shrink everything around her. She wishes her new husband would sleep at night like other old men. Can't you stay in your bedroom? she thinks. Can't you let me have a moment? I want this night to myself. Mr. Killian's wheelchair has stopped its whirring noise outside her closed door.

The baby's crying starts again. Or maybe she can hear the cries now that the wheelchair's electric motor is quiet. Kayta imagines the baby on its back with its hands and feet twitching in the cool desert air. It would have perfectly shaped hands, perfectly shaped feet. Babies are so tiny. They are like miniature old men. Kayta loved playing with Viktor's hands and feet. She would look at them and touch them and kiss them.

There is the metal-on-metal sound of a key slipping into the lock. A click and turn. Her new husband guides the electrical wheelchair into the room and parks himself beside her king-sized bed. She can smell him, the oranges and the mothballs. The moonlight is silver across the burgundy Persian rug and the pine floor. Mr. Killian locks Kayta's bedroom door at night. We must protect you from the desert animals, Mr. Killian says. The desert animals can sneak into your room, he says. Kayta doesn't believe that. She believes her new husband locks her door to keep her from leaving and going into the desert.

Where's the baby's mother? Kayta is thinking. Some women should never be allowed to bring babies into the world. Some women need to wear a sign around their necks that says, Don't marry me. I would be a dangerous mother. The baby's crying seems weaker now, as if the desert is taking its energy, its life. I want to see you, it says. I am in the desert, it says. I am waiting, and I miss you.

Kayta has opened one eye just enough to see Mr. Killian. He is removing his white terry cloth robe. Mr. Killian is naked. He climbs out of the chrome and gray leather wheelchair and onto her bed. His body has no hair and his skin is a smooth pink. Kayta feels him crawling on top of her. He weighs nothing. Mr. Killian isn't much more than little bones and a bald head. Kayta doesn't know whether to brush her new husband away or offer Mr. Killian her breasts and let him feed until he is full and sleepy and ready to let her alone.

Blind Margo is sleeping on a narrow mattress beside the gray stone fireplace. She sleeps in her black dress and stockings. The nights are cool in Zov'kiv, and the fireplace has warm red ashes that bring light to the room. The mattress is wrapped in a dark blanket and smells of sour milk.

How do the blind dream? The villagers want to know.

I dream with what I have, Blind Margo tells them. There are no colors, she says. But I have what my fingers and skin feel, the temperatures, the people and the things in my life. There are fragrances and voices and the shapes without faces.

Tonight Blind Margo is dreaming about her Kayta. Blind Margo feels the warmth of the sand on her bare feet and the cool desert air on her face. She can hear the sound of an owl, and its call is distant and repetitive. This place has the smell of an Odessa beach but without the water of the bay. Kayta has written many letters from Lubbock, Texas, America. Antosha has read these letters to Blind Margo. Kayta's letters are about her new husband and his ranch and the desert. There are letters about food, hamburgers with cheese and lettuce and tomatoes, French fries with salt and vinegar. Kayta writes how she misses Zov'kiv and her Viktor. There are many letters about Kayta's Viktor. Blind Margo doesn't understand why Kayta didn't cry or go to Viktor's funeral. What mother doesn't feel heartache when her child dies? The sound of the owl has become a baby's cry. The baby is close, Blind Margo knows it, so very close. She hunches down. Her hand begins feeling the warm sand around her. Blind Margo shifts one foot forward then the other. Her small heavy body tilts back and forth like a duck. She inhales a quick breath as her fingers touch and envelope the baby's arm.

Kayta pretends to sleep while Mr. Killian locks her bedroom door from the hallway and begins guiding his electric wheelchair back to his own room.

She is up right away, pulling off the window screen, climbing out onto the roof of the front porch. Kayta shuts her eyes tight and jumps. The loose ties of her pink silk bathrobe flap and twist in the fall. Her right shoulder and right hip strike the ground hard enough to make tiny white flashes behind her eyes. The air has an electrical stink like Mr. Killian's wheelchair when the motor goes bad. Kayta is sure she will faint but hears the baby crying somewhere on the desert side of the highway. Wind swirls sand over the porch and sidewalk. Sand stings her face and her bare legs. A burning pain in her right hip won't let her run. She settles on a fast limping walk. Headlights from passing cars and trucks shine on her then glare down the road and into the night. What must the drivers imagine when they see me? Kayta thinks. A big monster woman with her pink silk robe and her big bare feet, what must go through their minds? Look at her, they say. Look at those big arms and those big wide hips and those legs that are too white and too thick and don't seem to end. Then Kayta thinks, Do they know I am trying to find a baby left in the desert?

Blind Margo is dreaming about holding a baby in a desert. The sun has made you sick, she says to the baby. You must have been here a long time, she says. In the dream the baby is lying against her left arm. Blind Margo is touching the baby's face with her fingertips. She must paint her dream for new objects to show themselves. As Blind Margo touches the baby, a dark silhouette of its face appears. The air is cool, and wind rushes warm sand over her bare feet. Blind Margo lowers her head and puts her cheek to the baby's face. I can feel the heat on you, Blind Margo says. I can feel the way your heart is working. A baby's heart shouldn't work that hard. The baby smells of urine and feces. Its thin body quivers. A terrible sadness swells inside the old woman's chest. Blind Margo says, What will you do with your future, Kayta? What fortune will you make of this?

The baby and Kayta are inside Boedy Dorsey's truck. Kayta's new husband likes to sit on his porch and wave to the passing trucks, and the trucks honk back twice. Mr. Killian would say that Mr. Dorsey's truck is an eighteen wheeler. The Big Boy, Mr. Killian calls it.

Five minutes ago Kayta was standing in the center of the highway with a sick baby in her arms and daring Boedy Dorsey's Big Boy to run her and the baby down. Go on and do it, Kayta thought. We will be in a better place than we are now. Instead of running her down Mr. Dorsey stopped his truck and wanted to know what a woman and a baby were doing in the middle of the road at night. Then he called University Medical in Lubbock on his cell phone and said he was bringing them a real sick baby and the biggest mama he had ever seen.

The baby is stinking so bad that Mr. Dorsey turns off the air-conditioner in the cab and rolls down his window and tells Kayta to roll down her window too. Mr. Dorsey wears a red baseball cap with a white P in the front. He has fat gray sideburns and a mustache down to his chin and a stomach that presses against the black steering wheel. He is chewing bubble gum, or that's what it smells like to Kayta.

What's wrong with your baby? Mr. Dorsey says. He is looking at the road.

It's not my baby, Kayta says and feels the tears swell and fuzz her vision. The baby is still crying, breathing funny. It has a red sunburned face, arms, and legs. Its bottom lip has a puffy yellow blister. Kayta kisses the baby's forehead and says, Shh, quiet now.

Don't you worry, Mr. Dorsey says. Then he says, That University Medical is real good. They'll know what to do for your baby.

It's not my baby, Kayta says again and starts to cry but the crying has no noise. Her big white legs are pressed to the dashboard like Mr. Dorsey's stomach. She tucks her pink silk robe about her chest with a free hand. I found the baby in the desert, Kayta says. Can you imagine? What mother leaves her baby in a desert? What was she thinking?

I bet you're a fine mama, Dorsey says.

Kayta holds the baby close and remembers her Viktor. She touches her wet cheek and rubs the tears between her fingers and thumb. Kayta wants to tell Mr. Dorsey that this isn't her baby but she had a baby and she didn't want to see his casket go into the ground. Kayta wants to tell Mr. Dorsey that she was a good mother and her Viktor was a good baby.

The highway has no traffic and the sky is bright and clear with a half moon and many stars. The thought of traveling occurs to Kayta. She shuts her eyes and sees the pictures on her bedroom wall, the Houston skyline, the Statue of Liberty in oxidized green, the Colorado River bending through the canyon, the presidents cut into Mount Rushmore, and the Golden Gate Bridge. This is a Texas night, and she is in America.

Drought

Roz Spafford

WHEN IT STOPPED RAINING FOR GOOD, HE STARTED CARRYING A GUN. She didn't understand.

"Why do you need to take that thing?"

"Rattlers," he said, tipping his hat to her as if they were in a goddamn movie, and rode off.

But there had always been rattlers. He had not always carried a gun, in the holster he had made himself. He had not always carried a folding shovel behind his saddle.

He could make anything with his hands—repair a stirrup, mend a saddle blanket, set her gasping in the night, so loud she pressed her face into the pillow so as not to wake the baby. Though that had dried up along with the land. She didn't like to think of the gun—cold, black, heavy—in those hands.

The baby was whimpering—how long had she been awake? Chrissie went to get her—she was soaked—the sheets were soaked. More laundry. But at least the wet was still warm, and at least she still wet—so she was getting enough milk. Chrissie picked her up, set her on the changing table. The little cracks in the plastic pad were widening, but she couldn't replace it. The baby, Matilda after her grandmother, had learned to flip over and then to sit up, so Chrissie kept one hand on her while she reached for a diaper, a sleeper, a sweater. It was getting chilly. What would they do when it froze?

She put the baby down in the playpen so she could start stew. The meat would take all day to soften up. Matilda wailed, then stopped abruptly, watching the ribbons of light come through the blinds. Of light there was plenty.

The beef in the stew had disintegrated to ropy shreds when he came home, well past Matilda's bedtime, the fall evening having closed to dark long ago. He started to unload the gun, then asked, "Baby asleep?" When she nodded, he hung the holster up on a hook.

"Dinner?" she said, chilly.

"Sure." She reheated the corn bread in a frying pan with a little bacon grease. He smelled like whiskey, sharp and sweet, and he sat in his own dusk, staring at his hands. There was blood on his right shirt sleeve.

"What did you do to yourself?" Barbwire, she thought, but the sleeve wasn't torn.

"Nothin."

She watched him eat the stew in silence, trying not to twist her hands in her lap.

"How are things?" she asked, finally.

He shrugged. His neck had reddened, even in the thin November sun, and his shoulders stayed hunched halfway to his ears.

She counted to thirty, one hundred, five hundred, and then got up to put the stew away.

"We're out of everything," she said, looking in the fridge. "We need milk."

He grunted something that might have been yes.

The next day he put on a dress shirt she had ironed while the baby napped, and took the truck to town. Chrissie had almost given up speaking, except to the baby; she said only "Please remember milk. We've got to have milk."

Her own milk seemed thinner, more blue than white—she tried to remember to eat, but food stuck in her throat and the water tasted more and more like stone as the level in the well dropped. Usually when she went up to run the pump, she could see the sun glinting off the surface, would splash herself pulling up a bucket for a drink, but now she could count the seconds a stone took to fall in, and she had to ask Clay to add a length of rope to the bucket. Soon they would have to shut down the pipes ahead of the freeze and she would have to carry water, the baby and water, down the rocky path from the well to the house, then heat water on the stove for diapers. They couldn't afford to buy water. Nor formula: so she couldn't let her milk dry up.

He came back from town with a freezer in the back of his truck, a grim smile set on his face.

"What's that?" she said. "We can't afford that."

"Can't afford not," he said, and rolled it off the track down a ragged ramp, heaving it into the corner of the barn.

"How did you pay for it?

"Credit at Central Commercial. Vultures at the bank say if they start giving second loans to every rancher in the county, they'll dry right up. But Central has feed, too. We'll need it."

This being the longest sentence Clay had said in some weeks, Chrissie held her breath. But as he seemed disinclined to say more, she said, "How will we pay it back?"

"Cross that bridge," he said.

She went down to the barn and looked into the freezer, square and blank as death.

"We'll need to put a lock on it when Mattie learns to walk," she said to his back as he sat at the table.

"Yep," he said. He had changed his shirt and was eating some cold stew.

"I would have heated that for you."

"It's OK."

"Where are you off to now?"

"Still trying to move the cattle down." They had a winter pasture where it didn't snow, though "pasture" was hardly the word for the cracked land, speckled with creosote and cactus, just a few tufts of grass along the rim of the sand wash. Nothing grew deep; a layer of caliche under the topsoil kept what rain there was from soaking in. Still, in a good year, cattle could winter here. But now, with the drought—now they would have to ship those that could walk as far as the corral by the highway.

Clay had maybe waited too long to move the cattle—but there had been a little water in the mountain pastures, none in the desert.

"Can't you get help?"

"Can't pay."

"Bill Logsdon would come. You've done enough for him."

"I'm only finding two, three at a time, all day long. If they can walk, only takes just me to herd 'em on down."

"If they can't?"

Clay just looked at her. From the bedroom, Matilda started to wail.

"Could you get her for a sec? I was just going to the garden."

He nodded, and Chrissie took the pan of rinse water from the dishes outside, trying not to spill any on the stone steps. She poured a cupful on each carrot plant, still waving hopeful lacy fronds in the breeze, and promised the squash she'd be back. Maybe she could blanch the carrots and freeze them, so they wouldn't have to buy so many vegetables in the winter. The squash would hold outside till it froze, then inside for a couple of months.

Later that afternoon, while Mattie drowsed, she risked a shallow bath.

She plugged the empty tub, kneeling on the cold porcelain, and washed her hair under the tap with a thimbleful of Dr. Bronner's—she hated the mint smell, with its false cheer, but it didn't hurt the plants and the garden was still dry. A little soap got in her eyes, and for the rest of the night, they were so dry she felt as though she had been crying.

Clay came home on time, still silent but a little less rigid. When she asked him how the cattle were, he said, "the same." She had made shepherd's pie from the stew, burying it in mashed potatoes. Worrying about her milk, she was trying Mattie on a little solid food and the mashed potatoes would do. Maybe she could mash squash and freeze it, so they wouldn't have to buy that baby food in jars.

After dinner, she washed the dishes in just a couple of inches of water, still feeling guilty about the bath. If she had run the well down, silt would discolor the water for days, and she would have to drain the water heater to wash diapers.

Clay had untangled Mattie from her high chair and was waltzing her stiffly around the living room, humming "The Streets of Laredo." When he handed her to Chrissie, his eyes were narrow, perhaps wet. "I just want to do right by her," he said. "I just want to do right."

That night, she wore her summer nightgown to bed, and when Clay turned away from her as usual, she rubbed his clenched shoulders.

"Please, honey," she said.

"We can't," he mumbled into the pillow.

"I'm safe," she said.

"Nothing is safe," he said.

When Clay rode home the next day, he went straight to the barn, coming up to the house an hour later. He must have washed in the horse trough; his chest was bare and his boots splashed with water.

"Where's your shirt," she said. "I'll wash it."

"Soaking," he said. "I'll wash it in town," he said. "We can't spare the water."

"Can we spare the money?" she said.

"More money than water. Pack up them diapers, too."

"You don't have to do that—we could come with you if you're driving."

"Won't kill a man to wash some diapers."

In the morning she sent him off with the diapers in a pail, bundles of sheets like the round segments of a snowman, two pairs of his Levi's in a pillowcase. "Wash everything on hot," she said. "It needs it."

Once the sound of his truck died down, she wound a long shawl she had made around her chest and shoulders and tucked the baby into it against her chest, knotting the ends around her waist. She walked into the barn quietly, as if someone were watching, and peeked in the freezer. It was layered half-full with steaks and roasts, awkwardly wrapped in wax paper, even a liver in a plastic bag.

The next night he came home at sunset but stayed down at the barn until long after the moon rose, casting a cold eye on the barnyard. She waited up, shivering, a sweater over her nightgown. He came in and sat down at the table across from her.

"Are we to eat our own, then?" she said, finally.

"You'd rather they died for nothing?"

"You can't save them?"

"Christine I have been carrying calves across my saddle to water and when I get them there, they can't stand up to drink. I have poured water from my own canteen into their mouths and they are too played out even to swallow. I can't save anything."

She put her hand on his hand, running her thumb along his blood-rimmed cuticles. Her mouth was dry. They sat, as if frozen, listening to the wind.

The Last Day of the Boom

JUSTIN ST. GERMAIN

WE'D BEEN TALKING ABOUT WHAT WE WOULD DO IF WE WON THE LOT-tery, Ricky and Choobies and me. The Powerball was up to a couple hundred million dollars, so all of our parents and everybody at the Wheel and just about every other loser in Tombstone had bought tickets, thinking they might hit it big and finally get the hell out of town. After work, Ricky used his fake ID to buy us some tickets and a thirty-pack, even though the lady behind the counter at Circle K knew he wasn't twenty-five and his name wasn't Maurice and he'd never seen Pennsylvania and he must have stole the license from some tourist, which he had.

"Tell you what I'd do. I'd buy a new motorcycle," Ricky said, kicking gravel towards the old Yamaha sitting in the corner of the yard with a hole where the carburetor should have been. Ricky's place was way up near the top of Skyline Hill, so we could see the whole town. We'd watch the cars, counting as they passed the Circle K lights on the far end and took the highway through town, past the motels and past the palm trees out front of the high school and finally past the sign that told you it was thirty more miles to Bisbee, until their taillights disappeared over the rise. It took about a minute and a half if they weren't speeding.

"You could just pay me for that one," Choobies said. He'd sold the Yamaha to Ricky for three hundred bucks a year ago, but Ricky sucked water through the carb trying to cross the gulch after a monsoon, and of course he never paid.

"I'd buy the whole town," I said. "So I could burn it." It wasn't true. I didn't hate Tombstone, even though I knew I was supposed to. We didn't mean a lot of the things we said; it was like we were practicing.

"Wouldn't be the first time," Ricky said, and then he did his tour guide voice: "After the Campbell and Hatch's fire in 1881, the town had burned to the ground twice in two years. But the town folk rolled up their sleeves and built again . . ."

Ricky had worked at the Historama for a month, taking tickets for the show. Ever since, he liked to get drunk and retell the stories about Ed Schieffelin and the Gunfight at the OK Corral, as if he was the only one who grew up hearing all that shit. You couldn't walk down the boardwalk without running into a sign telling who got killed there and when and who did the killing.

"I won that money, I'd be long gone by the time anybody heard," Choobies said. "I'd send you guys a postcard from Hawaii." He hit the heel of one hand off the other so it looked like a rocket taking off.

I walked over to where Ricky was sitting on the low stone wall and bummed a cigarette and a light off him, then went back and sat next to Choobies on his truck's tailgate. Nobody said anything for a while and I knew it was about time to go home, since I had school in the morning, but I didn't feel like leaving just yet. It was a pretty nice night, with the full moon sitting up in the sky shooting out light so it hurt to look at it, like a chrome hubcap on a sunny day. We could see the whole thin road that ran up one side of Skyline, past the chain-link cages that covered the mine shafts, then past Ricky's driveway near the top and back down the other side into town. If the cops showed up, we'd see them in time. So I was glad when Choobies went and turned on the stereo in his truck, then grabbed us each another beer from the cooler on his way back, because it meant we'd be sticking around a while longer. He put on a Mexican station. The sound of trumpets came out the windows.

"What'd your mom want when she called?" Ricky said. "She sounded upset."

"Bet she wanted to know when I was coming over," Choobies said, flicking the tab on his can. He always wisecracked about how he wanted to bang my mom.

It took me a second to remember what Ricky was talking about. I was draining the deep fryer at the Wheel when Ricky walked into the kitchen and told me my mom was on the phone. I meant to tell them about it right away, but we were closing up the restaurant and we were all in a hurry to get out of there, and I still had to finish cleaning the ice cream machine. I forgot all about it myself until he brought it up.

"I guess a letter from Eastern came in the mail."

"Was the envelope fat or thin?" Choobies held his hands together and pulled them apart to show how fat he meant.

"She didn't say. Wants me to open it myself." I'd been picturing a thick envelope made of heavy, official paper, but after he pressed his hands together it shrank in my mind.

"Well, if it's fat, that means you got in for sure," Choobies said, rubbing the hair on his upper lip. He was a year younger than me, three years younger than Ricky, but he was half Mexican, so he could almost grow a mustache.

"How the hell would you know?" Ricky said.

"Better than you. At least I'm going to graduate high school," Choobies said, pointing a thumb inward at his chest.

"I would have graduated if they'd let me do work study," Ricky said. I didn't say anything. There was no harm letting him think it, even though he'd been fired from most of his jobs before he even got a paycheck, much less school credit.

"You gonna go?" Choobies asked me. He rubbed his palms against his greasy jeans.

"What else would I do?" I thought of the smell that stuck to my clothes after working in the kitchen, like somebody put out a mesquite fire with a bucket of grease. Sometimes I didn't get hungry for a whole day after seeing all that bloody meat everywhere. I couldn't do that for the rest of my life. If I did all right at Eastern, I could transfer to a real university in a couple of years.

Choobies walked over to the edge of the yard and looked out at the town. His jaw worked like it did when he was thinking, and it made his cheeks puff out even more than usual. That's how he got his nickname—his real name was Chris—because he was a porker all through grade school and he was always chewing on the insides of his mouth. Made him look like an over-grown baby, like the kind of kid you'd call a name like Choobies.

"But it's *Thatcher*," he said. "Nothing but Mormons and cow shit up there."

He was right about that. I'd seen the campus when we went to play Thatcher High in football, and the place didn't have a hell of a lot going for it. It was only a junior college. But I didn't exactly expect Stanford to come knocking—like my guidance counselor said, college is college.

"What would you guys do?" I asked.

"I don't know, man. I just couldn't leave all this," Choobies said, holding his stubby arms out toward the town. "I'd miss it too much." He was being a wise ass, but a little part of me agreed with him anyway.

Ricky kicked his dirty white sneaker across the gravel.

"What about you?" I said to him.

His head shook. "It ain't my choice to make." He paused. "I'm not leaving, that's for sure. Not now." I wanted to ask what he meant by that, but I knew he'd tell us if he wanted to.

"Sarah's pregnant," he said. The moon was above his head, and I half expected it to fall right on him.

"You're shitting me," I said. Ricky shook his head again and smiled tight and thin. He smiled a lot when things went wrong in his life, whenever his Tempo broke down or he got fired again, but this time he looked different, kind of sick. His teeth stuck out from his mouth like the fangs on a javelina.

"Been meaning to tell you for a few days. Guess I was waiting for a good time."

I still hadn't really swallowed the idea when Choobies chimed in from beside me.

"Well, it ain't mine. Scout's honor." He held up three fingers and laughed. He'd dated Sarah for a couple weeks freshman year, before Ricky, and I guess he thought it was funny. His laugh petered out as his face moved from me to Ricky. Choobies had a knack for cracking wise at the worst possible times. Sometimes when he would say shit like that to his dad, I'd hear the yells from my house, all the way across the street.

"Is she sure?" I asked.

"Yeah, pretty sure. Her sister bought her a pregnancy test. It turned blue." His head hung dark below his shoulders. I couldn't see his face. It seemed like his words were coming from somewhere else than his mouth, like from the sky, maybe.

"Congratulations, man," I said. Choobies said the same. Neither of us meant it, and we all knew it. But it was what we were supposed to say. We knew how it worked.

I scraped rust off the tailgate and rubbed it between my fingers until they turned a shiny brown. Choobies threw pebbles at the "No Dumping" sign by the road with the middle blasted out by a shotgun round. Ricky drank the rest of his beer and threw the can in the bushes.

"What are you planning to do?" I asked.

"We sure as hell ain't getting married, if that's what you mean."

"You're going to keep it?" Choobies blurted.

Ricky lit a cigarette, sucked the first drag in deep, and pointed it at Choobies. "What the fuck do *you* think? You know Albert." Smoke leaked out his mouth as he talked. Sarah's dad, Albert Lopez, was the preacher at the Church of Christ, where all the born-agains went. Like most of the town, Mom and I were Catholic, and it was a good thing, too, because Albert scared the shit out of me. The guy was built like a barrel cactus, even looked sort of like one when he got pissed off and the gray hair around his ears stuck out, like needles.

"Does he know?" I asked.

"Don't think so. He hasn't showed up to kill me yet."

"What about her mom?"

"Yeah. She's the one going to tell Albert. Might get ugly if Sarah told him herself."

"I can't believe you're going to have it," Choobies said. He hadn't talked for a while. We'd almost forgot he was there.

"What else are we supposed to do, Choobs? Kill our own kid?" Ricky drew the edge of his hand across his stomach, like he was cutting himself open.

"'Course not," I said, although the first thing I thought of was the Planned Parenthood at the end of a strip mall over in Sierra Vista, with the red awning and dark windows.

"Why the hell not? You think it's any better to have it?" Choobies said.

"You trying to tell us that you could do that to your own flesh and blood?" I said. Ricky had fucked up good, but he didn't need the third degree, from Choobies or anybody.

Choobies put his hands out at his sides like he was checking for rain. "If it was me, I would have worn a rubber." He said it like it was the easiest thing in the world, and I guess it was for a guy who'd never been naked in a sweaty backseat without one. Choobies had never scored, and we gave him a hard time about it.

Ricky did his Historama voice again: "After the fact, Choobies said he would have worn a rubber." He snorted and went back to his normal voice: "You don't need a rubber, Choobs. You couldn't get pussy at the animal shelter."

As I laughed, I heard a wheezing noise coming from beside me, on Choobies' side of the tailgate. It sounded like he was sucking up air to save it for something.

"Yeah, well at least I didn't knock anybody up." Choobies leaned back when he said it, crossing his arms and squinting.

Ricky got up and rubbed his hands together. He hacked some phlegm from his throat and spit it into the weeds at the base of the wall. "Is that right, Choobs? So if you're so smart, why don't you know when to shut your face?"

"Cut it out." I could see where things were headed, and I didn't feel like playing peacemaker again. Those two did that shit all the time. Once a month they'd get into one of their half-assed shoving matches where they dared each other to throw a punch until I broke it up. So far that had always ended it, because neither one of them messed with me after what happened at the boonie party with the Benson kid.

Ricky took his lighter out of his pocket and ran it across his jeans so it made a zipping noise and sparks flew onto his thigh. I imagined him catching on fire and running around the yard in flames, wondered what Choobies and I would do to save him. The furnace rattled to life inside the house.

"You going to move out of here, then?" I asked him, nodding toward the porch full of shadows.

"Yeah, when I hit the Powerball," Ricky said with a smirk.

"At least you've got a good plan," Choobies said.

Ricky pretended not to hear, but there was no stopping Choobies. He had a way of taking things personal, of taking wrongs done to other people and making them his. Earlier that night, on the way back from the beer run, he'd screamed "Cochinos!" at some Border Patrol agents searching a car by the overpass. I never understood it, myself. We all had enough to put up with, Choobies' old man and my mom's asshole boyfriends and now Ricky with a kid on the way. We didn't need to go chasing other people's problems.

"You going to get a real job?" Choobies asked Ricky.

"I've got a real job."

"You're a busboy," Choobies said.

"You act like you're running the place," I said. "You're a dishwasher."

"Whatever, Sam. You know he's just going to fuck that kid's life up. He can't even take care of himself. Look at this place—would you want to grow up here?" Choobies swept his hand in front of him, nearly hitting me in the stomach. I wondered what he was pointing at—the rusting junk on the porch, the cigarette butts in the yard, the whole town—but then I realized it didn't much matter.

"I *did* grow up here."

He took a long pull off his beer. "But you're leaving."

I hadn't thought of it that way. I'd been treating the letter like I'd always treated the future, thinking it would never really happen. I tried to picture myself in Thatcher, taking notes in classrooms, eating in the cafeteria, trying to bang Mormon girls. But I couldn't see myself anyplace but our trailer outside town, the kitchen at the Wheel, or right there on Choobies' tailgate in Ricky's yard.

"It's not that far away. I'll come back plenty. Plus you'll still have Ricky." I tried to believe it, and sort of did, because we'd stayed friends through all kinds of shit. I'd had four step-dads by the time I could drive, Choobies' real dad beat the snot out of him all the time, and Ricky kept losing jobs until he owed us both so much money we finally had to get him a job at the Wheel. I'd always figured that in twenty years, we'd all be sitting inside where it was warm, bitching about our kids and wondering what they were doing out at one in the morning on a school night.

"Ricky?" Choobies said, pointing. "He's gonna have a *baby* to take care of, for chrissakes."

"You think I don't know that, Choobies?" Ricky said. "You think I don't realize? Why do you think I'm out here getting drunk in the middle of the night?"

"He'll figure it out," I said. I was starting to feel weird talking about Ricky like he wasn't there when he was sitting right across the yard. I slapped Choobies on the back. "It'll be fine."

He swiped my hand away and shot up off the tailgate. "It's going to be just *fine*, huh?" he said in a mocking voice. "Everybody's just going to *figure it out!*" His arms flailed at his sides like he was trying to take off.

I stood and grabbed hold of his sweatshirt. It was still wet from the dishwater. "Sit down, Choobies. Sit down and shut up."

"You're so full of shit, Sam. Who do you know ever just figured it out? Where's your dad?"

I felt the heat in my throat, and the tears came up behind my eyes like they do when I start to lose it. I wanted to take Choobies apart. I tried to make myself remember that night at the party, when the Benson kid kept talking shit about Tombstone, until I had to break his jaw to shut him up. After they pulled me off him he was still trying to talk, blood leaking out his ragged mouth, but nobody could tell what he was saying. The rage went away, quick as it came, and it left me sort of empty. I felt like I had proved something.

Ricky was talking.

"Sam . . . hey, Sam." He snapped his fingers at me. "I was you, Choobies, I'd take that back. His eyes are watering—you know how he gets."

"Apologize for what? It's just the truth. You, too, Ricky—you ought to know better. You think your dad figured it all out? Where the fuck is he?"

"Ohio." The word fell out of his mouth. Normally Ricky would have come at Choobies hell bent for leather if he said a thing like that, but he just slumped farther down on the wall. I started to think about where our dads were right then and knew Choobies was right. I pictured Ricky's dad in some cornfield or whatever they had in Ohio, and then I thought about my dad, how I didn't even know where he was anymore. How he'd left me here in a goddamned ghost town, cooking ribs for a bunch of tourists who tucked their pants into their boots, watching a bunch of dickheads I hardly knew try to be my new dad.

"You can go fuck yourself with your high and mighty, Choobies," I said. "I'll take having no dad over having yours." I knew I shouldn't have said it, even while I was saying it. But that only made it feel better.

Choobies shrugged like he was putting on a real heavy backpack. He looked at the sky and I saw that his eyes were wet.

"There you go, Sam. Looks like you figured it all out."

It got quiet again, only this time it felt different. A cloud went over the moon and everything went darker. Choobies staggered to the truck and reached into the back to get a beer out of the cooler. He was so short that he had to lean way over, bracing himself on the bed rail with his other hand. I watched him, wondering where we could go from here. Then his hand slipped on the primered metal and he lost his balance and fell face-first into the bed with a yelp and a crash.

Ricky and I laughed so hard we fell to our knees in the dirt. We laughed and pointed and stopped laughing, then looked at each other and busted up again. Choobies dusted himself off, told us to go to hell, and said he was leaving.

"Some friends you are," he said. He got in his truck and slammed the door. I was thinking about trying to stop him because he was probably too drunk to drive, but the Datsun didn't start anyway. The engine just clicked— he'd left the stereo on too long. His key chain jingled as he turned the key over and over. Then he slapped the dashboard and stuck his head out the window.

"I need a jump," he said, like it was all one word.

Ricky and me looked at each other.

"Don't look at me," I said. "You know what happened to my cables." We'd ripped them in half a month before when we tried using them to tow Choobies' truck out of a ditch.

"Some friends you are," he said again. "You guys ain't good for shit." He got out of the truck and kicked the fender. He must have liked how it felt, because he kicked it again, and again, and next thing you know he was rearing his leg all the way back and just whaling on it. The steel toes of his boots clanged against the metal. He started yelling curses and some sounds that weren't even real words and something about nothing ever working right.

Finally Choobies stopped kicking and walked over and sat back down on the tailgate and didn't say anything or even look at us. Ricky went to get himself a beer and shot me a grin on his way by. As he leaned into the truck bed, he started talking in his Historama voice.

"But little did Choobies know how dangerous his truck could be," he said. He pretended to slip and threw himself over the rail, squealing and thrashing around. It cracked me up, but Choobies got all pissed off and started cussing at us and waving his arms around and hopping like a pigeon.

Then his head fixed on the Yamaha and he walked real fast across the yard. He grabbed the handlebars and started pushing it toward the street.

"What the fuck?" Ricky said.

"Choobies," I yelled. "Where you going with that thing?"

"I'm taking my bike," was all he said.

"Come on back, man," Ricky said. He elbowed me, then cupped his hands toward Choobies. "Wouldn't want you to fall and hurt yourself!"

Choobies flipped us off. He was under the streetlight by then, next to my shitbucket Volkswagen. He swung a leg over the seat and started pushing the bike with small steps, his toes barely reaching the ground, until he picked up some speed and pulled his feet onto the pegs and coasted out of the streetlight and into the dark. I wondered where he thought he was going on a broken motorcycle that could only coast downhill.

"You ever seen anything like this?" I asked Ricky as I searched the hill with my eyes, looking for Choobies.

He stuck out his jaw and blew smoke up past his eyes. "This town makes people do some crazy shit." His thumbs tugged at the edges of his pockets as he started up with his Historama voice again. "When the mines played out, Tombstone threw a party . . ."

It was a line from the last scene of the Historama, when the town's silver boom ended. We all knew the story: one night in 1886, just right across the street from Ricky's yard at the old Grand Central works, the pumps that pulled water out of the mines caught fire. The pumps burned and the shafts flooded, and now all the silver and some of the miners were buried a quarter mile beneath our feet.

I guess those pumps were loud as jackhammers, so when they went quiet around sundown and the fire lit up the hill, everybody knew the jig was up. They say it was the biggest night the town ever saw. Barkeeps rolled whiskey barrels onto the boardwalks, whores danced on balconies, and miners staged mule races down Allen Street. The next morning, the last of the silver left in the prospectors' pockets. They took the town for all it was worth and left it with nothing.

I heard gravel crunch in the street. Choobies limped toward us and stopped in the middle of the yard. His sweatshirt had a big tear in the shoulder and he was keeping weight off one of his legs. He traced his mustache with his fingers. His knuckles were bloody.

"So what the hell happened to you?" I said.

"Where's the bike?" Ricky said.

Choobies pointed to a spot in the dark about halfway down the hill. "In the bushes right past the bend. I wrecked it." He smirked. "That thing's kind of hard to ride with no motor."

I asked him if he was all right and he shrugged.

"I guess. Didn't break nothing."

"Want me to take you home?" I said.

"No hurry. It's too late. My dad'll get there first." He nodded toward the bottom of the hill, where the bars on Allen Street were letting out and all the drunks stumbled past the false fronts of the gift shops. They wore hats and dusters and carried replica guns on their belts, a bunch of cowboy posers drunk enough to believe their own act. The whole place looked like some sorry-ass fun park.

Choobies sat down. I sat next to him. There wasn't any more room on the tailgate, so Ricky leaned against the side of the truck. We sat there and watched the streets empty and the lights shut off until only the fake gas lamps and moon were left to see by and the town looked scrubbed clean and different somehow.

"I don't know what the hell I'm going to do now," Choobies said. I thought it was weird that out of the three of us, he was the one to say it, and Ricky must have thought the same thing.

"Me neither," he said.

I looked down the tailgate at my friends' faces. They looked old and new at the same time, like the town.

"Me too," I said. "Me neither."

I cut the engine at the top of the driveway and let my car coast over the gravel. The tires crunched in the night. We creaked to a stop in front of my house and got out, closing the doors as quiet as we could, hoping not to wake my mom.

Across the street, Choobies' dad's old Chevy sat cockeyed in the driveway.

"You can stay here if you want," I whispered. "Sleep on the couch. I'll take the floor."

He shook his head. "I'll take my chances."

I told him I'd see him tomorrow and he started walking. He crossed the street and paused at the bottom of the steps, looking up at the door's lit window. He looked even smaller than usual standing there like that, and part of me wanted to shout across the street and tell him just to sleep on my damn couch already. Choobies didn't always need to be so stubborn. He could sneak in through his bedroom window in the morning before his old man woke up, and nobody would be the wiser. But Choobies' hand turned the knob and he stepped through the door.

I walked up our steps and the motion lights on the side of the trailer kicked on, blasting light in my face. I stopped and blinked and looked in the window. The TV was on, some infomercial with lots of big families in big houses, and in the glow I saw Mom asleep on the couch under a Mexican blanket, alone. The room was warm when I walked inside. It smelled like old milk. A big white envelope sat on the coffee table. I walked over and picked it up, weighing it in my hand. At first it felt heavy, but the longer I held it, the lighter it felt, and finally I couldn't tell which it was, or which I wanted it to be. The day behind me felt long, like a small lifetime, and finding out didn't seem like any way to end it. The letter would still be there in the morning.

I put it down and switched off the TV. I usually slept on the couch so Mom could have the bedroom, but as I stood in the dark room with the porch lights shining on her face and her tangled hair, I didn't want to wake her up. I wanted to stay right there, watching over her, until the morning. I wanted to, even though I knew I couldn't, and I knew I couldn't, even though I didn't know why.

Road to Nowhere

James Terry

THE MARKERS RAN DUE EAST FROM AN UNUSED DIRT ROAD NAMED Maverick straight towards the mountains, their fluorescent orange ribbons bright as poppies against the pale browns of the desert. It was mostly mesquite bushes and grama grass on this side, the occasional yucca and dried-up ocotillo. Clarence's new bulldozer plowed through it all like a hot spoon through margarine.

It had been nearly a year coming. First the County had cut his budget, leaving him barely enough money to maintain his existing equipment, let alone buy anything new. So he'd applied for a project completion grant from the State. The only problem was that there hadn't been any projects in need of completion. Clarence had remedied that by creating Enchanted View Road SE. He knew there to be a tract of county land seven miles southeast of town, out near the base of the Floridas, already platted for development. Sooner or later it would need an access road. He'd gotten the records from the County Clerk, had his usual guy do the survey, drafted the bid himself—he requested $100,000, knowing he'd be lucky to get half that—and got his old high school drinking buddy Tom Reed, now the County Commissioner, to backdate the proposal by a year. Next he'd phoned Ike Crawford, who in his autumn years as state senator was trying to seal his legacy as the champion of Luna County roads. Crawford said he'd see what he could do when the legislature reconvened in January. Road projects being low on the list of priorities for the State in a recession, he wasn't able to get a slot in the capital outlay calendar until late February. At the urging of a personal memo from the governor, who owed Crawford a favor for his help in the last election, the chair of the finance committee made sure that the merits of financing the completion of a rural road in one of the least populous counties in the state, a road that probably wouldn't have a tire anywhere near it for decades to come, were not seriously debated. In the end, "Enchanted View Road Completion" was apportioned $50,000. Clarence called in his order the very next day, only to be told that there was a backlog on the track loaders— "The Israeli army cleaned us out"—and he'd have to wait six to eight weeks. Four months later the bulldozer finally arrived.

Some people might have said that what he'd done was dishonest, but Clarence didn't see it that way. The department had needed a new bulldozer and he'd found a way to get it one. To his mind, taking advantage of the law was a whole lot different than breaking it. And to prove, if only to himself, that he had every intention of using the bulldozer to complete the road he'd invented, he chose the very next morning to take it out to the site and get started on it.

The mesquite roots were the only thing that gave him any resistance at all. Some of them were as long as thirty feet, snaking out stiff as dead tree branches just below the surface. He snagged the bushes in the teeth of the rippers and gunned it straight up, and the roots leapt through the dirt, thumping and snapping as he dragged them off to the side of the road path.

The sun beating down hard on him, baking his cracked knuckles a deep coppery brown, Clarence took a break just after noon. He lifted his hat and wiped his brow with his sleeve. As he was digging out the used-up dip from his right cheek to pinch a fresh one in, he noticed something in the distance, some little man-made structure. It was white, or close to it. He took off his sunglasses and squinted but still couldn't make it out clearly. Whatever it was it looked like it was right in the path of his road.

He cut the engine and got down and set out walking up the gently sloping bajada, weaving around the bushes as he went. Up close Clarence wasn't as big as he looked from a distance. It was his belly that gave people the impression that he was a man of stature. The pride and confidence that ten years as head honcho of the Luna County Road Department had given him exaggerated his natural swagger, pulling his shoulders back, curving his arms parenthetically around him as they swung through their arcs, shifting the brunt of his weight to the back edge of his bootheels, all of which tended to push his belly out tight against the long-sleeve polyester business shirts he favored. It wasn't a beer gut, for when he did drink, which wasn't as often as he liked to let on with the men, he went in for the harder stuff. Nor was an unhealthy diet to blame. Barb made sure of that. She always trimmed the fat from their steaks, used low-fat margarine and 2 percent milk. The fact of the matter was that, like Clarence himself, his belly wasn't actually as large as the impression it left in people's minds.

It turned out to be a small camping trailer, a sixteen- or eighteen-footer by the looks of it, white, the lower third of it banded aqua green. The door in the side appeared to be open, or missing altogether. As Clarence came nearer he observed that the hoist was resting on a stack of rocks and that the tires appeared to be inflated, indications that this wasn't just another old wreck that someone hadn't bothered to dispose of properly. Even so, he wasn't expecting it when someone stepped across the doorway.

Clarence stopped and stood there for a moment, eyes fixed on the camper. He turned his head and spat. He wasn't fond of coming across people out in the desert. Nine times out of ten there was a good reason they were out there instead of with the rest of civilization, namely they weren't normal. They were outcasts—fugitives of the law, wetbacks, religious fruitcakes, kooks of one stripe or another. The last thing he wanted was to spook some nutcase with a gun.

He considered things for another moment or two, squinting against the sun, marveling how out of all the miles of open desert to choose from they had gone and parked the thing directly in his road path. Then he carried on up the bajada, clearing his throat every now and then so as to make his presence known.

When he was an easy stone's throw from the camper, he stopped and hooked his thumbs over his front pockets and called out.

"Hey there."

A moment later a woman appeared in the doorway. The first thing Clarence noticed was her belly. By the looks of it she was a good six or seven months pregnant. She looked young but there was a hardness in her face, something gaunt and weary in the way she peered out at him, her black hair tied back tight against her skull. She was wearing a pale yellow cotton print dress that went clear down to her ankles, like something worn a hundred years ago.

Clarence stared at her for a full five seconds, then he lifted his hat a little to show his cordiality and said, "Afternoon, ma'am."

"Howdie," she replied, staring back at him suspiciously.

"This your trailer?"

"Me and my husbunt," she said.

A bunch of plastic milk jugs and various other plastic containers full of water were lined up along the front of the camper. Off to one side sat some apple crates that appeared to be full of rocks.

"Name's Clarence Bowman. I'm with the Road Department."

"Howdie," she said again.

He waited a moment for her to say her name or anything at all to explain what she was doing out there in a camper in the middle of nowhere. She didn't.

"Is your husband around?" Clarence asked.

"He's out."

Clarence scuffed his boot around a little in the dirt.

"Well, we're fixin to put a road through this way," he said, nodding toward the camper and beyond. "See them stakes over yonder?"

She squinted.

"What for?"

"Oh," Clarence grinned, as if letting her in on some private joke, "just plannin ahead."

Her expression didn't change. Clarence turned his head to spit but caught himself in time.

"Mind if I have a look around?" he asked.

"Make yourself at home," she said.

He thanked her and walked around to the back of the camper. It had an Oklahoma license plate with an out-of-date registration sticker. Some blackened tin cans and half-melted plastic marked the spot where they had been burning their garbage. He spat there, then walked around to the hoist. The tire tracks led off to the north.

A few minutes later he came back around to the front. She was still in the doorway, leaning her right hip against the frame. He noticed now that she was barefoot. She raised her hand again and looked down at him. Clarence kept a respectful distance.

"Your husband workin in town is he?" he asked her.

"Nah, he's up there gettin rocks," she said, referring with the back of her head to the mountains.

"Rocks?"

"He's a rock collector. We had us a place in Muskogee with a museum and all but it burnt down."

"Sorry to hear that."

She didn't look all that sorry herself.

"When ya'll startin on that road?"

"I'm down there now doing some clearin."

"You want us to move?"

"Well," he said, giving it a little thought, "it'll be a while yet before I'm up this far."

"We ain't supposed to be here much longer," she said.

Clarence nodded. He raised his hat.

"You have a good day now, ma'am," he said and turned to leave.

"I'll tell my husbunt you stopped by," the woman said.

Clarence turned back and winked, then carried on down the bajada.

"Modern-day Okies," Ruby cackled when Clarence told her about his encounter in the desert. He knew it would get a rise out of her. She was forever reading some trashy paperback novel about trashy people doing trashy things to each other. She was sixty-two years old and had spent thirty of them running the office at the Road Department, which mostly entailed filing papers and talking to her daughters long-distance on the county dime. On her desk sat an array of framed photographs of her grandchildren in their infancy, red-faced babies not long from the womb, their eyes and mouths and nostrils identically shaped little lozenges of perplexity. She had a big jowly face with a mass of bronze hair that she tinted herself every three months and sculpted every morning with a wire hairbrush and a fog of hairspray. She smoked two packs of menthol cigarettes a day and had a voice like a bullfrog.

The one thing Clarence could always count on from Ruby was her cynicism. It was perfectly in tune with his own. She expected only the worst of people and was seldom disappointed.

"The husband's some kind of rock hound," Clarence said.

"Rocks for brains sounds more like it."

Sometimes Clarence wished Barb could take a few lessons from old Ruby. When he told her over supper about the people in the camper she started right in with the pity.

"That's no place for a pregnant woman to be stuck all alone." She set her fork on her plate and looked at Clarence as if he had parked the woman there himself. "Out there without a car. That isn't right. She could fall down and hurt herself and there'd be no one there to help her. No phone, nothing."

"Well, I don't think they intend on startin a family out there," Clarence said.

"What kind of a man goes and leaves a pregnant woman alone all day in a camper in the middle of the desert at the height of summer without any electricity or running water?"

"Them old things run on propane," Clarence said, cutting into the foil of his baked potato. "Matt Hertz used to have one. Refrigerator and everything. They'll probably only be there a couple days anyhow. The husband's some kind of rock collector."

"I don't care if he's John D. Rockefeller. That's no way to treat a pregnant woman, Clarence."

Barb believed that the world was a good place and that people were good too, even when they did bad things. She had a knack for talking to complete strangers as if they had been next-door neighbors all their lives, and more often than not the stranger couldn't help but respond in kind. This frustrated Clarence to no end whenever they went to the mall in Las Cruces. Inevitably she would strike up a conversation with the cashier in Sears, or the people in line with them at the corn dog place, or some old man resting beside her on the bench. It didn't matter what the subject was—the weather, the price of gas, her aching feet—she always got them talking. Sooner or later she would start talking about Clarence or their daughter Shelly or some other private matter that Clarence didn't feel was any stranger's business, and he would shift around and clear his throat in an attempt to remind her that they didn't know this guy from Adam. The worst was when she started rattling off the names of friends and other Deming people as if they were common knowledge to the whole of humanity. "How the hell is he supposed to know who Rhonda is?" Clarence would say irately once they were alone again. But these small frustrations aside, it was this trusting, generous, sometimes downright naive nature of Barb's that had captured Clarence's heart nearly twenty-five years ago and never let go.

"Did her ankles look swollen?"

"How should I know? I wasn't lookin at her ankles."

"Well was her face all puffy?"

"No, she looked half-starved if you ask me."

"Good Lord," she shook her head. "Doesn't that just make you sick?"

"Why should I give a damn if people want to live like gypsies. It's a free country."

Barb shook her head sadly and picked up her fork and stabbed her potato to let out some of the steam.

Clarence figured that was the end of it. He should have known better.

The next morning as he was pulling out of the driveway, Barb scuttled out in her pink housecoat with a carton of Vivaway "Female Vitality" in her hand. Clarence stopped the truck and rolled down his window.

"Here," she said, "take this out to that woman."

"Oh, for Pete's sake."

"Just do it, Clarence. She needs it."

"I'm not out there makin house calls."

"It won't kill you," she gave him her irritated, maternal glare. He sighed and grabbed the carton and put it on the seat. She stood in the driveway and watched him drive away.

The sight of the new bulldozer basking in the morning sunlight, yellow as the yolks of fresh duck eggs, filled Clarence's heart with gladness. The feeling stayed with him all morning as he worked clearing the brush. For Clarence there was no greater joy than starting a new road. There was something so promising about it. It was the work of civilization, of man taming unruly Mother Earth. What could be more important work than that? Whatever frustrations he may have had to suffer along the way, it was all worth it when he looked out and saw that nice straight stretch of fresh, clean dirt cutting across all that wild desert brush.

Shortly after noon he cut the engine and walked back to the truck to have his lunch. He sat in the hot silence of the cab, eating his turkey sandwich, a carton of Female Vitality resting beside him on the seat.

"Vivaway," it said in bold white letters across the blue-and-pink box; and beneath it, in smaller letters: "For a New Tomorrow."

Clarence picked up the carton.

"Female Vitality," he grumbled, shaking his head with sufferance. He turned the carton around and read: "Designed to support proper balance of the female reproductive and glandular systems." He read the ingredients, a long list of strange-sounding roots and herbs. He read everything else, the recommended intake, the claims and disclaimers, the company's mailing address, etc.

The desert heat wafted in through the open windows, stinging Clarence's cheeks. He sat for some time, staring at the mountains, trying to picture some guy out there looking for rocks, leaving his pregnant wife stranded in a sweltering trailer. Then, with an annoyed grunt, he grabbed the carton and set out up the road path.

He stopped about twenty feet short of the camper and loudly cleared his throat. The woman came to the door. She was in the same dress as yesterday.

"Afternoon, ma'am," Clarence said. "Sorry to bother you again. My wife asked me to give you this." He walked up to the door. The woman went to take a step down, then yanked her bare foot back from the hot metal.

"Watch yourself there." Clarence handed the box up to her. She took it and looked it over curiously. Clarence's face was almost level with her belly, and he couldn't help but notice how her navel was poking out against the stretched fabric of her dress.

"It's supposed to be good for . . . well, uh, somethin or other," he said with an embarrassed little smile.

She thanked him.

"I don't know if it works or not," he added. "I guess some people think it does or she wouldn't be sellin so much of it. Our garage is full of the stuff."

"I'll give it a try," she said, slipping her feet into a pair of blue plastic flip-flops just inside the door.

Clarence stepped back and surveyed the desert.

"It's a hot one today, ain't it," he said.

She stepped down cautiously onto the metal step, then settled in the doorway in a familiar way. He noticed now that her eyes were an unusually light brown, almost the color of the desert sand, as if their natural color had been bleached out of them.

"I told Trevor you was puttin a road through here," she said. "He got a kick out of that. Puttin a road out here."

"You'd be surprised at some of the places we've put roads," Clarence said. "My crew's down near the border as we speak, workin on a five-miler. That one's just about nowhere to nowhere, too. You got a road department, you got to make roads. Sooner or later someone'll need them."

She looked at him and scratched her ankle. Clarence took note that they weren't at all swollen.

"Why ain't you with them?" she asked him.

"Huh? Oh. Well, I figured I'd give this new dozer a spin, have a look out this way," he said, glancing out at the desert.

She didn't say anything.

Clarence was just about to say he'd better be on his way when she asked him if he was thirsty. He gave it some thought.

"I can't say as I am at the moment."

"We got some cola. I'm gonna get me one. You want one?"

"Well," he said, stroking his mustache, "if you're going to the trouble."

"It ain't no trouble," she said and smiled. It was the first smile he'd seen on her, and it put him a little more at ease.

She stood up and went in. Clarence turned his head and spat and scuffed some dirt over the wetness. He stepped over to one of the apple crates and had a look at the rocks. There were a few rough geodes, but most of it looked worthless to him: shale and quartz and plain old chunks of granite. She came back to the doorway, handed him the can, and sat back down.

"Nice and cold," Clarence said, opening it and taking a sip. It was awful. The can said "Cola" on it.

"Mighty nifty, these old campers, runnin on propane."

She sipped her cola and looked at him.

"How long you been married?"

That took Clarence aback a little. He reached up and adjusted his hat.

"Oh, going on twenty-two years, I reckon."

"Shee, now that's a long time. We only been married a year," she said. "Seems like a lot longer," she added a moment later with a twitch of her lips. "Any kids?"

He told her about Shelly being in college in Las Cruces.

"I'm expectin myself," she said.

"I kinda figured."

She looked down at her belly as if she hadn't noticed it before.

"Ah, hell," Clarence said, patting his gut proudly, "you got nothin on me."

That almost made her laugh. Or else the single grinning bob of her head was as far as laughter went with her. Clarence drank as much of the cola as he could stomach and was about to thank her and get going, but again she thought of something else to say to keep him there talking to her.

"We went down to some little Mexican town last night," she said.

"That'd be Palomas."

"Wildest thing I ever seen. Not ten feet from America. A whole different world. Everyone was lookin at me. Every beady little eye. They'd liked to have gobbled me up."

"What'd you all go down there for anyway?"

"To get Trevor's medication. He said it was cheaper down there. Course they didn't have his brand. I could've told him that myself."

Clarence nodded. He glanced up at the mountains. From that vantage they were stunning to behold, a curtain of blue-gray granite blocking out the entire eastern sky, so sharp and clear that it seemed he could reach out and touch them. It gave him a pleasant floating sensation just to look at them, as if all that mass piled up in one spot were exerting a gravitational pull on his insides.

When he glanced back down at her he noticed that the hem of her dress was hitched up to her knees and that her legs were spread enough for him to see that she wasn't wearing any underwear. He caught an eyeful of black pubic hair under the pale dome of her belly before he quickly looked away. He glanced out across the bajada nonchalantly, as if mulling something over in his mind.

"Well," he said a moment or two later, "I best be pushin off."

When he glanced at her again, her dress was back over her knees.

"You take care," she said.

It took him most of the following morning to think of an excuse to go back up to the camper. His boots made a dry sucking sound in the sand as he followed his own footprints up the bajada, scattering jackrabbits as he went. Already the walk was shorter than before, thanks to the progress he'd been making with the clearing, but it was still nearly half a mile to the camper.

This time he walked right up to it and knocked lightly on the side. He heard some racket like the clanking of utensils in a pot, then she came to the door. She was holding a can opener in her right hand.

"You're gettin to be a regular neighbor," she said. She stood in the doorway with her hips cocked left, looking down at him as if he were some exasperating kid come to sell her something. She was in the same dress again.

"My wife was curious to know if that stuff I brung you did you any good."

That wasn't true. Last night over dinner Barb had asked him if he'd given it to the woman, but she knew better than anyone that you couldn't expect results overnight. Ideally it was best taken in conjunction with Good Life Revitalizer and Worry Away.

"It sure did," she said. "I feel like a million bucks. You thank her for me again."

Clarence couldn't help but grin at the obvious sarcasm in her voice.

"You want a drink?" she said.

"I should probably get on back," he said unconvincingly.

She turned from the doorway, ignoring his remark, and was back a moment later holding a clear, unlabeled bottle by the neck. The bottle was half-empty. She gave it a little shake.

Clarence looked back and forth a few times between the bottle, her belly, and her face.

"Well are you comin in or you just gonna stand out there in that heat all day?"

Clarence adjusted his hat, gave a little tug to the right arm of his mustache, then stepped up into the camper.

It was tiny inside and suffocatingly hot. The walls were all wood paneling, stained here and there from water leaks. Awkward stacks of apple crates full of rocks stood here and there at every wall. A dirty yellow curtain hung limply to one side of the back window, which was missing altogether its glass and screen. From the bare aluminum undersiding showing through a rectangular section low on the back wall, it looked as though some built-in furniture, probably a sofa, had been ripped out. In its place stood two metal chairs with torn olive green vinyl seat cushions. A few feet in front of them sat an overturned apple crate with some magazines on it.

Clarence was struck by the feeling, as intense as the first time he had entered a Mexican's home as a kid, that he didn't belong in there. Out of force of habit he took off his hat and looked around for somewhere to hang it before setting it on the seat of one of the chairs. He took off his sunglasses and put them in his shirt pocket.

"You'd never guess from the outside how roomy these things are," he said.

She was standing behind the narrow Formica counter that partially divided the living room, if it could be called that, from the tiny kitchenette. She scooted a Styrofoam cup his way and took a sip from hers.

"I don't guess that's water," Clarence said with a nervous chuckle, stepping over to get the cup.

"Trevor's daddy makes it," she said. "It's strong."

Clarence stepped over to the door and dug the remnants of his dip out with his forefinger and flung it to the ground. He took a sip and scowled. A glowing coal rolled down his esophagus and into his stomach.

"You ain't lyin," he said, eyes brimming with tears.

She grinned at him.

"Have a seat," she said.

"Nah, I sit all day. My back ain't so good."

He took another drink.

"This stuff is awful," he said.

"You get used to it."

"Whoa," he said a few seconds later as a warm breeze wafted across his brain. She smiled again. She seemed to be getting a kick out of him. He didn't mind. There was a part of him, not expressed often enough, that liked to play the merry fool.

"You know you ain't supposed to drink when you're pregnant," he said lightheartedly.

"You ain't supposed to fuck strangers neither," she replied, as if it were the most innocent thing in the world.

That made Clarence laugh—a quick sharp bark of a laugh. He stood there for a second, looking out the door, rolling the remark around his mind, in the end deciding it had to be a joke, odd as it was. He laughed again.

"No, I guess you ain't," he said, still looking out the door. A flying beetle buzzed by, a flash of iridescent green in the blinding sunlight.

He took another sip. He could see the strip of naked earth he'd already cleared, and the bulldozer at the edge of it, a speck of bright yellow in a sea of tan. His heart was pumping a little more forcefully than it should have been. He went to take another drink but there was nothing left in his cup.

At last he turned and looked at her. She was on the near side of the counter now, her arms down at her sides. She was staring at him intensely, not blinking at all.

"Your husband carry a gun?" Clarence asked, almost under his breath.

"He's got one in the truck."

Clarence walked over to her and set his cup on the counter. Her eyes hadn't left him for a second. He tried to look into them but they were too intense. He stared at her belly instead, his heart knocking hard against his sternum now. Then he slowly raised his right hand and set it on her stomach. The fabric of her dress was thin and he could feel the warmth of her body through it, even in that stifling heat. He brought his other hand up. Staring down in dumb amazement he watched his hands roam in tender circles around that lovely sphere. When his fingers grazed her belly button she inhaled sharply, then gradually let her breath back out.

"Would he use it if he was to walk through that door right now?" Clarence said without looking up.

"Right now he might not," she said, "but a minute or two from now he probably would."

With that she took a fold of her dress in each hand and slowly began to pull it up, pulling Clarence's eyes up with it as it passed her knees, slid up her pale skinny thighs, up over and around her bulging belly, exposing the fleshy pink clot of her belly button. Beneath it her thick black pubic hair spread out toward the top of her thighs, thinning to a fine line creeping toward her navel. She pulled the dress over her head and off.

The sight of her little freckly tits nearly touching the top of the white globe of her belly just about knocked Clarence over. He stepped back, balanced himself, and teetered there slack jawed, as if on the edge of reason. The dress dropped silently to the floor.

After that it was all panic and fluster, him clutching her ass and sucking at her tits, her fumbling with his belt buckle, both of them grunting and gasping in haste to be done with the preliminaries and find some place to fuck. In the end he turned her around and bent her down against the counter and got up into her from behind, his hands gripping her swaying belly as if for dear life as he banged away against the blunt knobs of her haunch bones. Finally he collapsed against her with a hoarse little bleat, panting, covered in sweat, the whole business having taken less than two minutes.

"Sweet Jesus," he gasped, and stood there for a while breathing hard, still inside her. "I don't even know your name."

When he got home that evening some of the ladies were already there for the Wednesday night Vivaway social. They looked up from their brochures and greeted him from the sofa with big, frivolous smiles. Barb came from the kitchen and kissed his cheek and told him his dinner was in the oven.

After his shower Clarence ate his supper alone in the kitchen, staring at the wall. He could hear the ladies arriving, chattering away, laughing, but for all intents and purposes he was still in the camper with Angela's pregnant belly in his hands.

"Now that's a strange sight," Barb squawked, all juiced up on Vivaway vision, when she came in half an hour later to get the snacks out of the refrigerator. Clarence had already washed his plate and the other dishes that were on the counter and was now in the middle of cleaning all the aluminum trays beneath the stove burners.

He mumbled something about burnt gunk.

"You can clean the rest of the kitchen while you're at it," she said on her way out the door.

He did. It was so clean when he finished that Barb had to bring all the ladies in to show them what kind of a man she had. Clarence heard it all from the deck chair on the back porch, where he sat thinking about the silence of the desert at night.

"Is there something you aren't telling us, Barb?"

"Hold on. What's this? He didn't dust the knife holder."

Clarence didn't return to Enchanted View Road for the rest of the week. Instead he joined his crew at the road site near the border. They had been on the site for two months already and were well into the paving. All the men had their jobs and didn't need Clarence loafing around telling them what to do. It was only when he was around, they always said, that they messed things up. As if to prove the point, Hector forgot to load the bitumen into the hopper, and they had to rip up fifty yards of fresh pavement. Still, Clarence felt grateful to be among his men again, good simple men, free of the burdens of shame. Of course they all knew about the Okies in the camper—Ruby had made sure of that—and they wanted to know more. What did the woman look like? What were they doing out there? Did they intend on staying? "How the hell should I know?" Clarence replied to all their questions, bewildered by how much energy it took to say it with just the right amount of feigned indifference.

By Thursday afternoon Clarence was starting to feel bored. Being around the men always got his upper lip twitching with barely restrained frustration. He had a variety of tactics for relieving this tension, one of them being tugging fitfully at the right arm of his mustache. He was also a master of the slow, disgusted shake of the head. Tapping the fingernail of his left pointer against the brass bull on his belt buckle was another. On those occasions when a series of relatively minor incompetences suddenly flared into a blazing display of ineptitude, he had no choice but to take off his hat and run his fingers through his thinning black hair in stonily silent disappointment.

By Friday morning all his twitchings and tappings and tuggings were back from vacation.

It was a long, dull weekend. He spent all day Saturday working on the front and back yard, mowing the grass, pulling weeds, clipping the shrubs. Sunday after church he settled into a golf tournament on TV. At one point Barb came up behind him and started rubbing his shoulders. Images of the camper, of Angela, of her pregnant belly, flashed across his eyes and flowed up Barb's fingers into her unsullied mind.

"Was that a hole in one?" she asked.

Clarence grunted. He knew what she was after. She always got frisky Sunday afternoons after church, when at last the world was pure again.

"Your shoulders sure are tense," she said. She massaged deeper. He could feel her breasts against the back of his head. A few putts later they were naked in the bedroom, Clarence trying to maneuver Barb into the doggy position. She resisted. She never liked doing it from behind. Clarence tried to tug her around but she wasn't having it.

"Why do you have to be so damn prissy about it?" he snorted. "Everyone else does it."

She turned around, her neck and face flushed with indignation.

"How do you know what everyone else does?"

"Ah, hell," he said and started getting dressed.

Monday morning Clarence checked in at the office and left his truck there and drove back out to Enchanted View Road in the big flatbed hauler. It was time to get the bulldozer out of there.

As he pulled up to the junction of the clearing he glanced out across the bajada. In his own truck he hadn't been able to see it from the dirt road, but the cab of the hauler was higher, affording him a clear view straight across to the mountains. Clarence sat there tugging pensively at his mustache. The fact of the matter was, they didn't even need the bulldozer down at the border site. They were well past that stage of things. They didn't need him either. If he didn't carry on with the clearing here, he had no option but to go back to the office and deal with the paperwork he'd been putting off for weeks. As much as he loved Ruby, he had no desire to be stuck in the office with her all day.

He pulled out his can of snuff and set a clump in his cheek. He managed to work until ten before the urge to go on up there and say his peace got the best of him. She must have heard him coming, for she was already at the door when he got there.

"Where you been?" she said, an accusatory tone in her voice that implied unfulfilled expectations.

"I had some business to take care of."

She nodded, not impressed. "Must've been pretty important."

On each of his previous visits the sun had been right in her face, but at this time of day she was entirely in the shadow of the camper, and it made her pale skin look almost blue.

"You all right?" Clarence asked her.

"Right as rain."

He glanced over at the crates of rocks, which had multiplied considerably since his last visit.

"Looks like your husband hit the mother lode."

She made no reply. She crossed her arms atop her belly. Her foot was tapping the floor. Clarence looked up at her.

"Is that the only dress you got, woman?" he said and immediately felt sorry he had. It was none of his business. Her foot stopped tapping.

Clarence lifted his hat and ran his fingers through his hair. He'd never felt such confusion. Pity one second, disgust the next. Ten seconds of dense silence hung in the air between them before she spoke again.

"You want a drink?" she said sullenly.

Clarence glanced down for a second then looked up at her again, his heart all knotted up in his throat.

"What the hell's wrong with you?" she said.

Clarence shook his head. He didn't know. He was on the verge of weeping.

"Get over here," she said.

He stepped up to her. She took off his hat and set it on her head. It was too big for her. It nearly covered her eyes. It only made the guilt and pity all the worse for Clarence seeing his hat on her like that.

All of a sudden he dropped to his knees and wrapped his arms around her legs and sank his face into her belly. He felt a stifled laugh ripple through her body. A moment later she was running her fingers through his hair, pulling his face hard against her. He reached under her dress and ran his hands up and down the backs of her legs, and whatever remorse he was feeling was quickly replaced by a sharp jolt of lust. She went on petting him as he stroked her legs. Then, knowing there was no sense fighting it, he pushed her dress up over her belly and put the knob of her navel into his mouth and proceeded to suck it like some big hairy baby at the nipple of an enormous breast, and the sounds that came from his throat were new to him and not entirely human.

They didn't bother with the drink. As before, they did it up against the counter. Clarence tried to take his time but it wasn't easy, what with the rush of premeditated adultery, the seediness of the camper, even the hard-to-forget fact that the husband carried a gun. Most of all it was her belly. He couldn't keep his hands off of it. He loved the way it hung down when she was bent over, the weight of it, the tightness, how it heaved forward and back in his hands, how it pulled taut the skin around her ribs and backbone, how soft and round and smooth it was, and even the knowledge that another man's fetus was the thing in his clutches did something to Clarence, made him feel more alive than he ever had before. And if there was one point on Angela's body that unleashed this feeling in him more than any other it was her belly button, or rather what it did to her when he touched it. He would push it in and twirl it around between his fingers, and she would let out a stifled, laughing cry, as if she were swallowing a scream, and her knees would start to jitter. He kept pressing it until she was moaning and whining like a sick dog. Clarence had never heard those kinds of sounds from a woman.

Afterwards they sat on the olive green chairs facing the open door. She was back to her terse, inscrutable self. They stared vacantly out at the desert, Clarence upright in the chair with his arms crossed in front of him, Angela reclining with her head against the back of the seat, her legs way out in front of her.

He started to say something, then stopped. He pulled out his can of snuff and pinched a fresh wad into his cheek.

"He don't like doin it with the baby in me," Angela said. "Says it'll give it brain damage."

Clarence shook his head and nearly chuckled, but she wasn't joking.

That wasn't the only thing that got Clarence thinking that the man had a screw loose. When he asked her about the rocks, what exactly her husband did with all of them, she told him again about the rock shop they'd had back in Muskogee. "Course he burnt it down himself to get the money from the insurance," she said, "only the insurance had done run out. So he stole five hundred dollars from his old man. That helped get us out here."

Clarence frowned in disgust, picturing Ruby's face receiving these new details, but he'd already started lying to Ruby, and to Barb, saying he hadn't paid the Okies any more visits.

It was a while before she spoke again.

"I shouldn't a come," she said. "He wanted me to stay back home but I didn't want to."

"Why not?"

"I can't stand my mama," she said. Again there was a long silence before she spoke again. She said they had been out in some desert in Texas for two months before coming here, that she thought she would go out of her mind out there, just sitting there day after day, nothing to do but stare out the door. "I'm fed up with it. This ain't no way to live."

"Why don't you all just stay in town at one of the RV parks? You could at least take a shower without having to use a bucket."

"We ain't got the money for that."

Clarence put his hand on her shoulder and gave it a sympathetic squeeze. It was strange feeling bone everywhere he touched on a woman. Barb was so much thicker and softer. All the hardness of Angela's life was right on the surface, in her bones and in her eyes. He leaned over and kissed her dry lips. That seemed to strike her as a novelty. She smiled, as one might at the sight of some exotic animal in a zoo.

It didn't cross his mind until the next morning, as he was ripping at a particularly tenacious mesquite bush, that maybe she was asking him, without coming right out and saying it—she seemed too proud for that—for money. He pondered this as he worked. He thought about that day she'd hitched up her dress and spread her legs. Considering all that had transpired he could no longer see that as an innocent oversight. Was she really just lonely and horny, or was there more to it? He thought about the various times she'd mentioned money, how she'd let him know how bad off she and her husband were, and it seemed to Clarence now that a certain awkwardness had lingered in the air following her remarks. He wondered if he ought to give her something, if that was the right thing, the noble thing, to do. But even if she did accept it, he couldn't see what good it would do. She couldn't exactly go out shopping. And the husband would immediately know something was going on if he ever found it.

This question, and the quandary it put Clarence in, remained unresolved in his mind as he made his way day after day up the bajada to see her. The shame had long since waned into a kind of guilty peace, the feeling that at last he too had joined the race of man, for whom there was no redemption. Here he was, screwing another man's wife, barely older than his own daughter, and pregnant to boot, and somehow it felt right, like he deserved it. Like God had put Angela out there in that camper for a reason, smack dab in the path of Enchanted View Road, and that reason was Clarence J. Bowman. A little gift for his life of hard work. A bonus.

Every day before setting out for the camper he took a minute to scope out the terrain through his binoculars for any sign of the husband, either in his truck or wandering around the mountains, but he never saw a thing. It was as if the man didn't even exist. She was usually sitting there on the step waiting for him. Clarence would go to his knees before her in the dirt, whisk off his hat and sunglasses, pull up her dress and start sucking on her belly button. More than once he felt a little kick against his lips that spooked the hell out of him but only made Angela giggle. Then, tearing him away from her navel, she would pull him up into the camper.

Afterwards they would sit and talk on the olive green chairs facing the open door. One of the magazines on the apple crate that served as a crude coffee table was an old *Better Homes and Gardens.* Angela said she liked to look at the pictures. One day as she sat there thumbing through it, she asked Clarence if he had a house. "Of course you do," she answered herself. That got Clarence telling her about the hot tub he'd put in a few years back, and how Shelly and her boyfriend had been the only ones who ever used it.

"You let your daughter bring a boy into your hot tub?"

"Yeah, me and Barb had a real argument over that one," Clarence frowned at the memory. "I said that ain't no place for teenagers of the opposite sex to be fraternizin half-naked. You're just askin for trouble. But Barb liked to think they were less likely to get up to no good under our nose than out in some parked car somewhere."

"She's right."

"That don't mean I got to like havin my daughter half-naked with some snot-nosed runt feeling her up behind my back."

Angela grinned at him.

"You got a jealous streak in you."

"Yeah, when it comes to Shelly."

"You got a picture of her?"

Clarence pulled out his wallet, a big fat rattlesnake skin thing nearly three inches thick, full of credit cards, receipts, notes, bills, business cards. He showed her the picture. It was one of Shelly's prom pictures. She was in a white satin dress with a big pink ribbon around the middle. She had blue mascara on.

"She takes after her mother," he said.

Next to it was an older Kmart studio photo of Clarence and Barb. He was in a dark brown suit with a striped tan-and-brown tie, his hair slicked back. She was thinner and her hair was down to her shoulders. Her glasses were smaller then. She and Clarence were smiling, gazing out into the great blue beyond.

"Now if that ain't the picture of wedded bliss, I don't know what is," Angela quipped.

"Yeah, well, we used to have a lot of fun when we was younger," Clarence replied, ignoring the touch of sarcasm in her voice. "Used to go to the dances all the time. Hell, I ain't complainin. It's just part of life. You ain't meant to have fun all the time. I done had my fun. I don't need anymore."

Angela looked at him.

"Ain't I your fun?"

Clarence set his hand paternally on her knee and smiled.

Meanwhile, the road progressed. Sometimes while he was clearing he'd look up the bajada (he was close enough now for an unobstructed view) and see Angela in the distance, outside the camper doing something—hanging some of the husband's clothes out to dry, taking their garbage out to burn, or just standing there watching him work—and he'd feel that this was the way things were meant to be: the man working the land, his home over yonder, his woman there with a child on the way. It got him thinking about civilization in general. What was it good for? What was everyone working so hard for? What was the point of all these computers and telephones and wall-to-wall carpeting and all the debt you had to get into to pay for it all? He didn't have any answers. He knew Reagan had beat the Russians, which pretty much proved that capitalism was a good way to run things, but sometimes he wondered if it wasn't just a little bit out of hand.

Most days she was happy to see him, but on a few occasions she seemed to be suffering from some pregnancy-related discomfort and wasn't up for any sex; she only wanted to talk. When Clarence asked her if she was taking her Female Vitality, she laughed.

"Is it me you're concerned about or yourself?"

"Come on now," he said.

Those were the days he felt the least comfortable being there in the camper with her, as if friendly conversation were the greater violation. Sometimes he would hear something outside and ask her to be quiet for a second, and he'd sit there, listening, but it was usually a small plane passing overhead, or nothing at all.

"The more I see of this life," she said on one of those moody days, a Friday afternoon, "the more I think it's a cruel thing bringin a new one into it. Nothin but lies the moment we take our first breath. Is that what my baby's got to look forward to? A life of lyin and cheatin? Is that the way it's gonna be?"

"I've got no complaints," Clarence said.

"Then you're just plain dumb."

"Dumb hell. I'm the smartest guy I know."

Clarence was itching to get back to the bulldozer, to the nice, clean, predictable lines of the road. But she had more to say.

"So after I'm gone you're just gonna carry on with your wife like nothin ever happened and never mention a word of it?"

"That's right."

Angela shook her head in disgust.

"What kind of life is that? Carryin that lie around inside you the rest of your life? And her probably carryin her own lies too."

"My wife ain't carryin around any lies worth a damn."

"How do you know?"

"Because I know."

"She could be out there fuckin someone right now, goin door to door, and you wouldn't even know it."

Clarence smiled at the thought.

"She hasn't got it in her."

"Same thing Trevor thinks."

She got up and walked over to the counter and poured herself a cup of liquor. She stood there drinking it almost spitefully, staring at Clarence. He'd told her more than once that drinking was the worst thing you could do to a baby in the womb. It annoyed him that she didn't seem to care.

"I've seen what it can do to you," she went on. "Carryin secrets around. It eats a hole in you. Trevor wouldn't need them pills if he just got rid of all the stuff inside his head. He won't even tell me, his own wife. I said to him, 'All right we'll swap secrets. You tell me what you done in Vietnam and I'll tell you somethin you don't want to hear.' He said I didn't have anything he didn't want to hear. Well, now I do, don't I? Maybe it's time we had us a little truth swap."

"Vietnam?" Clarence sat bolt upright, aghast at the sound of that word. "You're tellin me you're married to a Vietnam vet?"

"So what?"

"Jesus, girl. Are you nuts?" He stared at her. "He must be thirty years older than you."

"Well you ain't exactly no spring chicken yourself."

"I ain't the one married to you."

Clarence stood up and ran his fingers through his hair. He picked up his hat and put it on his head. He walked to the door. He turned and looked at her. "Why didn't you tell me your husband was a goddamn Vietnam vet?"

"What difference does it make?"

"Every difference in the world."

More than once he had come across Vietnam vets living out in a trailer or a shack in the desert, exiled from humanity, as if silence and isolation had become the essential nutrients of their troubled souls. There was something in their eyes that cut right through Clarence, no matter how seemingly friendly they were.

"This ain't me," Angela carried on, oblivious to the state she'd put Clarence in. "I need people. I need people to talk to. This is prison. I've thought about it a lot and this ain't no different from prison at all. It's worse. At least in prison you've got other prisoners to talk to."

Clarence looked her squarely in the eye and said, "Well why don't you just go on home?"

"I ain't got any money. How am I supposed to go back without any money? What am I supposed to live on? I can just hear Mama now, 'I told you not to marry that crazy bastard.'"

"Well how much you need? You could take the bus."

"How should I know? What difference is it to you anyway?"

Clarence opened his wallet and took out a fifty and handed it to her. She looked at it, looked at him.

"Get the hell out of here, you goddamn sonofabitch."

"Hold on, now, Angie. It ain't that way at all."

"Get out!" she shouted.

He did. He turned and walked out the door and didn't look back.

Monday morning he drove the flatbed hauler out there again. He thought about her as he walked up the path to the bulldozer. He wished it had ended on a better note, but he wasn't about to make the same mistake twice.

He and Barb had had the nicest weekend. Friday night they'd gone out to dinner and rented a video. Saturday afternoon they drove out to the pond at the El Paso Natural Gas Plant, like they used to when they were dating, and walked around it holding hands, talking about Shelly. Sunday at church Clarence felt his soul being cleansed by the word of God. Afterwards he made love to Barb the way she liked it, front to front, and he apologized for being grumpy lately, blaming it on his frustrations with his crew. He vowed to himself that he would never betray her again.

He had just settled into the seat of the bulldozer when he noticed some movement from the camper. He glanced up to see Angela in the doorway trying to signal to him with a hand mirror. But because the sun was behind her the mirror wasn't catching any light.

"What in God's name?" Clarence muttered as he watched her trying without success to get a sunbeam onto him. He was sorely tempted to ignore her, just fire up the bulldozer, turn it around, and drive it down the road without looking back.

He sat there for several minutes, waiting for her to give up and go back inside the camper, but she just stayed there in the doorway, pivoting the mirror. There was something conciliatory, something pathetic, in that futile gesture, and Clarence wasn't one to turn a blind eye on someone trying to set things right.

He cursed himself as he got down and set out for the camper. He wasn't too far from it when he noticed that all the crates of rocks were gone. That put a hitch in his stride. He instinctively surveyed the surrounding area for the truck, sensing changes afoot.

She had dispensed with the mirror by the time he reached her. He stopped short of the camper, hooked his thumbs over his front pockets, and looked her over without comment, figuring the burden of speech was on her this time.

"We're leavin tomorrow," she stated flatly.

Clarence looked over to where the crates had been.

"Where is he?" he said.

"Gettin some stuff in town."

"Why didn't you go with him?"

"What do you think?" she said.

Clarence turned his head and spat.

She settled down in the doorway with her feet out on the step. Clarence looked up at the mountains. The sun was just breaching the crests and there was still a hint of coolness in the air.

"Sorry I yelled at you," she said after a while.

"Forget it."

An image of the camper gone, the road path clear at last, flashed across Clarence's mind, and it pleased him.

"Where you all off to?" he asked her.

"What's the next state over?"

Clarence turned his head and looked out across the desert. The shadows lay long westward of the bushes, insects flitting in the angled sunlight.

"Woman, if you don't know that."

She stepped down from the camper and walked over to him, her flip-flops thwacking her heels with every step.

"I told you I was sorry," she said, taking hold of his hands. "Or ain't my apology good enough for you?"

Clarence looked her in the eyes.

"I told myself I was finished with you."

She pulled his hands forward and set them on her belly. She started moving them around in circles.

"You can be finished tomorrow," she said.

Clarence closed his eyes and, despite his determination not to, began to reconsider things. The sound of her breath as his palm grazed her navel settled it. *One for the road*, he thought.

She led him over to the camper, and he followed her up the steps and in. She went straight to the counter. As his eyes adjusted to the dimness he saw that she was holding a pistol in her hands. It was pointed at him.

Clarence stood there looking at her, offended by the notion that she thought he was someone she could point a gun at.

"What in God's name do you think you're doing?"

"Get them pants off," she said.

Clarence stared at her, not knowing whether to laugh or get mad.

"If it's money you're after, all you have to do is ask."

"You're a fool," she said.

Clarence stared at her for a few seconds, then turned to step back out the door and be on his way. She fired. The blast, or the shock wave it sent down his spine, knocked his hat off and opened a small hole of sunlight in the wall a few feet to the left of his head. The bang echoed through his brain as if through an empty canyon, gradually leveling out to a high-pitched ringing in his left ear.

Clarence slowly turned back around, his hands instinctively rising. "Off," she said. He quickly unlatched his belt buckle and lowered his pants. "All the way," she said. He pulled off his boots and took his pants off and stood before her in his boxers and socks. "Sit on the chair," she said, pointing with the pistol. He went over and sat down. She backed her way to the door, keeping the pistol pointed at him, and stepped down.

She took the keys from the front pocket of Clarence's pants and the wallet from the back. She opened the wallet and pulled out the photographs of Barb and Shelly. She tucked them into the front of her dress and tossed the wallet aside. Until that moment Clarence had been more pissed off than afraid. Now he felt a cold wave of fear roll through him. If she had taken the money, or the entire wallet, that would have been something he could understand.

"What do you want?" he said, his mouth suddenly dry.

She smiled. "I wish you could see your face."

She draped his pants over her shoulders and turned and set out walking down the road path, the gun in her right hand, Clarence's keys in her left.

When she was about fifty yards away, Clarence got up and went to the door.

"Hey!" he yelled. "Give me my goddamn pants back, you crazy bitch!"

She didn't look back. He watched her walk down to the bulldozer and step up into the seat. She sat there for what seemed like several minutes, looking down at the controls.

Then Clarence heard the rumble of the engine firing up, saw the black exhaust belch from the stack. He watched in stupefaction as the blade jerked up, rose to its full height, then began descending again. The engine revved. The bulldozer jerked backwards. It stopped. More time passed. She seemed to be pushing and pulling everything. The blade rose again. Then the dozer jerked forward and stayed in motion.

Clarence stood there in a kind of trance, watching his bulldozer drawing nearer, as one watches in silent awe the needles of lightning flashing in a distant storm. She was bearing down on him with the same dispassion, and there was something both awful and beautiful in her placid face coming at him above the mud-encrusted blade.

It was the sound of a yucca stalk cracking less than fifty feet away that snapped Clarence out of it. He reached for his boots and frantically yanked them on. He grabbed his wallet from the floor, picked up his hat, and jumped out the door, scrambling out of the way just in time to see the blade dig into the side of the camper. The camper leapt up with a piercing squeal. Everything inside flew up and slammed into the back wall. The teeth of the treads caught the undercarriage and gnawed the floor to splinters as the bulldozer rolled up and over the camper, flattening it to rubble as it climbed through it and out the other side.

She managed a wide turn out into the desert and circled her way back around to the road and carried on down it. Clarence stood there bare legged, mouth open, watching her, and as she receded down the road atop his bulldozer it seemed to him as if the sky itself was ripping wide open before her.

What to Do with the Dead

DON WATERS

MELVIN, MY COWORKER, SOMETIMES TALKED GHOSTS WHILE PREPAR-
ing a burn.

"So look, friends say it's strange, but there's a clause in my will for
Springer," he told me. "And I wanted your opinion about it," he went on,
"whether or not, you know, it's strange?"

Springer was a large part of Melvin's life, a calico I'd heard much about.
I didn't have an opinion one way or the other. To me, whatever Melvin
wanted: fine. Though I'd only known him a short time, it was clear Melvin,
a squat, fortyish, high-foreheaded man, was a champion of animal com-
panionship. I'd also heard talk from the grounds crew that Melvin was a
refugee fresh from a war-torn marriage, which helped explain his devotion.

"It's decided that when Springer goes there's a spot for him in my enter-
tainment center," he said, adding, as if to impress me, "behind glass."

Melvin tapped the retort's gauge, inspecting the temperature. A glowing
ball of orange light filled the retort's small rectangular window as it climbed
toward sixteen hundred degrees.

"And when I go, I've requested that Springer be mixed in with me. For
interment I've decided—"

Melvin lifted his hand, his ginger-colored eyes widening. He carefully
scanned the plain industrial room.

"Did you feel that?" he asked. "The breeze?"

He was talking ghosts again and I didn't like it. I didn't believe in ghosts,
or spirits, or gods. I painted. Life was filled with too many choices.

Melvin massaged his forearms, saying, "Now that was something."

I was across the room on a hard metal stool, trying to copy down the delivery addresses of yesterday's burns. A black binder hung via wire from the wall. Lists of names corresponded to dates of death. Attached was a pencil, a chipped nub, which gave my hand cramps.

The pencil's tip hovered over a street that didn't match my directory. I didn't recognize the name. In fact, where the hell was Choking, Nevada? I looked at the form again. Mary Ellis, age thirty. Requested delivery address: Choking. A joke? I was more annoyed that I didn't know where Choking was than by the fact that Mary Ellis was a thirty-year-old overdose.

All together, there were four deliveries, including the capsule now resting on the retort's mechanical lift.

"Who's going in?" Melvin asked.

I picked fuzz from my lip. "A man named Edward Yoo."

"Makes sense, another Chinese bribe," Melvin said. "The man's restless. I hope his family gave him a spendy send-off. That was probably him, just now, Edward Yoo."

I wanted to ask Melvin how he figured that, but didn't.

Every few weeks we had one, a money box. I'd learned from Melvin it was old country tradition to place cash and gifts with the dead to satisfy the spirits. I'd seen a few overeager families stuffing bodies with thousands of dollars. They packed mouths full of twenties; they folded rigor-mortised hands around hundreds. Out of respect I never explained to them what they didn't need to know. That the retort was an elaborately designed, computerized machine that recycled cinerary vapor through a series of funnels, and in the end, the only thing left was heat, not smoke. All that cash was incinerated over and over, and what remained was an imperceptible translucent streak shimmering from the chimney.

The retort's glow colored Melvin's pupils gold. He stepped behind the control panel and said, "How'd he die?"

"Car crash, it says."

Melvin said, "Well, help me carry him home."

I was working on a bubble. I blew it, and gum bonded to my upper lip.

Melvin tipped his head. "At what point did you get so weightless?" he asked, which was funny of Melvin, a funny thing to ask.

~⌐

Each hundred pounds required an hour to incinerate. During the three days a week I worked, I'd discovered the job required a lot of standing around.

Estimating from Mr. Yoo's weight, I thought he was an hour and a half, give or take. At the end of a life, I'd come to realize, some of us are reduced to six pounds of gray powder with two bored men pacing around our processed bones in a concrete room.

Earlier, on my drive to work, the sky had in it a purple tone I hadn't noticed before. I thought about replicating the crushed-grape color on an abandoned urn.

Melvin patted a boxy bulge over his heart. "Duty calls," he said.

"Mel, wait," I said. He pulled back the door. I said, "Did you feel that?"

"Oh, Mister Hilarious," Melvin said.

While Melvin stepped outside for a smoke, I removed acrylics, bowls, blotched towels, etc., from my footlocker and headed to the vault. The stairs to the basement were bordered by solemn cement walls that brought to mind a nuclear silo. The heavy steel door to the vault was open. Stepping inside, I smelled cinder. I briefly wondered whom I was breathing.

Newer burns were on the floor, stickered for delivery. These wood, stone, and bronze urns all had destinations: mortuaries, residences, a reserved spot on a flight to the Midwest. But it was the others that interested me. Lining a shelf along the back wall rested my blank templates, small cardboard tombs that held the remains of the unknown and the forgotten.

We had a contract with the county. Twice a week the coroner's minivan pulled up and rolled the bodies in. Some mornings, I'd arrive at work to find five or six horizontals already waiting. I'd also find Melvin, locked in the side room, talking to himself. Without names with which to invent a face, no birth dates, the bodies were mysteries. Our only clues were the coroner's forms, which listed causes of death. Suicides, mostly: gunshots, hangings, the filleted arms of the depressed. It was a transient city, and I figured these numbers were normative.

I was part of its transience, and I'd grown to appreciate the town's gaudy, burned-neck sensibility. Elementally it was a gambling town, what I considered a full-scale, interactive Dali. We were practically cut off from the rest of the universe by a vast desert to the east and, to the west, a looming mountain range.

I'd relocated for reasons. The living was cheap, the sun shined three hundred days a year, and—it was becoming a pattern—yet another girlfriend had X-ed me from her life, a woman I believed I'd loved, who said in the course of our airless, tearless discussion that I'd always lacked ("was immune to" were Christine's words) emotional depth, which I just did not get.

In a few short months my hobby had transformed the vault into a lush underground island. I'd decorated nearly half of the indigent urns with a single impressionistic detail, whatever I could multiply from memory. An aspen leaf, a rivulet, green patches of forest. It was good for my mood; plus, Melvin liked it. He said my pastime showed real heart, unlike the delivery guy before me. Melvin had mentioned the guy had the habit of disappearing to the bathroom and communing with aluminum foil packets of crystal meth.

Melvin slammed the door upstairs and scraped around. Soon I heard low, sad strains from a radio.

On the far side of the vault, packed in a corner, were the paid-for castaways, an oak receptacle, a fancy cone-looking thing, etc. Their only purpose now, it seemed, was to take up space. Looking at these urns, I always conjured up the image of a battered widow talking incoherently to a white wall. I'd think, I don't know why: here's what's left of a wife beater; here's the remains of a child molester. Someone had requested and paid for incineration. Someone had chosen a specific urn, but for whatever reason—malice, I suspected—the property went unclaimed.

The decision to use heat and light, a sixteen-hundred-degree oven, was an act of forced closure. And to erase almost all physical evidence of a person and abandon them to an underground cement vault struck me as . . . But it was just as well.

Delivering the dead was part-time and the pay was miserable, which made it perfect when going for broke. My move from New York had an attached aim. I wanted to earn less than thirteen grand by tax-filing season in order to qualify for subsidized housing.

Around town there were scores of government-sponsored apartment complexes—hovels, essentially, but they made ideal base camps. Cut-rate, no maintenance; it certainly wasn't a way to live forever. In any case, my time was largely spent outdoors, rustling inspiration from desolation. I was trained as a landscape painter, and desert was fascinating study. Desert defined the limits of civilized space. It offered an unobtrusive canvas in which everyday matter diminished or enlarged in proportion to the day's light. (I discovered detail in its lack of; I found lines in its shapeless barrens.) Anyway, there were just too many painters in New York painting New York, so when Christine chopped me off at the knees, I finally decided to place art on the top shelf of my life. But subsidized eligibility required poverty.

There were ample famine-level listings in the local Help-Wanteds— dishwasher, lawn mower, etc. One ad, however, grabbed my attention. My reason for applying? I liked the gothic typeface on the name "Sunset View." I was also intrigued by the miniature logo, what appeared to be a Ming vase with wings.

I arrived in my van. The crematorium was at the bottom of a bronze hill hidden under a spattering of ancient oaks and surrounded by the sprawling, sunbaked lawn of a cemetery.

The manager, a man named Peter, escorted me into his office. Peter was one of the unlucky ones. He had a deformed cranium. It appeared that at some early fetal stage his brain had shifted bone to the right side of his skull, spawning a remarkable protrusion.

I handed Peter a résumé. He shot me a look of naked surprise.

He said, "Usually folks forget to bring a pen."

Peter began the interrogation. He asked me what it meant to graduate in fine arts? I told him I painted trees. For some reason, he winced.

Finally, Peter said, "What's your temperament when it comes to bullshit?"

"Excuse me?"

"Okay, all right, fine." He was beginning to look upset, and I tried to decipher the reason. "You have a car?" he asked.

I gestured out his window. He stole a sideward glance at my van parked in the lot. I'd painted fat, swollen cumulus clouds across the side.

"Understand this," Peter said. "Some are hard deliveries." He leaned back executively in his leather chair, lacing his fingers together. "Say you hand over an urn to a grieving wife and she smacks you across the face. Not your fault, clearly, we see all kinds, but what do you do?"

I was startled by the question, but I appreciated the fact he'd put it out there. "Nothing," I said, speaking the truth.

"Sure, okay, fine," Peter said.

Peter drove me around the grounds in a golf cart topped with a lemon yellow canopy. As he pointed things out, Peter kept his head tilted to the left, as if compensating for the bulge on the side opposite.

We stopped at the crematorium. Peter threw a manual in my lap, said I should know a few things. When we stepped inside, the retort was preheating. Peter looked around, growing pissed off again. He opened the door to a side room, and a short man was sitting in a metal chair. The man was covering his ears with his hands.

"That's Melvin."

Peter led me downstairs to the vault. When I saw the dull brown boxes, the wall of containers stacked like bricks, my first thought was: mine. I thought, as Peter rambled: all mine. It was in my nature to renovate. A gray room, a vacant wall, I saw potential.

He pointed at the shelf. "At the end of the year these get dumped in a common grave. Melvin usually performs an amateur ceremony," Peter said. "No one ever attends, obviously."

~~~

I stood back, examining my painted cube of liquid purple. I pictured my collection of colored vessels disappearing under a pile of copper dirt while Melvin held open a Bible, speaking of nonexistent things. It was a disappointing thought.

Impermanence, as a notion, frightened me. I quietly clung to the belief, foolishly perhaps, that through art there was the slim possibility of a life beyond, a second life made eternal by the white light on a gallery wall. After all, who wanted their legacy to be a distant echo?

The skin beneath my fingernails was stained indigo from my work. I tossed my brush into a white salad bowl. A violet mist drifted through the water.

After a while, Melvin clambered down with a dolly, rattling my nerves with each stair.

"Mr. Yoo is cooling," Melvin said. Standing safely outside the door, he placed his hands on his hips and studied the newest addition. "Springer would like it," he said.

It required a day to dry, and I decided I liked it too. I considered painting the rest of the top shelf different moods of sky, creating atmosphere above the leaves, rivers, and hills.

Melvin quickly began packaging the urns marked for the day's delivery. Counting Edward Yoo, there were three mortuaries on my list, one house visit. We wrapped the urns in parchment and then placed each into a cardboard box with winged logos printed on the sides. Melvin, in a hurry, sealed boxes with packing tape. Whenever he visited the vault he moved with purpose. He worked decisively, guardedly, as though the vault's door was some sort of demarcation line that he'd crossed.

From a back pocket, I removed my list.

"It says on this one." I touched the box with the cherry wood urn in it. "It says Choking, Nevada," I said to Melvin. "Where's that?"

Melvin looked distant. "I've heard of Maybe, California," he said.

We loaded my van and spread a map across the hot pavement. Melvin bent to inspect it and his finger traveled east, across dried lake beds, over old mining towns. Unbelievably, his finger kept moving, until at last it stopped four inches from where we were now crouched.

"That can't be right," I said.

"Looks that way, Julian."

"That's at least two hundred fifty miles across the desert," I said. And it was. Choking was a miniscule black crumb in the middle of the state.

"Who's the delivery?" Melvin asked.

"Ellis, Mary," I said, unsure why I'd said her name that way. "She was my age."

Delivering urns to residential addresses was not my favorite activity. Each time I jotted down a residence on the paperwork, I noted the cause of death, the date of birth. I wanted to know how much of a storm to expect on the drop-off. Early century dates, even mid-century, a '28, a '48, those never registered with the same impact as the occasional times I came across a birth year close to mine. "She was a thirty-year-old suicide," I said.

"A real shame," Melvin said. He stood up, and I heard his knee pop. "You'll be back late. Tonight, I guess. Me and Springer have a date with TV."

"Fantastic," I said.

"Bring your paints. Look at it that way. Make it an excursion."

I said, "Christ."

"Lord's name in vain," Melvin said.

~⌒◡

Midday, and the heat was punishing inside the van. I leaned over to the passenger side, where dozens of cassettes were scattered across the floor. A thrift shop near my studio sold the things for a nickel. I noticed that a Lynyrd Skynyrd had melted into a futuristic molten sculpture. I located the tape I was searching for, cranked it up.

Naturally, I tried not to think about it. That there was a graveyard behind my seat. Some days there were eleven, twelve cardboard boxes behind me, so to keep it manageable I invented opinions. Today, I wondered, did they like my painted van?

Mr. Yoo thought, yes.

Kids liked it too; they waved. Drivers honked. Then there were the tough guys, their car doors primed gray, who usually stared until a stoplight flashed green.

Mortuaries were easy drop-offs. I rang a bell, a door opened. A strict face stared out. The city was fifteen minutes anywhere via the freeway, and by early afternoon Mr. Yoo and two others had been safely transported.

With house calls it was typical for someone to break down. A small child once answered the door, saw the box that contained his father, screamed at me, and then darted upstairs. I'd developed a stock response when situations got tight. "Yeah, yeah, yeah," I'd say slowly, accompanied by a few head shakes. One elderly woman had led me inside, prepared Earl Grey tea, and wrapped my palm around a large tip. Thankfully, I'd never been assaulted, as Peter had warned, but when one woman answered her door holding a spatula, she proceeded to smack the cardboard box until I dropped it.

I fueled up at Milo's, a mini-mart I frequented. It was near the I-80 on-ramp, and I figured I'd kill an hour, wait while the heat let up. I slid open the van door and threw a Tijuana-bought blanket over the last box, that of Mary Ellis. There was a quick sting in my bottom lip as I reconsidered. I took her with me.

Aligned neatly along the front wall like chromium tombstones was a row of blinking Quartermania slots. I noticed that my stool at the end was empty. That particular machine had once paid me five Benjamins from candy-bar change. Following that single payout, my synapses were prone to light up whenever I'd sit for a pull or two. I turned two twenties into quarters, and Mary Ellis slid in by my feet.

Sitting on the next stool was a short, obese woman whose breasts hung low and met in her lap. I fed the hungry mouth five quarters, got nothing.

In terms of aesthetics, Milo's was antichic. Fishing gear was sold alongside up-all-night trucker tablets, and puffs of smoke drifted in DNA patterns from ashtrays situated between the other gamblers. In New York, sure, I gambled. A Knicks game, a friend's poker table, a few hundred lost, whatever. Christine detested it. She said the money should go toward "trips." But at Milo's, I figured, my gambling was justifiable; it was another way to pick up tax-free cash. At the casinos, anything over six hundred was reportable. They made you fill out forms.

The woman sitting on the adjacent stool startled me by talking. "You from here?" she asked me.

I wasn't in the habit of fraternizing while losing my money. I inserted another quarter, picturing small walruses hiding beneath her loose T-shirt.

I said, "Me?"

"Yeah, silly, you," she said. She tugged back her lever, and I glanced at her zipped-open fanny pack. From the look of her cache, she was wealthier than me.

I said, "Poughkeepsie, originally."

"What kind of name is that?" she said.

The woman kept talking, spending, burrowing into her pack.

It was incredible. My machine was loose. Seven dollars in quarters and in a single pull it paid out again: one hundred and fifty-two dollars on three lined-up strawberries and a peach.

I collected my winnings from the cashier and returned for Mary Ellis. I lifted her from the floor.

"Have you heard of a place called Choking?" I asked my gambling neighbor.

"Sure, nothing there," the woman said. She looked up and I was struck by a pair of mesmerizing emerald eyes. She said, "But yeah, I've heard of it. It's a ghost town."

Desert was notable for its sterility, which was terrific for rendering on canvas, but the infinite wasteland grew tiresome. I steered east until the last signs of civilization melted from my windows and new backdrops exposed themselves. Umber, mountainous slopes were pockmarked with a million dots of gnarled sage. And the heat, even in the late afternoon, was relentless.

I passed one, two, sixty monstrous eighteen-wheelers. With the windows down, the growl of their churning engines filled the van. A faint trace of pleasure came each time I trumped one of the beasts. I wondered what unimportant things they were hauling, growing more aware with each mile that their loads couldn't match the gravity of mine. For forty miles I tried placing the name. And, finally, it arrived: Charon, the gangster who required payment to cross the Styx. We do have our myths. The Greeks laid coins on the eyes of their dead while the Chinese bribed spirits.

I cycled through cassette tapes. Most I'd tossed in the back to clear space for Mary Ellis' box on the passenger seat. But when my music selection wore thin, there was nowhere to hide when my mind wanted to stumble over pebbles of memory. A still shot of Christine as she wrote poems; her long delicate fingers; how she'd wanted children; how at times I missed her.

The sky turned the same purplish hue as earlier in the day. And the farther I drove the more frustrated I became by the skeletal figures of crooked power-line poles paralleling me. Eventually, after a few hours, a faded green sign directed me to a two-lane highway. All at once the landscape's canvas enlarged, lengthened, and I'd never felt more alone. The middle-of-nowhere town was seventy more miles down a flat, empty road.

The only thing my stereo picked up was a country station, old pity music drowned by static. As the miles on the marker signs ticked downward, the station's reception improved. A man's gravelly voice introduced a song. The crackle in his throat brought to mind the sound of sticks breaking. The song was Waylon Jennings, and I turned it up.

Approaching town, I noticed a drab, fenced-in, jail-like compound set off from the main highway down an ill-paved road. Above the compound hovered a two-hundred-foot radio tower.

Choking was a Xerox copy of images I'd only seen in history books. Four brick buildings were padlocked, boards nailed over their windows. I crept along with the address in my hand. The only places open, apparently, were an auto body shop, the United Church of Choking, and a Chinese restaurant, Wok Here.

I pulled over. Odd that there wasn't a road sign for Highway 6.5. Odder still was the matter that there was a highway halved and decimal-pointed.

I drove to the end of town, or what someone had once designated a town, and turned the van around. I didn't enjoy the thought of wasting my afternoon, guzzling sixty in gas, and getting lost.

From a pay phone in the auto shop's dirt lot, I called Melvin at the crematorium. After no answer, I tried Peter's office. I got his machine. I hung up when I heard his weird angry message. To the west, the sun was beginning to fall, and I noted the way the tips of hills darkened and turned the color of plums.

I walked toward the auto shop's open garage. A young guy in khaki overalls stepped from behind a demolished car propped up by tireless rims.

I said, "Highway 6.5?"

"You're on it," he said.

I tried to digest this. I was on Highway 6, not Highway 6.5. I gave the guy the address.

"Oh, that's back aways, maybe three miles," he said. "That radio tower you passed. Between here and the station is Highway 6.5."

Choking, I decided, was the right name for the place.

I backtracked and drove down the poorly paved road, stopping in front of a gate. A ten-foot chain-link fence topped with spirals of rusty razor wire encircled the small brick compound. I wondered who would want to break in. Perhaps someone didn't want to get out. Behind the building was a trailer, its paint peeling, and parked beside it was an older-model sports car, dents in its side.

I carried Mary Ellis to the gate and pushed a button on a box. Blinds in a window split into a sharp V as someone looked out.

A buzzer sounded.

Another buzzer was implanted in a black grille door. I was gradually beginning to feel that the cardboard box in my arms—Mary Ellis—was live ordnance.

The door swung open, and an unshaven man with a thick shock of white hair stepped onto the stoop. He was in his sixties, I guessed, with all-around stubble flecked by spots of red.

I said, "Mr. Ellis?"

He steadied his hand by holding it with the other. There was a shake in it. "What's this about?" he asked. I recognized his gravelly voice. He'd been talking to me through my radio.

I gave him my name. Softly, I told him where I was from.

Mr. Ellis responded by closing his eyes, laying two trembling fingers on both. After a moment, his eyes opened.

"That my daughter?" he said.

I told him, yes.

"Set her down right there, please," he said.

As requested, I placed Mary Ellis on the stoop. Then I thought about leaving, quickly. Mr. Ellis squinted over my shoulder, toward my van. I turned to leave, and Mr. Ellis said, "You thirsty, Julian? A drink?"

His trailer was sparsely furnished. Except for a few charred ovals crusted to the stove top, the place was immaculate. Sharp ammonia fumes clung to the air. Out on the stoop, I'd been somewhat afraid to decline his offer, considering. Hanging on the wall was a warped poster of a ranchero strumming a guitar.

I asked for water. Instead, Mr. Ellis filled two shot glasses with cheap vodka and handed me one. He leaned a shoulder against the refrigerator. With each sip, his lips pulled back and I saw gums.

"Ten years Mary's been gone," Mr. Ellis told me. "The first time she left, she was maybe nineteen. Ran away with an older man, Warren, used to drive limos, a real son of a bitch."

On the refrigerator, pegged by an ochre magnet, I saw a snapshot of a young family dressed in their Sunday best. The clothes were from a different decade, and there was a crease down the center of the photo. I recognized Mr. Ellis without the milk in his hair, but it was the girl beside him, and the woman next to her, who captured me. The girl looked to be in her early teens. Curtains of red hair framed her round, cherubic face.

"When I got that phone call and heard how it happened," Mr. Ellis said, "I thought about it, you know, the way people think about those things. Thinking about it now too." He sipped and I saw more gums. "Anyway, when I wired money I didn't expect this." He pointed his glass at me. "You."

I studied the photograph again, memorizing Mary's eyes. I wanted them to speak. An unexpected ache sealed my throat, and I coughed vodka back into my glass.

"Careful," Mr. Ellis said. He looked over my shoulder at his little home. I asked him what he thought about it, about Choking. "Quiet, you know, but I have my music," he said.

Standing next to her father, her face beaming, Mary had her hand wrapped around his arm. I wanted Mr. Ellis to mention the girl's mother, tell me about her, but he didn't.

Mr. Ellis said, "I can't accept that box, Julian. Or, what I mean is," he said, "I know Mary wouldn't have wanted to come back. There's nothing here she liked. I mean is, you can find Mary a decent resting place back in town, I hope?"

I told him about the common grave, the small informal ceremony.

"Let's do that," he said, and he drained his glass. I placed my vodka, unfinished, on the counter.

"Time to get back to the station, son," he said. "We're running dead air."

In front of the compound, I dug my key into the cardboard box and ripped away parchment paper. I handed the urn to Mr. Ellis.

"It's a nice color," he said.

I didn't have anything, so I said nothing.

One final time Mr. Ellis held his daughter, and I noticed, though I wasn't certain, a look of injury enter his eyes. If there were tears, they didn't come. Maybe ten years without her had bled the man dry.

Then, unexpectedly, Mr. Ellis smiled, and he handed me the urn. His fingers had lost their quiver. He took out an orange pill bottle and poured three white tablets into his steady palm. He shook out a few more until the bottle was empty.

"Care to join me?" he said.

The ache from a moment before busied itself into anger as I pictured the young red-haired girl in the picture standing beside this man. I couldn't move. I simply stared at him.

One by one, Mr. Ellis popped the pills into his mouth. It wasn't enough to do serious damage, just enough so that he wouldn't feel anything. He held the empty pill bottle with three fingers, as if he were pinching a shot glass. He moved the bottle to his lips. "To women," he said to me, winking, and he tipped his head back and swallowed. He pulled open the black grille door, and when it closed, I heard the snap of a lock.

In the van I sat listening to static, waiting for a song to play. A minute of silence turned into fifteen, and I reached for the ignition. Several miles down the road a grim voice crackled from my speakers. As I listened to Mr. Ellis set up a song, I thought of what Melvin had asked. When had I gotten so weightless?

What to do with the dead, what to do with Mary Ellis. Even though I liked my painted collection of boxes, it was painful to imagine Mary's urn tossed into the common grave with them. I listened until the station dissolved into atmospheric clicks. A few high beams illuminated the van, but otherwise, we were alone, wordless. We drove.

Blackness filled the night sky, and I decided to exit the highway, driving until I found a dirt road, a quiet little piece of nowhere. A mile or so from pavement, I stopped the van. Brush scraped my knees, and the cherry wood felt slick and cold against my fingers.

Although there was little to see within the void, I knew we were surrounded by sand, by granite rock, by mountains that had ground down into a sea of sharp, beige grains. Perhaps in another thousand years, I thought, there would be water here again, a lake.

I poured Mary into a mound at my feet. Deduct what I'd spent on gas, and ninety dollars was all that remained of my slot winnings. I knew it wasn't much, but it was what I could offer. I returned from the van with the fiery eye of my cigarette lighter and the seven tattered bills burned swiftly on top of her ashes.

A warm space opened in the blackness, as gray strings of smoke drifted upward, and I hoped it carried Mary. I hoped to deliver her safely. The fire died out, a perfect emptiness descended, and I looked up, watching pieces of feathery ash vanish into a sky pulsing with fragments of white light.

Man-O-War

Claire Vaye Watkins

THE FIFTH OF JULY. MILO SLUNK OUT AND SNIFFED AROUND THE DRY lake bed while Harris loaded his find into the truck. The bitch was a pound mutt—mostly Lab, was the old man's guess—and the abandoned stash was a good one, like last night's festivities never got to it. At least fifteen Pyro Pulverizer 33-shot repeaters, a load of Black Cat artilleries and Screamin' Meemies, some Fortress of Fire and Molten Core mortars, probably three dozen Wizard of Ahhhs, and one Man-O-War, a hard-to-find professional-grade shell pack, banned even on Paiute land after an Indian boy blew his brother's face off in '99. It was a couple grand worth of artillery, all told. The largest pile Harris had ever found.

Every Fourth of July kids from Gerlach, Nixon, Lovelock, and Indian kids from the Paiute res came out to the Black Rock with their lawn chairs, coolers of Miller, bottles of carnival-colored Boone's Farm for the girls. They built themselves a bonfire, got thoroughly loaded, and shot off fireworks. The lake bed had no trees, no brush, no weeds to catch fire, just the bald bottom of an ancient inland sea. They dumped their Roman Candles and Missile Heads and Comet Cluster shells and Komodo 3000 fountains in a heap away from their encampments, out of range of the fires, then trotted out there whenever they wanted to light them off.

Except out here the night got so dark and the kids got so loaded they'd forget where they stowed their fireworks. They'd forget they even had fireworks. They'd drink like men, like their fathers and uncles, like George fucking Washington, take off their shirts and thump their chests and scream into the wide black space. Pass out in their truck beds and let their tipsy girlfriends drive them home all in a line. Leave their stash for an old man to scavenge come sunup.

Harris moved quickly now, working up a sweat as the sun burned the haze from the valley. He unbuttoned his shirt. Finished loading and ready to leave, he called Milo. He slapped his thigh. He whistled. But Milo didn't come.

Scanning, Harris could barely make out a shape in the distance, warped by the heat waves already rising from the ground. He drove to it, keeping an eye on Ruby Peak so he'd know his way home. Out here a person could get turned around and lose his own trail, each stretch of nothing looking like the next, east looking like south looking like west, not knowing where he came on the lake bed, and not knowing how to get home.

The shape in the distance was Milo, as Harris thought it would be, bent over and sniffing at a heap of something. The truck rolled closer and stopped. Harris got out, softly shutting the door behind him.

"Come here, dog," he said. But Milo stayed, nosing the pile.

It was a girl—a young girl, Mexican—lying on her side, unconscious. Maybe dead. Harris circled her. She wore cutoffs, the white flaps of pockets sticking out the frayed bottoms. She was missing a shoe, a thick-soled flip-flop. A white button-up man's shirt tied in a knot exposed her pouchy belly. Her navel was pierced, had one of those dangly pink jewels nestled inside. Rising below the jewel was a bruise, inky purple, the size of a baseball. Or a fist.

Milo licked at the vomit in the girl's black hair, matted to her head. Harris pushed the dog away with his boot and crouched over her. He laid his hand on the curve of her calf. Her skin was hot; the early morning sun had begun to burn her. She was breathing, he saw then, but barely. Her lips were dry and cracked white as the lake bed itself. No doubt she hadn't had any water in God knows how long. Her dark fingernail polish was chipped. Fifteen years old, maybe sixteen, but she was wearing a truckload of makeup and he couldn't tell with these kids anymore.

Harris shook the girl gently, trying to wake her. He looked around and saw no one, only dirt and mountain and sky. He poured some water from his jug and wet her lips with it. It was an hour and a half to the trailer clinic in Gerlach, and they couldn't do much more for her than he could. His knees popped as he hoisted the girl and positioned her body across the seat of the truck.

"Let's go," he said, and slapped his thigh. Milo came then, slowly: sharp ears, bad eyes, bad hips, a limp of one variety or another in all four legs. Harris squatted and lifted the dog to the bed of the truck.

The truck sped for six, seven miles over the white salt crust of the lake bed. Harris watched absently for dark spots of wet earth. When it had the chance, the Black Rock held moisture, as if it remembered when Nevada was mostly ocean, as if it was trying its damnedest to get the Great Basin back underwater. It would be hard—shit, near impossible—to dig the truck out of the mud by himself, even with the squares of carpet he kept in the bed for traction. And there was no time for that.

The tires of the Ford crunched the dirt, leaving a pair of faint tracks. Harris turned and followed two tire-wide ruts of crushed sagebrush. The road shifted from weed to dirt to gravel. Harris bent and put his face to the girl's. He felt her breath against his cheek. He turned once to check on Milo, her tail wagging against the fireworks he'd forgotten he'd come for.

The road shifted twice more: to State Route 40, that hot belt of shoulderless asphalt, and then to Red's Road, the ten-mile stretch of gravel that led up the alluvial fan to Harris's slumped brick house.

Harris carried the girl inside. She didn't stir when he laid her on the couch, or when he slipped her remaining sandal from her softly curled toes. Milo milled underfoot, sniffing at the sandal on the floor where Harris set it. "Don't even think about it," he said. The dog retreated to sulk in front of the swamp cooler.

Figuring it would make her more comfortable, Harris unknotted the girl's shirt. Though he'd already seen the twin juts of her pelvis and the slope of her stomach—she wasn't leaving much to the imagination—his hands fumbled and his breath went shallow while he buttoned the wrinkled flaps back together, not sure what he would say if, at that moment, she woke.

But she woke only once that afternoon, delirious. It was all he could do to make her drink, tap water from the Mason jar sliding down her stretched neck, wetting her chest, pooling in the divots above her collarbones. While she slept he checked on her often, felt for a fever, held a moist washcloth to her forehead and cheeks. He cleaned the puke out of her hair by dabbing at it with damp paper towels. All the while the bruise on her abdomen seemed to throb, to shape shift.

There was only so much he could do. He tidied up the house while she slept, washed the dishes, made his bed, trimmed Milo's nails. He could not remember the last time he'd had a houseguest, if the girl could be considered such. At least sixteen years. And though she was unconscious, having the girl there cultivated a bead of shame in him for the years of clutter he'd accumulated, with no one to get after him. The living room was walled with hutches and shelves and curio cabinets that had once been full of trinkets long since removed by Carrie Ann, off for another long stay at her sister's while he sat smoking on the porch, too angry or afraid to ask what she needed with her Kewpie dolls in Fallon. The shelves now held his rock collection: igneous feldspars, quartzes, olivines, and micas on the east wall; sedimentary gneiss and granoblastics on the built-in along the north; shale, siltstones, breccias, and most conglomerates along the west wall, minus the limestones, gemstones, and his few opals, which he kept in the bedroom.

Plastic milk crates lined the edges of the room, full mostly of chrysocolla chunks pickaxed from the frozen rock above Nixon the previous winter. A few were marbled with nearly microscopic arteries of gold. Dusty, splitting cardboard boxes were stacked four and five tall near the coat closet and in front of it, full of samples to be sent to the lab in Reno for testing, to tell whether or not his claims had finally paid off, whether he might augment his miner's pension. The rusted oil barrels on the porch and wheelbarrows out front overflowed with dirty schorl and turquoise and raw malachite in need of cutting and tumbling, specimens enough to supply a chain of rock shops from here to San Francisco.

Harris tried straightening up, but there was nowhere to put it all. Even the single drawer of his nightstand was filled with soapstone and milky, translucent chunks of ulexite waiting to be labeled.

He kept an eye on the lake bed too, though whoever left the girl would most likely know better than to come looking for her. It was a hundred and six degrees by ten a.m. The only person with any business out here this time of year was Harvey Bowman, a jack Mormon from Battle Mountain, and that was because the government paid him for it. But Harris knew full well that Bowman kept his BLM Jeep parked at the Mustang Ranch, a hundred and fifty miles away, where the trailers had swamp coolers chugging on the roofs and it was never too hot for sex. Bowman got laid more than Brigham Young himself.

The lake bed was dead. Whoever left the girl out there wasn't coming back, and anyone who wanted to find her didn't know where to look. For this Harris found himself strangely pleased.

For dinner he fixed a fried bologna sandwich and a bowl of tomato soup. He was in the kitchen, fishing a dill pickle from the jar with his fingers, when the girl woke.

"Where's my shoe?" she said, propping herself up with her arm.

"That is your shoe," said Harris.

She looked down. "So it is." Her face turned sickly and Harris rushed to her just in time for her to dry heave into the pickle jar. The girl lifted her head and looked at Harris squatting in front of her. Her face hardened. Out of nowhere she stiff-armed him in the gut, toppling him back on his haunches. Biled pickle juice sloshed down the front of him.

The girl looked wildly to the door.

"Relax," said Harris, rubbing his ribs where she'd hit him. "I'm not going to hurt you. I found you on the lake bed. This is my house. I live here. You've been out all day."

He got to his feet and slowly handed her the Mason jar from the windowsill, and a dishrag to wipe her mouth. "Here." She eyed the jar, then took it. Three times she drained it, sometimes coughing softly, and each time he refilled it.

"Thanks," she said finally. "What's your name?"

"Edwin Harris," he said. "Bud," he added, though he hadn't been called that in years.

She looked around, assessing, it seemed, the house and its contents in light of their belonging to an old fart who wanted to be called Bud. Harris asked her name. "Magda," she said. "Magdalena. My mom's a religious freak."

"Magda, you're lucky to be alive," he said. "The hell you doing out there alone?"

She dabbed her mouth with the dishrag and looked lazily about the living room, swirling the last bit of water around the bottom of the jar. "Drank too much, I guess," she said, giving a little shrug. "Happy birthday, America."

He nodded and went to his bedroom for a clean shirt. Drank too much. That's what he'd figured, at first. Kids partied on the lake bed year-round. Harris often heard the echoes of the screeching and thumping they called music. Out here they could see the headlights of Bowman's BLM Jeep coming from fifty miles away, if it came at all. The whole area was off limits, but most kids knew as well as Harris did that paying one man to patrol the entire basin, from the north edge of the lake bed all the way to the Quinn River Sink, almost a thousand square miles, was the same as paying nobody.

He returned to the kitchen. This girl seemed different from those kids, somehow. She was beautiful, or could have been. Her features were too weary for someone her age.

Magda motioned to the dog, lying in front of the swamp cooler. "Who's this?"

"Milo," he said. "She found you. You likely got heatstroke. You should eat." He brought her a mug of the soup and refilled her water.

She took a bit of soup up to her lips, nodding politely to the dog. "Thanks, Milo." She looked around, not eating, spooning at her soup as though she expected to find a secret at the bottom of the mug. "You're a real rock hound, no?"

"I do some lapidary work," he said.

"You at the mine?"

"Used to be. I retired."

Magda set her soup on the coffee table. She picked up a dusty piece of smoky quartz the size of a spark plug from the shelf beside her and let it rest in her palm. "So, what do you do out here?" she asked.

"I make by," he said. "I got a few claims."

"Gold?"

He nodded and she laughed, showing her metal fillings, a solid silver molar. "This place is sapped," she said and laughed again. She had a great laugh, wide mouthed and toothy. "The gold's gone, old-timer."

"Gold ain't all gone," Harris said. "Just got to know where to look." He pushed the mug toward her. "You should eat."

Magda regarded the soup. "I don't feel good. Hung over."

Milo lifted herself and settled at Harris's feet. Harris scratched the soft place behind her ear. "I drove you in from the lake bed," he said, gesturing out front. "I got a standard cab. Small. You didn't smell like you drank too much. Didn't smell like you drank at all."

Magda set the quartz roughly on the coffee table and leaned back into the couch. "That's sweet," she said dryly.

Harris walked to the pantry and returned. He set an unopened sleeve of Saltine crackers in Magda's lap. "My ex-wife ate boxes of these things."

"Good for her," said Magda.

"Especially when she was pregnant," he said. "I suppose they were the only thing that settled her stomach. Used to keep them everywhere, on her nightstand, in the medicine cabinet, the glove box of my truck."

Magda touched her belly, then quickly moved her hand away. She considered the Saltines for a moment, then opened the package. She took out a cracker and pressed the salted side against her tongue. "You can tell?" she asked, her mouth full.

Harris nodded. "What, twelve weeks or so?"

The question bored Magda, it seemed. She shrugged, as though he'd asked whether she wanted to bust open a geode with a hammer and see what was inside.

Carrie Ann had taken a hundred pictures of herself at twelve weeks. Polaroids. The film had cost a fortune. She wanted to send them out to family but, as with so many of her projects, she never got around to it. So for months the photos slid around the house like sheets of gypsum. After she lost the baby, when he couldn't stand the sight of them anymore, he collected every last one, took them to work, and, when no one was around, threw them into the incinerator.

He took the quartz into his own hand now and pointed it at Magda's abdomen. "You want to tell me who did this to you?" He spit on the crystal and with his thumb buffed the spot where the saliva landed.

"It was my boyfriend," she said. She snapped another cracker in half with her tongue. "But he only did it because I asked him to."

Harris felt instantly sick. "Why'd he leave you then?"

"Because he's a fucking momma's boy. He'd just finished when we saw BLM coming. That ranger goes to Ronnie's church. We're not supposed to be together." She smiled. "He said he'd come back for me."

"Hell of a plan."

"You think I don't know that? He just took off." She folded another cracker into her mouth.

"He could have killed you, hitting you like that."

"What were we supposed to do? His mom was threatening to send him to Salt Lake to live with his grandma just for going out with me."

"What about your folks?"

"Forget it."

"Jesus," Harris said softly.

"I tried him." Magda laughed. "La Virgen, too. Nothing."

Harris decided to let the girl be a while. He turned on the AM jazz station and had his evening smoke on the porch. Through the screen door came Dizzy Gillespie, Charlie Parker, Fats Waller, Artie Shaw. When he returned, Magda was biting into the last Saltine in the sleeve. "Can we turn this off?" she said, and without waiting for an answer hit the power button on the radio.

Harris went to the pantry and brought out the whole box of Saltines. He set it on the coffee table. "You want, you can take these with you." She eyeballed the box. "I'll give you a ride," he said. "We got to get you home."

"I know. It's just, I'm still feeling a little sick." She combed her fingers through her hair. "I wonder would the ride upset my stomach even worse, you think? Probably I should stay here, just for the night. If that's okay with you, Bud."

This was a lie, he knew, though her face gave up nothing. He didn't like the prospect of explaining to the authorities why he was hiding a runaway. And there were her parents to consider. If he had a girl, he'd beat the living shit out of anyone who kept her overnight while he was looking for her. The county was full of men—fathers—who'd do the same or worse.

And yet he said nothing, only sat for a moment with his hands on his knees and then walked to the linen closet to get the girl a quilt and a clean pillowcase. He'd take her home. First thing in the morning. The girl smiled up at him as he handed her the linens. What was one night?

His sleep was fitful and often interrupted. He had to piss constantly these days and crossed the hall as quietly as he could, hoping the girl would not notice. When he did sleep he dreamt vile scenes of stomachs and fists, babies and blood. Once he woke sure he'd heard the throaty chafe of Magda's accent at his bedroom door. *Levanta.* Around four a.m. he started to a faint knock, imagined. An erection strained against his shorts. It'd been some time since he was blessed with such and so he quietly took advantage. After, he slept soundly through the remaining nighttime hours.

Harris rose in the early violet of the morning, antsy with a feeling like digging on a fresh plot of land. He dressed in clean blue jeans, white cotton socks, boots, and a fresh white tee shirt. He tucked an unopened pack of filterless Camels into his breast pocket, poured himself a mug of coffee, and walked quietly through the living room to the porch, so as not to wake the girl.

Carrie Ann had been gone since the spring of 1991, having cleared her Kewpie dolls and floral china out of the curio cabinets, wrapped them in newspaper, married a state trooper she'd met in Fallon while she was—yes— staying at her sister's. She'd long since moved with the man to Sacramento. Their miracle baby was almost sixteen. And still Harris accommodated her by smoking outside.

He'd stirred the shit a little when, a new bride, she forbid him from smoking in the house. He went on about a man's home being his own and hadn't he earned the right, but in truth he didn't mind being shooed outdoors. He was even patient later, when she implied that his smoking—combined with his single glass of bourbon in the evening—was the reason they were having such a hell of a time conceiving again, that he ought to take better care of himself, and finally that he didn't give a shit whether they made a baby or not. But it could not be said that Harris made things easy for his young wife. He never held Carrie Ann's temper against her—in his head he forgave her before she even apologized—but just the same he never let on how it soothed him when she let off steam, that seeing her angry was effortless next to seeing her hurting. And where was the harm, he figured, in letting his hotheaded wife guilt herself into a steak dinner, a foot rub, a blow job?

Somewhere in their bickering Harris decided to cut back, to exercise a grown man's discipline. But what was once discipline had over the years become mindless routine, four smokes a day: morning, after lunch, midafternoon, and sundown. His cigarettes helped mark the passage of time, especially on days that seemed all sun and sky, when he scolded poor Milo just to hear the sound of his own voice. The dependable dwindling of his cigarette supply reassured him that he hadn't been left out here, that eventually he would have to ride into town and things would still be there, that the world hadn't stopped whirling.

Magda was awake now, and he could hear her shifting on the couch. He rubbed his cigarette out on the side of the Folgers can he kept on the porch and dropped the butt inside. In the living room, the sun was filtered through the yellowed paper window shades, lighting the room warmly. Harris let the screen door swing shut behind him. Magda's lids lifted at the soft *shwack*.

She arched her back, stretching catlike. "Morning," she said.

"Coffee?" he said.

She made a face and pulled the old quilt up under her arms. She'd slept in her clothes. "Mind if I shower?"

"We should get you back."

"Come on, Bud. I reek." She looked up at him, smiling sweetly. "You don't want to ride in that cab with me."

It had been a long time since a woman had tried to convince him of anything. "Be quick," he said. "Hot water don't last but twenty minutes. Pump leaks." She shuffled down the hall, still wrapped in the quilt. He called down after her. "I apologize for the hard water."

"It's all right," she said, poking her head out the bathroom door, her shoulders already naked. "We got hard water, too."

Steam soon billowed from underneath the door, thickening the air in the hall. Water beaded on the metal doorknobs and hinges. Harris heard the squeak of her bare feet pivoting against the porcelain. From what he'd seen of her while she slept, it wasn't difficult to imagine the rest. He busied himself cleaning the coffee maker and filling Milo's water dish, though the dog preferred to drink from the toilet.

Eventually, the pipes squealed closed and the bathroom door opened. Harris turned to see Magda standing in the doorway, one of his thin maroon bath towels tucked around her like a cocktail dress, her hair wet-black, curling at her shoulders, her bare collarbones. She held her dirty clothes in a wad under her arm. Milo limped to her. The girl bent and scratched the dog under the chin. Without looking up, she said, "Mind if I borrow some clothes?"

Harris was uneasy at the idea of her pilfering his drawers, her fingers running over the flecks of mica among his graying underwear. But better that than him choosing clothes for the girl. "Go ahead," he said. "Bedroom's on the left."

"Bud." She turned, smiling, strands of wet hair clinging to her skin. "This house's got four rooms. I been in three of them."

When Magda emerged from the bedroom she wore a black tee shirt, a pair of tall white socks pulled to her knees with the heels bulging above her ankles, and Bud's royal blue swim trunks. They were old, like everything in this place—except Magda herself—with yellow and white stripes running up the sides. They were short, even on her small frame. She must have hiked them up.

She stood in the doorway dipping the pad of her middle finger into one of his dented pots of Carmex and running the finger over her lips until they glistened.

"What are we doing today?" she said.

"Doing?"

"Let's go swimming," she said. "Bet you know all the hot springs."

"Swimming? Sweetheart, this ain't sleepaway camp."

She sat cross-legged in the recliner, setting it rocking and squeaking. "You're too busy?"

The only thing he'd been busy with in two years was her. "Somebody's bound to be looking for you."

"Nobody's gonna come looking for me," she said. She got up and walked out the door.

Harris wished something painful she was right. He wiped his hands dry on a dishrag and followed her out to the porch.

"Come on now. We have to get you home."

"I'm not going home."

"Why not? Because you did something dumb? Because your novio's a sonofabitch? That don't mean nothing. Plenty of girls your age get into this situation."

"Bud," she said, turning to him and squinting in the sun.

"What about your parents? They're probably scared out of their minds."

"Bud," she said again.

But he went on, partly because she needed to hear it and partly because he didn't at all mind the sound of someone else's voice saying his name over and over again. "Shit, kid, if I was your dad—"

"You're not."

"I'm just trying to say—"

"Bud, you're a fucking idiot," she said, laughing that mean laugh into the open expanse of valley. "You think I'm worried about my *boyfriend*? The Mormon *virgin*?" She laughed again. "I told Ronnie we got pregnant by taking a fucking bath together. Want to know what he said? 'I heard that happens sometimes.'" She lifted the tee shirt and swept her hand across her belly, her bruise, the way a person might brush the dirt from a fossil to expose the mineralized bones underneath.

Harris said, "Who, then?"

"Don't ask me that." She put her middle finger into her mouth and scraped some of the black polish off with her bottom teeth. "Please don't."

They stood staring a long while, her at the valley and him at her. He watched her come right up against crying, then not, instead saying, "Fuck," which was what he wanted to say but his mouth had gone dry.

"It's all right," he said, finally. "Let's go for a swim."

She looked to him. "Really?"

"I'll get you some shoes."

~~~

They left Milo behind and took Route 40 in the direction of town for fifteen miles, and even though Harris kept saying, "It's all right," he could tell Magda didn't trust him. She sat stiff, with her right hand on the door handle, and wouldn't look him in the eye until he took the Burrow Creek turnoff and Gerlach began to shrink behind them.

Some heifers were grazing on the long swaths of bluegrass and toadflax that had sprung up on either side of the spring, bright plastic tags dangling from their ears. The truck rolled to a stop at the edge of the alkali field, and a few of them lifted their heads to notice, but most kept their mouths pressed to the ground, chewing the dry grasses. Harris shut off the truck. "Here we are."

"It's beautiful, Bud. I didn't even know this was out here." Magda got out of the truck and shuffled through the tall grass in Harris's bed slippers. Harris followed her to where the water ran downhill from the spring to a clear, rock-bottomed pool.

"It's Indian land," he said. "Technically."

She pulled the slippers and socks from her feet. "Those Indians have all the luck."

He sat and watched her dip herself into the water, clothes and all. Wet to her waist, she turned to him. "You coming?"

"Nah."

She stumbled on a loose rock and slipped further down into the water. "Come on. Aren't you hot?"

Harris shook his head, though he was burning up.

Magda pinched her nose and dipped her head under, pushing her hair from her face with her free hand. When she came up she said, "That feels good." She paddled a weak breaststroke over to a half-submerged boulder and hoisted herself onto it. She lay there on her back, the wet clothes pasted to her body.

Harris looked away. He dug his fingers into the dirt around him—a habit—looking absently for something to catch the glint of the sun. Magda sat up and said, "What were you like as a kid, Bud?"

"Oh, I don't know."

"Come on. It's just us. What kind of stuff did you do?"

"Regular kid shit, I guess." He sifted a handful of dirt through his fingers.

"Like?"

"I used to sleep outside. With my friends. My best friends were these brothers. Lucas and Jimmy Hastings. Their folks had a cattle ranch, out by where the fairgrounds are now. We'd go out on their land."

"But what did you *do?*"

"We just talked, I guess. Shot the shit."

"About what?"

He pinched a dirt clod between his fingers. "About moving away. We were just kids."

"To where?"

"Reno, mostly. Or Salt Lake. Sacramento. San Francisco. New York. They were all the same to us back then. The big city." Harris laughed at himself a little, recalling. "We used to stay up all night, just listing the places you could take a girl in a city. One of us guys would say, 'To the park.' And another would say, 'A museum.' And another would say, 'The movies.' That was our favorite, the movies. Whenever somebody said the movies, we'd all together say, 'The movies,' all slow. Like a goddamn prayer."

Magda slipped from the rock into the water and went slowly under. Harris let himself watch this time, watched her belly submerge, her small breasts with his tee shirt clinging to them, then her shoulders, her jaw and lips. She arched her back under the water and pushed herself to the surface again, leading with her sternum, the ruts of her ribs visible beneath the soaked cloth, her nipples tight and buttonish. Drops dripped from her brows, her eyelashes, the tip of her nose, the outcropping of her bottom lip. She gathered her hair in her hand and wrung the water from it.

"What?" she said, like she didn't know.

Looking again to his fingers buried in the earth he said, "I haven't thought of the Hastings brothers in thirty years. Sounds stupid, to say that's what we did around here."

"No, it doesn't," she said. "That's what we do now."

On the drive back, Magda unbuckled her seat belt and took off the slippers. She leaned against her door and stretched her bare legs across the seat between them. Soon she was asleep with her head against the window, one long line from her stretched neck down to the bottom of her bare feet. A damp mineral smell filled the cab. Their bodies bounced lightly from the washboard road, and her raisined toes sometimes touched his thigh. He went hard again. Good Lord, he thought, sixty-seven years old and behaving like an adolescent.

After a dinner of boiled hot dogs, Harris smoked his evening cigarette on the porch and watched the sunset burning in the distance. The sky settled into strata of pale blue atop gold and flame-orange and a swath of clouds colored lavender and coral and an indigo so dark they seemed hunks of coal hovering above the range. Nearest the sun the sky was the wild red of a wound, like the thing had to be forced below the horizon. A single sandhill crane moved soundlessly across the sky. A sunset was nothing, Harris knew, dust particles, pollution, sunlight prismed by the slant of the world. Still, it was pretty.

Magda was trying with no luck to teach Milo to fetch a stick, oblivious to the dazzle going on behind her. When they'd dismounted from the truck that afternoon, Milo was sulking under the porch. It was Magda who finally coaxed her out. She'd used his Leatherman to cut the thorns off the mesquite branch she was now hurling into the rocky yard. But Milo only ambled over to the stick, lay down beside it, and soothed her bloody gums by gnawing on it for a while. Magda was stubborn. She slapped her thighs and said, "Come, Milo. Milo, come!" over and over again. When the dog finally did come, she came slow and stickless. Finally, Magda lost hope. She sat beside Harris and looked out on the lake bed. "What were you doing out there?" she said.

"I live out here."

"You live *here*. What were you doing out *there*?"

He thought a while. "I'll show you," he said. "Stay right here. Don't move."

He went around the back of the truck and muscled the old tailgate down, an action that seemed to get more difficult each year. Harris had been coming out to the lake bed every July fifth, searching for fireworks near the burnt remains of plywood and grocer's pallets, since 1968, when he was one of those wild jackasses. Since he woke up with an ache behind his eyes and realized he'd left a paycheck's worth of Roman Candles out on the lake bed and called his future ex-wife, Carrie Ann, and whispered into the phone so his mother wouldn't hear, "Morning, Honey Bee. Where'd you stash my keys?" He told Magda all this, more or less.

"You had a wife?" she said. "Where is she now?"

"Doesn't matter," he said. Then, "Sacramento."

"City girl."

"I guess."

"I'm sorry."

"Don't be. It was a long time ago." He turned to the girl, gripping a shell pack as big as his torso. The Man-O-War.

For the next forty minutes, Harris scrambled up and down the adjacent hill setting the fireworks, sometimes returning to the shed for a tube of PVC pipe, sandpaper, or duct tape. His back flared as he bent to wedge a stub of pipe into the ground or twist two fuses together. His sinuses stung with the brackish smell of sulfur. He glanced down the hill at Magda. She sat on the first porch step, leaning back, her arms propped behind her. He saw Carrie Ann sitting in that same spot, waiting for him to get home, passing her time knitting or shucking corn. Harris pressed the image below the horizon of his mind. They were fine now, him and Carrie. She'd gotten her baby. Harris sent the child birthday cards with fifty-dollar savings bonds inside. *Love, Uncle Bud*, they read. He couldn't complain, not in good conscience. They'd been given a second chance, Carrie and he, and were free to do with it what they pleased.

With the fuse hissing behind him, he hurried down the hill and sat beside Magda. She had her tee shirt lifted up under her breasts and one palm pressed to her bare stomach. She was bent, examining her midsection, looking for something.

"Watch," he said, nodding to his handiwork on the hill.

But she kept her face turned down to her abdomen. "It's probably dead, don't you think?"

"Come on, now," he said, too late to be of comfort. "Don't think like that."

"It is," she said. "I know it." He began to speak, but the first shell ignited, then and shot into the air above them, sparks streaming behind it. They both started at the sound and Harris, with the quickness of a gasp, put his arm around Magda. The little comet went dark for a moment, then exploded—*boom*—into a sizzle so big it seemed to light the whole sky. The sound ricocheted around the valley and returned to them—*boom*.

"See that?" he said. "That green? That's barium powder." He pressed her into him and held her there. She did not pull away.

Another shell rocketed into the sky—*boom*—raining down a brilliant hissing red.

He bent his face to her ear. "Strontium," he whispered.

"I'll be glad," she said. "If it's dead, this will all be over."

He held her tighter and said only, "Shh," before the next shell shot up, even higher than the others, as if propelled by the sound. It expanded—*boom*. Multicolored tendrils radiated from the center and made loops in the air like buzzards, descending. Silence took root between them.

A fourth shell and a fifth shot from the hill. They burst—*boom*—*boom*—into two spheres of light, one a steady-burning fountain of blue, and the other, wiry spokes of purple turning orange.

"What's that one?" Magda whispered.

"The blue is copper," he said. "Pure ground copper."

The last four shells whizzed into the air, all at once. When they burst—

boom—boom—boom—boom—Magda jumped a little and buried herself into him. Harris turned to see her face, his home, the whole wide valley lit by dazzling yellow light. He held her.

"And that one?" she whispered.

"That," he said. "That's gold."

That night, Harris watched her sleep. His own worn bedsheet was roped around her, twisted through her arms and between her legs. Alone in his bed—he had insisted—she looked delicate as a salt crystal. Moonlight fell in through the window, catching the angles of the specimens on the night-stand. In this light her belly looked bigger. Was that possible? In these few days? Or was she right? His wife had said, *I knew it. I felt the baby go.* Had that stupid kid done the job? No. Though he'd seen what the boy did to her, saw with his own eyes the blood bloomed up under her skin—she looked bigger. She did. She would need a doctor. A hospital. He would make the calls. They would drive to Reno. The doctor would tell her, Yes, you are getting bigger. The doctor would tell her, It is not over. It is only just beginning. She would need vitamins. Though he knew better, deep down in the bedrock of himself, he couldn't help it. He thought, She will need a stroller. She will need a car seat. How the barren cling to the fertile. We, he thought, we will need a crib.

Harris took one last pull on his cigarette and stubbed it out on the sole of his boot. It was morning. He dropped the butt into the Folgers can. He would wake Magda soon, tell her to get dressed, that they were going to Reno. But instead of going inside, he scanned the lake bed, as he had every day since she came to him. From where the house was perched, high up on the alluvial fan, the valley below seemed to unfurl and flatten like a starched white sheet. The sun was rising, illuminating the peaks of the Last Chance Range to the west, starting its long trip across the Black Rock. He stopped. Something was different in the distance. A small white cloud of dust billowed on the hori-zon. It grew. At its eye was a speck. A truck.

"Morning," said Magda, startling Harris as she joined him on the porch. She caught sight of the dust cloud unfurling below them and squinted. "What's that?"

"You tell me," said Harris. "Probably been crossing the lake bed since sunup. Circling right about where I found you."

"Oh, fuck," she said. "It's my dad." She began to pace the porch like a wild animal. "Fuck, fuck. Fuck." She looked as though she might cry.

Then, as if it had heard her, the truck turned toward Route 40, toward Red's Road, the washed-out path that dead-ended at Harris's driveway. His heart beat like a herd of mustangs charging at his rib cage.

"Get in the house," he told her. "He doesn't know you're here. Go to the bedroom. Shut the door. Don't come out. I'll take care of it." He half believed this.

The truck lumbered up the long, steep gravel driveway, the way you'd drive if you were concerned about dusting out your neighbors. Harris rummaged frantically through a wheelbarrow. He found a large hunk of iron ore, heavy and angular, easy to grip.

He kept the ore in his right hand and sorted through the rocks with his left, wanting to seem busy when the man arrived. He organized the rocks in piles on the ground according to size. The truck was halfway up the driveway—close enough to see them—when Harris heard the swing and *shwack* of the screen door. He tried not to turn too quickly, but jerked his head, panicked, only to see Milo ambling out to him. He almost hit her.

The truck—a black Ram, a dually with some sort of decal looping across the rear window—stopped at the edge of what Harris considered his yard. A man climbed out. He wore a rodeo buckle the size of a serving platter, a wide cream-colored Stetson, sunglasses, and ornately tooled caiman shit kickers.

Harris knew the man. His name was Castaneda. Juan, Harris thought, though he couldn't be sure. He'd worked with him at the mine. He was a foreman, like Harris.

They'd spoken. On breaks in the pit. On the Newmont bus back into town. They'd talked sports—Pack football, March Madness. They'd discussed the fine tits on the teenage girl behind the counter at the Shell station where they parked. Castaneda had talked about his kids. Harris had seen pictures, grimy creased things pulled from a leather billfold. All girls. Beautiful, Harris had said, and meant. And this man, he'd smiled wide as the ocean and said, I know. Harris gripped the ore so tight his fingertips went white.

"Morning," said Harris. Then, too quickly, "Help you?"

"Morning," said Castaneda, removing his hat but leaving his sunglasses. There was not a gray hair on his head. "Hope so." He approached with a bounce. "Harris, right? How's the sweet life, brother?"

"Can't complain."

"You strike it rich yet?"

Harris kept sorting, kept his wieldy rock in his right hand. He lifted his head and looked to the man, then to the white-hot lake bed, and then, squinting against the sun, to the hill behind his house. At its crest he could just make out the PVC pipes from last night, toppled and scorched. "You come out here to prospect?" he said. "Cause this is BLM land on all four sides. You'd be digging for Uncle Sam."

"Prospect? Ha. No, sir. I'm no rock hound," said Castaneda. "I'm hunting chukar. Thought an old-timer like you might know the good spots." Castaneda nodded to his truck.

"Chukar." Harris stood upright and faced the man. He wiped sweat from his top lip and caught the acridity of nicotine on his fingers. "Don't know of no chukar around here." Because there weren't any chukar around here, not until White Pine County at least. Only thing you could hunt out here was rattlesnake.

"Well, shit," said Castaneda. He reached behind him and adjusted his belt. "Probably got the wrong gun for chukar anyway." He brought around a revolver, a .44 glinting in the summer sun. He held it limp in his palm, as if he only wanted to show it off. But Harris knew better than that. Standing there with a rock in his hand like a goddamn child, he at least knew better than that.

Just then, Milo began to snarl and bark. But she didn't bark at Castaneda, with the gun flat in his palm, looking earnestly to Harris. She was disoriented, maybe heat blind. The dog was barking at Harris.

Castaneda raised his voice above the dog. "I don't know what she told you," he said.

"Who?" said Harris.

Milo kept on.

"Don't make this hard," said Castaneda. "She's a good girl. She's just got an overactive imagination."

A sudden tinny blood taste came to Harris's mouth. "There's nobody else here."

"Oh?" said Castaneda, smiling now. "You lighting off fireworks all night by yourself then?" He began to laugh. This was where Magda got her laugh. "There's nowhere else for her to be, brother."

Harris took a step toward the man, the ore hot in his hand.

Castaneda nodded to the rock. "Don't."

"You son of—"

He raised the hand that held the gun. "You don't want to take that thought any farther." Harris stopped.

Castaneda tucked the gun into the waist of his Wranglers. He walked past Harris, stepping carefully over the piles of specimens where they'd been set in the dirt. An oily aftershave smell followed him. He went into the house. Minutes later—too fast—Castaneda emerged with Magda, his hand on the small of her back. Her face was limestone, it was granite. She did not look at Harris. Castaneda walked her around to the passenger side of the truck and opened the door in the manner of a perfect gentleman.

"Wait," she said before getting in. "I want to say good-bye." Her father nodded and took his hand from her. She walked over to Milo. The dog went quiet. Magda squatted and rustled both her hands behind Milo's limp ears. She put her mouth to the dog's muzzle and said something Harris could not hear.

"She wants to stay," Harris called in a strange-sounding voice.

Casteneda grinned and turned to Magda. "Is that so?"

Magda shook her head and looked to Harris pityingly, as though it was he who needed her.

Harris gripped the iron ore. Why not? he wanted to ask her. But he knew. What could this place give to anyone?

Magda returned to her father's truck. Castaneda took her hand and helped her in. Before he shut the door he smiled at his daughter and rubbed his hand along the back of her neck. It was brief—an instant—but Harris saw everything in the way the man touched her. His hand on her bare neck, the tips of his stout fingers along the black baby hairs at her nape, then under the collar of her shirt. His shirt. From where he stood, he saw all this and more.

The truck pulled away and began its descent to the bald floor of the valley. Milo resumed her barking. Harris told her to shut up, but she went on. Rhythmic, piercing, incessant. The old man had never heard anything so clearly. He felt a steady holy pressure building in him, like a vein of water running down his middle was freezing and would split his body in two. He lunged at the dog. He wanted ore to skull. He wanted his shoulder burning, his hand numb. He wanted the holes that had been her ear and eye growing wider, becoming one, bone crumbling in on itself like the walls of a canyon carved by a river. He wanted wanted wanted.

He took hold of the scruff of the dog's neck. He tried to pin her beneath his legs but she yelped and wormed free, and instead he fell back on his ass.

He dropped the ore in the dirt. Milo scrambled behind the wheelbarrow where he'd been sorting. He reached up and grabbed the wheelbarrow's rusted lip and tried to pull himself up. The wheelbarrow tilted toward him, then toppled, sending Harris to the dirt again. Rocks rained down on him. A flare of pain went off in his knee and in the fingers of his left hand, where a slab of schorl crushed them.

He sat breathing hard, surrounded by heavy, worthless minerals. He took his wrecked fingers into his mouth. Then he fished his Zippo from his pocket and lit a cigarette. He breathed in. Out. The Ram shrunk to the blinding white of the lake bed. He stayed there for some time, smoking among the hot alluvial debris, the silt and clay and rocky loam. He watched a fire ant stitch through the gravel and into the shadow of the overturned wheelbarrow, then he watched the truck. A pale cloud of dust behind it swelled, then settled, then disappeared. She was gone. And all the while Milo's unceasing yowl ricocheted through the valley, returning to him as the *boom* of the fireworks, the *levanta* Magda never whispered, the twin cackles of the Hastings brothers bounding over the cattle range, as every sound he'd ever heard.

Visitation

BRAD WATSON

LOOMIS HAD NEVER BELIEVED THAT LINE ABOUT THE QUALITY OF despair being that it was unaware of being despair. He'd been painfully aware of his own despair for most of his life. Most of his troubles had come from attempts to deny the essential hopelessness in his nature. To believe in the viability of nothing, finally, was socially unacceptable, and he had tried to adapt, to pass as a believer, a hoper. He had taken prescription medicine, engaged in periods of vigorous, cleansing exercise, declared his satisfaction with any number of fatuous jobs and foolish relationships. Then one day he'd decided that he should marry, have a child, and he told himself that if one was open-minded these things could lead to a kind of contentment, if not to exuberant happiness. That's why Loomis was in the fix he was in now.

Ever since he and his wife had separated and she had moved with their son to southern California, he'd flown out every three weeks to visit the boy. He was living the very nightmare he'd suppressed upon deciding to marry and have a child: that it wouldn't work out, they would split up, and he would be forced to spend long weekends in a motel, taking his son to faux-upscale chain restaurants, cineplexes, and amusement parks.

He usually visited for three to five days and stayed at the same motel, an old motor court that had been bought and remodeled by one of the big franchises. At first the place wasn't so bad. The continental breakfast offered fresh fruit, and little boxes of name-brand cereals, and batter with which you could make your own waffles on a double waffle iron right there in the lobby. The syrup came in small plastic containers from which you pulled back a foil lid and voilà, it was a pretty good waffle. There was juice and decent coffee. Still, of course, it was depressing, a bleak place in which to do one's part

266

in raising a child. With its courtyard surrounded by two stories of identical rooms, and excepting the lack of guard towers and the presence of a swimming pool, it followed the same architectural model as a prison.

But Loomis's son liked it so they continued to stay there even though Loomis would rather have moved on to a better place.

He arrived in San Diego for his April visit, picked up the rental car, and drove north up I-5. Traffic wasn't bad except where it always was, between Del Mar and Carlsbad. Of course, it was never "good." Their motel sat right next to the 5, and the roar and rush of it never stopped. You could step out onto the balcony at three in the morning and it'd be just as roaring and rushing with traffic as it had been six hours before.

This was to be one of his briefer visits. He'd been to a job interview the day before, Thursday, and had another on Tuesday. He wanted to make the most of the weekend, which meant doing very little besides just being with his son. Although he wasn't very good at that. Generally, he sought distractions from his ineptitude as a father. He stopped at a liquor store and bought a bottle of bourbon, and tucked it into his travel bag before driving up the hill to the house where his wife and son lived. The house was owned by a retired Marine friend of his wife's family. His wife and son lived rent-free in the basement apartment.

When Loomis arrived, the ex-Marine was on his hands and knees in the flower bed, pulling weeds. He glared sideways at Loomis for a moment and muttered something, his face a mask of disgust. He was a widower who clearly hated Loomis and refused to speak to him. Loomis was unsettled that someone he'd never even been introduced to could hate him so much.

His son came to the door of the apartment by himself, as usual. Loomis peered past the boy into the little apartment, which was bright and sunny for a basement (only in California, he thought). But, as usual, there was no sign of his estranged wife. She had conspired with some part of her nature to become invisible. Loomis hadn't laid eyes on her in nearly a year. She called out from somewhere in another room, "'Bye! I love you! See you on Monday!" "Okay, love you, too," the boy said, and trudged after Loomis, dragging his backpack of homework and a change of clothes. "'Bye, Uncle Bob," the boy said to the ex-Marine. Uncle Bob! The ex-Marine stood up, gave the boy a small salute, and he and the boy exchanged high fives.

After Loomis checked in at the motel, they went straight to their room and watched television for a while. Lately his son had been watching cartoons made in the Japanese anime style. Loomis thought the animation was wooden and amateurish. He didn't get it at all. The characters were drawn as angularly as origami, which he supposed was appropriate and maybe even intentional, if the influence was Japanese. But it seemed irredeemably foreign. His son sat propped against several pillows, harboring such a shy but mischievous grin that Loomis had to indulge him.

He made a drink and stepped out onto the balcony to smoke a cigarette. Down by the pool, a woman with long, thick black hair—it was stiffly unkempt, like a madwoman's in a movie—sat in a deck chair with her back to Loomis, watching two children play in the water. The little girl was nine or ten and the boy was older, maybe fourteen. The boy teased the girl by splashing her face with water, and when she protested in a shrill voice he leapt over and dunked her head. She came up gasping and began to cry. Loomis was astonished that the woman, who he assumed to be the children's mother, displayed no reaction. Was she asleep?

The motel had declined steadily in the few months Loomis had been staying there, like a moderately stable person drifting and sinking into the lassitude of depression. Loomis wanted to help, find some way to speak to the managers and the other employees, to say, "Buck up, don't just let things go all to hell," but he felt powerless against his own inclinations.

He lit a second cigarette to go with the rest of his drink. A few other people walked up and positioned themselves around the pool's apron, but none got into the water with the two quarreling children. There was something feral about them, anyone could see. The woman with the wild black hair continued to sit in her pool chair as if asleep or drugged. The boy's teasing of the girl had become steadily rougher, and the girl was sobbing now. Still, the presumptive mother did nothing. Someone went in to complain. One of the managers came out and spoke to the woman, who immediately but without getting up from her deck chair shouted to the boy, "All right, Goddamn it!" The boy, smirking, climbed from the pool, leaving the girl standing in waist-deep water, sobbing and rubbing her eyes with her fists. The woman stood up then and walked toward the boy. There was something off about her clothes, burnt-orange Bermuda shorts and a men's lavender oxford shirt. And they didn't seem to fit right. The boy, like a wary stray dog, watched her approach. She snatched a lock of his wet black hair, pulled his face to hers, and said something, gave his head a shake and let him go. The boy went over to the pool and spoke to the girl. "Come on," he said. "No," the girl said, still crying. "You let him help you!" the woman shouted then, startling the girl into letting the boy take her hand. Loomis was fascinated, a little bit horrified.

Turning back toward her chair, the woman looked up to where he stood on the balcony. She had an astonishing face, broad and long, divided by a great, curved nose, dominated by a pair of large, dark, sunken eyes that seemed blackened by blows or some terrible history. Such a face, along with her immense, thick mane of black hair, made her look like a troll. Except that she was not ugly. She looked more like a witch, the cruel mockery of beauty and seduction. The oxford shirt was mostly unbuttoned, nearly spilling out a pair of full, loose, mottled-brown breasts.

"What are you looking at!" she shouted, very loudly from deep in her chest. Loomis stepped back from the balcony railing. The woman's angry glare changed to something like shrewd assessment and then dismissal. She shooed her two children into one of the downstairs rooms.

After taking another minute to finish his drink and smoke a third cigarette, to calm down, Loomis went back inside and closed the sliding glass door behind him.

His son was on the bed, grinning, watching something on television called *Code Lyoko*. It looked very Japanese, even though the boy had informed him it was made in France. Loomis tried to watch it with him for a while, but got restless. He wanted a second, and maybe stronger, drink.

"Hey," he said. "How about I just get some burgers and bring them back to the room?"

The boy glanced at him and said, "That'd be okay."

Loomis got a sack of hamburgers from McDonald's, some fries, a Coke. He made a second drink, then a third, while his son ate and watched television. They went to bed early.

The next afternoon, Saturday, they drove to the long, wide beach at Carlsbad. Carlsbad was far too cool, but what could you do? Also, the hip little surf shop where the boy's mother worked during the week was in Carlsbad. He'd forgotten that for a moment. He was having a hard time keeping her in his mind. Her invisibility strategy was beginning to work on him. He wasn't sure at all anymore just who she was or ever had been. When they'd met she wore business attire, like everyone else he knew. What did she wear now, just a swimsuit? Did she get up and go around in a bikini all day? She didn't really have the body for that at age thirty-nine, did she?

"What does your mom wear to work?" he asked.

The boy gave him a look that would have been ironic if he'd been a less compassionate child.

"Clothes?" the boy said.

"Okay," Loomis said. "Like a swimsuit? Does she go to work in a swimsuit?"

The boy stared at him for a moment.

"Are you okay?" the boy said.

Loomis was taken aback by the question.

"Me?" he said.

They walked along the beach, neither going into the water. Loomis enjoyed collecting rocks. The stones on the beach here were astounding. He marveled at one that resembled an ancient war club. The handle fit perfectly into his palm. From somewhere over the water, a few miles south, they could hear the stuttering thud of a large helicopter's blades. Most likely a military craft from the Marine base farther north.

Maybe he wasn't okay. Loomis had been to five therapists since separating from his wife: one psychiatrist, one psychologist, three counselors. The psychiatrist had tried him on Paxil, Zoloft, and Wellbutrin for depression, and then lorazepam for anxiety. Only the lorazepam had helped, but with that he'd overslept too often and lost his job. The psychologist, once she learned that Loomis was drinking almost half a bottle of booze every night, became fixated on getting him to join AA and seemed to forget altogether that he was there to figure out whether he indeed no longer loved his wife. And why he had cheated on her. Why he had left her for another woman when the truth was he had no faith that the new relationship would work out any better than the old one. The first counselor seemed sensible, but Loomis made the mistake of visiting her together with his wife, and when she suggested maybe their marriage was indeed kaput his wife had walked out. The second counselor was actually his wife's counselor, and Loomis thought she was an idiot. Loomis suspected that his wife liked the second counselor because she did nothing but nod and sympathize and give them brochures. He suspected that his wife simply didn't want to move out of their house, which she liked far more than Loomis did, and which possibly she liked more than she liked Loomis. When she realized divorce was inevitable, she shifted gears, remembered she wanted to surf, and sold the house before Loomis was even aware it was on the market, so he had to sign. Then it was Loomis who mourned the loss of the house, which he realized had been pretty comfortable after all. He visited the third counselor with his girlfriend, who seemed constantly angry that his divorce hadn't yet come through. He and the girlfriend both gave up on that counselor because he seemed terrified of them for some reason they couldn't fathom. Loomis was coming to the conclusion that he couldn't fathom anything; the word seemed appropriate to him, because most of the time he felt like he was drowning and couldn't find the bottom or the surface of this body of murky water he had fallen, or dived, into.

He wondered if this was why he didn't want to dive into the crashing waves of the Pacific, as he certainly would have when he was younger. His son didn't want to because, he said, he'd rather surf.

"But you don't know how to surf," Loomis said.

"Mom's going to teach me as soon as she's good enough at it," the boy said.

"But don't you need to be a better swimmer before you try to surf?" Loomis had a vague memory of the boy's swimming lessons, which maybe hadn't gone so well.

"No," the boy said.

"I really think," Loomis said, and then he stopped speaking, because the helicopter he'd been hearing, one of those large, twin-engined birds that carried troops in and out of combat—a Chinook—had come abreast of them a quarter mile or so off the beach. Just as Loomis looked up to see it, something coughed or exploded in one or both of its engines. The helicopter slowed, then swerved, with the slow grace of an airborne leviathan, toward the beach where they stood. In a moment it was directly over them. One of the men in it leaned out of a small opening on its side, frantically waving, but the people on the beach, including Loomis and his son, beaten by the blast from the blades and stung by sand driven up by it, were too shocked and confused to run. The helicopter lurched back out over the water with a tremendous roar and a deafening, rattling whine from the engines. There was another loud pop, and black smoke streamed from the forward engine as the Chinook made its way north again, seeming hobbled. Then it was gone, lost in the glare over the water. A bittersweet burnt-fuel smell hung in the air. Loomis and his son stood there among the others on the beach, speechless. One of two very brown young surfers in board shorts and crew cuts grinned and nodded at the club-like rock in Loomis's hand.

"Dude, we're safe," he said. "You can put down the weapon." He and the other surfer laughed.

Loomis's son, looking embarrassed, moved off as if he were with someone else in the crowd, not Loomis.

⁓〜

They stayed in Carlsbad for an early dinner at Pizza Port. The place was crowded with people who'd been at the beach all day, although Loomis recognized no one they'd seen when the helicopter had nearly crashed and killed them all. He'd expected everyone in there to know about it, to be buzzing about it over beer and pizza, amazed, exhilarated. But it was as if it hadn't happened.

The long rows of picnic tables and booths were filled with young parents and their hyperkinetic children, who kept jumping up to get extra napkins or forks or to climb into the seats of the motorcycle video games. Their parents flung arms after them like inadequate lassos or pursued them and herded them back. The stools along the bar were occupied by young men and women who apparently had no children and who were attentive only to each other and to choosing which of the restaurant's many microbrews to order. In the corner by the rest rooms, the old surfers, regulars here, gathered to talk shop and knock back the stronger beers, the double-hopped and the barley wines. Their graying hair frizzled and tied in ponytails or dreads or chopped in stiff clumps dried by salt and sun. Their faces leather-brown. Gnarled toes jutting from their flip-flops and worn sandals like assortments of dry-roasted cashews, Brazil nuts, ginger roots.

Loomis felt no affinity for any of them. There wasn't a single person in the entire place with whom he felt a thing in common—other than being, somehow, human. Toward the parents he felt a bitter disdain. On the large TV screens fastened to the restaurant's brick walls, surfers skimmed down giant waves off Hawaii, Tahiti, Australia.

He gazed at the boy, his son. The boy looked just like his mother. Thick bright orange hair, untamable. Tall, stem-like people with long limbs and that thick hair blossom on top. Loomis had called them his rosebuds. "Roses are *red*," his son would respond, delightedly indignant, when he was smaller. "There are orange roses," Loomis would reply. "Where?" "Well, in Indonesia, I think. Or possibly Brazil." "No!" his son would shout, breaking down into giggles on the floor. He bought them orange roses on the boy's birthday that year.

The boy wasn't so easily amused anymore. He waited glumly for their pizza order to be called out. They'd secured a booth vacated by a smallish family.

"You want a Coke?" Loomis said. The boy nodded absently. "I'll get you a Coke," Loomis said.

He got the boy a Coke from the fountain, and ordered a pint of strong pale ale from the bar for himself.

By the time their pizza came, Loomis was on his second ale. He felt much better about all the domestic chaos around them in the restaurant. It was getting on the boy's nerves, though. As soon as they finished their pizza, he asked Loomis if he could go stand outside and wait for him there.

"I'm almost done," Loomis said.

"I'd really rather wait outside," the boy said. He shoved his hands in his pockets and looked away.

"Okay," Loomis said. "Don't wander off. Stay where I can see you."

"I will."

Loomis sipped his beer and watched as the boy weaved his way through the crowd and out of the restaurant, then began to pace back and forth on the sidewalk. Having to be a parent in this fashion was terrible. He felt indicted by all the other people in this teeming place: by the parents and their smug happiness, by the old surfer dudes, who had the courage of their lack of conviction, and by the young lovers, who were convinced that they would never be part of either of these groups, not the obnoxious parents, not the grizzled losers clinging to youth like tough, crusty barnacles. Certainly they would not be Loomis.

And what did it mean, in any case, that he couldn't even carry on a conversation with his son? How hard could that be? But Loomis couldn't seem to do it. To hear him try, you'd think they didn't know each other at all, that he was a friend of the boy's father, watching him for the afternoon or something. He started to get up and leave, but first he hesitated, then gulped down the rest of his second beer.

His son stood with hunched shoulders waiting.

"Ready to go back to the motel?" Loomis said.

The boy nodded. They walked back to the car in silence.

"Did you like your pizza?" Loomis said when they were in the car.

"Sure. It was okay."

Loomis looked at him for a moment. The boy glanced back with the facial equivalent of a shrug, an impressively diplomatic expression that managed to say both "I'm sorry" and "What do you want?" Loomis sighed. He could think of nothing else to say that wasn't even more inane.

"All right," he finally said, and drove them back to the motel.

~⌒

When they arrived, Loomis heard a commotion in the courtyard and they paused near the gate.

The woman who'd been watching the two awful children was there at the pool again, and the two children themselves had returned to the water. But now the group seemed to be accompanied by an older heavyset man, bald on top, graying hair slicked against the sides of his head. He was arguing with a manager while the other guests around the pool pretended to ignore the altercation. The boy and girl paddled about in the water until the man threw up his hands and told them to get out and go to their room. The girl glanced at the boy, but the boy continued to ignore the man until he strode to the edge of the pool and shouted, "Get out! Let them have their filthy pool. Did you piss in it? I hope you pissed in it. Now get out! Go to the room!" The boy removed himself from the pool with a kind of languorous choreography, and walked toward the sliding glass door of one of the downstairs rooms, the little girl following. Just before reaching the door the boy paused, turned his head in the direction of the pool and the other guests there, and hawked and spat onto the concrete pool apron. Loomis said to his son, "Let's get on up to the room."

Another guest, a lanky young woman whom Loomis had seen beside the pool earlier, walked past them on her way to the parking lot. "Watch out for them Gypsies," she muttered.

"Gypsies?" the boy said.

The woman laughed as she rounded the corner. "Don't let 'em get you," she said.

"I don't know," Loomis said when she'd gone. "I guess they do seem a little like Gypsies."

"What the hell is a Gypsy, anyway?"

Loomis stopped and stared at his son. "Does 'Uncle Bob' teach you to talk that way?"

The boy shrugged and looked away, annoyed.

In the room, his son pressed him again, and he told him that Gypsies were originally from some part of India, he wasn't sure which, and that they were ostracized, nobody wanted them. They became wanderers, wandering around Europe. They were poor. People accused them of stealing. "They had a reputation for stealing people's children, I think."

He meant this to be a kind of joke, or at least lighthearted, but when he saw the expression on the boy's face he regretted it and quickly added, "They didn't, really."

It didn't work. For the next hour, the boy asked him questions about Gypsies and kidnapping. Every few minutes or so he hopped from the bed to the sliding glass door and pulled the curtain aside to peek down across the courtyard at the Gypsies' room. Loomis had decided to concede they were Gypsies, whether they really were or not. He made himself a stiff nightcap and stepped out onto the balcony to smoke, although he peeked through the curtains before going out, to make sure the coast was clear.

The next morning, Sunday, Loomis rose before his son and went down to the lobby for coffee. He stepped out into the empty courtyard to drink it in the morning air, and when he looked into the pool he saw a large dead rat on its side at the bottom. The rat looked peacefully dead, with its eyes closed and its front paws curled at its chest as if it were begging. Loomis took another sip of his coffee and went back into the lobby. The night clerk was still on duty, studying something on the computer monitor behind the desk. She only cut her eyes at Loomis, and when she saw he was going to approach her she met his gaze steadily in that same way, without turning her head.

"I believe you have an unregistered guest at the bottom of your pool," Loomis said.

He got a second cup of coffee, a plastic cup of juice, and a couple of refrigerator-cold bagels (the waffle iron and fresh fruit had disappeared a couple of visits earlier) and took them back to the room. He and his son ate there, then Loomis decided to get them away from the motel for the day. The boy could always be counted on to want a day trip to San Diego. He loved to ride the red trolleys there, and tolerated Loomis's interest in the museums, sometimes.

They took the commuter train down, rode the trolley to the Mexican border, turned around, and came back. They ate lunch at a famous old diner near downtown, then took a bus to Balboa Park and spent the afternoon in the Air & Space Museum, the Natural History Museum, and at a small, disappointing model railroad exhibit. Then they took the train back up the coast.

As they got out of the car at the motel, an old brown van, plain and blocky as a loaf of bread, careened around the far corner of the lot, pulled up next to Loomis, and stopped. The driver was the older man who'd been at the pool. He leaned toward Loomis and said through the open passenger window, "Can you give me twenty dollars? They're going to kick us out of this stinking motel."

Loomis felt a surge of hostile indignation. What, did he have a big sign on his chest telling everyone what a chump he was?

"I don't have it," he said.

"Come on!" the man shouted. "Just twenty bucks!"

Loomis saw his son standing beside the passenger door of the rental car, frightened.

"No," he said. He was ready to punch the old man now.

"Son of a bitch!" the man shouted, and gunned the van away, swerving onto the street toward downtown and the beach.

The boy gestured for Loomis to hurry over and unlock the car door, and as soon as he did the boy got back into the passenger seat. When Loomis sat down behind the wheel, the boy hit the lock button. He cut his eyes toward where the van had disappeared up the hill on the avenue.

"Was he trying to rob us?" he said.

"No. He wanted me to give him twenty dollars."

The boy was breathing hard and looking straight out the windshield, close to tears.

"It's okay," Loomis said. "He's gone."

"Pop, no offense"—and the boy actually reached over and patted Loomis on the forearm, as if to comfort him—"but I think I want to sleep at home tonight."

Loomis was so astonished by the way his son had touched him on the arm that he was close to tears himself.

"It'll be okay," he said. "Really. We're safe here, and I'll protect you."

"I know, Pop, but I really think I want to go home."

Loomis tried to keep the obvious pleading note from his voice. If this happened, if he couldn't even keep his son around and reasonably satisfied to be with him for a weekend, what was he at all anymore? And (he couldn't help but think) what would the boy's mother make of it, how much worse would he then look in her eyes?

"Please," he said to the boy. "Just come on up to the room for a while, and we'll talk about it again, and if you still want to go home later on I'll take you, I promise."

The boy thought about it and agreed, and began to calm down a little. They went up to the room, past the courtyard, which was blessedly clear of ridiculous Gypsies and other guests. Loomis got a bucket of ice for his bourbon, ordered Chinese, and they lay together on Loomis's bed, eating and watching television, and didn't talk about the Gypsies, and after a while, exhausted, they both fell asleep.

When the alcohol woke him at 3 a.m., he was awash in a sense of gloom and dread. He found the remote, turned down the sound on the TV. His son was sleeping, mouth open, a lock of his bright orange hair across his face.

Loomis eased himself off the bed, sat on the other one, and watched him breathe. He recalled the days when his life with the boy's mother had seemed happy, and the boy had been small, and they would put him to bed in his room, where they had built shelves for his toy trains and stuffed animals and the books from which Loomis would read to him at bedtime. He remembered the constant battle in his heart, those days. How he was drawn into this construction of conventional happiness, how he felt that he loved this child more than he had ever loved anyone in his entire life, how all of this was possible, this life, how he might actually be able to do it. And yet whenever he had felt this he was always aware of the other, more deeply seated part of his nature that wanted to run away in fear. That believed it was not possible after all, that it could only end in catastrophe, that anything this sweet and heartbreaking must indeed one day collapse into shattered pieces. He had struggled to free himself, one way or another, from what seemed a horrible limbo of anticipation. He had run away, in his fashion. And yet nothing had ever caused him to feel anything more like despair than what he felt just now, in this moment, looking at his beautiful child asleep on the motel bed in the light of the cheap lamp, with the incessant dull roar of cars on I-5 just the other side of the hedge, a slashing river of what seemed nothing but desperate travel from point A to point B, from which one mad dasher or another would simply disappear, blink out in a flicker of light, at ragged but regular intervals, with no more ceremony or consideration than that.

He checked that his son was still sleeping deeply, then poured himself a plastic cup of neat bourbon and went down to the pool to smoke and sit alone for a while in the dark. He walked toward a group of lawn chairs in the shadows beside a stunted palm, but stopped when he realized that he wasn't alone, that someone was sitting in one of the chairs. The Gypsy woman sat very still, watching him.

"Come, sit," she said. "Don't be afraid."

He was afraid. But the woman was so still, and the look on her face he could now make out in the shadows was one of calm appraisal. Something about this kept him from retreating. She slowly raised a hand and patted the pool chair next to her, and Loomis sat.

For a moment the woman just looked at him, and, unable not to, he looked at her. She was unexpectedly, oddly attractive. Her eyes were indeed very dark, set far apart on her broad face. In this light, her fierce nose was almost erotic.

"Are you Gypsy?" Loomis blurted, without thinking.

She stared at him a second before smiling and chuckling deep in her throat.

"No, I'm not Gypsy," she said, her eyes moving quickly from side to side in little shiftings, looking into his. "We are American. My people come from France."

Loomis said nothing.

"But I can tell you your future," she said, leaning her head back slightly to look at him down her harrowing nose. "Let me see your hand." She took Loomis's wrist and pulled his palm toward her. He didn't resist. "Have you ever had someone read your palm?"

Loomis shook his head. "I don't really want to know my future," he said. "I'm not a very optimistic person."

"I understand," the woman said. "You're unsettled."

"It's too dark here to even see my palm," Loomis said.

"No, there's enough light," the woman said. And finally she took her eyes from Loomis's and looked down at his palm. He felt relieved enough to be released from that gaze to let her continue. And something in him was relieved, too, to have someone else consider his future, someone aside from himself. It couldn't be worse, after all, than his own predictions.

She hung her head over his palm and traced the lines with a long fingernail, pressed into the fleshy parts. Her thick hair tickled the edges of his hand and wrist. After a moment, much sooner than Loomis would have expected, she spoke.

"It's not the future you see in a palm," she said, still studying his. "It's a person's nature. From this, of course, one can tell much about a person's tendencies." She looked up, still gripping his wrist. "This tells us much about where a life may have been, and where it may go."

She bent over his palm again, traced one of the lines with the fingernail. "There are many breaks in the heart line here. You are a creature of disappointment. I suspect others in your life disappoint you." She traced a different line. "You're a dreamer. You're an idealist, possibly. Always disappointed by ordinary life, which of course is boring and ugly." She laughed that soft, deep chuckle again and looked up, startling Loomis anew with the directness of her gaze. "People are so fucking disappointing, eh?" She uttered a seductive grunt that loosened something in his groin.

It was true. No one had ever been good enough for him. Even the members of his immediate family. And especially himself.

"Anger, disappointment," the woman said. "So common. But it may be they've worn you down. The drinking, smoking. No real energy, no passion." Loomis pulled against her grip just slightly but she held on with strong fingers around his wrist. Then she lowered Loomis's palm to her broad lap and leaned in closer, speaking more quietly.

"I see you with the little boy—he's your child?"

Loomis nodded. He felt suddenly alarmed, fearful. He glanced up, and his heart raced when he thought he saw the boy standing on the balcony looking out. It was only the potted plant there. He wanted to dash back to the room but he was rooted to the chair, to the Gypsy with her thin, hard fingers about his wrist.

"This is no vacation, I suspect. It's terrible, to see your child in this way, in a motel."

Loomis nodded.

"You're angry with this child's mother for forcing you to be here."

Loomis nodded and tried to swallow. His throat was dry.

"Yet I would venture it was you who left her. For another woman, a beautiful woman, eh, *mon frère?*" She ran the tip of a nail down one of the lines in his palm. There was a cruel smile on her impossible face. "A woman who once again you believed to be something she was not." Loomis felt himself drop his chin in some kind of involuntary acquiescence. "She was a dream," the woman said. "And she has disappeared, poof, like any dream." He felt suddenly, embarrassingly, close to tears. A tight lump swelled in his throat. "And now you have left her, too, or she has left you, because"—and here the woman paused, shook Loomis's wrist gently, as if to revive his attention, and indeed he had been drifting in his grief—"because you are a ghost. Walking between two worlds, you know?" She shook his wrist again, harder, and Loomis looked up at her, his vision of her there in the shadows blurred by his tears.

She released his wrist and sat back in her chair, exhaled as if she had been holding her breath, and closed her eyes. As if this excoriation of Loomis's character had been an obligation, had exhausted her.

They sat there for a minute or two while Loomis waited for the emotion that had surged up in him to recede.

"Twenty dollars," the woman said then, her eyes still closed. When Loomis said nothing, she opened her eyes. Now her gaze was flat, no longer intense, but she held it on him.

"Twenty dollars," she said. "For the reading. This is my fee."

Loomis, feeling as if he'd just been through something physical instead of emotional, his muscles tingling, reached for his wallet, found a twenty-dollar bill, and handed it to her. She took it and rested her hands in her lap.

"Now you should go back up to your room," she said.

He got up to make his way from the courtyard, and was startled by someone standing in the shadow of the Gypsies' doorway. Her evil man-child, the boy from the pool, watching him like a forest animal pausing in its night prowling to let him pass. Loomis hurried on up to the room, tried to let himself in with a key card that wouldn't cooperate. The lock kept flashing red instead of green. Finally the card worked, the green light flickered. He entered and shut the door behind him.

But he'd gone into the wrong room, maybe even some other motel. The beds were made, the television off. His son wasn't there. The sliding glass door to the balcony stood open. Loomis felt his heart seize up and he rushed to the railing. The courtyard was dark and empty. Over in the lobby, the lights were dimmed, no one on duty. It was all shut down. There was no breeze. No roar of rushing vehicles from the 5, the roar in Loomis's mind canceling it out. By the time he heard the sound behind him and turned to see his son come out of the bathroom yawning, it was too late. It might as well have been someone else's child, Loomis the stranger come to steal him away. He stood on the balcony and watched his son crawl back onto the bed, pull himself into a fetal position, close his eyes for a moment, then open them. Meeting his gaze, Loomis felt something break inside him. The boy had the same dazed, disoriented expression he'd had on his face just after his long, difficult birth, when the nurses had put him into an incubator to rush him to intensive care. Loomis had knelt, then, his face up close to the incubator's glass wall, and he'd known that the baby could see him, and that was enough. The obstetrician said, "This baby is very sick," and nurses wheeled the incubator out. He'd gone over to his wife and held her hand. The resident, tears in her eyes, patted his shoulder and said, for some reason, "You're good people," and left them alone. Now he and their child were in this motel, the life that had been their family somehow dissipated into air. Loomis couldn't gather into his mind how they'd got here. He couldn't imagine what would come next.

Publications Reviewed

The following online and print journals, magazines, books, and newspapers were consulted for this volume:

12th Street, Abraxas, African American Review, Afro-Hispanic Review, AGNI, Alaska Quarterly Review, Alimentum, Alligator Juniper, Ambit, American Letters & Commentary, American Literary Review, American Scholar, American Short Fiction, Another Chicago Magazine, Antigonish Review, Antioch Review, Antipodes, Apalachee Review, Appalachian Heritage, Arkansas Review, Arroyo Literary Review, Artful Dodge, Arts & Letters, Ascent, Asia Literary Review, Atlantic, Austin Chronicle, Baltimore Review, Bat City Review, Bellevue Literary Review, Bellingham Review, Beloit Fiction Journal, Berkeley Fiction Review, Best New American Voices 2009, Bilingual Review/Revista Bilingüe, Bird Dog, Bitter Oleander, Black Clock, Blackbird, Black Warrior Review, Bloom, Blue Mesa Review, BOMB, Boston Review, Boulevard, Briar Cliff Review, Brick, Bridges, Brilliant Corners, Burnside Review, Cadillac Cicatrix, Callaloo, Calyx, Canteen, Carolina Review, Carve Magazine, Cavalier Literary Couture, Cerise Press, Chandrabhāgā, Chariton Review, Chattahoochee Review, Chelsea, Chicago Reader, Chicago Review, Cicada Magazine, Cimarron Review, Cincinnati Review, Collagist, Colorado Review, Commentary, Concho River Review, Conduit, Confrontation, Conjunctions, Copper Nickel, Crab Creek Review, Crab Orchard Review, Crazyhorse, Cream City Review, CT Review, CutBank, CUTTHROAT, Daedalus, Dalhousie Review, Dappled Things, Denver Quarterly, descant (Forth Worth), Descant (Toronto), Dialogue: A Journal of Mormon Thought, DIAGRAM, Dirty Goat, Dislocate, Dispatch, Dos Passos Review, Downstate Story, Drash, Ecotone, Electric Literature, Eleven Eleven, Elixir, Ellipses, Epiphany, Epoch, Esquire, Event, Exile, Exquisite Corpse, Failbetter.com, Fairy Tale Review, Farallon Review, Fence, Fiction, Fiction International, Fifth Wednesday Journal, First Intensity, First Line, Five Points, Florida English, Florida Review, Flyway, Fourteen Hills, Fourth River, Front Range Review, Front Porch, Fugue, Gargoyle, Georgia Review, Gettysburg Review, Gingko Tree Review, Glimmer Train, Global City Review, Grain, Granta, Great River Review, Great Western Fiction, Green Mountains Review, Greensboro Review, Grist, Guardian, Gulf Coast, Hanging Loose, Harper's Magazine, Harpur Palate, Harrington Gay Men's Literary

Quarterly, Harrington Lesbian Literary Quarterly, Harvard Review, Hawaii Review, Hayden's Ferry Review, Heat, Hemispheres, High Desert Journal, Hobart, Home Planet News, Hopkins Review, Hotel Amerika, H.O.W. Journal, Hudson Review, Idaho Review, Image, Indian Literature, Indiana Review, Interim, Iowa Review, Iron Horse Literary Review, Isle, Isotope, the Journal, Jubilat, Juked, Kalliope, Kean Review, Kenyon Review, KGB BAR LIT, Knee-Jerk, Lake Effect, Landfall, La Petite Zine, Lapham's Quarterly, Laurel Review, LBJ: Avian Life/Literary Arts, Ledge, Legal Studies Forum, LIT, Literary Review, L Magazine, Long Story, Louisiana Literature, Louisville Review, Main Street Rag, Make, Malahat Review, Mandorla, Mānoa, Maple/Ash Review, Marginalia, Massachusetts Review, McSweeney's, Memoir (and), Meridian, Michigan Quarterly Review, Mid-American Review, Minnesota Review, Mississippi Review, Missouri Review, Mizna, Montana Quarterly, n + 1, Narrative, Natural Bridge, Nevada Review, New Delta Review, New England Review, New Letters, New Madrid, New Ohio Review, New Orleans Review, New Renaissance, News from the Republic of Letters, New South, New Yorker, New York Review of Books, New Texas, Nimrod International Journal, Ninth Letter, Normal School, North American Review, North Dakota Quarterly, Northwest Review, Notre Dame Review, Obsidian III, One Story, Ontario Review, Open City, Opium, Other Voices, Overland, Overtime, Oxford American, Oyez Review, Paris Review, Passager, Paterson Literary Review, Paul Revere's Horse, Pearl, PEN International, Permafrost, Persimmon Tree, Persona, Phoebe, Pilgrimage, Pilot, Pinch, Pindeldyboz, Ping Pong, Platte Valley Review, Pleiades, Ploughshares, PMS poemmemoirstory, Porcupine, Portland Review, Post Road, Potomac Review, Practice: New Writing and Art, Prairie Fire, Prairie Schooner, Predicate, Prick of the Spindle, Prism International, Provincetown Arts, A Public Space, Puerto del Sol, Quarterly West, Queens Quarterly, Quercus Review, Raritan, Realms of Fantasy, Red Cedar Review, Red Ink, Redivider, Red Rock Review, Red Wheelbarrow, Reed, Regarding Arts and Letters, Review of Contemporary Fiction, Rio Grande Review, River Styx, Rock & Sling, Rosebud, Ruminate, Sakura Review, Salamander, Salmagundi, Salt Flats Annual, Salt Hill, Santa Fe Writers Project Journal, Santa Monica Review, Saranac Review, Saturday Evening Post, Seattle Review, Seneca Review, Sewanee Review, SFWP.org, Shenandoah, Sierra Nevada Review, Silent Voices, Silk Road, Sinister Wisdom, Skidrow Penthouse, Slake, Slice, Snow Monkey, Sonora Review, South Carolina Review, South Dakota Review, Southeast Review, Southern Humanities Review, Southern Indiana Review, Southern Quarterly, Southern Review, Southwestern American Literature, Southwest Review, Spork, Stand, Storyglossia, StoryQuarterly, Stress City, StringTown, Subterranean, Subtropics, Sun, Swink, Swivel, Sycamore Review, Talking River Review, Tampa Review, Terra Incognita, Terrain.org, Texas Review, Thema, Third Coast, 13th Moon: A Feminist Literary Magazine, Threepenny Review, Tin House, Tonopah Review, TriQuarterly, Tusculum Review, Upstreet, Vanitas, Virginia Quarterly Review, Walking Rain Review, War, Literature, and the Arts, Washington Square, Water-Stone Review, Weber: The Contemporary West, West Branch, West Coast Line, Westerly, Western Humanities Review, Whiskey Island Magazine, Whitefish Review, White Fungus, William and Mary Review, Willow Springs, Witness, Women's Studies Quarterly, Workers Write!, Writer, World Literature Today, Yale Literary Magazine, Yale Review, Yellow Medicine Review, Yemassee, Zahir, Zoetrope, Zone 3, ZYZZYVA

Notes on Contributors

SALLIE BINGHAM published her first book, a novel, two years after graduating from Radcliffe College. She has published seven novels, four collections of short stories, many plays, and a memoir in the years since then. Her most recent book, *Mending: New and Selected Stories*, was published by Sarabande Books in October 2011. It was favorably reviewed in the *New Yorker*, among other places, and is an Editor's Choice in the *New York Times*. In August 2014, Sarabande Books will publish *The Blue Box: Three Lives in Letters*, a nonfiction narrative based on the lives of her mother, grandmother, and great-grandmother, spanning the mid-nineteenth century to the mid-twentieth century. She has lived in Santa Fe since 1991.

RON CARLSON is the author of ten books of fiction, most recently the novel *The Signal*. His short fiction has appeared in *Esquire, Harper's*, the *New Yorker, Gentlemen's Quarterly, Epoch*, the *Oxford American*, and other journals, as well as in *The Best American Short Stories, Best of the West: New Stories from the Wide Side of the Missouri, The Pushcart Prize, The Norton Anthology of Short Fiction*, and other anthologies. Among his awards are a National Endowment for the Arts Fellowship in Fiction, the Cohen Prize at *Ploughshares*, the McGinnis Award at the *Iowa Review*, and the Aspen Foundation Literary Award. He directs the Graduate Program in Fiction at the University of California–Irvine.

EDDIE CHUCULATE (Creek/Cherokee) is an Oklahoma native but considers northern New Mexico a second home. His debut collection of short fiction, *Cheyenne Madonna*, was published in 2011 by Black Sparrow Books in Boston. A former journalist, he earned an MFA in fiction at the Writers' Workshop at the University of Iowa and a Wallace Stegner Fellowship in creative writing at Stanford University. His story "Galveston Bay, 1826" was selected for *The PEN/O. Henry Prize Stories* in 2007 and was juror Ursula K. Le Guin's favorite story in the collection.

NATALIE DIAZ was born and raised in the Fort Mojave Indian Village in Needles, California. After playing professional basketball in Europe and Asia for several years, she completed her MFA from Old Dominion University in 2007. Her first book of poetry, *When My Brother Was an Aztec*, was published by Copper Canyon Press in 2012. She currently lives in Mohave Valley, Arizona, and works with the last elder fluent speakers of the Mojave language to revitalize it within the Fort Mojave community.

MURRAY FARISH lives in St. Louis, Missouri, where he teaches writing and literature at Webster University. His stories have appeared in such publications as *Epoch*, the *Missouri Review*, *Low Rent*, and *Black Warrior Review*. His first collection, *Inappropriate Behavior*, will be published in 2014 by Milkweed Editions.

LAURA FURMAN was born in New York and educated in New York City public schools and at Bennington College. Her first story appeared in the *New Yorker* in 1976, and since then her work has appeared in the *Yale Review*, the *Southwest Review*, *Ploughshares*, the *American Scholar*, *Preservation*, *House & Garden*, and other magazines. Her books include three collections of short stories, two novels, and a memoir. She has received fellowships from the New York State Council on the Arts, the Dobie Paisano Project, the Guggenheim Foundation, and the National Endowment for the Arts. Series editor of *The PEN/O. Henry Prize Stories* since 2002, she selects the twenty winning stories each year. For many years, she taught writing and literature at the University of Texas–Austin. Her newest collection is *The Mother Who Stayed: Stories* (Free Press, 2011). She lives with her husband and son in West Lake Hills, Texas.

DAGOBERTO GILB's latest book is *Before the End, After the Beginning* (Grove Press). He is the author of seven previous books, including *The Flowers*, *Woodcuts of Women*, and *The Magic of Blood*. His fiction and nonfiction appears in a range of magazines, most recently the *New Yorker*, *Harper's*, and *The PEN/O. Henry Prize Stories 2012*. Gilb is writer in residence at the University of Houston–Victoria, where he is also executive director of Centro Victoria, the university's center for Mexican American literature and culture.

CAITLIN HORROCKS is author of the story collection *This Is Not Your City* (Sarabande Books, 2011). Her stories have appeared in the *New Yorker*, *The Best American Short Stories 2011*, *The PEN/O. Henry Prize Stories 2009*, *The Pushcart Prize XXXV*, the *Paris Review*, *Tin House*, *One Story*, and elsewhere. Her work has won awards including the Plimpton Prize and a Bread Loaf Writers Conference fellowship. A former Theresa A. Wilhoit Fellow at Arizona State University, she currently lives in Grand Rapids, Michigan, where she teaches at Grand Valley State University and is a fiction editor at West Branch.

PAULA MCLAIN received an MFA in poetry from the University of Michigan and has been a resident of Yaddo and the MacDowell Colony. She is the author of two novels, *The Paris Wife* and *A Ticket to Ride*, two collections of poetry, and a memoir, *Like Family*. She lives in Cleveland with her family.

DAVID PHILIP MULLINS is the author of *Greetings from Below*, a collection of stories. He is a graduate of the Iowa Writers' Workshop, and his work has appeared in the *Yale Review*, the *Massachusetts Review*, *New England Review*, *Cimarron Review*, *Ecotone*, *Folio*, and *Fiction*. He has won the Mary McCarthy Prize in Short Fiction, the International Walter Scott Prize for Short Stories, and the Silver Pen Award from the Nevada Writers Hall of Fame and has received awards from Yaddo, the Sewanee Writers' Conference, and the Nebraska Arts Council. He lives in Omaha, Nebraska, where he is an assistant professor of creative writing at Creighton University.

KENT NELSON has published four novels and five story collections and has had stories anthologized in *The Best American Short Stories*, *The Best American Mystery Stories*, *The PEN/O. Henry Prize Stories*, and *Best of the West 2010: New Stories from the Wide Side of the Missouri*. He has run the Pikes Peak Marathon twice (7,814 feet) and has a North American bird list of 754 species. He lives in Ouray, Colorado.

MICHAEL ONOFREY is from southern California. He now lives in Japan. His stories have appeared in *Cottonwood*, the *Evansville Review*, *Imagination & Place: An Anthology*, *Natural Bridge*, and the *William and Mary Review*, as well as in other literary journals and anthologies in the United States, Canada, Japan, and Scotland. He is currently working on a novel.

KIRSTIN VALDEZ QUADE is from northern New Mexico. She earned her MFA from the University of Oregon and was a Wallace Stegner Fellow at Stanford University. Her work has appeared in the *New Yorker* and *Best of the West 2010: New Stories from the Wide Side of the Missouri*.

RON SAVAGE has published more than one hundred stories worldwide. He is the recipient of the Editor's Circle Award in Best New Writing and was nominated for the Pushcart Prize. He also has been a guest fiction editor for *Crazyhorse*, and he's the author of the novels *Scar Keeper* (Hilliard & Harris) and *Sharing Atmosphere* (Black Matrix). His short story collection, *Loving You the Way I Do* (Black Lawrence Press), was published in 2012. His work has appeared in *Film Comment*, the *North American Review*, *Shenandoah*, the *Baltimore Review*, and the *Magazine of Fantasy and Science Fiction*. Find him online at http://www.ronsavage.net or http://www.facebook.com/ron.savage2.

ROZ SPAFFORD was raised on a cattle ranch in northwestern Arizona, a place where words were as precious as water. For a number of years, she taught writing at the University of California–Santa Cruz. She now works in Toronto. Her book of poems, *Requiem*, was awarded the 2008 Gell Poetry Prize from Writers & Books in Rochester, New York. "Drought" received the 2010 David Nathan Meyerson Prize from the *Southwest Review*.

JUSTIN ST. GERMAIN grew up in Tombstone, Arizona. He attended the University of Arizona and was a Wallace Stegner Fellow at Stanford. His fiction has appeared in *ZYZZYVA*, *Best of the West 2010: New Stories from the Wide Side of the Missouri*, and elsewhere, and his memoir, *Son of a Gun*, was published by Random House. He lives in Albuquerque and teaches at the University of New Mexico.

JAMES TERRY's fiction has appeared in numerous places and has been nominated for the Pushcart Prize and the PEN/O. Henry Prize. "Road to Nowhere" belongs to a forthcoming short story collection called *Kingdom of the Sun*, set in his hometown of Deming, New Mexico. Other stories from the collection have recently appeared in the *Georgia Review*, the *Dublin Review*, the *South Dakota Review*, the *Connecticut Review*, and *Fiction*. He presently lives in Edmonton, Alberta, with his wife and son.

DON WATERS is the author of the short story collection *Desert Gothic*. He has been awarded fellowships from the Christopher Isherwood Foundation, the Lannan Foundation, and the Iowa Writers' Workshop. He lives in Portland, Oregon, and Iowa City.

CLAIRE VAYE WATKINS was born in Death Valley in 1984 and raised in the Nevada desert. Her work has appeared in *Granta*, the *Paris Review*, the *Hopkins Review*, *Sycamore Review*, *Hobart*, *One Story*, *Glimmer Train*, *Ploughshares*, *Las Vegas Weekly*, *Las Vegas City Life*, and *Best of the West 2011: New Stories from the Wide Side of the Missouri*. She has received a William Ralston Scholarship from the Sewanee Writers' Conference and a Presidential Fellowship from the Ohio State University, where she received her MFA. A graduate of the University of Nevada–Reno, she is an assistant professor of creative writing at Bucknell University. Her collection of short stories, *Battleborn*, was published by Riverhead Books in 2012.

BRAD WATSON is the author of *Last Days of the Dog-Men*, *The Heaven of Mercury*, and *Aliens in the Prime of Their Lives*. He's held fellowships through the National Endowment for the Arts, the Lannan Foundation, and the Guggenheim Foundation. His books have received awards from the American Academy of Arts and Letters, the Great Lakes Colleges Association, the Southern Book Critics Circle, and the Mississippi Institute of Arts and Letters. *The Heaven of Mercury* was a finalist for the 2002 National Book Award in Fiction. *Aliens in the Prime of Their Lives* was a finalist for the St. Francis College Literary Award and the PEN/Faulkner Award in Fiction.

Credits

287